D1190498

TIM WAGGONER

YOUR TURN
TO SUFFER

FLAME TREE PRESS
6 Melbray Mews, London, SW6 3NS, UK
flametreepress.com

US sales, distribution and warehouse:
Simon & Schuster
simonandschuster.biz

UK distribution and warehouse:
Marston Book Services Ltd
marston.co.uk

Thanks to the Flame Tree Press team, including:
Taylor Bentley, Frances Bodiam, Federica Ciaravella, Don D'Auria,
Chris Herbert, Josie Karani, Molly Rosevear, Mike Spender,
Cat Taylor, Maria Tissot, Nick Wells, Gillian Whitaker.

The cover is created by Flame Tree Studio with
thanks to Nik Keevil and Shutterstock.com.
The font families used are Avenir and Bembo.

Flame Tree Press is an imprint of Flame Tree Publishing Ltd
flametreepublishing.com

A copy of the CIP data for this book is available from the British Library
and the Library of Congress.

HB ISBN: 978-1-78758-518-8
US PB ISBN: 978-1-78758-516-4
UK PB ISBN: 978-1-78758-517-1
ebook ISBN: 978-1-78758-520-1

Printed and bound in Great Britain by Clays Ltd, Elcograf S.p.A.

TIM WAGGONER

YOUR TURN TO SUFFER

FLAME TREE PRESS
London & New York

This one's for David Lynch, dreamer of the dark and wondrous.

PROLOGUE

"Can I ask you a question?"

Lorelai Palumbo – who preferred to be called Lori – didn't register the man at first. She'd just left work, and her mind was on the last client she'd had, a twelve-year-old boy named Stevie. He'd been struck by a hit-and-run driver, after running into the street in an attempt to catch his new chiweenie puppy, which had made a mad dash for freedom when he'd opened the front door to go out to play. The dog had escaped being hit, but Stevie hadn't been so lucky. He'd needed multiple surgeries, and the bones of his right arm and left leg were held together by so much metal he joked that he qualified to be called a cyborg now. Today hadn't been his first physical therapy session, but it had still hurt like hell, so much so that he was in tears by the end of it, and she felt as if she'd been torturing the poor boy. But Stevie wasn't the only thing occupying her thoughts. After Stevie and his mom left, her supervisor, Melinda Dixon, had gotten on her ass about taking it too easy on the boy toward the end of his session.

We have to help them fight through the pain, Melinda had said. *Help them not be afraid of it. But in order for that to happen, we first have to let them feel it. All of it.*

Melinda's words had infuriated her, especially because she feared the woman was right. She hadn't intentionally gone easy on Stevie, but seeing him cry like that had torn at her heart, so she wouldn't have been surprised if she'd subconsciously backed off and not made him work as hard as she should've.

And if all that wasn't enough, she was also thinking about last night's phone conversation with Justin.

Just because I'm not comfortable with your ex-boyfriend staying at your place until he 'gets on his feet,' doesn't mean I'm insecure. I think my reaction is perfectly reasonable, given the circumstances.

The accumulated stress had given her a headache, a bad one. Her head pounded like hell, and she was beginning to see flashes of light in the corners of her vision. She was on the verge of triggering a stress-induced migraine, and if she didn't want to lie in a dark room for the next three days feeling as if her head was going to explode any second, she needed to take some Fiorinal – and fast. She'd been meaning to get her prescription refilled, had even called it in, but with one thing and another, she hadn't stopped by the pharmacy to pick it up yet.

Stupid, stupid, stupid!

Luckily, the pharmacy was only a couple of blocks from where she worked. She'd decided to walk instead of drive. She knew from experience that her headache would worsen faster if she tried to drive, so she wasn't going to get behind the wheel of her car until she got some Fiorinal into her system. The medicine made some people drowsy, but she'd been taking it so long that it didn't affect her that strongly. Still, she might call Justin and ask him to drive her home – assuming he still wasn't too pissed off at her. Screw it. She didn't feel like dealing with him right now. She'd call an Uber instead.

So, with Stevie, Melinda, Justin, and her raging headache on her mind, if the man hadn't stepped in front of her and repeated his question, she most likely would've continued walking down the sidewalk, passing him by without ever noticing him. But she definitely noticed him now – had to stop abruptly to avoid colliding with him, in fact.

He was in his sixties, maybe seventies. He had a neatly trimmed white mustache and wore a brown suit with a garish yellow tie. He wore a fedora, and she couldn't tell if his hair was as white as his mustache or if he was bald. There was nothing particularly remarkable about him, nothing *concerning*. At least at first glance. But then she saw the haunted look in his eyes, and a chill rippled down her spine. He looked as if he'd seen something awful, and her first thought was that the man was in shock. That, or he was insane.

He smelled of a cologne she didn't recognize, as well as the lingering scent of tobacco. He was a smoker. The combined smells turned her stomach, and caused her head to pound even harder. The pain was so intense that for a moment she thought she might throw up on the man. She didn't, but it was close.

She saw something move in the man's eyes then, dark threads that passed across the whites like fast-moving storm clouds. Then they were gone. She put them down to a visual hallucination caused by her migraine, and she forgot about them.

His words registered on her consciousness then – *Can I ask you a question?* – and without thinking about it, she said, "No." She quickly stepped around him and continued down the sidewalk, moving at a faster pace than she had before.

Her reaction to the man had been an instinctive one, without thought or consideration. Her head felt as if it was going to split open any second, and that look in his eyes, as if whatever he had seen that had bothered him so was playing on an endless loop in his mind, had warned her not to talk to him.

She couldn't stop herself from glancing back over her shoulder at the man, even though she knew that by doing so she might encourage him to approach her again. He stood on the sidewalk looking at her, a sad expression on his face, but he made no move to come after her.

She looked forward once more.

You need to get your medicine, she reminded herself. *Besides, he was probably going to try to sell you something, maybe ask for a donation to a church or charity.* Either way, he'd be used to people not wanting to talk to him, right? He wouldn't take her rejection personally.

Would he?

An SUV drove past then, and late-afternoon sunlight flashed off its windshield, piercing her eyes like a pair of white-hot metal spikes. The pain in her head intensified, driving out all thoughts of the man who'd tried to ask her a question. Squinting to block out the light, she continued down the sidewalk toward the pharmacy and the relief that awaited her within.

CHAPTER ONE

Where the hell is the garlic powder?

It was a week after her terrible migraine. Lori stood in the baking aisle of FoodSaver, a plastic shopping basket gripped in her left hand, purse slung over her right shoulder. The basket contained ingredients for her dinner – wheat pasta, low-sodium marina sauce, grated parmesan cheese, vegetable-oil-based margarine, and a package of French bread she'd picked up in the store's bakery section. She was going to make spaghetti tonight, and she planned to accompany it with what remained of the chardonnay she'd picked up earlier in the week. Larry wasn't going to be home this evening. He actually had a gig, the first one in a couple weeks, and Justin had to work late tonight. She was on her own, and she intended to enjoy this rare night of solitude. She'd go home, make her food, pour the wine, and sit on the couch and eat while she watched the new season of her favorite comedy series that had dropped on Netflix today. There was a problem, though. She always made garlic bread to eat with spaghetti – she *hated* the premade frozen kind – but how was she supposed to make her own without any goddamn garlic powder?

She faced the shelves where containers of spices had been arranged in neat rows and organized alphabetically by the ingredients they held: allspice, anise, basil, bay leaves, black pepper.... Garlic powder should've been between fennel seed and ginger, but it wasn't. Not only was it absent, there wasn't an empty space where it should've been. She'd bought garlic powder here before. Did FoodSaver not carry it anymore? No, that was crazy. Garlic powder wasn't some exotic spice with a hard-to-pronounce name that no one had heard of. It was a normal, everyday ingredient that people used all the time. It made no sense for it not to be here.

Maybe someone put it in the wrong place, she thought.

She started at the beginning – allspice – and slowly read the label of each container on the shelves. She knew she was being foolishly stubborn. She could have spaghetti without garlic bread, probably shouldn't eat it in the first place. There were enough carbs in the pasta as it was. She didn't need the extra in the bread. But once she'd fixed her mind on something – such as creating a perfect night for relaxing – she didn't give up easily. Besides, she *needed* to relax. Melinda had busted her metaphorical balls at work today for going too hard on an elderly woman who'd recently undergone hip replacement surgery. This after chiding her for going too easy on Stevie last week. She wished the woman would make up her goddamn mind on how hard she wanted Lori to work her patients. She went through the spices all the way to the end – vanilla extract – without finding garlic powder. She knew it was going to be a wasted effort, but she decided to go through the spices a second time, in case she'd somehow missed the garlic powder. She'd barely started when she heard the sound of a shoe scuffing the tiled floor to her right.

She didn't stop her second search to look at the person. She figured it was just another shopper, making his or her way down the aisle, searching for baking ingredients. Whoever it was, she hoped they had better luck locating items than she was having. The person came closer until only a foot separated them. She could see her – it was a woman – in her peripheral vision, and while she was annoyed by the woman's physical proximity, she was determined to finish her second scan of the spices.

You're a stubborn thing, her mother had once told her. *Goddamn right,* she thought and smiled.

"Confess."

The woman spoke so softly that at first Lori wasn't sure she had heard correctly. For that matter, she wasn't certain that the woman had been talking to her at all, but she looked over at her just in case—

—and immediately wished she hadn't.

The first thing Lori noticed about the woman was her eyes. They were too large for her face, and they were watery, so full of moisture that tears should've been running down her cheeks, but somehow it remained in her eyes, as if the woman held it there by some trick. But the worst part was the woman's pupils. Instead of being round, they were black horizontal rectangles. *Like goats' eyes,* she thought. There was something wrong with the skin around those eyes, too. It seemed soft, doughy, more like putty than flesh. She imagined she could reach out with an index finger and push those eyes back into the woman's head without any resistance, and the putty-flesh would flow inward to cover up the spaces where the eyes had been.

Lori was by no means a physician, but as a healthcare professional, she'd had a certain amount of medical training, and she'd never seen or heard of any condition that could account for the woman's bizarre eyes. The rest of her looked normal enough. She was of medium height – about the same size as Lori – and wore a pale-blue sweatshirt, jeans, and sneakers. Lori guessed she was in her early forties, although the weird skin around her eyes made her seem older. She wore no makeup, and her shoulder-length brown hair looked as if it hadn't been washed in a while. A strong ripe scent of body odor emanated from the woman, as if she were surrounded by a dense cloud of stink. The only other odd detail about her – so minor that it seemed unimportant compared to the others – was the nail of her left pinky finger was painted red. Her other nine fingernails were devoid of polish.

Lori was so taken aback by the woman's appearance that she didn't fully register her words.

"I don't understand," she said.

The woman – goat eyes fixed on Lori – took half a step forward. The smell of her body odor became more intense, and Lori wrinkled her nose and half turned her head in a vain attempt to mitigate the stench's effect.

"Confess and atone – or suffer."

The woman's voice was sandpaper-rough, and her breath had a strangely fruity smell. Lori wondered if she were ill.

The woman leaned her face closer to Lori, and although it wasn't, couldn't be possible, her rectangular pupils rotated in opposite directions. Startled, Lori stepped backward quickly, colliding with the spices on the shelves and knocking a number of them to the floor. She lost her grip on her shopping basket, and it fell to the floor as well, tipping over as it landed, the ingredients for her dinner spilling forth. Her purse slipped off her shoulder and slid down to her forearm, but she managed to keep it from falling.

The woman stared at her a moment longer, but made no further effort to come closer. Then, without saying anything more, she turned and started walking down the aisle, away from Lori. She walked with slow, shuffling steps, and it seemed to take a long time before she reached the end of the aisle, turned, and was lost to sight.

Lori hadn't realized she'd been holding her breath until her lungs began to ache. She inhaled deeply, and instantly regretted it. The combined smells of the woman's strong body odor and her strange fruity breath still suffused the air. She wanted to get out of there, and she was tempted to leave her groceries where they'd fallen, haul ass out to the parking lot, jump in her Honda Civic, drive off at full speed, and never come back. But she didn't. She wouldn't have been much of a physical therapist if she didn't know how to keep going when the going got tough – or in this case, bizarre.

She slid her purse back up to her shoulder, then knelt down and began picking up items and putting them back into the plastic shopping basket. She breathed shallowly to minimize the impact of the woman's stink, and she tried not to think about those goat eyes and how they had appeared to rotate in their sockets. No, it hadn't been the eyes themselves that moved. Only the pupils had rotated. She wasn't sure how she knew this, but she did. Still, did it matter? Either way was equally fucked up.

Once she'd retrieved her meager supply of groceries, she picked up the spices she'd knocked down and put them back in their proper places on the shelves. Feeling better now that she'd restored at least a small bit of order to the world, she picked up the shopping basket and headed toward the self-checkout. She still didn't have any garlic powder, but it didn't matter anymore. She intended to buy the groceries, but right now the notion of making food – let alone eating it – nauseated her. All she wanted to do was go home, put her groceries away, and take a long hot shower, using copious amounts of body wash to cleanse the woman's stink from her skin and hair. She'd toss her uniform into the wash as well. And if she couldn't get the stench out of the fabric, she'd throw the uniform away. She had others.

Look forward, push onward.

She told her patients this, but it was something of a personal mantra for her as well. It had gotten her through a lot in her life, and it would get her through an encounter with a crazy woman in FoodSaver. But despite her determination to put the incident behind her, she heard the woman's rough voice speak once more in her mind.

Confess and atone – or suffer.

*   *   *

Lori left the store, carrying her groceries in a single plastic bag that dangled from her left hand. A pleasant breeze caressed her body, and the sky was a bright, clear blue. Small trees had been placed throughout the parking lot, and while most of their leaves were still green, some had begun to change color. A few dry ones had fallen, and they made soft skittering sounds like small insects as the wind blew them across the asphalt. The scene wasn't perfect, of course. It was the tail end of the evening rush hour, and while downtown Oakmont, Ohio, was hardly a busy metropolitan hub, the traffic flowing past FoodSaver was steady, and the air held the faint tang of exhaust fumes.

It would smell worse if the wind wasn't blowing, she thought, and she reminded herself to be thankful for small graces. Not that she was religious. Her parents were more or less devout Lutherans, but both she and her sister had stopped going to church years ago. She still considered herself spiritual, though, in a loosey-goosey nondenominational way. Besides, it never hurt to appreciate the good things in life, even the small ones.

The lot was full for a Tuesday night, and she'd had to park farther away from the store's entrance than she usually did. That was okay, though. She had an app on her phone that recorded the number of steps she took in a day and how many calories she burned by walking. So as far as she was concerned, the more she walked, the better. Her car was parked close to the street, next to a tall lamppost. She always tried to park next to one, day or night. She could more easily find her car that way, and at night the illumination was a good security measure. She headed straight for her Civic, feeling better with every step she put between herself, the grocery, and the goat-eyed woman. Maybe by the time she got home, her appetite would've returned.

As she passed a pair of SUVs parked next to each other, a flash of movement caught her eye. Without thinking, she turned to look in that direction, and she saw...something. It moved too fast for her to get a good look at it, but she had the impression of a tall person with thin arms and legs, dressed entirely in black. But whoever it was slipped in front of the vehicles with silent, liquid grace, blocking her view. It happened so fast that she wasn't certain she'd seen anything at all. It had probably been her imagination, she decided. She'd been creeped out by the goat-eyed woman, and now she was seeing sinister shadows flitting around the parking lot.

She frowned. That was odd. Why did she think it was *sinister*? The way it moved? Or.... An image came to her then of the dark figure she'd glimpsed. Originally, she'd thought she'd seen a person dressed in black: black long-sleeved pullover, black pants, black shoes.... But now she realized that the figure – she was having an increasingly hard time thinking of it as a person – had been black all over. The hands had been black, and so had the head. It was as if the figure had been garbed in a black skin-tight outfit that completely covered its body, making it look like a living shadow.

It was a ridiculous thought, but she walked faster, and although she felt an itch between her shoulder blades, as if someone was watching her, she didn't turn around to look, too afraid of what she might see.

★　　★　　★

Neal Goodman was tired.

He'd started working at seven this morning, and – with the exception of the half hour he'd taken for lunch – he'd worked straight through until five. To someone looking in from the outside, the work of a dentist hardly seemed strenuous, and it wasn't as if he spent his days digging ditches or anything. But bending over to peer into patients' mouths and holding your arms up while working on their teeth hour after hour took a physical toll. His lower back ached, and the base of his neck was so sore that it hurt to turn his head in either direction. The joints in his hands throbbed thanks to his arthritis, and it was all he could do to maintain his grip on the steering wheel of his Volvo. When he got home, he'd have to do his best to hide his discomfort from Rosie. If his wife saw how badly he was hurting, she'd start nagging him about retiring again. He would turn seventy this January, and while he liked working – even if it was getting harder on his body as time passed – Rosie was beginning to wear him down.

You've been a dentist for almost forty years. You've had your own practice – a very successful one for thirty of those years. You've earned a rest, and you should take it before you're too old to enjoy it.

It was this last part of her argument that was the most effective. Aside from some aches and pains, he was in good health for a man of sixty-nine. But how long would his health hold up? How much time did he have left before his life ended? He wasn't by nature a morbid man, but he was a realist. With luck, he'd live another decade, but more than that? Maybe not. And even if he *did* live into his eighties, would he still be strong and healthy enough both physically and mentally to keep enjoying his life, or would he end up parked in some assisted-living facility, marking time until his old body finally had the good sense to give up the ghost? The latter outcome seemed more likely.

Maybe he should make an appointment to talk with his financial advisor to see if it was feasible for him to retire at the end of the fiscal year. If nothing else, it would make Rosie happy and keep her off his back, at least for a little while.

That decided, he started thinking about what he might do with his newfound leisure time. Go on a cruise, maybe. Rosie had always wanted to take a cruise to Alaska. He had no idea why the notion appealed to her so. She *hated* winter. Maybe he could talk her into going someplace warmer, like the Caribbean. He'd seen commercials for Caribbean cruises on TV, and they'd always looked—

His train of thought broke as he realized he was approaching FoodSaver. He remembered that Rosie had asked him to stop there on his way home and pick up…something. He hadn't written it down because it was such a normal thing to pick up – like milk or bread – that he figured he wouldn't forget it. But of course he had. He could stop anyway, go inside, and hope that being in the store would jog his memory. Or he could pass FoodSaver by, continue on home, and when Rosie asked if he'd gotten what she'd asked for, he could say he'd been too tired to stop. She might feel sorry for him then and let him off the hook. Calling her and asking her to remind him what he was supposed to get wasn't an option. She worried about him enough as it was. He didn't want her to think he was starting to show signs of dementia. Passing by FoodSaver because he was too tired to stop was one thing. But forgetting the single ordinary item she'd asked him to pick up? She'd take that as an early symptom of Alzheimer's. Best just to go on home.

He'd eased up on the gas while debating with himself, but now that he'd made his decision, he increased pressure on the accelerator and his car began to pick up speed. He saw something out of the corner of his eye then, and he reflexively turned to see what it was.

A woman, wearing jeans and a pale-blue sweatshirt, stood at the entrance to FoodSaver's parking lot. At first, he thought she was waiting on someone to pick her up – a bus or an Uber – but then, for reasons he wasn't quite clear on, he understood that she'd been waiting for him. He locked eyes with her, and for an instant, it was as if time came to a screeching halt. The woman was at least a dozen yards from him, but he saw her as if in close-up, every detail clear and vivid – especially her oddly shaped pupils. Her face was impassive, but there was something about her that spoke of grim purpose. And then, as quickly as time had slowed, it returned to normal speed.

He took his gaze off her, looked forward, and was startled to see a man standing on the road directly in his path. No, not a man. A shadowy *thing* shaped like a man. It had a head, torso, arms, and legs but otherwise was completely featureless: a silhouette come to life. It was tall, limbs long and lean, and it made him think of the way a person's reflection could be stretched in the warped glass of a funhouse mirror. Neal didn't have time to brake or swerve. All he could do was tighten his grip on the steering wheel and grit his teeth. He wanted to close his eyes – wanted to do this very much – but they remained open as he struck the dark figure.

Except he didn't.

There was no sudden jolt, no horrible meaty *thump* of his Volvo hitting whatever it was. He saw a flash of darkness rushing toward him, felt a blast of cold course over and through his body, and then he was past the shadow thing. He looked at his rearview mirror and saw the creature – whatever it was – standing on the street behind him, seemingly unharmed.

He passed through me, Neal thought. *Or I passed through him.*

The cold he'd felt.... That had been the instant his body had come into contact with the shadow's substance. Somehow the thing was insubstantial enough to pass through glass and metal but still solid enough to affect him as it moved through him. He wondered how—

Pain slammed into his chest with sledgehammer force. His left arm stiffened and went numb, and his left hand slipped off the steering wheel. He couldn't breathe, and his vision narrowed to tiny pinpoints of light surrounded by darkness. Without realizing he was doing so, he pressed the accelerator all the way to the floor, and his right hand – which had a white-knuckled grip on the steering wheel – turned hard to the left. His Volvo swerved into oncoming traffic, and the driver of a white pickup gave an angry blast of the vehicle's horn as Neal cut in front of it. Neal missed colliding with the pickup by less than a foot, and his Volvo bounced over the curb, went over the sidewalk, and roared into FoodSaver's parking lot, continuing to pick up speed as it went.

Neal was in agony, teeth gritted, lower lip caught between them, flesh bitten, blood pouring out of his mouth. But a part of him was detached from the pain, was merely observing what was happening, not scared so much as confused. He'd had a checkup less than a month ago, and the doctor had said he was in good shape for a man of his age, and she'd said his heart sounded strong and healthy. But if what the doctor had told him was true, how could this be happening? It took more than a few weeks to develop heart disease, didn't it?

He saw another woman, this one wearing a blue uniform top and carrying a small bag of groceries. He was heading straight for her, and she turned to look at him, her expression one of terrified disbelief.

Toilet paper, he thought. *I'm supposed to get toilet paper.*

★   ★   ★

Lori was two-thirds of the way to her car when the sounds of a blaring car horn and screeching tires caught her attention. She looked toward the street, expecting to see an accident take place, most likely involving someone who was about to discover why it wasn't advisable to ride another driver's ass during rush hour. But instead of witnessing one vehicle rear-end another, she saw a Volvo swerve into FoodSaver's parking lot and come barreling toward her, engine racing.

It's not going to stop, she thought. This realization was devoid of emotion at first, as if what was happening was no more remarkable than her noting it might rain soon. But this emotional numbness lasted only for a second before panic exploded inside her. Her body wanted to freeze, to remain motionless in the hope that the car would miss her, like a small animal in the presence of a larger, hungry predator. It was the hardest thing she'd ever done, but with an effort of will, she made her body move. She was closest to the row of cars on her right, and while their shelter tempted her, if the Volvo slammed into the vehicles, she might be caught between two of them and squashed like an oversized bug. Instead, she ran toward the vehicles on her left. They were farther away, but the Volvo was angled to her right, and as fast as the vehicle was going, the driver would, most likely, end up striking one or more of the cars in that direction. So left it was. She ran all out, adrenaline flooding her system and providing her with strength and speed.

She caught a glimpse of the driver as she ran in front of his car – ashen face, wide, staring eyes – and then the Volvo flashed past her, veered toward a parked minivan and slammed into it head-on. She continued running, not looking back to check what was happening, wanting only to get as far away from danger as fast as she could. She heard a tremendous crash of metal striking metal, the impact so loud and violent that the vibrations in the air made her teeth rattle. The Volvo's engine cut out then, and aside from the soft ticking sounds coming from beneath its crumpled hood, there was silence.

Believing that the worst of the danger had passed, Lori stopped running and, more than a little winded, turned to see what had happened. The Volvo had plowed into the minivan so hard that it appeared as if the two vehicles had fused into a single mass of twisted metal. The air was thick with the scent of engine exhaust and burning oil, as well as the tang of spilled gasoline from the Volvo's ruptured tank. She knew she should stay back, should call nine-one-one and report the accident, but she found herself hurrying toward the damaged vehicles in case someone was hurt – which seemed more than likely – and needed assistance.

When she reached the Volvo, she saw that the driver had been wearing his seat belt and remained buckled into place. The vehicle's airbags had activated, but they were already mostly deflated, their work done. The impact had driven the dashboard inward, and the steering wheel now pressed tight against the driver's chest. Even with the protection of the airbag, it looked as if he'd been badly injured. Besides being pinned back against the seat by the steering wheel, his head had smashed into the driver's-side window. The impact had broken the glass, and most of it had fallen to the ground, giving her an unobstructed view of the large bleeding gash over the man's left temple. He was bleeding from his mouth, too. She didn't know if that was due to internal injuries he'd sustained or if he'd bitten his tongue during the collision. But as bad as those injuries looked, she could tell by his pallor and the way he was struggling for breath that he was probably having a heart attack. She didn't know if the attack had caused him to veer wildly into the parking lot or if the attack had been brought on by the accident, but either way, he was in serious trouble.

"Hold on," she said. "I'll call for help."

As she pulled her phone from her purse, she gave the van a quick glance and was relieved to see it appeared unoccupied. She quickly called nine-one-one, but as it began ringing on the other end, the man's head flopped to the side and he looked up at her.

"Her…eyes…" he whispered, "like a…goat's." This was followed by a hissing exhalation of air, and although his own eyes remained open, Lori no longer saw any sign of life in them.

A woman's voice spoke in her ear.

"Nine-one-one. What's your emergency?"

Lori tried to speak, but words wouldn't come.

Her…eyes…like a…goat's.

She felt a sick crawling sensation in the pit of her stomach. She continued holding the phone to her ear, and she heard the dispatcher repeat herself, more loudly this time.

"Nine-one-one. What's your emergency?"

Lori still couldn't answer. She had the sensation she was being watched, and she looked around. Cars on the street were passing by slowly as their drivers tried to get a good look at the accident and satisfy their morbid curiosity. A few drivers had pulled to the side of the road, and a couple were getting out of their cars, probably intending to offer what help they could. She didn't pay attention to any of the witnesses or looky-loos. Her attention was focused on the goat-eyed woman who stood on the sidewalk next to the street, staring at her. The woman's mouth moved, and although she was too far away for Lori to make out her words, she knew what she said.

Confess and atone – or suffer.

*   *   *

As the prime witness to the accident, Lori had to stay at FoodSaver and give a statement to the police officers who arrived to investigate. She told them everything that had happened – except for seeing the shadowy figure and the goat-eyed woman. She told herself the woman had nothing to do with the accident, and as for the shadow thing…it had only been a product of her imagination. Besides, she feared the officers would think she was crazy if she told them about the encounters.

When the officers were finished taking her statement, they asked her to remain at the scene in case they had more questions. Lori said she would – she was too shaken up to drive yet anyway – and she sat on the sidewalk outside the store, back against a brick wall, knees hugged to her chest, purse on the ground next to her. She felt a headache coming on, and she dry swallowed a Fiorinal in hopes of forestalling it. She watched as a pair of paramedics removed the old man from his Volvo, laid him on the ground, and began CPR. A layperson might've wondered why they bothered, but Lori knew that as long as someone wasn't obviously beyond saving – like if they were decapitated – paramedics would do everything they could to revive that person for as long as they could, just on the chance their efforts might save his or her life. Lori feared the old man was beyond medical help, though.

Before he'd died, the old man had spoken about goat eyes. Lori was certain he'd been speaking of the same woman who'd confronted her inside the grocery, but there was no sign of her now. A small crowd had gathered to watch the police and paramedics do their work, but the goat-eyed woman wasn't among them. That was a huge relief. Lori didn't think she'd be able to stand it if the woman approached her now to once more deliver her incomprehensible message.

A fire truck had pulled into the parking lot along with a pair of police cruisers and the paramedic van. She assumed the firefighters had come to hose down the area around the Volvo to dilute and disperse the gasoline that had leaked from the damaged vehicle, but since the paramedics were still trying to revive the man at the scene, all they could do for now was stand around looking bored. The emergency lights of the first responders' vehicles were all activated, and as dusk edged its way toward night, their colors seemed to become brighter and more garish. As she stared at the lights, doing her best not to think of anything in particular, she saw a van turn into FoodSaver's lot. It had a small satellite dish attached to the roof, and *Action News* was painted on the side. The driver pulled up close to the police cruisers and parked. Three people got out – a pair of men, and a woman wearing a skirt and a blazer. Lori didn't watch the news, whether national or local. She found it too depressing. She didn't recognize the woman, but she knew she was a reporter, and that meant she'd want to interview any witnesses to the accident. Especially the woman the Volvo had almost hit. It would only take a few moments for the news crew to get ready to start recording, and once they found out who Lori was from the police, they'd hurry over to get her firsthand account of the accident. No fucking way was she going to stick around for that.

She picked up her purse, stood, and went inside FoodSaver. Forcing herself to walk at a normal pace in order not to draw any attention, she made her way to the back of the store. There was no exit for customers here, but there was a pair of swinging doors with *Employees Only* written on them. She pushed through the doors without hesitation and found herself in FoodSaver's storage area. She saw stacks of empty cardboard boxes that hadn't been broken down yet, as well as wooden pallets containing boxes of non-perishable items. The boxes were labeled – paper towels, breakfast cereal, potato chips – but there was no one present to open them and remove their contents. She figured that whoever had been working back here had gone out front to watch the action after the accident had happened. This meant there was no one to see her, let alone stop her, as she walked toward the receiving dock. The dock's large door was shut, but there was a regular-sized door next to it, and this was the one she went to. She found it unlocked and she opened it, half expecting an alarm to sound, but she didn't hear anything. She stepped outside and closed the door behind her. There were several dumpsters back here, some for trash, some for recycling cardboard. The trash stank of rotten meat and sour milk, and her stomach roiled at the smell. She hurried past the dumpsters toward the west side of the building. She walked around the corner and continued on, going slowly, careful to remain close to the wall. She kept going until she could peek out into the parking lot.

She saw the reporter speaking to the police, one of the men recording her with a camera while the other stood by, watching. The paramedics had strapped the old man to a backboard and lifted him onto a gurney. They wheeled him to their vehicle and got him inside. One of the medics remained in the back with the old man, while the other closed the rear doors, jogged to the front, and climbed into the driver's seat. A second later, the vehicle's engine roared to life, its emergency lights came on, and its siren began blaring. The vehicle started moving, slowly at first, but once the driver pulled onto the street, he hit the accelerator and sped off.

Lori knew they would take the man to the nearest hospital, which was in Ash Creek, about fifteen miles away. The news cameraman had stopped filming the reporter's discussion with the police officer and shot footage of the paramedics leaving. When they were gone, the firefighters started preparing to wash away the gasoline that had leaked from the Volvo, and the cameraman began filming them.

She drew back and, as she'd done before, she sat on the ground, back to the wall, knees hugged to her chest, purse resting next to her. She wondered what it must be like for the paramedics, knowing that the patient you were transporting was almost assuredly nothing more than a collection of bones and dead meat, but needing to pretend that some small spark of life might be hiding somewhere within him in order to do your job properly. She couldn't imagine anything more depressing, and she was glad she was a physical therapist. The patients she worked with might be in pain – sometimes quite a lot – but they were alive. They could heal, maybe not all the way, and maybe their bodies would never get back to the point they were before whatever had happened to break them. But they could get better. They could *improve*. That was a hell of a lot more than the old man would ever be capable of.

She'd ridden in the back of a paramedic vehicle only once in her life – back in high school – and once was enough. She unconsciously reached down to rub her right knee, and although there was no reason for it to hurt, she felt a distant, dull throb. The pain drew her attention to her hand, and she quickly removed it from her knee.

Look forward, push onward, she reminded herself.

* * *

Lori remained hidden until everyone – the police, the firefighters, the reporters – had left, and both the Volvo and the minivan it had struck had been towed away. As she left her hiding place and walked to her Civic she kept watch for the goat-eyed woman, but thankfully she was nowhere in sight. Lori got into her car and pulled out onto the street, and she was halfway home before she realized she had no idea what had happened to the groceries she'd bought for dinner. She didn't remember dropping them when she'd run to avoid being hit by the old man, but she must have. Someone probably picked them up and threw them away when cleaning the accident scene. It wasn't much of a loss. She had no appetite whatsoever.

She thought of the old man and wondered if the doctors in the ER had been able to revive him, or if he was – and this seemed far more likely – lying on a table in the hospital's morgue, waiting to be autopsied. The idea saddened her. She wished the man no ill will. Sure, he'd almost run her down, but that had been an accident.

Hadn't it?

It was close to nine o'clock when she pulled into the ridiculously named Emerald Place. Whoever had come up with the name had been going for some kind of *Wizard of Oz* vibe, as if this was a place of enchantment instead of a collection of dull-looking brown-and-gray buildings housing cramped one- and two-bedroom apartments.

Be it ever so crumbled, there's no place like home.

It wasn't especially late, but all the parking spots in front of her building had been taken, and she was forced to park two buildings down. She trudged to her building – which lay uphill from where she'd parked – her legs protesting with every step. As a physical therapist, she was usually on her feet during work hours, and today had been no exception. Plus, she felt emotionally drained from the events at FoodSaver so, all in all, she was wiped out. No longer did she want to sit on the couch and watch television. All she wanted to do was climb into bed, curl up under the covers, and sleep for a week. Maybe two.

The sidewalk was lit by a series of lampposts that gave off dim yellow light. She wasn't certain if the effect was supposed to be aesthetic, or if the company that owned the complex kept the outside lights low at night to save on electricity. She'd never been comfortable with the meager light the sidewalk lights provided. It left too many shadows untouched around the trees and hedges that were positioned between the sidewalk and the buildings. Shadows in which anyone could be lurking – muggers, rapists, goat-eyed women who made cryptic pronouncements…. She remained alert as she walked, continually swept her gaze around to check her surroundings, listened intently for the slightest sound that might indicate someone was watching her from the concealment of darkness.

After what had happened at FoodSaver tonight, she was even more nervous about the shadows than usual. She pictured the dark form that she'd seen right before the old man's car had come racing toward her. The thing had been like an omen of ill fortune, or a harbinger of doom. Yes, she'd managed to escape unscathed, but that had been a matter of luck as much as anything else. If she'd hesitated so much as a split second, she might well be lying on an autopsy table in the hospital morgue, next to the old man in the Volvo.

Instead of looking away from the shadows, she peered more closely at them, trying to discern any distinct shapes within their mass of black. She had the impression of silent, squirming movement, of dozens of dark forms writhing over and around each other. It reminded her of when she was a child and her parents would take her and her younger sister, Reeny, to play miniature golf. The course was set up as a twisting, turning maze of fake miniature mountains, and a pond wound in and around the holes. There were large koi in the water, and for a dime you could buy tiny brown pellets from a vending machine to feed them. She and Reeny would always beg their parents for change to buy fish food, and once their hands were filled with the hard little pellets, they would walk to the wooden railing that separated the course from the pond and throw the food out over the water as far as they could. The pellets would come pattering down like raindrops, and the koi would rise up from the water in a roiling mass to fight over the food in mindless desperation. That's what the shadows seemed like to her now – giant, over-eager black fish, all squirming hungry energy as their slick surfaces slid over each other with wet whispers.

She wondered which she'd rather see again the least: the shadow creature or the goat-eyed woman. She decided it was a toss-up. They'd both been equally disturbing in their own way.

The shadows remained where they were as she continued walking, and she didn't feel the itchy-crawly sensation on the back of her neck that indicated someone's eyes were on her. She walked up to her building without incident, opened the door – which creaked on old, dry hinges – and stepped inside. The building was small and had no real lobby, just a narrow hallway and a set of stairs leading up to the second floor. The lights inside were fluorescent, much brighter than those outside, almost too bright. Even during the daytime she had to squint when she came and went from her apartment. The building's interior exuded a faint chemical smell, as if some kind of cleaning fluid had been used recently. She'd never seen anyone washing the faded, threadbare carpet, though, and she had no idea what caused the smell. It was always present and always the same, never stronger, never weaker. She only really noticed the odor when she was out in the hall, though, so she could live with it.

The residents' mailboxes were located in a central area outside the rental office, but she hadn't felt like stopping and checking hers tonight. Whatever bills and junk mail that waited for her would keep until tomorrow.

The building only had two levels, and her apartment was located on the second floor. She held on to the thin metal railing as she ascended the stairs, more out of habit than any real need for support. There were two apartments on the ground floor and two on the second. Hers was 2B. She walked to her door — which was painted a particularly ugly avocado green — fished her keys out of her purse, opened the door, stepped inside, then quickly closed and locked it behind her. She didn't consider herself paranoid exactly, but leaving the door unlocked, even for a short time, seemed like an unnecessary risk to her. And after what had happened tonight, she wanted the feeling of security being in her own place, locked door between her and the rest of the world, provided.

She flipped the light switch next to the door, and the floor lamp in the living room came on. This light was soft and warm, much better than the hallway's fluorescents, and she sighed, relieved to be home. But her relief was short-lived. As she walked into the living room, she saw it was a mess. A comforter lay in a bunched-up mass on the couch, and a bed pillow lay on the floor between the couch and the glass coffee table. The table was littered with detritus — empty corn chip bag, a bowl coated with salsa residue, a half-eaten chocolate bar, and three empty cans of a highly caffeinated energy drink, along with several books and magazines stacked in a lopsided pile. She knew from experience that the pages in the reading material would be dog-eared, and probably stained with salsa, too. Larry was far from the tidiest roommate she'd ever had. She didn't want to go into the kitchen. God only knew what sort of state he'd left it in before heading out to play his gig.

A duffel bag lay on the floor next to the couch. It was open and clothes — T-shirts and underwear, mostly — stuck partway out of it. Back when they'd both shared the same bed, she'd spent too much time picking up after him. But since they'd broken up, he'd become more considerate.

Yes, he'd left a mess behind when he'd gone off to play his gig, but at least it was a *contained* mess. That was a major improvement.

The first time she'd confronted Larry about being a slob, he'd tried to play it off as no big deal. *I'm a creative type. We live in our heads, not in the real word, you know? Besides, what does it matter where stuff is? On a shelf, on the floor.... Is one place inherently better than the other?*

She'd felt like strangling him then. Sometimes she wished she had.

She'd first met Larry Ramirez when he'd accompanied one of his clients – a deaf man who'd undergone multiple back surgeries – to physical therapy. Larry was a sign language interpreter in his day job, and he served as the communication channel between his client and Lori. She'd found him funny and charming, not to mention handsome, and after the fourth PT session for his client, she'd asked him out. He wasn't her patient so it wasn't exactly unethical for her to go out with him, but it did skirt the boundaries of professionalism. They'd had dinner then gone back to her place to have a drink. She made it a rule not to sleep with guys on the first date, but she'd broken that rule with Larry. They started dating regularly after that, and three months later, when the lease on his apartment was up, she asked him to move in with her.

Larry didn't only sign for the deaf; he was also a jazz guitarist who sometimes played with a group and sometimes played solo. She wasn't the biggest fan of jazz, but she thought he played beautifully, and she loved to watch him perform, whether in a group or on his own.

She'd learned one other thing about him early on. He was bisexual. He'd told her not to worry, that he was currently in a 'girl phase'. She'd never dated anyone who was bisexual before, and she *was* worried. She feared he'd eventually get tired of her and go into a 'guy phase', but she decided to put her fears aside and see where their relationship went. It lasted for the better part of three years before she'd decided they made better friends than lovers. When she told Larry, he'd agreed at once, and while she'd been relieved that he'd taken it so well, she'd also been disappointed that he didn't seem at least a little bit sad. He'd always been a go-with-the-flow type, but she would've liked to think their relationship had meant something more to him.

Larry didn't have a steady job. As both an interpreter and a musician he got paid by the gig and, after they broke up, he hadn't been able to afford his own place right away. She'd told him he could continue to stay with her until he'd saved up enough money to move out. That had been nine months ago, and he was still sleeping on her couch every night. Not counting those nights when he stayed out partying with friends or having sex with whoever he was seeing at the time. She kept hoping he'd enter into a long-term relationship with someone and move into their place, but he rarely slept with anyone more than a handful of times in a row.

She'd once asked him why he kept moving from one short-term relationship to another.

It's hard to find anyone who holds my interest very long, you know? He'd smiled and added, *You were the last interesting person I dated.*

The last part had probably been bullshit, but it had made her feel good nonetheless.

It was sometimes frustrating – and more than a little weird – to have her ex as a roommate, but they made it work, more or less. And while she wanted him to get back on his feet and leave, she knew she'd miss him when he was gone.

She sighed.

"Girl, you ought to have your head examined."

She thought of the goat-eyed woman and the shadow thing she'd seen lurking in FoodSaver's parking lot and regretted her choice of words.

CHAPTER TWO

She got ready for bed, a process that normally took half an hour, but she hurried and was done in fifteen minutes. She usually slept in her panties and an oversized T-shirt, and tonight she had on a XXL red-and-gray OSU shirt so large it hung down to her knees. She'd only just gotten into bed and slid under the covers when her phone rang. She'd forgotten to turn the ringer off when she'd placed it on her nightstand, and she was tempted to ignore it, but what if it was important, maybe even an emergency?

"Fuck," she muttered. She snatched the phone off the nightstand and answered it without checking the display to see who it was.

"Hello?"

"Hey, beautiful."

It was Justin. She hadn't wanted to talk to anyone, but now that she heard his voice, she was glad he'd called, and even more glad she'd chosen to answer.

"Hey yourself."

"Sorry I didn't call earlier. I just got home from work. We had a backlog of tests that needed to be done, and Arlene insisted the techs stay late tonight and get caught up. You know how she is when we get even a little bit behind."

Arlene was Justin's supervisor at BioChem Diagnostics, and while Lori had never met her, she'd heard Justin complain about the woman on numerous occasions.

Lori was tempted to tell Justin everything that had happened to her that night, but she was reluctant to talk about the goat-eyed woman, the shadow thing, and the old man in the Volvo. When you put all three together, they sounded outlandish, and Justin was too logical to accept the trifecta of weirdness she'd experienced tonight. And even if he were inclined to believe everything she said, she still didn't want to talk about it, not yet. She wanted to try to forget it all, at least for now.

A few weeks after she and Larry had decided to be just friends, Lori had been ready to date again. She'd never tried a dating service before, but Reeny swore by them, since that's how she'd met her husband, Charles, so Lori decided to give it a try. She researched which online dating services had the highest success rate in matching people, chose one, signed up to the service, and filled out a profile. When it came time to upload a photo, she couldn't decide which one to use, so she'd ended up asking Larry to help her pick one – which was all kinds of weird. He told her to go with a picture of her that appeared on the PT practice's website. In it, she was wearing her uniform and working with a patient. *Don't worry about privacy issues,* Larry had said. *We can blur the guy's face.* She was looking at the camera and smiling while she held the patient's feet to the floor so he could do some sit-ups. *It's a good picture. You look really pretty in it, and it shows you're a caring person.*

She hadn't been certain the photo was a good choice, but she decided to trust Larry's opinion and uploaded it. She received her first message from a potential suitor within fifteen minutes. She received a lot of messages over the next few days, and while she'd been encouraged at first by the responses, they soon became overwhelming – and there were more than a few creepers in the mix. One guy asked if she would send him pictures of her feet, and another asked if she was into breast bondage. She hadn't known that was a thing, and when she looked it up on the Internet she immediately regretted it. Not only did it not look like any fun, it looked like it *hurt.*

She was about to cancel her account and give up on the entire idea of online dating when she received a message from a man named Justin Nguyen. She almost didn't open it, but she had a friend in middle school named Justin. His last name had been Reed, but he'd been a good kid, so she figured, what the hell. Maybe the universe was trying to tell her something. She opened the message, which was a friendly, polite one – no inquiries about which fetishes she might be into – so she checked out his profile. She liked what she saw, sent him a message, and they met for coffee several days later. It wasn't love at first sight or anything, and she didn't feel any immediate sexual attraction toward him. But he was nice and funny and smart, and unlike Larry, he seemed to have his shit together. She decided to go out with him a second time, then a third, and they'd been dating steadily ever since, coming up on seven months now. She still wasn't sure she was *in* love with him, but she cared for him a great deal and she enjoyed his company, and that was enough for now.

"Want to have coffee tomorrow morning before work?" she asked. "My treat."

They both worked in offices downtown, but their buildings were a couple of blocks apart. There was a Starbucks between them, and they'd often meet there around seven a.m., especially if they hadn't seen each other the day before. They'd have coffee and breakfast – a scone for him, a piece of fruit or yogurt for her – and they'd chat about anything and everything, from work to world events. Getting together like this always reminded her of their first date, and she loved starting her day this way. She hoped Justin would say yes. After tonight, she could use a little normalcy.

"Sorry, I can't."

She waited for him to go on, to explain why he couldn't have coffee with her tomorrow. Not that he *had* to give her a reason. She didn't believe in being the kind of girlfriend who kept constant tabs on her boyfriend, but he almost always explained what was going on if he couldn't get together with her. He didn't say anything right away, though, and she started to wonder if something was wrong. But before she could ask if he was okay, he went on.

"I've got a doctor's appointment in the morning. It's just a checkup, but if I cancel, it'll be weeks before they can fit me in again. Maybe longer."

There was nothing about this that she found unreasonable, which made her wonder why Justin sounded defensive, as if he were expecting her to challenge his explanation.

"No problem," she said. "Maybe we can do it the day after tomorrow."

"Sure. Yeah. Sounds great."

He sounded distracted, and she wondered if he was just tired. He had said he'd had to stay late at work tonight. Still, something seemed off, and she couldn't put her finger on what it was. Then she remembered something. Hadn't he seen his doctor earlier in the month? And hadn't that appointment also been for a checkup? Why would he need another so soon? The answer, of course, was that he wouldn't – which meant something else was going on. Was he cheating on her, maybe seeing someone else for coffee tomorrow? Or maybe he was spending the night at her place tonight, whoever *she* was, and he didn't want to leave her any earlier than he had to tomorrow morning. No, that didn't make sense. *Justin* had called *her*. If he was at someone else's place, or if someone was at his, why would he call her? Neither of them were teenagers and while they texted or spoke most days, it wasn't uncommon for a day to go by now and again without any contact between them. When that happened, she'd never worried about it, so there was no reason for him to think she'd get suspicious if he didn't get in touch tonight. *Unless* he was feeling guilty about cheating and needed to set up an alibi in order to decrease his anxiety about being discovered.

She almost laughed then. After all the weird shit that had gone down at FoodSaver, she was being paranoid. Maybe she simply misremembered the last time Justin had gone to the doctor. Or maybe one of the appointments was with his physician and the other was with his dentist. Whichever was the case, she highly doubted Justin would cheat on her. He believed there was a right way and a wrong way of doing things, and that the right way – whatever it was – should be followed. *Always*. It was a trait that made him extremely good at medical testing, even if it did make him overly conventional and a bit boring sometimes. No, if he had wanted to see someone else, he would've broken up with her first. She was certain of that. He wasn't like Larry, who could be balls deep inside someone he'd just met before it occurred to him that the person he was currently dating might be displeased by his actions.

Then again, things weren't always the way they seemed, were they?

"I hate to do this," Lori said, "but I should go. I'm exhausted. How about I call you after work tomorrow night? Maybe we could have dinner."

"Sounds good."

He still sounded distracted, as if he was only partially paying attention to their conversation. It occurred to her then that maybe he'd called because he'd wanted to talk about something important, only now that they were on the phone together he was having second thoughts.

"Is there something wrong?" she asked.

He immediately became defensive again. "What? No, why would you ask that?"

"You seem a little preoccupied tonight, that's all. It's not like you." Another thought occurred to her then. "Are you still upset about our conversation last week?"

"Which conversation?" He sounded honestly puzzled.

"The one where you lectured me about continuing to allow Larry to stay here."

She could've said the *latest* conversation about Larry, since his continued presence in her life was a sore spot with Justin – especially the fact that they technically still lived together. She'd assured him a dozen times over that she and Larry were just friends. Larry had taken it upon himself to talk to Justin as well, explaining that he had nothing to worry about. Not only were he and Lori better off as friends, he was currently in a 'guy phase'. Each time Lori addressed the issue with Justin, he seemed reassured, but only for a while, and then his jealousy would build once more until he could no longer contain it. She really couldn't blame him. If their positions were reversed, she was sure she'd be just as insecure as he was, if not more. But she couldn't just kick Larry out to make Justin feel more comfortable. Could she?

"I can honestly say that Larry was the furthest thing from my mind tonight," Justin said, his tone sharp. "But now that you've brought up the subject, what is your *friend* doing tonight? Or maybe I should ask *who* he's doing."

Lori was shocked. Justin was an even-tempered person for the most part, and even when he became angry – which he always did when Larry came up in conversation – he'd never gotten mean like this before, and she found herself reacting with her own anger.

"What do you want me to say? That's he's in bed with me right now, head buried between my legs, sucking on my clit while his fingers piston in and out of my vagina like he's some kind of human vibrator?"

She was shocked as much by her own words as she'd been by Justin's. She'd never spoken to him like this before, had never spoken to *anyone* like this before. What the hell had gotten into her?

"Sorry," she immediately apologized. "Like I said, I'm tired. But if it makes you feel any better, Larry's playing a gig tonight, and I don't...."

She trailed off when she realized she was speaking to dead air. Justin had hung up on her. She started to call him back, then thought better of it. They could both use the rest of the night to cool off before they talked to each other again. Still, she didn't want to leave things the way they were, so she sent Justin a quick text.

I didn't mean to snap. I'll be more pleasant after a good night's sleep. She hesitated a moment, and then added, *Love you.* Not *I love you. Love you* was something you said to friends and relations. *I love you* was a commitment, one she wasn't ready to make yet.

She sent the text, then turned off her phone's ringer and placed it on her nightstand. If there were going to be any emergencies tonight, the world would just have to get along without her.

She turned off her nightstand lamp, rolled onto her left side – her preferred sleeping position – and closed her eyes. Given everything that had happened since she'd left work tonight, she expected she'd be too wound up to fall asleep immediately, and she was right. She tossed and turned for a while, but eventually sleep did find her. Later, she would wish it hadn't.

★   ★   ★

"That's it, Lori! Take it all the way to the goal!"

Lori barely registered Coach Anderson's words. She was in the Zone, and being in the Zone felt damn good. It was like everyone else in the world had ceased to exist, like she was the only person left. It was just her and the sun and the breeze and the grass and the ball. And, of course, the goal. She knew there was a goalie protecting it – Aashrita Dhawan, her best friend in all the world – but she didn't actually see her. Aashrita wasn't invisible to her, not exactly. But then again, she kind of was. The rest of the girls on their team were on the field, wearing their blue jerseys and black shorts, but half also wore green vests so they could be identified as the opposing team for this afternoon's practice. But all of them, Aashrita included, existed on the periphery of Lori's awareness, present but not important. All that mattered was her, the ball, and the goal.

Lori was seventeen. She'd started playing recreational league soccer in grade school, and she'd kept at it, eventually winning a place on the high school girls' team when she was a freshman. She loved the game, loved pushing her body to its limit and beyond, loved the excitement of competition, loved the emotional high of victory, and she loved supporting her teammates and being supported by them in turn. Losing wasn't much fun, naturally, but even then she still loved the game. She'd seen a bumper sticker once on an old battered pickup: *My worst day fishing was better than my best day doing anything else.* Replace *fishing* with *soccer,* and that's exactly how she felt about the sport. She hoped to continue playing in college, but when she'd shared this ambition with Coach Anderson, she'd said that if Lori really wanted to play at college level, she needed to be more aggressive on the field, take more chances, give her all on each and every play. *You're a good player,* Coach Anderson had told her, *but if you want to make it in college, you've got to be great.* So heeding her coach's advice, she'd stolen the ball from Ashley Boone – which, to be honest, hadn't been all that difficult – and now she was charging toward the other team's goal, and while this was only practice and her opponents were in truth her teammates, she intended to show them no mercy. *Mercy is for the weak,* her father had told her on numerous occasions, and Lori knew that if she wanted to be college soccer material, she had to avoid being weak in any way. *No fear, no mercy, no pity,* she thought.

Her blood sang in her ears as she ran, her body operating like a superbly maintained high-performance machine, arms and legs pumping, controlling the ball as she drove toward the goal, almost as if the ball was part of her. She'd read about people having tunnel vision, where they hyper-focused on something to the exclusion of all else, but she'd never experienced it before now.

When she had closed to within fifteen feet of the goal, she lined up her shot – high and to the left, toward the one area of the goal that Aashrita always had trouble covering. She was about to make her kick, would've done so in another second, two at the most, when suddenly an East Indian girl wearing a green vest appeared in her vision. It was as if Aashrita had materialized out of thin air. She was way outside of the goal and charging just as hard toward Lori as Lori was charging toward her. Lori had time for a single thought – *This is going to hurt like a bitch* – and then she and Aashrita collided.

When she thought back on this moment in the years to come – which wasn't often – she had no memory of actually striking Aashrita. One instant she saw her friend only inches from her face, Aashrita's expression one of fierce determination, and the next Lori was looking up at blue sky and clouds and wondering why her ears were ringing so bad. Then the pain hit her and she heard a scream split the air. It was a moment before she realized the scream had come from her mouth. She hurt all over, but the worst pain was centered in her right knee. It felt as if the bone had been replaced with molten fire, the sensation so intense, so far beyond any type of pain she'd ever experienced, that she wasn't sure there was a word for it.

Her eyes were squeezed shut and tears streamed down her face to wet the grass on either side of her head. She didn't see Coach Anderson, but she heard the woman blow her whistle – a signal for the other girls to take a knee – and then she heard pounding footfalls as the coach ran toward her.

"Lori! Are you okay? How badly are you hurt?"

She opened her eyes and tried to focus on Coach Anderson's face, but her eyes were filled with tears, and she could only see a watery, distorted image of the woman. The light hurt her eyes, caused her head to start throbbing and the ringing in her ears to intensify, so she quickly closed them again.

"Check on Aashrita," she said, hissing the words through her pain.

She feared her idiotic desire to be the baddest badass soccer player on the team had resulted in her friend being hurt, maybe seriously so. And if that was the case, she didn't think she'd be able to live with the guilt.

To hell with soccer, she thought. Playing in college wasn't worth it, not if it meant having to hurt anyone who stood in her way.

"A noble sentiment."

Startled by the voice – a male's, one she didn't recognize – she opened her eyes.

The pain was gone. Her head no longer pounded, the ringing in her ears had ceased, and the fire in her knee had been extinguished. The relief was so great that it was almost as overwhelming as the agony it replaced, and she drew in a gasping breath. Her vision was clear once more, and she saw she sat alone in the back seat of a car – a big one, a Cadillac or limousine – and she was her current self again, thirty-four, and wore a long-sleeved robe made of sheer white fabric. She was naked underneath, and her breasts and nipples were quite visible. Suddenly uncomfortable, she crossed her arms over her chest. The seats were upholstered in fine black leather, luxuriously soft, but cold, and her gossamer-thin robe did little to insulate her body from it. The vehicle's only other occupant was the driver. He – Lori assumed the driver was male based on the voice she'd heard – wore a hooded red robe. She couldn't see the back of his head, but she could see his hands gripping the steering wheel. They were broad and thick fingered, the backs covered with hair so thick it almost looked like fur. The nail of the pinky finger on his left hand was painted red, the same shade as his robe.

Like the goat-eyed woman in FoodSaver, she thought.

The radio was on, but all that came out of it was static, the volume turned low so it was almost inaudible. There was a rhythm and cadence to the sound, almost as if it were words spoken in some alien language that she could barely perceive, let alone understand. She turned to look out the right passenger window and saw nothing but blackness. She might've thought the window had been painted over, but she had the impression there was depth to the darkness, that it stretched outward for miles, all the way to some unseen horizon. She leaned closer to the window and looked upward. There were no stars in the empty black sky, and it seemed the darkness continued on to infinity. It made her feel very small, and she tightened her arms around herself as she shivered.

She looked forward, and through the vehicle's windshield, she saw headlight beams illuminating a glossy obsidian surface. *We're on a road,* she thought, one without any identifying features. *No billboards, no dividing line painted down the middle. Nothing.*

"Where am I?" she asked. "What's going on?"

The driver answered without turning to look at her.

"Where you are is the Nightway. What's going on is that I'm taking you to the Vermilion Tower. My associates and I want to have a little chat with you."

The man's voice was devoid of emotion, almost robotic. She leaned forward to look at the rearview mirror, hoping to catch a glimpse of his features in its reflection. She expected him to have goat eyes, like FoodSaver woman. He had no eyes, though, only patches of smooth skin where eyes should be. As she watched, the patches pulsed, as if in time with his breathing. He smiled then, his teeth a gleaming unnatural white.

"I suggest you relax and enjoy the ride."

The no-eyed man turned his attention back to the obsidian road that stretched out before them.

Lori's detached calm was beginning to give way to nervousness. All of this – her nakedness, the road, the car, the driver – had seemed like a dream, or perhaps a hallucination brought on by some powerful drug. But her mind was starting to clear now, and she couldn't shake the feeling that maybe, just maybe, this was real. She tried to remember how she'd gotten here, but nothing came to her. She remembered being on the soccer field, running toward the goal that Aashrita protected, remembered how they'd crashed into each other.... She frowned. That had happened in high school, seventeen years ago. How.... She realized then that she had been dreaming. That day on the practice field had changed her entire life. She'd torn her anterior cruciate ligament – her ACL – the tissue that connected the thighbone to the shinbone. She'd needed surgery, followed by months of physical therapy. It was nine months before she was able to return to full physical activity. By then she was in her senior year, and although the doctor had given her the green light to return to playing soccer, she was no longer interested in it. Partially because she wanted to avoid another serious injury, but also because she had a new passion. After going through physical therapy and experiencing firsthand what it could do to help someone heal, she'd decided to enter the profession. She eventually graduated with her bachelor's in PT, then went on to get her master's in the discipline. As for Aashrita.... She didn't want to think about her right then, and so she turned her mind back to the problem at hand.

She had dreamed about her soccer injury, but that dream had ended with her lying on her back on the grass, knee hurting like a motherfucker. Now she was here, with no apparent transition between. That meant this *was* a dream. She'd simply transitioned from one scenario – a realistic one drawn from her own life – to a more unrealistic one, where a man with no eyes chauffeured her down a black road in a sunless, starless world. And where she was wearing a see-through robe to boot. This scenario had all the hallmarks of a dream that was rapidly sliding into nightmare territory. So why didn't it *feel* like a dream?

She rubbed her right hand across the leather of the seat to test its reality. She jerked her hand back when she felt the leather ripple beneath her fingers, as if her touch excited it. Her bare ass was on this leather, or whatever it was, separated only by sheer cloth. She imagined the seat rippling beneath her butt, as if caressing her, and the thought turned her stomach. She resolved to sit very, very still. Aside from the radio, the car was quiet, and she wondered if the vehicle had an engine or was propelled by other means. The ride was smooth, too, as if the obsidian surface of the Nightway was perfectly flat and highly polished.

She began to tremble, as much from fear as from cold. She wanted to ask the driver to stop and let her out, but she said nothing. Not only did she think the eyeless man would refuse her request, if he *did* allow her to leave the vehicle, where could she go? The car's lights were the only source of illumination she'd seen in this place so far. Once she was standing on the side of the road alone, and the driver had put enough distance between them, she would be swallowed by darkness as complete as that in a cavern far beneath the surface of the earth or at the bottom of the deepest part of the ocean; places light had never touched and never would. Where could she go? How would she find her way? And what if there were other things out there in the darkness with her, things she couldn't see, but which could detect her by sound or smell, things that were *hungry*?

No, better to remain where she was. If this was a dream, it didn't matter what she did. Nothing could harm her here. And if this was real – even if only partially – the longer she remained inside the car, the safer she'd be. She hoped.

She sat back and felt a wave of revulsion as the leather behind her shuddered upon her contact with it. She told herself to keep still, ignore the obscene sensation, and focus on the world outside the window, but that didn't help. There were no landmarks to see, nothing to indicate the passage of time or the vehicle's movement. The blackness was eerie and absolute, but sometimes she had the impression of things moving on either side of the road, shadows within shadows, and more than moving – they were watching as well. Watching and waiting and hoping that the car edged a little too close to the side of the road, close enough to reach out and grab it.

Occasionally they passed vehicles going in the opposite direction. Some were four-wheeled machines that more or less resembled cars she was familiar with, but others looked like nothing she'd ever seen before. One looked as if it had been built from the hollowed-out exoskeleton of a praying mantis the size of a semi-truck. Another was an amorphous mass of sparkling fog, in the center of which crouched the silhouette of a figure that held only the most rudimentary resemblance to a human form. The strangest was something that resembled a carriage made from raw meat, pulled by a pair of creatures that resembled horses that had been turned inside out.

She wasn't certain how much time passed. It could've been minutes, it could've been hours. But eventually she became aware of a faint red glow in the distance ahead of them. She fixed her gaze upon it and watched it grow larger as they approached. Eventually, they were close enough for her to begin to make out details. It was a gigantic spire, although without any objects around it for comparison, its size was difficult to judge. It *felt* big, though. Skyscraper-big. A curling organic-looking spiral, it reminded her of a narwhal's jutting horn, only it was wider at the bottom and continued getting narrower until it came to a point at the top. It was clear to see how the Vermilion Tower had gotten its name. The spiral gave off its own crimson light, which seemed to smolder amidst the darkness, like the coals of a fire that hadn't quite burned out yet. The light pulsed slowly, as if in time to the beat of an enormous heart. She wondered then if the spiral truly was a horn, and if so, if it was attached to some unfathomably large creature buried vertically beneath the ground. Maybe the behemoth was long dead and only its skeleton remained, or perhaps it still lived and was only slumbering, waiting for the right moment to wake and burst free from the ground that imprisoned it.

The driver slowed as they approached the tower. He activated his right turn signal – an action Lori found so absurd she nearly laughed – and pulled off the road. The surface they now drove on wasn't as smooth as the Nightway, and the car juddered as the driver pulled up to the tower. He stopped, parked, and turned off the car. The headlights flicked off, but the pulsing scarlet light emanating from the tower provided enough illumination for Lori to see. Her skin looked blood-red in the tower's light, and she was surprised to find the effect beautiful in its way.

The driver got out of the car and opened one of the passenger doors for her to disembark.

What if I refused? she wondered. Would the eyeless man grab her by the arm and pull her out of the car? Or would he stand there and wait until she chose to come out, regardless of how long it took? Either way, she'd end up leaving the car, so she saw no point in putting it off. She climbed out, acutely aware that her naked body was fully visible through the thin fabric of her robe. Once outside, she crossed her arms over her chest again, even though the man who'd brought her had no eyes with which to examine her body. She covered herself more for psychological comfort than anything else.

The ground felt rough and pebbly beneath her bare feet, and when she looked down, she saw the area around the tower's base looked more like animal hide than soil, the thick, tough skin of some large mammal like a rhino or elephant. This reinforced her impression that the tower was in truth the horn of some buried creature, and she shuddered at the thought that she stood upon the skin of some unimaginably vast horror.

The driver closed the passenger door then faced Lori.

"Follow me," he said, and then he walked toward the tower. After a moment's hesitation – perhaps solely to give herself the illusion that she had a choice in the matter – she followed. A sound emerged from beneath the car's hood, a soft, high-pitched tone that made Lori think of an unhappy dog's whine. It was crazy, but she thought the car was expressing sadness over her departure.

The air was chilly, like a late fall morning in Ohio, and it had a curious stale quality, like a room that had been closed for years. *Dead air,* she thought, and the description seemed apt.

The eyeless man led her to the tower's base. Now that she was close to it, she could see the tower was smooth and shiny, as if it were made of pearl, or a substance very much like it. She felt an urge to reach out and run her hand along its surface, but she resisted. She sensed touching the tower's outer surface would be bad, although she had no idea why it should be so. Still, she heeded her instinct and kept her arms crossed over her chest.

There was no apparent door in the tower's base, but when the eyeless man waved his hand in the air inches from its surface, the pearl-like substance flowed away like liquid, forming a semi-circular opening large enough for both of them to enter.

She thought he might turn to her, smile with his too-white teeth, say *After you,* then gesture for her to precede him. But he didn't. Instead he walked into the tower without waiting to see if she would follow.

This was it – her chance to escape.

She could run off into the darkness, take her chances with whatever might be out there waiting for her. She heard a quiet chorus of whispers then, like a sudden strong breeze, but she felt no stirring in the dead air. She could make out what sounded like words.

Yes, yes! Come to us, come! We will welcome you with our claws and mouths and our sharp-sharp teeth!

She looked back at the car that had brought her here. It looked something like a cross between a limo and a hearse, and while its surface appeared dark crimson in the light pulsing from the Vermilion Tower, she thought the vehicle was likely painted black – the blackest black that had ever been created, darker than night, despair, hopelessness, and sin. Could she steal it – get in, slide behind the wheel, and drive away from the tower, and try her luck on the Nightway? If this was a dream, she'd wake up eventually, and if it wasn't, at least she'd be away from this place and whatever awaited her within.

She didn't know if the vehicle needed a key to activate its engine. She hadn't heard the eyeless man remove a key from the ignition and slip it into a pocket of his robe as he got out of the car. But maybe the car only needed a keyless remote to turn it on, in which case, the eyeless man probably still had the remote on him. But this car wasn't an ordinary vehicle. It seemed to possess some kind of independent life of its own – *and* she thought it liked her. If she got in, maybe it would activate its engine for her, only too happy to assist its newfound friend.

She thought then of the way the car's back seat had rippled under her hand, and she wondered what the car might do once she was alone inside it.

What can it do? she thought. *It's just a machine, for Christ's sake.*

She took a step toward it, the driver's-side door swung open, and a low thrumming sound like the purr of a large cat filled the air.

She stopped, stood for a moment, reconsidering. Her grandmother had loved to dispense bits of homespun wisdom via folksy sayings. Lori had come to loathe them as a child, but as an adult, her grandmother's words came back to her now and again, and she often found them pertinent to her life. Once of those sayings was, *Dance with the one that brung you.* In this case, she thought that was excellent advice.

She turned and entered the tower, the semicircular door flowing closed behind her.

The eyeless man was nowhere in sight.

She expected the inside of the tower to resemble the outside, walls, floors, and ceiling made of the same pearl-like substance, all of it pulsing with burning-coal light. But the interior was made of gray stone blocks, with illumination provided by burning wooden torches, set into rusty iron sconces at periodic intervals. The fire that blazed from the torches seemed perfectly ordinary at first, but it took her only a few moments to realize the flames gave off no heat or smoke. Frowning in puzzlement, she walked up to the closest torch and reached toward the dancing fire burning at its tip. When her fingers were within an inch of the flames – and feeling no warmth at all – the fire bent toward her hand and engulfed the flesh. She screamed as pain erupted in her hand, and she jerked it away from the flames, taking a couple steps back for good measure, as if she feared the fire might stretch out and attempt to burn her once more. It stayed where it was, though she could almost hear the crackling sound of laughter, as if the torch flame was amused by what it had done.

She cradled her injured hand to her abdomen and looked down to examine it. She expected to find her skin red and blistered, but her flesh was smooth and undamaged. But if that was the case, why did her hand hurt so goddamn *bad*?

"The Flames of the Intercessor burn from the inside out."

She spun toward the speaker of these words and saw the eyeless man facing her. His tone had been one of amusement and his mouth formed a crooked smile.

An instant ago, the corridor had been empty, with no sign of the man. Now here he was again, as if he'd materialized before her. Who knows? Maybe he had.

"You entered the tower willingly," the eyeless man said. "That is a point in your favor. Come with me."

He turned and began moving down the corridor in a strange gliding motion. The hem of his crimson robe extended all the way to the stone floor, concealing his feet. Although given the odd way he moved, and the fact that she heard no sound of shoes touching the floor as he traveled, she wasn't certain he *had* feet.

She might've shivered at this thought, but her hand hurt too much for her to feel anything else. Still cradling her hand to her abdomen, and no longer caring that she wasn't concealing her breasts, she followed after the eyeless man.

CHAPTER THREE

She opened her eyes to darkness, instantly alert, but not knowing why. She felt her mattress beneath her, the comforter over her, and she realized she was in her bed, in her apartment. It was night, and she had been sleeping. Dreaming, too. She thought of the drive to the Vermilion Tower, thought of the Nightway, the eyeless man, the fire that burned her from the inside out. It had seemed so real, but now she was awake, and the nightmare was over. She felt too wired to return to sleep right away, but she didn't care if she'd be up the rest of the night. A little sleep deprivation was a small price to pay to escape that awful—

Her thought was cut off by the sound of a *thump* coming from somewhere in her apartment. The living room, maybe. She understood that she hadn't woken because her dream-slash-nightmare had become too disturbing. She'd woken because she'd heard a noise, probably a previous *thump*. She was a light sleeper, had been since her parents had brought her home from the hospital, at least to hear them tell it. She always woke when Larry got home after a night gig. He was usually drunk, or close to it, and while he wasn't known for being ninja-quiet in the best of situations, he was even louder when he had alcohol in his system.

Ordinarily, she'd have been irritated by his clumsy noisiness, might've called out for him to keep it down. He'd call back, saying *Okay,* and he'd be quiet for a couple minutes, and then he'd start being noisy again, as if she'd never said anything at all. But tonight she was glad he was home. After the nightmare she'd had, she was grateful that she wasn't alone in the apartment any longer.

I'll go out, say hi, see how the gig went, she thought. And if Larry was in a talkative mood, if he wanted to stay up and regale her with stories of how many good-looking men and women had attended the show, and laugh about all the ways he and the band had screwed up their performance, she'd listen to every word, ask questions, encourage him to add more details until the sun came up and her nightmare became a distant – if unpleasant – memory.

She threw off the comforter, moved into a sitting position, then put her feet on the floor and stood. After dreaming of being semi-nude, she was self-conscious about how much of her bare legs were visible below the T-shirt – not to mention that she only had a pair of panties on underneath – but Larry had seen her naked more times than she could count. Since they'd ceased being a couple, he had never tried to make a move on her, not once. She had no reason not to trust him. Still, she was tempted to grab a pair of sweatpants from the dresser and slip them on before leaving her bedroom. She decided against it. Larry knew she didn't sleep in sweats, and he'd know something was wrong if he saw her in them. She didn't want to tell him about her dream, wanted to let the memory of it fade in the way dreams did. So, bare-legged and braless, she walked to the bedroom door, opened it, and stepped out into the short, narrow hallway.

The hallway housed a small linen closet as well as a half-bath, but that was all. From here, she normally could see into the living room – when the lights were on, that is. They were off now, and the apartment was pitch black. Larry never went to bed right away after coming home from a gig. Even if he'd had a few drinks – or more than a few – he was too wired from performing to sleep. He'd stay up two, three hours, texting friends and watching YouTube videos on his phone, listening with earbuds so he wouldn't wake her. Maybe he'd drunk more than usual and had passed out on the couch moments after entering. He snored, though lightly, when he slept sober, louder when he fell asleep drunk. But she heard no breathing, let alone any snoring.

Maybe the noise she'd heard had come from another apartment. It wasn't as if the walls and floors were soundproof. She could often make out conversations taking place in the adjoining apartments, especially when said conversations devolved into shouting matches. If Larry was zonked out, she didn't want to bother him, and if the thumps had come from another apartment, they didn't concern her. She started to turn and head back into her bedroom when she thought of something. When Larry came in late, he sometimes forgot to lock the door. One time, he'd been so drunk and exhausted that he'd left the damn door open all night while he slept belly-down on the living room floor. They'd been lucky someone hadn't tried to rob them – or worse.

If Larry *had* collapsed on the couch – or fallen to the floor – he might have passed out before closing the door. She should go out into the living room and check to make certain the door was closed, and if it wasn't, she'd close and lock it herself. If she didn't check, she knew she'd keep obsessing over the door, and there would be no way she'd get back to sleep tonight. Without realizing it, she crossed her arms over her breasts as she'd done in the nightmare, and started toward the living room, moving slowly so as not to trip in the darkness.

There were lampposts behind the apartment building, the same kind as the ones out front. Both the first- and second-floor units had sliding-glass patio doors close to the kitchen. Lori used hers as a dining area, keeping a small round table with a pair of chairs in front of the patio door. The ground-floor apartments had individual fenced-in patios, while the upper apartments had wooden decks they shared with the unit next door. They each had a small space where residents could sit and hang out, the spaces bisected by a single set of wooden stairs that led down to the ground. Vertical blinds covered Lori's patio door at night, but slivers of light usually managed to sneak through the spaces between the slats, illuminating the living room and kitchen, at least a little. There was no light now, though, which was weird because the blinds were old and some of the slats didn't close all the way. Maybe there was something outside the patio door, blocking the light. She wanted to tell herself the thought was ridiculous, but after what she'd experienced tonight at FoodSaver the idea didn't seem foolish at all.

She took several steps into the living room, stopped, and whispered, "Larry? Are you home?"

No response.

She didn't want to speak much louder in case he was here and sleeping, but she could feel the first stirring of panic in her mind, and so she said his name again, speaking in a normal – if strained – voice.

"Larry?"

Still no response.

Even louder now, almost yelling.

"Larry!"

Nothing.

Either he was *really* out of it – like alcohol-poisoned and unconscious out of it – or he wasn't here. There was only one way to know for certain.

She uncrossed her arms and reached out toward where she thought the wall was, hoping to find one of the switches that turned on the living room's ceiling light. Her fingers found the wall and slid back and forth across its flat surface, but she couldn't find the switch. She could've sworn there was a light switch somewhere around there. But if there was, she couldn't find it. Maybe the switch wasn't there now. Maybe something had happened, maybe her apartment had *changed*.

Stop it, she told herself. *Just. Stop. It.*

She took in a slow, deep breath. Held it. Let it out just as slowly.

Okay, so she couldn't find the switch for the ceiling light. There were other ways to check for Larry's presence.

She started moving toward the area where she thought the couch was located, half bent over, both hands stretched out before her, ears straining to detect any hint of Larry's breathing. She walked for what seemed too long a time. Surely she should've reached the couch by now, or at least reached *something* – a wall, the chair next to the couch…. But she continued walking without encountering anything, and a terrible thought occurred to her. What if when she left the hallway, she'd somehow stepped onto an endless dark plain, like the land on either side of the Nightway in her dream? What if the Nightway and the Vermilion Tower were real, and her apartment – her entire life on Earth – was the dream? Was she lost in the lands beyond the Nightway, doomed to wander aimlessly until some deadly predator caught wind of her scent and decided to approach her in order to satisfy both its curiosity *and* hunger?

She felt a sudden sharp pain in her shins, and she let out a squeal of fright. It took her an instant to realize she'd walked into the glass coffee table in front of the couch.

"Fuck," she muttered beneath her breath. But despite the pain, she was relieved to have struck the coffee table. The pain told her that she was in her apartment and that everything was normal. *Probably going to have a of couple bruises tomorrow.* That was a small price to pay for a little reassurance, though.

She crouched and searched with her fingers until she felt the edge of the coffee table's surface. Keeping one hand on the table to guide her, she walked around it until her left leg bumped into the couch. She stretched out her right hand and felt the cushions. No Larry. She kept her hand on the couch as she made her way around to the floor lamp sitting next to it. She found the switch and turned on the light. She forgot to look away and bright illumination stabbed into her eyes. She squeezed them shut and turned her head away from the lamp. Her eyes watered and tears slid down her cheeks. She felt a spike of pain behind her eyes, and she feared she might be on the verge of triggering another goddamn migraine.

Don't borrow trouble, her mother always said. It was good advice, and she told herself not to worry about her head. Either she'd get a migraine or she wouldn't.

She opened her eyes slowly to give them a chance to adjust to the light. She had to blink several times to clear the tears from her vision, but once she'd done this, she was able to see well enough. What she didn't see was any sign of Larry. The front door was closed and locked, and that was a relief.

Whatever had caused those thumps, she hadn't heard any more of them since leaving her bedroom. The noises had most likely been caused by one of the building's other residents – as she'd suspected – and it seemed they'd stopped doing whatever it was they'd been up to. She was just on edge after everything that had happened tonight, that's all. Best to forget about the mess, go back to bed, and try to return to sleep. She had work in the morning.

She glanced at the door once again. She was tempted to engage the chain lock for an extra measure of security, small though it might be. But if she did that, Larry wouldn't be able to get in when he finally made it home. He might figure fuck it and go sleep in his car. It wouldn't be the first time. But there was an equally likely chance he'd pound his fist on the door and call her name until she woke and came out to let him in. She didn't want to deal with a loud, drunk, and angry Larry tonight. She'd leave the chain off.

She turned back to the lamp, intending to turn the light off, but she changed her mind. What would it hurt to leave the light on out here for the rest of the night? Maybe she'd sleep with her nightstand lamp on, too. She hadn't done so since she'd been a little girl, but if having a light on in her bedroom helped her get through the rest of the night, she'd do it. Hell, she'd install a fucking spotlight in her room if it would—

Her thoughts were interrupted by a soft clattering.

Her gaze was instantly drawn toward the sound, and she saw the vertical blinds over her patio door undulate slowly, stirred by a breeze.

She felt a fresh jolt of fear. A breeze meant the patio door was open. Had Larry left it like that when he'd departed for his gig? She hadn't checked the patio door to make sure it was locked before she'd gone to bed, had she? She couldn't remember, but she didn't think so. If the patio door was open, that meant that someone else *could* be in her apartment right now. Maybe multiple someones.

She stood there, frozen, unable to decide what she should do next. She could call nine-one-one, but she'd left her phone on her nightstand, and she'd have to return to her bedroom for it. And if she did call for help, what could she say? *I heard a couple thumps, and when I checked, I discovered my patio door was open. I'm scared. Can you send someone to check if the Boogeyman snuck in?* She'd feel ridiculous if the police showed up, checked her entire apartment, and found nothing.

There's no sign of an intruder, ma'am. You're perfectly safe.

She imagined the officer saying these words with a slight sneer, as if he or she was angry with the overly nervous woman who'd wasted their time because she thought she'd heard something scary – upon awakening from a nightmare, no less. Then again, she'd be an idiot to continue investigating on her own, going into the small kitchen, stepping out onto the patio. That was the kind of dumb move people in films made, and more often than not, their stupidity resulted in their deaths. Better to be embarrassed than dead, she decided.

She started walking back toward the bedroom, moving slowly and quietly, continually gazing back at the patio door as she went. Another gust of wind stirred the blinds, this one stronger than the first, causing them to ripple and rattle more loudly than last time. The sound made her jump and she stopped walking and stared at the patio door.

That's when she saw the first hand reach through the blinds. It was shadow-black, with long, multijointed fingers that ended in sharp, curving claws. It was the same sort of hand the shadow thing she'd glimpsed in the parking lot of FoodSaver had possessed. Was it the same creature? Had the thing somehow followed her home? She thought of the thumps she'd heard, and now she realized she knew what the sounds had been someone – or something – pounding on the glass of the patio doors from the outside. The door *had* been closed, and maybe the shadow creature had been trying to force it open, perhaps pounding the glass in frustration until it finally succeeded.

A second hand emerged from between the blinds, identical to the first. Then came a third, a fourth, a fifth…. Six, seven, eight, nine…. She lost count after that as hands continued thrusting through the blinds. Within seconds the rectangular space that marked the patio door's opening was filled with ebon-clawed hands, all of them reaching toward her, fingers flexing, claws softly scratching against one another, as if the creatures were attempting to sharpen them before attacking. She'd been right about something blocking the light from the lamps behind the building, and now she knew what that something was.

She heard whispering then, a sound that might have been an autumnal wind, but which might also have been a chorus of voices speaking words that she couldn't quite make out. Then one of the shadow creatures entered the apartment, seeming to slide between the blinds' slats as if it were momentarily two-dimensional. But once it was inside the room, standing between the patio door and the dining table, it regained mass, like a black balloon inflating itself. This creature looked exactly like the one she'd seen at FoodSaver, might even have been the same one. It was impossible to tell. The thing had no apparent sensory organs, but its featureless face was pointed at her, and she had the impression that it was well aware of her presence. It stood for a moment, regarding her, and then it gripped the edge of the small round table with its clawed hands and flipped it over. The sound of the table hitting the floor shocked her out of her paralysis, and she turned to flee. In her peripheral vision she caught sight of the shadow creature heading toward her, claws upraised, as others of its kind entered the room, knocking the dining table's two chairs over as they came.

She ran.

Her bare feet pounded on the carpet of the short hallway as she dashed toward her bedroom. She heard no sounds of pursuit coming from behind her, but she didn't know if the shadow creatures made any noise as they moved – the one at FoodSaver hadn't. But she wasn't dumb enough to believe the things weren't chasing after her, and she was damn sure she wasn't going to look back over her shoulder to check. When she reached her bedroom, she dashed inside, slammed the door shut behind her, and locked it. She then hurried to her nightstand to snatch up her phone. Before she could start to input numbers, one of the creatures crashed into her bedroom door, hitting it so hard she heard wood crack. The creatures might look like shadows and move just as silently, but it seemed they could pack a wallop when they wanted to.

More pounding at the door now. She pictured a mass of shadowy forms filling the hallway, clawed hands curled into fists, all of them pounding on her bedroom door, desperate to get at her. It wouldn't take the things long to break down the door and flood into the room. She preferred not to be there when it happened.

She darted toward her bathroom and reached it at the exact instant that the bedroom door burst open. She spun around, shut the bathroom door, locked it, then plopped down on her ass in front of it. She turned, braced her bare feet on the toilet bowl's cold porcelain, and pushed her back against the door. She didn't know how long she'd be able to keep the shadow creatures from reaching her, but she hoped it would be long enough.

Heart pounding, head throbbing, breath coming in ragged gasps, she pressed nine-one-one on her phone's screen and then held the device up to her head with a shaking hand. For an instant she feared that the call wouldn't go through, that the shadow creatures possessed some kind of ability to block her phone's signal, and she was relieved when she heard the sound of ringing as her phone tried to connect.

Before the dispatcher on the other end could answer, dozens of hands began pounding on the bathroom door, striking so hard that she could feel the impacts juddering through her bones and teeth. She experienced a draining sensation then, a sudden weariness, as if her strength was deserting her. Her legs began to tremble, and she feared she wouldn't be able to keep the door closed much longer.

"No," she said. "Please, no...."

And just like that, the pounding stopped. It didn't taper off, one pair of hands stopping, followed by another and so on. All the hands discontinued striking the door at the exact same instant, as if the shadow things had received some kind of signal to break off their attack.

"Nine-one-one. What's your emergency?"

Lori was so relieved she started crying, and when the dispatcher once again asked what her emergency was, she almost couldn't speak.

"Someone's broken into my apartment," she said, voice soft and breathy. "I've locked myself in the bathroom and I'm hiding from them."

"Hold on. Someone will be there soon. Give me your address."

Lori did, and the dispatcher told her to remain on the line while she contacted officers closest to her location. Lori said she would, and while she waited, she listened, trying to hear if the shadow creatures were still gathered outside the bathroom, perhaps hoping to trick her into thinking they were gone so she'd open the door and they could get at her. She heard nothing, though. Maybe they *were* gone.

A soft rapping sounded on the door, and she screamed.

"Lori? Are you okay?"

It was Larry.

In an instant, she was on her feet. Still holding on to her phone with her left hand, she unlocked the door with her right, opened it, and threw herself into Larry's arms. She hit him so hard, he staggered back a step before hesitantly bringing up his arms to hold on to her.

"What's wrong?" he asked.

She tried to speak, but all that came out was a sob, which was swiftly followed by more tears. She began trembling then, and Larry held her tighter as she cried.

*   *   *

Lori and Larry were sitting on the couch when someone knocked on the door. Lori held a mug of tea in her hands – Larry had made it for her – and while she'd drunk very little of it, she found the mug's warmth comforting. She turned her head toward the door, but before she could start to get up, Larry gave her hand a gentle squeeze, then rose from the couch and headed to the door.

Larry was tall and thin, with a stubbly beard and thick black hair that was always in need of a trim. He wore T-shirts, jeans, and sandals, regardless of the weather, and tonight his shirt was black with the iconic red Rolling Stones lips on the front. His battered guitar case was propped up in the corner next to the couch, where he usually kept it. He tended to practice when she was at work, and it had been a long time since she'd heard him play. She was surprised by how sad this realization made her feel.

Larry unlocked and opened the door to reveal a pair of uniformed police officers, one man, one woman. The man spoke first.

"We got a call that someone broke into your apartment."

Both officers looked Larry up and down, and the woman wrinkled her nose. After a night of performing, Larry always smelled like sweat, alcohol, cigarette smoke, and marijuana. Not exactly the best first impression to make on a couple of cops.

"Yeah," Larry said.

He opened the door all the way and stepped aside so the officers could enter. They did so, immediately noting Lori's presence, as well as sweeping their gazes around the apartment to take everything in. Once the officers were all the way inside, Larry closed the door. He didn't lock it again, though.

The male officer looked to be in his thirties. He was stout, broad-shouldered, and his head was shaved. His facial features were unremarkable, his expression emotionless, almost bored. The female officer was about a decade older than her partner, as well as a few inches taller, and she possessed a runner's build – lean and strong. Her brown hair was straight and cut short, and she wore minimal makeup and no jewelry.

"I'm Officer Rauch," the man said. He nodded toward his partner. "And this is Officer McGuire."

Lori and Larry gave the officers their names. McGuire took a notebook from her shirt pocket and wrote down the information.

"Which of you called to report the incident?" she asked.

"I did," Lori said. She didn't rise from the couch. She felt weary, although less so than she had earlier. But that wasn't the reason she didn't get up. She still wore only her oversized T-shirt and panties, and she'd pulled the shirt over her bare legs as far as she could to cover them. She felt uncomfortable at the idea of Officer Rauch staring at her legs, and he was bound to notice she was braless if she started moving around. Maybe she was being foolishly modest, but she didn't care.

"As calm as you both seem to be, I take it that the intruder is no longer on the premises?" McGuire asked.

"I don't think so," Lori said.

"I got home right after she called," Larry said. "I didn't see anyone."

McGuire nodded. "Okay. It doesn't hurt to be thorough, though." She looked at her partner. "Ralph?"

"On it."

Officer Rauch gave the living room another once over before heading for the small kitchen. Larry looked at Lori and mouthed, *Ralph Rauch?*

She knew what he was thinking. It sounded more like the name of a cartoon character than a police officer. She smiled briefly at the thought.

As Rauch headed for the kitchen, McGuire said, "Lori, tell me what happened here tonight."

Lori nodded and began talking. Larry stood off to the side, listening, brow furrowed. She'd already told him a short version of what had occurred, but this was his first time hearing the details. Not that Lori provided all of them. She knew if she told the officers everything that had happened, they'd write her off as a kook, or worse, haul her in for a psych eval. She told McGuire about hearing the thumps, but she omitted any descriptions of the shadow creatures, and instead spoke of 'someone' who'd been in the living room when she'd left her bedroom to check if Larry had come home yet. As for the rest of her story, she told a modified version of the truth. The 'intruder' had chased her to her bedroom and broke through the locked door. She'd then hid inside the master bathroom, and the intruder had tried to break through that door as well. The next thing she knew, Larry was knocking on the door and asking if she was all right.

As she told the edited version of her story, Officer Rauch headed down the hall and into her bedroom, continuing his search of the apartment. She was uncomfortable with the idea of a strange man inspecting her bedroom and bathroom, but she knew he was only doing his job. Still, it was in its own way as creepy as the shadow things that had come after her.

Officer McGuire made notes on a pad as Lori spoke, stopping her a couple times to clarify some points. When Lori was finished, Rauch returned to the living room.

"The bedroom door was forced open," he said. "Caused some slight damage. I'm going to look at the patio door, see if there are any signs it was forced open too. Then I'll check the deck and take the stairs down to the ground, see if I can find anything."

McGuire nodded, and Rauch walked toward the open patio door. As he passed the couch, Lori noticed two things about him. One was that there was a trio of lines on the side of his neck. At first she thought they were wrinkles of some sort, although the man seemed too young for that. But when he drew in a breath, the lines parted, and she realized they were openings in his flesh, like a fish's gills. They closed once more when he exhaled. The second thing she noticed was that the nail on the pinky finger of his left hand had been painted red.

She'd taken Fiorinal while she and Larry had waited for the police to arrive, but now she felt a sharp, stabbing pain between her eyes. She began trembling, shaking so hard that tea sloshed over the side of her mug. She tried to put the mug down on the coffee table, but her hand was shaking so badly that Larry rushed forward to help her. He gently removed the mug from her hand and placed it on the glass surface of the table. A small pool of spilled tea gathered around the base of the mug, almost as if it were leaking. *Or bleeding,* she thought.

She watched Rauch push the vertical blinds aside with the back of his hand, probably to avoid leaving fingerprints. He examined the lock on the patio door for a moment, and then stepped out onto the deck. When he released the blinds, they swayed back and forth, clacking softly against one another. She heard the heavy tread of his boots on the wooden deck, followed by the sound of him going down the stairs.

McGuire said something then, but her words didn't register on Lori's consciousness. She was still staring at the swaying blinds, thinking about Rauch's opening and closing gill slits, and especially about his red pinky nail.

"Ms. Palumbo?"

McGuire spoke louder this time, and Lori's head jerked in her direction.

"I'm sorry. What did you say?"

"I asked if there are any details you can give us about the intruder. Gender? Race? What the person was wearing? Did the person say anything?"

It wasn't one intruder. It was at least a half dozen, and they weren't human. They were monsters made entirely out of shadows, with multijointed limbs and clawed hands. Oh, and they made these weird whispery sounds, like they were talking, but if they were, I couldn't understand anything they said.

"None of the lights were on," she said, "so I didn't get a good look at whoever it was, and the person didn't say anything. Sorry."

McGuire's lips pursed, as if she was irritated by Lori's answer, but she dutifully jotted it down on her pad.

Lori regretted calling nine one one now. She'd done so in a panic, but now that she wasn't gripped by mortal terror, she could think more clearly. What good could the police possibly do? If she'd hallucinated the shadow creatures, she needed a psychologist, not a cop. And if the things had been real, what could human police officers do to protect her? But that wasn't the worst. The worst part was the gills on Rauch's neck and his crimson pinky nail. By calling nine-one-one, she'd invited one of *them* into her apartment. She had no idea who *they* were, exactly, but she knew they were connected to the shadow creatures somehow.

Her eyes narrowed as she scrutinized McGuire. Was she one of *them* too? She looked the woman over from head to toe, trying to ascertain if there was anything odd about her. One of her nostrils was larger than the other, and she had a small scar at the right corner of her mouth. Neither feature was on a par with neck gills in terms of weirdness, though. It didn't appear that McGuire was one of *them*. Unless she was simply better at disguising her true nature than Rauch was. But if she wasn't one of *them*, wouldn't she have noticed her partner's gill slits? They weren't the sort of feature that was easily overlooked. Maybe you didn't have to be one of *them* to work with *them*.

McGuire turned to look at Larry.

"And you didn't see or hear anything when you came in?" she asked.

"That's right. I put my guitar down and headed for the hall bathroom. I thought I heard Lori crying. Her bedroom door was open – which I thought was strange since she never leaves it open when she sleeps – so I went inside. The bedroom was empty, so I knocked on the bathroom door. A moment later, Lori came out." He shrugged then, as if to say he had no idea what had happened here tonight.

"And your relationship to Ms. Palumbo is...?"

"I'm her ex-boyfriend. We're just friends now, and I'm staying with her for a while until I can get my own place."

McGuire made a few more notes on her pad. She then looked to Lori once more.

"How would you describe the way your relationship to Mr. Ramirez ended?"

Lori frowned. "What do you mean?"

"Was it a mutual thing, or did one of you bring up the subject first? Would you say the breakup was civil or was it acrimonious?"

Lori exchanged a puzzled look with Larry before answering.

"Like Larry said, we're friends now. Good ones. I know that's rare, but...." A thought occurred to her then. "Are you asking if *Larry* was the intruder?"

"Not necessarily," McGuire said. "But if Mr. Ramirez does harbor any resentment toward you, he might've been tempted to scare you as a way of getting back at you. And it could have had nothing to do with your breakup, could simply have been a practical joke that went too far." She faced Larry once more. "Maybe when you discovered she'd already called nine-one-one you were too embarrassed to tell her you were the one who scared her. If it *was* you, this is your chance to confess before this goes any further. Admit you did it, apologize to Ms. Palumbo, and we all call it a night. What do you say?"

Lori wanted to defend Larry, to tell McGuire that he'd never play such a cruel joke on her, no matter how much anger and resentment he might have felt. He wasn't that kind of person. But she couldn't speak. Something that McGuire had said – one word, actually – had stopped her cold. That word was *confess*. McGuire hadn't put any special emphasis on the word, but it had stood out to Lori nevertheless. She remembered what the woman – Goat-Eyes – had said to her. *Confess and atone – or suffer.*

Larry looked at her as if he expected her to stick up for him. When she didn't, his expression fell, and he faced McGuire once more.

"I wouldn't do anything like that to anybody, let alone a friend."

McGuire looked at him for a moment, as if trying to gauge whether or not he was telling the truth. Finally, she nodded. "Have either of you touched anything since you reported the incident? The bedroom door? The patio door? The table or chairs?"

"No," Lori said.

"Me neither," Larry said.

McGuire jotted their responses down on her pad.

Lori heard the sound of boots on the wooden stairs outside. Rauch was returning.

He pushed his way past the blinds as he reentered the apartment. The lines of his gills were faint now, so much so that she almost couldn't make them out. She dropped her gaze to his left hand. The nail of his pinky finger remained just as red, though.

Rauch stopped when he reached McGuire.

"The bedroom door was definitely forced open," he said, "and the lock on the patio door is broken. I didn't see anything out of the ordinary on the deck or stairs. Nothing on the ground at the foot of the stairs, either."

When Rauch finished speaking, his neck gills opened and closed one time, the action occurring so quickly, Lori almost missed it. She looked at McGuire's face and then at Larry's. Neither showed any reaction. Maybe she was seeing things, minor hallucinations brought on by the stress of everything she'd experienced tonight. But the shadow things hadn't been hallucinations, though, had they? Rauch said both the bedroom door and the patio door showed physical signs of having been opened by force. If the shadow creatures hadn't been real, then who or what had broken into her apartment?

"I'm going out to the cruiser," Rauch said. He looked at Lori. "We need to get a crime scene tech in here to take photos of the evidence and dust for prints."

The last thing Lori wanted was to have more strangers in her apartment tonight – especially if any of them happened to have red-painted pinky nails.

"Okay," she said.

Rauch held her gaze a moment longer, and there was something in his eyes that she couldn't name, but which disturbed her greatly. A coldness, almost a loathing, as if the very sight of her offended him on some deep level. Then it was gone, and he turned, opened the door, and stepped out into the hall. He didn't close the door, and McGuire made no move to close it for him.

Lori was shaken by Rauch's glare, and she wanted – no, *needed* – to get away from McGuire and from Larry, too. She needed a few minutes by herself.

"I need to use the bathroom," she said. "There's one in the hall. I can use it instead of the one in my bedroom."

"No problem," McGuire said. She smiled then, and Lori tried to gauge whether there was anything sinister in that smile. It seemed genuine, but how could she be sure?

She rose from the couch without returning McGuire's smile. Larry looked concerned, so much so that she expected him to offer to escort her to the bathroom. But he said nothing, and Lori walked down the hall by herself. When she reached the bathroom, she turned on the light, stepped inside, then closed and locked the door behind her.

She took in a shuddering breath and let it out. The madness that she'd encountered at FoodSaver had followed her home – not just in the form of the shadow creatures, but also in the form of Officer 'Gill-Neck' Rauch. If one of *them* was a cop, who could she turn to for—

Her thoughts slammed to a halt as something registered on her consciousness. She turned toward the mirror over the sink and saw there were letters on the glass, written with a substance she couldn't identify. It was thick and greenish-gray, like snot, and it smelled like rotting vegetable matter. She held her breath as she read the words.

You know what you did. Confess and atone – or suffer. It was signed, *The Cabal.*

A small whimper escaped her throat, and she began to tremble.

CHAPTER FOUR

Lori found herself once more walking through a torchlit corridor. It took her a moment to realize that she was back in the Vermilion Tower, following the crimson-robed eyeless man who'd brought her here. She frowned. She'd been somewhere else, hadn't she? Where – her mind cleared and she remembered the shadow creatures breaking into her apartment, remembered the police coming to investigate after she called nine-one-one. She especially remembered Officer Rauch and his highly disturbing neck gills. She remembered seeing a message written on her bathroom mirror, one she thought Rauch had left during the time he'd been away from the rest of them, checking her place out. She'd considered calling for Larry and Officer McGuire to come look at the message, but if Rauch denied writing it – which of course he would – she feared they'd think that *she* wrote it, and she'd seem even crazier to them than she already did. She'd cleaned the disgusting substance the message had been written in, wiped it off the mirror's surface using a hand towel and then used toilet tissue to get off the remaining residue. She'd tossed both the towel and the TP into the small plastic trash receptacle next to the toilet and then returned to the living room without peeing. If either Larry or McGuire noticed she hadn't actually used the bathroom while she'd been in there, neither said anything about it.

The crime scene tech – a gawky guy in his late twenties – arrived to do his thing soon after that. Lori had been relieved to see his left pinky nail hadn't been painted. By the time he finished and left with the two officers, it was almost four o'clock in the morning. She was surprised to discover it was so late. She'd completely lost track of time. Larry closed the patio door, although he couldn't lock it, of course, then returned to the couch, sat, and held her. She didn't think she'd fall asleep, was way too wired, but she remembered feeling drowsy and closing her eyes after only a few minutes.

And now she was here, in the Vermilion Tower once more. It was weird. She couldn't remember ever having a multipart dream like this, one that picked up exactly where it had left off. She didn't want to consider the possibility that this wasn't a dream, that it was some kind of...what? Alternate reality? If sure *felt* real. Cold stone beneath her bare feet, a damp chill on her skin.... She still wore the flimsy, see-through gown with no underwear beneath, and she once more crossed her arms over her chest. Modesty seemed foolish here, but it offered her some small measure of control, and she'd take what she could get.

"Where are you taking me?" she asked.

The eyeless man — who she was starting to think of as the Driver — didn't stop walking or look back at her as he answered.

"To the Chamber of Revelation."

The words meant nothing to Lori, and since she couldn't see any other option at the moment, she continued following the Driver. It seemed they walked for a long time, but eventually the corridor ended at a pair of large doors fashioned from some nightblack wood that Lori couldn't identify. Two thick metal rings were bolted to the wood — one for each door — and the Driver took hold of the ring on the right and pulled. She expected the door's hinges to give loud creaking groans of protest, but they were silent, and the Driver easily opened the massive door as if it weighed nothing more than a papier-mâché prop. He walked in first, not looking back to see if she would accompany him or take this opportunity to make a break for it. She was tempted to do the latter, but she thought once more of the Nightway, of the vast dark plain it cut through, and of the unseen things that might dwell there. Running off now could very well be a form of suicide, and while dying might be preferable to what the Driver and his friends — the Cabal, if she could trust the word Officer Ralph Rauch had written in gray-green goo on her bathroom mirror — would do to her, she wasn't ready to kill herself just yet. She knew the old superstition that if you died in a dream, you died in real life too, and while she'd always thought the idea was nonsense, it didn't seem so to her now. Not at all.

She followed the Driver through the open doorway.

Whatever this place was, it was dark inside. The only light here was the flickering of torchlight coming from the hallway outside, and that was only enough for Lori to see the Driver's red-robed shape walking ahead of her. It was cold in here, so much so that if there'd been enough light, she was certain she'd see her breath mist in the frigid air. She hugged herself tighter, more concerned about warming herself than concealing her breasts now, but the action didn't help. She began shivering, and she was unable to make herself stop.

She had the impression that there was a large space around them, but she wasn't sure why she thought this. She could hear no sounds beyond her own breathing, but she nevertheless felt the pressure of being surrounded by a great deal of nothing. Was this the reason she'd been brought here? Was this dark place to be her prison, punishment for whatever crime the Cabal thought she had committed?

A small red pinpoint of light glowed to life in front of her face, and she stopped walking to avoid colliding with it. It became brighter as she examined it, and as soon as she was able to make out the features of the thing that was giving off the faint illumination. She expected it to be some kind of insect, like a firefly, but one whose abdomen glowed red instead of greenish yellow. But no bug lay at the heart of this crimson glow. Instead it was a tiny humanoid figure, something like an infant curled into a fetal position. Its body was distorted, asymmetrical, arms and legs different lengths and thicknesses, features stretched out of true, flesh covered with tumorous growths. The small humanoid's eyes were huge in proportion to the rest of its deformed body, and they were wide open and blazed with baleful red light, which accounted for the crimson glow surrounding it. How it floated in the air, she had no idea. It possessed no wings, and there was no sign that anything artificial held it aloft. No strings, no wire. The tiny thing's body didn't move – arms and legs remained motionless, fingers and toes didn't twitch or wiggle. And there was no way to tell if the creature's eyes were focused on her because of how they were glowing, or if it could see at all, for that matter. But she had the impression that it saw her just fine, and for some reason it didn't like what it saw. She could feel hatred radiating from it, rolling off in waves like heat from a blazing fire.

More crimson pinpoints of light glowed to life around her, at their core other miniature infants, all deformed in various ways, eyes all shining red.

Firebabies, she thought, and the name seemed fitting. They were ugly and beautiful in equal measure, and she was both fascinated and repelled by them. She wondered if there was a word for this mix of emotions. If so, she didn't know it.

At first there were only a few dozen, but more appeared, hundreds, thousands, maybe millions. They floated toward each other, packed tight together, and formed a single mass shaped roughly like a sphere. They rose into the air slowly, and their combined light illuminated the area around Lori in crimson. She was able to make out her surroundings, and she saw that her initial impression had been correct. She stood in a large open area like an auditorium, except instead of rows of seats surrounding her, there was an upward curving spiral ledge that circled around the chamber's wall.

I'm within the horn's inner core, she thought.

And she wasn't alone.

The Driver was there with her, although he'd continued walking as the firebabies appeared. Now he stood next to the far wall opposite her. He had turned around and faced her, his red-washed features devoid of any emotion. He was far from the only robed figure in attendance, however. Others stood on the spiral ledge, shoulder to shoulder, all facing her. Their numbers began at floor level and continued upward, one after the other, around and around, going on so far that the mass of firebabies – which now hovered directly above Lori – couldn't illuminate them all. The firebabies' eyelight was more like that of smoldering red coals than a blazing inferno, and because of this, she couldn't clearly make out the faces of the robed figures, even those close to ground level. But the shapes of their bodies varied widely, some looking perfectly human, others looking like…something else. Things whose limbs were too long, too short, too numerous, or more like animal or insect appendages. Their faces – what she could see of them in this light – were similarly twisted and alien. And while she couldn't see it, she felt confident that all of the red-robed figures had one feature in common – a crimson-painted pinky nail on their left hand. She wondered if the goat-eyed woman was among those assembled here. The gill-necked police officer, too. She didn't spot them, but she thought they might be here, watching her with the same cold, silent scrutiny as the others.

She heard a voice then, or rather a multitude of voices, speaking in unison.

"Confess."

The word reverberated throughout the chamber, and Lori winced at the accusatory anger behind it.

They're speaking through the firebabies, she thought. She knew what word was next.

"Atone."

Louder this time, angrier. The sound hurt her ears, the pain like that of a seriously bad ear infection. She clapped her hands over her ears to protect them, but the sound of her doing so sent fresh bolts of pain shooting deep into her ear canals, and she moaned. She gritted her teeth then, and pressed her hands tighter against her ears, not giving a damn if it hurt. She knew another two words were coming.

"OR SUFFER!"

This time the chorus of infant voices seemed to come from inside her brain, and the resulting pain of their furious shout caused her to release a scream of agony. She fell to her knees, hands still pressed against her head, as if to keep it from exploding. Her eyes were squeezed shut and she could no longer see them – the members of the Cabal – but she could feel the weight of their scrutiny on her, as if they were waiting for her to give them the response they were seeking. The problem was, she had no idea what that response might be.

The firebabies' combined voices seemed to echo forever in the auditorium, but eventually they faded. When they were finally gone, the pain in Lori's head – far worse than any migraine she'd experienced – began to lessen. She lowered her hands and opened her eyes. She rose to her feet, weak and shaky. She spoke then, raising her voice so the assembled Cabal members could hear her, although she had a feeling that she could whisper or even merely think her words, and they would all be able to hear her just fine.

"What is it that you think I've done?"

The firebabies remained silent as the Cabal gazed at her, faces impassive. She felt tears of frustration building and as they began sliding down her cheeks, she cried out.

"How can I confess if I don't know what I've fucking *done*?"

Still no response.

She looked to the Driver. He stood near the bottom of the spiral ledge, where it curved down to meet the floor. She went to him, trying to run but too weak and lightheaded to manage more than a fast shuffle. He said nothing as she drew near, but she saw that the patches of skin over where his eyes should've been were pulsating more rapidly than they had been earlier. She didn't know what, if anything, this might mean.

When she reached the Driver, she almost reached out to grab his arms, intending to shake him, as she demanded to know what the other crimson-robed men and women wanted from her. But at the last instant, she restrained herself. She sensed that touching the Driver would not be safe. Why this should be, she didn't know, and she preferred not to find out.

"Please, can you tell me what's going on? Why am I here? What do these—" she hesitated a second before continuing, "—*people* want?"

She hoped he would answer her. He'd spoken to her in the car with his own voice, so she knew he didn't need to speak through the mass of firebabies. Like the other members of the Cabal, his expression had been detached, almost clinical, up to this point. Then, without warning, the Driver slapped her. The strike was too swift for her to avoid, the impact so strong that it drove her to her knees. The pain hit her an instant later. It felt as if her jaw was aflame and she wondered if it was broken. She tried to look up at the Driver, but her vision had blurred out of focus, and she could only make out the crimson outline of him. She wanted to ask him why he'd hit her, but she feared that if she spoke, he'd hit her again.

She felt hands take hold of her arms and lift her to her feet. Her legs were too weak to support her, but whoever had hold of her kept her upright. Her head lolled to the left, and she saw a hazy image of a woman's face – a woman with goat eyes. She looked to the right and saw Officer Rauch, gill slits opening and closing, opening and closing, as if he was excited. Both wore the crimson robes of the Cabal. Deep inside, Lori was scared – fucking terrified – but the Driver's slap had left her conscious mind too dazed to feel much of anything. She returned her gaze to the Driver and waited to see what he would do next. But he did nothing. He simply stood, arms at his sides, and regarded her. His facial expression was indifferent, but his eye patches pulsated rapidly.

She heard a sound then, a grinding, like stone sliding against stone. The goat-eyed woman and Rauch roughly turned her around, and she saw that in the middle of the auditorium's floor, directly beneath the red-glowing mass of firebabies, an object was emerging. It wasn't rising through a hole, though. It was *growing*, the floor's substance flowing upward inch by inch to form the shape of a large X. Her jaw still felt as if it was on fire, and she could feel the flesh there beginning to swell. She blinked several times to clear her vision, and while it improved, it remained a trifle blurry. Had the Driver hit her so hard that she had a concussion?

When the X had fully emerged, there were soft rattling sounds, and manacles grew from the top and bottom of the X. She didn't need to ask what – or who – the restraints were for.

She tried to pull free of Goat-Eyes' and Rauch's grip, but they were too strong. That, or she was too weak. The two Cabal members dragged her toward the X-cross, and again she resisted, thrashing and kicking, but her efforts were feeble and ineffective. Goat-Eyes and Rauch pushed her against the cross and arranged her limbs in a spread-eagle position, then – moving with swift efficiency – they locked manacles around her wrists and ankles. When they were finished, they stepped to the sides of the cross. She slumped forward, the manacles keeping her from falling face-first to the floor. They were cold against her skin, and the edges hurt her wrists as the manacles now bore her full weight. She forced herself to stand upright, and although her legs still felt like spaghetti, she managed it. The pain in her wrists lessened immediately.

The Driver had only watched as his two colleagues had chained her to the X-cross, but now he stepped toward her, face still impassive, eye patches pulsating even faster. When he reached her, he stopped, grabbed hold of her nightgown's bodice, and ripped the flimsy thing off her, the fabric tearing as easily as if it were paper.

"There's really no point to it," the Driver said. He lowered his hand and let the torn gown fall to the floor. "It's not like it left anything to the imagination. Plus, it would just get in the way."

In the way of what? she thought, but she didn't really want to know and said nothing.

Several firebabies detached from the mass above her and drifted down to the discarded nightgown. They lowered to within inches of the fabric and trained their glowing gazes on it. Within seconds, small sections of the gown began to blacken and smolder, and then flames appeared. The firebabies floated upward to rejoin the others as the flames spread, growing larger and brighter. Within seconds, the entire garment was ablaze. As quickly as it had started, the fire burned itself out, and the gown was gone, reduced to a scattering of charred ash.

Lori's mental fogginess had mostly lifted now, and she raised her head to regard the assembled Cabal members – at least the ones she could see from this angle. They demonstrated no reaction to her being naked and chained before them, but maybe this kind of thing was old hat for them. She, however, felt exposed in a way she never had before. Hundreds of people were looking at her nude body, and she could do nothing to cover herself, couldn't hide from their silent, angry gazes.

It was her turn to get angry now.

"Let me go, you sick fuckers!" she shouted. "You have no right to do this to me! I haven't done anything wrong!"

The Cabal didn't react at first, then she heard a soft chuckle come from above her, from one of the firebabies, she guessed. It was followed by a second and a third, and then the entire floating mass of miniature infants was laughing. No more chuckling now, but rather full-throated roaring laughter, which sounded eerily adult coming from their tiny mouths.

Goat-Eyes and Rauch joined in the laughter, and while the Driver didn't, he did break out in a grin.

"Haven't done anything?" he said. "My dear, you've done *everything*."

Another object began to emerge from the floor, this one several feet in front of the X-cross. It was flat and rectangular, and as it rose, Lori realized it was a table. When it was all the way up, a number of smaller shapes formed on its surface, all aligned in neat rows. At first she couldn't tell what the objects were, but they quickly resolved into specific forms, and she saw they were tools. Some were simple things like hammers and knives, but others were more complex and made her think of medical equipment, and some were bizarrely complex, and she couldn't guess at their function. These were large and wicked looking, all edges and angles and teeth and spikes, and she suspected they had no analogue in the real world.

"The Intercessor provides," the Driver said. The firebabies repeated his words, almost as if it were a religious invocation.

The Driver stepped over to the table and perused the instruments displayed upon it. Goat-Eyes and Rauch joined him. They took their time, but eventually each selected one of the tools, pulling it free from the surface of the table with a tug. Goat-Eyes held something that looked like a speculum covered with inch-long spikes. Rauch held a knife with a blade that had been beveled to give it four separate cutting edges. At first, Lori thought the hand that gripped the knife trembled, but then she realized it wasn't Rauch's hand that was shaking – it was the blade. The thing quivered in Rauch's grasp, as if it couldn't wait to begin cutting into her smooth, unmarked flesh. The Driver had chosen a rod-like device that looked something like a cross between a huge dildo and a cheese grater. He touched a button on the base, and the device began to hum softly. At first she thought it was vibrating, but then she saw it begin to emit a faint orange glow, and she realized the device was heating up – and *fast*. If it kept going like this, it would soon be white-hot. The dildo-grater didn't have a protected handle, and she heard the sound of the Driver's palm flesh start to sizzle, and she smelled burning meat. The Driver's eye patches thrummed as quickly as hummingbird wings, and his mouth stretched into a wide smile.

Lori couldn't take her gaze from the trio of horrible instruments the Cabal members held. She felt cold inside, sick, and she shook her head in denial as the three stepped closer to her.

"Please," she said, her voice little more than a whisper. "Don't do this. *Please!*"

"I hope for your sake you figure all this out soon," the Driver said. "But not *too* soon. My friends and I would like to have a little fun first."

The three crimson-robed figures began their work then. Lori screamed, and while she couldn't be certain, she thought she heard the firebabies giggle with delight.

★   ★   ★

She opened her eyes.

She didn't scream, didn't throw herself off the couch as if desperate to escape. She simply lay there for several moments, head resting on one of the couch arms, the soothing warmth of a fuzzy blanket over her body. She was alone. She remembered Larry holding her as she fell asleep. Where was he?

Her phone lay on the coffee table in front of her and she reached for it to check the time.

Seven fifty-two.

Groaning, she pushed the blanket off her and sat up. She expected to feel her head pound in response to this action, but it didn't give so much as a twinge of pain. After the nightmare she'd had, she wouldn't have been surprised to wake up with a raging headache. Thank Christ for small favors. Her first client of the day wasn't scheduled until nine, but she double-checked her work schedule on her phone to make sure. Yep, nine. She was scheduled to work with Debra Foster today, and while Lori usually dreaded working with her, she'd do so today with a glad heart. Anything to take her mind off the shadow creatures and lunatics dressed in red robes.

She rose from the couch, her body protesting. She always felt achy if she fell asleep out here. The couch was secondhand – she'd gotten it from her parents when they'd decided to refurnish their house – and while it was comfortable enough to sit on, it played hell with her back whenever she slept on it.

A thought came to her then, that maybe she hurt this morning because of what had been done to her in the Vermilion Tower. Her dream hadn't ended as Goat-Eyes, Rauch, and the Driver began torturing her. It had continued for some time, and she recalled every horrible detail. The things they'd done to her…. She hurt *everywhere* this morning, outside *and* inside. She felt as if she'd been taken apart piece by piece, and every bit of her – skin, organs, bones – had been violated in unspeakable ways before being put back together. Except – she didn't feel exactly herself. It was like some of her pieces were missing, as if her torturers had forgotten to put a few back or perhaps had put them together in the wrong order, forcing some pieces to fit where they shouldn't, like the way someone frustrated with a difficult puzzle tries to jam a piece into a spot where it doesn't belong.

She shuddered and pushed the memories away. It had been a nightmare to end all nightmares, no doubt, but it hadn't been real. Then again, if she'd fully experienced pain in her dream – and she had, god, how she had – how was that any different from experiencing it in real life? Beyond the fact that she hadn't woken up with any injuries, of course. Pain was pain, however you experienced it, and the emotions she'd felt as the Cabal members had violated her body to the sound of the firebabies' delight – the shame, the humiliation, the absolute and utter *degradation* – had been real, and she still felt them now. It seemed to her that being tortured in her dreams was, in one way, worse than being tortured in real life. The next time she fell asleep, it could all begin again. She could be tortured night after night, rising whole the next day, like a warrior in Valhalla whose battle injuries healed each evening so he could fight anew in the morning, on and on for eternity. She didn't know if she could take another night like that, thought she might go mad, or maybe her heart would give out, her mind pulling the plug to keep from experiencing such agony again.

She knew the pains she felt were psychosomatic, a result of stress from the break-in combined with the emotional residue of her nightmare – not to mention watching a man die in FoodSaver's parking lot last night. She wasn't hurting because anything had really happened to her physically. There was no Nightway, no Vermilion Tower. But then again, the shadow creatures were real, weren't they? And if *they* were real, who's to say the rest of it wasn't real, too?

Forget about it for now, she thought. *You'll feel better after you get some coffee in you.*

She doubted it, but making coffee would give her something to do, so she started shuffling toward the kitchen. On the way, she tried calling Larry's name, but her mouth and throat were dry, her voice hoarse, and the sound that came out of her was little more than a croak. She doubted he'd have heard her if he was standing next to her, let alone if he was in the bathroom. She was going to try calling out for him again when she saw a folded piece of paper sitting on the counter in front of the coffee maker. She reached for it, then hesitated. What if it was another message from the Cabal? She thought if it was, she might start screaming and never stop.

Don't be such a baby, she told herself.

She picked up the note, gratified that her hands only shook a little as she opened it. She was immediately relieved to see Larry's handwriting, and she quickly read the message.

I didn't have the heart to wake you after the night you had. I got up early and cleaned (a little) so you wouldn't have to wake up to a total pigsty (ha ha). I've got a signing gig this morning at a conference for small business owners downtown. Sounds like a snooze-fest, but at least I'll get a check out of it. Call or text me if you need anything. I hope you have a good day!

Larry.

He'd drawn a small heart next to his signature. She knew it wasn't a romantic gesture. He always drew a heart next to his signature, even when signing official documents like contracts or tax forms. It was just part of who he was. Seeing it cheered her a little, and she put the note down on the counter, leaving it open so she could see the little heart while she made coffee.

She made a of couple slices of toast while the coffee brewed, and she decided to spoil herself a little and slather some blackberry jam on the bread. The dining table and its chair stood upright once more – Larry had righted them after the crime scene tech had departed. She didn't feel comfortable sitting at the table, though. The shadow creatures had knocked it over when they'd rushed through the open patio door. They'd *touched* it. She didn't think the things had poisoned the table or cursed it or anything. Then again, who knew what the creatures were capable of?

So you believe the shadow things are real, but the Vermilion Tower isn't? How can you choose to believe in one impossibility but not the other?

She drank her coffee and ate her toast standing at the counter. She loved blackberry jam, would eat one jar after another if she allowed herself, which was why she bought it so rarely, and when she did buy it, she saved it for a special treat. But she barely tasted it today, and she only managed to eat one piece of toast and a single bite of the second before she lost her appetite. She felt slightly nauseated, but she downed the rest of her coffee – appetite or not, she needed the caffeine – then put the uneaten toast down the disposal. She then rinsed her mug and put it in the dishwasher.

Normally she did yoga in the morning, following along to the routines on one of the DVDs she owned. As much as her body hurt this morning, she could use the exercise. But she wasn't sure she had the time, not if she didn't want to be late for her first client. A shower might do more good for her body than yoga today anyway. It would sure as hell be more soothing. But she was hesitant to head to the master bathroom. This was partially due to the fact that the shadow creatures had broken into her bedroom last night and pounded on the bathroom door as she hid there, terrified. But she was also reluctant because the lock on her patio door was broken. She'd call the rental office before she left and ask them to send someone to fix the lock, but it would likely be a while before a maintenance worker showed up. In the meantime, anyone could enter her apartment through the patio door. Anyone – or any*thing*. She didn't like the idea of standing naked in the shower, defenseless and wondering if someone had snuck into her apartment and was walking down the hallway, heading for her bedroom, intending to break the lock on the bathroom door and come rushing toward her.

The image brought a fresh twist of nausea, and for a moment she thought she might throw up her meager breakfast. She managed to keep it down, though. Did she have anything that she could use to keep the patio door closed? Some kind of metal or wooden rod that she could slip into the track so the door couldn't be opened? She couldn't think of anything.

She'd left her phone on the coffee table when she rose from the couch, and now she heard it vibrate against the table's glass surface. The sound was off, but since the phone only vibrated once, she figured she'd just received an email or text message. She walked over to the coffee table and stared at the phone. She regarded it warily, as if it were a poisonous insect that might sting her if she came too close. What if the message she'd received was another enigmatic taunt from the Cabal?

Fuck it, she thought and picked up the phone.

She unlocked the screen and sure enough, she had one text message. She took a deep breath to steel herself before opening it. It was from her sister, and she released her breath in a sigh of relief. She read the message.

Just checking in. Haven't heard from you in a few days. I hope things are going well with you and Justin! ☺ *Love ya! – R*

Reeny had been not-so-gently urging Lori to start dating again since she and Larry had ceased being lovers, and she was thrilled her sister had a new man in her life. Reeny might be the younger sister, but she acted as if she were older than Lori, was always trying to take care of her. Sometimes – okay, a lot of times – this irritated her, but today she was grateful for Reeny's concern. She wrote a text in reply.

I really need to talk. Can you meet me for lunch today?

Short and sweet. There was no way she could explain everything over text, and if she tried, Reeny would only get upset and start worrying that her sister was going crazy.

Maybe you are going crazy, she thought.

This was *not* a thought she wanted to examine further, and she buried it, afraid of where it might lead. She sent the text and, phone still in hand, headed for her bedroom. No shower this morning, but she'd clean herself as best she could with a washcloth. That way she'd at least be able to hear if anyone opened the patio door from outside. As for her hair, she'd do what she could, but if it looked like crap, the world would just have to deal with it.

She hurried into her bedroom, trying not to think about the shadow creatures breaking open the door last night and rushing toward the bathroom where she was hiding.

She failed miserably.

★　　★　　★

Get Moving! (complete with exclamation mark) was located in a shopping center near downtown. It was nestled between an optometrist and a foot spa. Lori had no idea exactly what a foot spa was. She imagined a place where people's feet were pampered in every way possible, and she had to admit that sounded good. Every time she pulled into the parking lot, she told herself that she should give it a try sometime, but so far she never had and, if she was honest with herself, she probably never would.

She parked several rows back from Get Moving!'s entrance. The up-close spaces were reserved for clients. Not only was that good business practice in general, but given the mobility issues their clients often had, it was a necessity. She checked her phone before getting out of the car, and she saw that Reeny had texted her back.

Lunch is on! The Thai place okay? Speaking of okay, I hope YOU are! Love, love, love ya! – R

Lori was so relieved to hear from Reeny that she almost cried. Now all she had to do was get through the morning until lunchtime. She didn't think talking to Reeny was going to solve her current problems, but it would make her feel better, and it would hopefully give her a better perspective on what had happened. Unless Reeny listened to her story and told her she was nuts and needed to check into a psych ward, pronto.

Just get your ass to work, she told herself. If she could manage to keep busy, she wouldn't have time to obsess over all the weird shit that had happened to her. That was the hope, anyway.

Reeny's was the only text she'd gotten since leaving her apartment. Nothing from Justin letting her know how his doctor's appointment went. She checked her voicemail app and found she had no new messages. Maybe Justin's appointment wasn't over yet. Or maybe he was still pissed at her after the way their phone conversation had gone last night. If she hadn't heard from him by lunchtime, she'd text him, or maybe call him on her way back from the restaurant.

She grabbed her purse, got out of her car, locked it, and started walking toward the office. It didn't look like much from the outside. *Get Moving!* was spelled out in large blue plastic letters above the entrance, which consisted of a narrow glass door and a side window with white letters painted on it enumerating Get Moving!'s services.

Physical Therapy
Free Assessments
Work Injuries
Pre- and Post-Surgical Therapy
Sports Injuries
Joint Replacement Therapy
All Major Insurance Accepted
Medicare Patients Accepted

Lori thought the letters on the window could've easily – and perhaps more honestly – spelled out *We do anything you need. Please give us money!*

She pulled the door open and stepped inside. No sound triggered to alert the staff that someone had entered – no tinkling bell or electronic tone. Such noises wouldn't be conducive to creating a calm, relaxing atmosphere. Katie Pope sat behind a curving front counter close to the entrance. She was African-American, in her late twenties, a touch overweight with a roundish face. She was pretty and her outgoing personality and charm attracted men to her in droves. Lori loved Katie, but she sometimes found the woman exhausting.

Across from reception was the waiting area, which consisted of a couch, chair, side table with lamp, and a round table upon which were magazines of various kinds for people to read. Lori was relieved to see the waiting area was unoccupied. She'd been afraid she'd see Debra Foster sitting on the couch, glaring at her because she'd gotten here before her. The woman was notoriously early and had no patience with anyone who wasn't. To her, 'Early is on time and on time is late' wasn't just a saying but her life's guiding principle.

"Morning," Katie said without looking up from her computer.

Lori was shocked. Every morning, Katie greeted her with a big, happy smile and a cheerful, *Hey, beautiful! Ready to kick some ass today?* and Lori would reply, *Always,* or, *You know it.* She'd never seen Katie like this before.

Katie and she weren't close friends, but Lori cared for her, and she was certain that something had to be wrong – *very* wrong – for her to be acting like this.

She stepped up to the counter. "Is everything all right?"

Katie looked up from her computer.

"I had the *worst* thing happen to me on the way to work this morning." Her lips pursed together. Katie made this face whenever she was unhappy – which was rare – but even then, she looked like she was affecting a sexy childish pout. But Lori knew the expression was genuine.

"What happened?" Lori asked.

"I was driving down Bartlett Avenue when this huge black car pulled up behind me."

Lori felt as if she'd been punched in the stomach when she heard the words *huge black car.*

"The driver came right up on my rear and stayed there for maybe a mile or more. At first, he made me nervous. I was afraid he might hit me. But then I got mad. I figured the jackass had no right to tailgate me like that. It didn't matter how late he was for work, you know?"

Lori nodded. She didn't want to hear any more of Katie's story, but at the same time, she *had* to hear.

"I got so mad that I decided to make him back off. I tapped my brakes, just enough to make the lights come on for a second. It was just a warning, right? Well, this guy got *really* pissed off when I did that. He stepped on the gas and hit my back bumper hard enough that my head snapped forward and back, and I had to fight to keep the rear end of my car from swerving."

"Jesus," Lori said softly.

She was afraid to ask Katie the question that was foremost in her mind, but she couldn't stop herself.

"Did you see him? What did he look like?"

Katie's brow furrowed. "I don't know. All I remember is he was wearing sunglasses."

Sunglasses . . . Lori thought. *To hide the smooth patches of skin where his eyes should be?*

She shuddered.

"He backed off then and started to pull around me. I didn't look over at him. I figured I'd only see him yelling at me, probably giving me the finger, you know? When he got far enough ahead, I figured he was going to swerve in front of me and then hit his own brakes, give me a taste of my own medicine, right? But he didn't. Do you know what he did?"

Lori didn't, of course, and part of her wanted to keep it that way. But she said nothing, only waited for Katie to continue.

But before she could go on, the front door opened and Debra Foster walked in. She bared her teeth when she saw Lori – her version of a smile.

"So you beat me here for once. Good for you."

Lori's own smile was strained. "Good morning, Debra. Ready to get to work?"

"Yep. Not that I think it will do any good. But you already know that."

Lori did.

Debra was in her early fifties, a stout, gray-haired, broad-shouldered woman who lived alone on a small farm outside town. She'd injured her left shoulder while cleaning out the stalls of her two horses, and she'd been coming to see Lori twice a week for the last three weeks, as prescribed by her physician. Debra believed that physical therapy was barely one step above voodoo.

I'm only here because my doctor said I have to do a month's worth of this crap before he'd write me a prescription for some heavy-duty pain pills. I don't expect anything I do here to make a goddamn difference, but if it gets me my meds, then I'll gut it out.

Lori had tried to tell her that with an attitude like that her condition was unlikely to improve – especially if she didn't follow up her sessions by doing the exercises at home. But Debra didn't pay attention to her warning, and Lori had given up trying to convince her. She'd decided to do what she could for the woman, and if Debra ended up with a chronic injury and an addiction to pain pills, it would be her own damn fault.

Lori turned to Katie, but the woman was once more engrossed in whatever was on her computer, a sullen expression on her face. Lori would have to hear the rest of her story later. She turned once more to Debra.

"Follow me on back to the exercise room," Lori said, doing her best to fake a friendly, enthusiastic tone.

"Might as well get this over with," Debra said.

Lori felt exactly the same way.

CHAPTER FIVE

For the remainder of the morning, Lori worked with one client after another with barely enough time to go to the bathroom or get a soda from the break room. She normally liked being busy – it made the day go faster – and she especially appreciated it today. She couldn't keep the shadow things, the Nightway, and the Cabal entirely out of her thoughts, but neither did she obsess over them.

When her last client, an elderly woman who'd just undergone her second hip replacement surgery, had left, she checked the time on her phone and saw it was eleven fifty-six. Almost lunchtime. She grabbed her purse and started to leave the exercise room – where some of the other PTs were still finishing up with clients – but before she'd gotten more than a few steps down the short narrow hallway that led to the front of the facility, she heard Melinda Dixon call her name.

"Lori!"

She stopped walking and closed her eyes.

Stay calm, she told herself and turned around as Melinda caught up to her. Melinda was a woman in her late fifties, tall and thin. Her hair had gone prematurely gray years ago, but she never colored it, and she wore it in a long braid down her back. Like Lori, she wore a short-sleeved smock and blue pants, but instead of sneakers – which the other PTs wore because they were on their feet all day – Melinda always wore black flats. Lori had no idea how Melinda's feet weren't killing her all the time. Maybe she regularly visited the foot spa next door.

"Yes?" Lori said, her tone wary.

She'd never gotten along great with Melinda. Get Moving! was Melinda's practice, and all the other PTs who worked there, Lori included, were her employees. The woman was a good PT, and she ran the practice well. She had a doctorate in physical therapy, while the other PTs – including Lori – only had master's degrees. Melinda had never come out and said she thought she was better qualified than her employees, but she didn't have to. The way she treated them made her feelings very clear.

"How did your session with Ms. Foster go today?"

The PTs wrote client reports that they submitted electronically to Melinda. Everything Lori had to say about Debra was in today's report on their session. She knew that Melinda read each and every report at the end of the day. If she spotted any typos or grammatical errors in a report, she returned it to the writer for revision. Lori wanted to tell Melinda that she had an extremely important appointment to get to, and she should go read her report about today's session with Debra if she was so damn interested in knowing what they'd done. But she knew that Melinda wouldn't react well to being snapped at. Who would? Besides, she was the boss, and she *did* have that bright shiny doctorate of hers....

"I'd say Debra took a couple steps backward today. She's still not doing the exercises I gave her to do at home, and her shoulder is really stiffening up. Her range of motion was more limited today than it was last week, and she was in considerably more pain."

Melinda nodded. "I watched the two of you working for a bit, and that's what it looked like to me."

Melinda was one of those people who it was impossible to read from facial expression or vocal tone. She could be ecstatic or royally pissed, but outside she came across as an emotionless robot disguised by a covering of human flesh.

"Did Debra complain to you about me?" Lori asked. Such behavior would be completely in character for her.

Melinda looked surprised. "Not at all. I noticed you were very low energy all morning, and at times it seemed as if you were merely going through the motions. I was wondering if there's something bothering you."

Lori's eyes caught a flash of movement, and her gaze was drawn to Melinda's shoulder. She'd thought she'd seen.... But she couldn't have. For an instant it had appeared that Melinda's braid had flicked to the side, as if she'd jerked her head to make it move. But Melinda's head had remained steady the entire time. Was she seeing things? If this had happened yesterday, she'd have said yes. But after everything that had happened since FoodSaver? She wasn't so sure.

"I appreciate your concern, Melinda, I really do. But I'm fine. Everything's fine."

Good job, she thought. *That sounded really convincing.*

Melinda's eyes narrowed, and Lori had the sense the woman was scrutinizing her, trying to peer into her brain to determine if she was lying. Melinda must've been satisfied with what she saw, for her eyes relaxed and she gave a thin-lipped smile.

"I'm glad to hear it. If you *were* unhappy, as your boss, I'd be required to do something about it."

Now it was Lori's turn to frown. "Such as?"

"Oh, I don't know. Tear off one of your tits with my teeth, or press a hot steam iron against your cunt and hold it there until the flesh has melted into a solid, charred mass. Something along those lines. I'm glad neither of those things will be necessary, though." She smiled. "Have a good lunch."

Without another word, Melinda walked past her and entered the billing office to speak to Dennis, the practice's business manager, her braid swaying as she walked.

Lori stared after Melinda. *What the actual fuck?*

She walked to the reception area, unable to believe what had just happened. She and Melinda might not exactly have been best friends, but the woman had never come close to speaking to her like that. What the hell had – and then it came to her. *They* had gotten to Melinda somehow. The Cabal. They'd done something to her, something that had made her say those vile, disgusting things.

All she wanted to do now was get the hell out of there and talk to Reeny. Her little sister was clear-headed and pragmatic. *Being a wife and mother teaches you to cut through a lot of bullshit,* Reeny had once told her. She hoped Reeny would be able to lend her some of that clarity. She sure as shit could use it right now.

She was so intent on leaving that she barely noticed Katie still working at the reception counter, typing away at her computer. She would've walked right past her and dashed out into the parking lot if the woman hadn't suddenly spoken.

"Do you want to hear the rest of my story or not?"

She sounded irritated, almost angry, and it was so unlike the Katie Lori knew that, despite her near frantic desire to be out of this place, she stopped. Katie took this as a sign to continue speaking, picking up the thread of her story exactly where she'd left off several hours ago.

"Like I said, I thought the guy in the sunglasses was going to pass me, pull in front of me, and hit his brakes. But when his car was even with mine, he rolled down the passenger-side window and threw something out. It hit the hood of my car with a loud thump, and I was so startled I slammed on my own brakes and swerved to a stop along the side of the road. I was damn lucky nobody rear-ended me, though I got a lot of dirty looks, raised middle fingers, and angry honks. The sonofabitch in the black car just kept on going. Fucker didn't even slow down."

The longer Lori stood there, the more she became aware of a sour-sweet odor hanging heavy in the air. She didn't know what was causing the stink, but it turned her stomach.

She knew she shouldn't ask, knew she'd regret it if she did, but she couldn't stop herself.

"What was it? The thing that he threw at you?"

"It bounced off my car and fell onto the road before I got a good look at it. But once my heart stopped racing, I hit my hazard lights and got out of the car to see what it was. I found it lying next to the curb about ten feet behind my car. It was a cat. A tabby. I figured it had already been dead when the guy in the sunglasses threw it out of his window. Its head was twisted all the way backward. That's not the sort of injury that could happen on impact, right?"

"I don't know."

Lori tried to keep from imagining the details of Katie's story, but she couldn't help it. She saw the blurred orange form of the cat fly out the window of the Driver's black car, heard the dull thump as it struck the hood of Katie's car and bounced off, saw it lying next to the curb, head twisted, neck broken. She felt weak, lightheaded, dizzy. She needed to get out of here, get out into the fresh air. She lurched toward the door, but before she could grab the handle, Katie said, "And do you know what the worst part was?"

Don't look back, don't look back, don't look back....

But of course she looked.

Katie had reached down and from somewhere behind the counter she brought up a ragged mass of blood-soaked fur. It was the cat from her story – part of it, anyway. Its lower half was missing and entrails hung down loose from the opening, the organs wet and glistening. Lori now understood what caused the foul order that was stinking up the reception area.

"He'd already eaten half of it, the greedy bastard."

Katie raised the tabby's remains to her mouth, sank her teeth into its chest, and began snarling and shaking her head, trying to tear a mouthful free. There was a horrible ripping sound as Katie pulled a hunk of bloody fur and meat from the cat's corpse. She pulled her head back and chewed vigorously, making awful smacking sounds, her lips and chin smeared with the animal's blood. After a moment, she tossed her head back and swallowed. Then she lowered her head and looked at Lori. She blinked several times as if she'd forgotten she was standing there.

"Where are my manners?" She held the cat out toward Lori. "Want some?"

Lori dashed forward and slammed her shoulder into the door. It swung violently outward, and she flung herself onto the sidewalk outside Get Moving! The door slowly closed behind her as she ran toward her car, but before it closed completely, she heard Katie shout.

"Be that way! It just means more for me!"

★   ★   ★

Lori's pad thai was cold by the time she finished telling Reeny her story. At first Reeny had eaten her Singapore noodles while Lori had talked, but she'd soon gotten so caught up in her sister's tale that she'd stopped eating and listened intently, leaning forward, eyes wide, lips slightly parted, as if she wanted to interrupt but forced herself to remain silent. By the time Lori finished speaking, her mouth and throat felt dry as desert sand. She reached for her glass of water. Her hand trembled so badly she feared she might drop the glass, so she lowered her hand to her lap. She'd have to live with her dry mouth for the time being.

Reeny didn't say anything right away. She just looked at her with that same expression, eyes wide, lips parted.

Reeny was shorter than Lori and had carried a little extra weight since having Brian a few years ago. She wore her straight blond hair short – *Easier to manage that way*, she'd once said – and kept her makeup to a minimum for the same reason. Today she was dressed in a white blouse, gray jacket and skirt, and low-heeled black shoes. She was a real estate agent, and always liked to look professional when she was working. Lori thought they must look odd together, she in her blue smock and Reeny in her business attire.

A Taste of Thai was a small, homey restaurant located a few blocks from the Cannery District. It had the funky, rundown look of a lot of establishments in this area of town – faded carpet, worn chairs, water damage on some of the ceiling tiles – but the food was always excellent and the staff efficient and friendly. It had been Lori and Reeny's go-to place since their early twenties. Lori had hoped that meeting here would make her feel comforted, safe. But she kept glancing around, surreptitiously observing the other customers and the waitstaff, examining their left hands and looking for red-painted pinky nails. So far she'd seen none, but every time someone new walked into the restaurant, she checked again. They were out there somewhere, the members of the Cabal, just waiting for the next opportunity to fuck with her. She could feel it.

It's not paranoia if they're really out to get you, she thought.

She felt guilty telling her story to Reeny. She didn't spend as much time with her sister as she should, and when they did manage to get together, it seemed she usually asked Reeny to help her with one problem or another. But today she couldn't help it. She *needed* to talk to someone about what had happened last night – and the weirdness that had occurred at work today – and who else could she turn to but her sister?

She smiled nervously at Reeny.

"You're awfully quiet."

Reeny started, as if Lori's words had brought her out of a daze.

"It's a hell of a lot to take in."

"I know. You probably think I've lost my mind."

She hoped Reeny would protest, would say she didn't think anything of the sort. Her silence hurt worse than Lori had expected.

"So everything was fine until the woman with the weird eyes started talking to you in the grocery store."

"Yes. No bizarre encounters, no strange nightmares. Not before her."

Reeny nodded slowly. Lori had the impression she did this more to give herself time to think than because she was agreeing with what she'd said.

"And you think this mysterious group – the Cabal – is behind all of this."

The idea sounded crazy coming from her sister, like sign-the-commitment-papers-and-lock-her-up crazy. But she nodded.

"And you believe that the things you dreamed about – the Nightway, the tower – are real."

Lori wanted to deny it, to tell Reeny that *of course* she didn't think that those dreams were real, or at least a different *kind* of real. She'd have to be insane to think that, right? But she said nothing, and Reeny went on.

"Do you think the Cabal—" she grimaced as she said the word, "—somehow got to Katie and Melinda and…what? Did something to them?"

That's exactly what she thought, but she said, "I don't know."

Reeny took a sip of water. *Another stalling tactic,* Lori thought. Reeny put her glass down on the table and sat back in her chair.

"If it was anyone else but you telling me all this, I'd think they were playing some kind of sick joke on me or they were…." She trailed off.

"Nuts," Lori finished.

Reeny nodded. "But unless you've suddenly developed a dark sense of humor – I mean *really* dark – or you've had a stroke or a psychotic break in the last couple days…."

Lori felt encouraged by her sister's words.

"Does that mean you believe me?"

"I didn't say that. I mean, come on. It's a lot, Lori. A whole fucking lot."

Lori felt disappointed, but she didn't blame Reeny. She was sure she'd feel the same if their positions were reversed. But before she could say anything else, Reeny held up a hand to stop her.

"But let's say for the sake of argument that it's true. It all seems to come down to that one message, the one that the Cabal gave you."

"Confess and atone," Lori said. "Or suffer." Speaking the words caused her to shudder.

"A lot of the things that have happened in the last day could count as you suffering, couldn't they? Like you're being punished for something you did."

Lori thought about this for a moment. Goat-Eyes had delivered the Cabal's message, and after that, everything had started going to hell for her. Almost getting hit in FoodSaver's parking lot by that poor man. The shadow creatures breaking into her apartment. Her nightmare of being tortured in the Vermilion Tower. Officer Rauch leaving the message on her bathroom mirror. Melinda and Katie turning psycho….

She supposed all of those incidents could be looked at as ways of making her suffer.

She nodded.

"And the Cabal wants you to confess to something you did – or at least what they *think* you did – and make amends for it somehow. So if you can figure out what they think you've done, then you can atone for it, whatever that entails. And once you do—"

"It'll be over," Lori finished.

"That would seem to be the logical conclusion. As logical as any of this shit can be, anyway. So whether this stuff is real or...I don't know, some kind of message your subconscious is trying to send you, it all comes down to the same question: What could you have done that the Cabal would think was so bad they need to punish you in both the real world *and* the dream world?"

Aashrita's face came immediately into Lori's mind, but she banished the image just as swiftly.

"I don't know," she said.

Reeny looked at her for a long moment. She might be the younger sister, but she'd always acted like the older of the two, and she could always tell when Lori was lying to her. She'd gotten even better at assessing her truthfulness since she'd become a mother. But Lori had banished the thought of Aashrita so thoroughly that she didn't remember having it in the first place. Eventually Reeny relaxed, evidently satisfied that Lori had told the truth.

"Then I suggest you figure it out fast and do whatever you need to in order to make it better. Otherwise, things are going to get worse. Probably a *lot* worse."

Reeny's warning wasn't phrased in the same language as the Cabal's, but her words were still chilling, so much so that Lori looked at her sister's left pinky finger. But the nail was free of polish. Reeny noted Lori's examination of her finger, but instead of getting angry that her sister would entertain the notion, however briefly, that she was a member of the Cabal, she looked sad and sympathetic.

"Promise me something," Reeny said.

"Anything."

"Go see someone, get a professional opinion about all this."

Lori bristled at the suggestion.

"You mean go see a shrink."

"Yes," Reeny said. "Do it to humor me, if nothing else. I'm worried about you, Sissy."

That had been what Reeny had called her when they were kids – *Sissy*. Lori had hated it back then, but she'd come to love the word over the years, and hearing it now brought tears to her eyes. She knew Reeny didn't believe her story. How could she? It was *insane*. But she loved Lori enough to talk as if she believed it, and her support meant everything.

"Please don't say anything about all this to Mom and Dad," Lori pleaded. "I don't want them worrying about me."

Reeny frowned, obviously unhappy with this request.

"*Please*," Lori said.

"Okay," Reeny agreed. "But if you—" she paused a moment before continuing, "—if things don't start getting better soon, I think Mom and Dad should know what's happening."

Lori didn't like this, but she knew it was the best she was going to get out of Reeny, so she nodded her acceptance. She felt a little better after talking, and she was able to keep her hand mostly steady as she lifted her water to her mouth and finally took a drink. She drained half the glass before putting it back down.

Their server came over to the table. He was a handsome Asian man in his mid-twenties. Lori didn't know if he was Thai, but from his slight accent she thought it likely. He eyed their full plates of food and then asked, "Is there something wrong?"

"Not at all," Reeny said. "The food here's always delicious. We just got carried away talking and lost track of time. Could we have a couple of to-go boxes?"

Lori envied how easily Reeny could talk to people. She'd always been socially skilled, even when they'd been children. She'd never had any trouble making friends and, later, getting dates, and her people skills served her well as a real estate agent. Lori did okay with people once she got to know them, but she was an introvert at heart. Interacting with people for too long a time exhausted her. Not Reeny, though. She drew energy from human contact, almost like she was a psychic vampire.

"Of course," the server said. He smiled, then turned and walked away.

"Did something about that smile seem off to you?" Lori asked.

"Off?"

"Not right. Like he wasn't *really* smiling at us, like he was faking it."

"You're starting to scare me," Reeny said.

Lori took her gaze off their departing server and met her sister's eyes. She saw concern there, but she saw wariness, too. *She doesn't trust me,* Lori realized. *She can't predict what I'll say and do next, and that scares her.* She needed to cool it with the paranoia, at least until they left the restaurant and went their separate ways.

She dropped her gaze to her plate of cold pad thai. "Never mind," she said.

She thought Reeny might make an issue of her comment about the server's smile, but instead she said, "What does Justin think about all... this?"

Lori kept her eyes on her food as she answered. "I haven't had a chance to tell him yet."

"So I know and Larry knows, but Justin doesn't. Your *boyfriend* Justin."

Lori still had no appetite, but she picked up her fork and began moving rice noodles around on her plate. "We talked on the phone last night after I got home from FoodSaver. We got into an argument before I could tell him what had happened, and he hung up. I haven't been able to get hold of him today."

Reeny shook her head. Before she could respond further, the server returned to their table with a pair of Styrofoam containers. He handed one to each of the women, and as he did so, Lori checked to make sure his left pinky finger was free of polish. It was.

The server placed the check on the table and then with another smile that Lori thought was less than genuine, he left. Once he was gone, Reeny scowled at her, and she knew her sister had noticed her checking the man's little finger. She didn't comment on it, though.

"I'm not surprised you and Justin haven't talked yet. You guys have a lot of trouble communicating."

This was the *last* thing Lori needed right now. Reeny wasn't Justin's biggest fan, and she'd made no secret that she thought he wasn't right for Lori. She thought he was too self-focused, almost to the point of being neurotic.

"This stuff isn't the kind of thing you can communicate easily over the phone." She hated how defensive she sounded, but whenever Reeny was critical of Justin – which was often – Lori felt a need to defend him. Or maybe she was defending her choice of him as a boyfriend. She felt that by making excuses, she was only confirming Reeny's assessment, but she couldn't stop herself.

Reeny seemed to sense this wasn't the time to dig into Lori's relationship problems, and she changed the subject. "Are you planning to go back to work today?"

Lori thought of Katie's bloodstained mouth, saw her offering the remains of the cat and asking, *Want some?* "No fucking way. As soon as we're done here, I'll call in sick."

Melinda would be pissed at the disruption in the afternoon's schedule. Katie — assuming she wasn't running around outside looking for more cats to eat — would have to call all of Lori's clients for the rest of the day and reschedule their appointments. Lori didn't care, though. She couldn't bring herself to return to Get Moving! She didn't know if she'd ever be able to go back.

The server returned for their check, and Reeny took a credit card from her wallet and handed it to him along with the bill. He took them with a smile and headed off again. Lori wanted to watch him closely as he departed, wanted to search for a sign — however small — that something was wrong about him. But she knew what Reeny would think if she did, and she forced herself not to look at the man as he walked away from their table. Reeny's eyes narrowed as if she sensed Lori's struggle, but she didn't remark on it.

"Thanks for picking up the tab," Lori said.

"My pleasure. So if you're not going back to work, what are you going to do with yourself the rest of the day?"

"I don't know. I haven't thought about it yet."

Normally, she might've gone home, but her apartment didn't feel safe anymore. Even if one of the maintenance workers had replaced her patio door's lock, there was no reason to think that the shadow creatures couldn't find some way into her apartment again. And if they didn't make another attempt to break in, if she fell asleep and took a nap, she might find herself back in the Vermilion Tower, picking up exactly where she'd left off, with the Cabal torturing her. And she had no idea how long Larry's signing gig would last today. There was a good chance he'd be home when she got there, and while she'd find his presence a comfort, they weren't a couple any longer and she thought it best to maintain a certain amount of emotional distance between them. Given how scared she was right now, it would be all too easy to fall back into old patterns of behavior, to seek a return to what they once had, simply for the solace that such closeness might bring. Larry might be in a 'guy phase' right now, but that didn't mean he wouldn't be tempted to fall back into bed with her if she gave him the opportunity. No, it would be best to keep him at arm's length for a while – for both their sakes.

She needed to find somewhere to go, somewhere she could think in peace and try to begin sorting out this mess, without having to worry about what weird thing might confront her next. She had no idea where that might be, though.

"You could hang out with me," Reeny offered. "I'm showing a house at one-thirty, and I have to pick up Brian at preschool at three. He'd love to see you. You know how much he loves his Aunt Lorlee."

When Brian had first started talking he'd pronounced her name *Lorlee*, and that's what he'd called her ever since. Lori loved that her nephew had a special name all his own for her. She was tempted to take Reeny up on her offer. She didn't want to be alone, and god knew she could use Reeny's emotional support. But she didn't want to drag Reeny into the insane mess her life had become. Who knew what the Cabal might do to them in order to punish her? No, she couldn't do that to Reeny.

"Thanks, but I think I'd rather keep handling this on my own for a little while longer. Once I figure out what's happening to me, maybe I can come up with some way to counter it."

"I'm not sure that's such a good idea." Before Reeny could say more, the server returned with her credit card and handed it to her, along with a final bill and a black pen to sign it.

"I hope you both have a wonderful day," he said, and gave them a final smile before going off to see to other customers.

Fat chance of that, Lori thought.

When Reeny finished adding a tip and signing the check, she held it up as if to inspect her work, make sure her signature was neat and legible, her math accurate. As she did this, Lori saw a message scrawled onto the back of the bill in black ink.

Confess and atone – or suffer.

She almost told Reeny about the message, but she decided not to. As much of a relief as it had been to tell her sister about everything that had happened, she wondered if it had been wise. What if by talking to Reeny, she ended up bringing her to the attention of the Cabal? As long as Reeny believed she was delusional and that the Cabal wasn't real, they'd have no reason to harass her.

She hoped.

★   ★   ★

They walked into the parking lot together. They hugged, and Reeny made Lori promise to call if things got worse. Lori said she would, though she suspected Reeny knew this for the lie it was. Reeny climbed into her red Nissan Altima, started the engine, then after a last worried look and a wave, she backed out of the space, put the car in gear, and drove off. Lori got in her Civic and turned on the engine, but she sat there for a moment, thinking, trying to decide on her next move. She was still debating when her phone rang, startling her. She almost didn't check to see who was calling, afraid to find it was someone from the Cabal. But the phone's display screen indicated it was Justin, so she answered it.

Instead of saying hello, she said, "Justin?" as if unsure it was really him on the other end.

"Hey."

His voice was subdued, but it was him.

Before he could say anything else, she said, "I'm sorry about last night. I shouldn't have snapped at you like that."

He didn't respond right away, and she thought he was still angry with her. She was going to apologize further, but he said, "I got the CT scan results this morning."

She was confused. She'd known he'd had a doctor's appointment, but he'd said nothing to her about needing a CT scan.

"Justin, what are you—"

"I didn't want to say anything to you until I was sure. I didn't want to worry you unnecessarily. Maybe I shouldn't have done that. Maybe I just wanted to pretend that everything was normal for a little while longer, you know? Still, that's no excuse for keeping you in the dark like I did. Sorry."

Lori was stunned. After everything that had happened since last night at FoodSaver, she'd come to expect that her life was going to continue to get increasingly fucked up. But finding out that her boyfriend had some kind of ongoing medical issue – evidently a serious one – that he hadn't told her about seemed equally as surreal as sadistic occultists in blood-red robes and black cars traveling an ebon road beneath a starless sky.

"What's wrong?" she asked.

"I've been feeling rundown for a couple months, so much so that I've been guzzling coffee by the gallon trying to stay functional. It helped, but not as much as I'd hoped. I decided to go to the doctor for a checkup, and the doctor ordered a series of tests. X-rays indicated the presence of shadowy masses on my lungs, so the doctor ordered a CT scan."

The word *shadowy* caught her attention as much if not more than *masses*. She imagined night-black multijointed fingers entering Justin's mouth, reaching down into his lungs, infecting them with darkness.

"It looks like cancer," Justin said. "How bad it is, we won't know until we do a biopsy. I've got one scheduled for next week. But the doctor's already talking about aggressive chemotherapy, so I know he thinks it's pretty bad."

Lori wanted to say something to comfort Justin, but nothing came to her. What can you say to someone who's just told you that their body has betrayed them in one of the most horrible ways imaginable?

"Where are you? I want to see you."

In an awful way, she was almost glad Justin had called her with this news. It gave her something to focus on besides herself and the shitshow her life had become in the last twenty-four hours. She would go to Justin, comfort him as best she could, and in so doing hopefully forget – if only for a little while – about the Cabal. She knew this was selfish, that it made her a terrible person, but there it was.

"I'm at work. I wanted to try to keep the rest of my day as normal as possible, take my mind off—" he paused, "—off *it*. It's not really working, though." He let out a mirthless laugh.

She wanted to tell him to leave work so they could be together, but she didn't. Doing so would be focusing on her needs, not his. Maybe she wasn't so selfish after all.

"Then how about after work? I could come over to your place."

Justin almost never came to her apartment. Even if Larry wasn't there, his *presence* was – at least that's what Justin said – so when they spent time together, it was usually at his condo.

"Sure," he said, voice devoid of emotion. "That would be great."
Another pause, then, "I should go. I've got a lot of stuff to do this afternoon."

"Okay. I'll come over around six. Sound good?"

He didn't respond to her question, and she wondered if he'd even heard it.

"Bye," he said, then disconnected.

Normally, he told her he loved her when he said goodbye to her over the phone. It always made her uncomfortable, but now that he hadn't said the words, she was surprised by how much she missed hearing them.

She put her phone back in her purse and sat there for several moments, trying to absorb what Justin had told her. Her initial reaction was that he was too young to get cancer. She knew this wasn't true, though. Cancer could strike at any time during a person's life, and while she associated lung cancer with smoking, she also knew that a person who'd never touched a cigarette could also contract it. Still, she couldn't escape the nagging feeling that Justin's diagnosis was related to the Cabal somehow. Perhaps they'd caused his cancer in order to punish her further. She recognized this as another egocentric thought – that she was trying to make Justin's cancer about her when she should be thinking about him. And even if the Cabal wanted to harm Justin to punish her, it wasn't as if they'd made him sick overnight. He hadn't told her he was getting a CT scan, but he would've had to have had it done at least a few days ago in order to get the results this morning. It took time for a pathologist to examine the scan's results and then send a report to Justin's doctor. Whatever abilities the Cabal possessed, they couldn't reach backward in time to give Justin cancer. Then again, who knew what they could do and what sort of unnatural laws governed their actions?

If Justin's cancer had been caused by the Cabal, however they'd managed it, that meant no one she knew was safe. They'd already done something to Katie and Melinda. Who else might be next? Reeny and her family? Their parents? Larry? Her clients at the clinic? She couldn't let any harm come to them, but she had no idea how to prevent the Cabal from hurting them

Or did she?

She remembered Reeny's words about the Cabal.

If you can figure out what they think you've done, then you can make amends for it, whatever that entails.

Like in a twelve-step program, Lori thought. She'd never gone through such a program herself, but she'd worked with clients who had. She couldn't remember which of the twelve steps making amends was, but she knew it was an important one. Maybe Reeny had been on to something. At least it gave her a place to start. But who had she wronged to such a degree that she needed to formally apologize to them? She was hardly a perfect human being, but she didn't careen thoughtlessly through life, causing damage to others along the way. She wasn't impulsive, always tried to think through her actions and anticipate their consequences before doing anything. She worked hard to avoid hurting anybody. So what could she possibly have done that the Cabal considered so bad that it warranted harassing her? No, more than that – *torturing* her. There wasn't anything she could think of.

That's not exactly true, and you know it.

Maybe she thought about the consequences of her actions these days, but she hadn't always been that kind of person, had she?

Aashrita.

The moment she thought the name, her mind fought to snatch it back, to drag it down into the depths of her consciousness and bury it once more, as it did whenever she thought of Aashrita. But she didn't let it happen this time. There was too much at stake.

Aashrita, she thought. *Aashrita, Aashrita, Aashrita.*

She backed out of her parking space, then headed for the road—

—and Woodlawn Cemetery.

CHAPTER SIX

Debra Foster parked her blue Ford Mustang – with a bumper sticker that said *I'd rather be in the saddle* – in front of Get Moving! at roughly the same time as Lori and Reeny left A Taste of Thai. She was pissed off, but that wasn't anything special. She was always pissed off about something. At the moment, she was angry that she couldn't find her goddamned reading glasses. She'd looked everywhere for the fucking things, but she'd had no success locating them. When she'd been younger, she thought that old people who wore their reading glasses tethered to a loop of string around their necks were pathetic. Obviously, they were so damned senile they'd lose their things if they didn't keep them on their person at all times. Now she was one of those old people – although she no longer considered being in her fifties as old – and she misplaced her reading glasses often.

She wasn't certain that she'd had them with her when she'd arrived for her physical therapy appointment with Lori, but she'd decided to retrace her steps and see if she'd accidentally left them somewhere. She was going in reverse, so she'd start at Get Moving! and if she didn't find her glasses here, she'd return to the diner where she'd eaten breakfast this morning and see if she'd left them on the table when she'd departed. She knew she could simply buy a new pair. Non-prescription ones didn't cost much, and you could find them at any grocery or pharmacy. But it was the principle of the goddamned thing. They were *her* glasses and she was determined to find them, even if she had to spend the rest of her day driving all over the fucking town.

Lori had once commented on her stubbornness, saying that if she directed it toward her physical therapy, kept up with her exercises at home, she'd be sure to see results. Debra knew the woman had only been doing her job, but she'd almost told her to go fuck herself just the same.

She turned off the car, and when she moved to open the driver's-side door a bolt of white-hot pain lanced through her left shoulder. She'd been taking over-the-counter painkillers and anti-inflammatories like they were candy for the last several weeks, but they only did so much to blunt the pain. She drew in a hissing breath, muttered, "Fuck," and pushed the door open. She got out of the car slowly, hoping to avoid setting off any more pain, and then gently closed the door behind her. Even though she used her right hand to do this, her shoulder gave a twinge, but it wasn't nearly as painful as before, and she counted this as a minor victory.

She knew her injury was her goddamned fault. She'd kept horses ever since she'd been a little girl, and she'd been cleaning stalls all this time. The sawdust you put down in a horse's stall absorbed their urine when they pissed, and when they pissed, they pissed a *flood*. They were big animals, after all. The sawdust grew sodden and heavy, and when you shoveled it into a bucket to remove it, you had to be careful not to put in too much at a time, or else the bucket would be too heavy to carry. Last month, there'd been a stretch of several days when it had rained like a sonofabitch – strong winds, lightning, thunder, the whole fucking deal – and she'd kept the horses, a quarter horse named Lucky and a Friesian named Gustav, in the barn until the storms finally blew over. When she let them out into the field, she had days' worth of manure and urine-soaked sawdust to clean up. She'd been impatient, and instead of filling buckets up halfway, dumping them outside, and returning for more, she filled them up full to overflowing and struggled to lift and carry them out of the barn. She knew better, that was the hell of it, but she'd done it anyway, and in the process fucked up her shoulder big time.

She lived alone – sharing living space with another person would irritate the hell out of her, and she knew she'd be no picnic to cohabitate with either – so she had no one to help her with the chores around the farm. Thanks to her goddamned shoulder, everything took twice as long for her to do now. She was convinced her shoulder would eventually heal on its own, but in the meantime, she needed better meds to help her function. Her fucking doctor insisted she try physical therapy for a month before the bastard would prescribe heavy-duty painkillers and muscle relaxers for her, and while she resented the hell out of him for it, she was determined to get through the stupid therapy and get her drugs. The staff at Get Moving! were nice enough, if a little too fanatical in their devotion to the great god of Physical Rehabilitation, but she still hated going there, and she resented the fact that she had to return. One visit a day was way more than enough for her.

But she needed her fucking glasses, couldn't read a goddamned thing without them.

When she walked into Get Moving!, the first thing she noticed was an odd smell. She'd lived in the country all her life, and she knew the smell of meat starting to rot, knew the smell of spilled blood. The mingled odors triggered an alarm in her subconscious, but she was so damned pissed about her glasses that she ignored it. The woman who was always at the front – Debra could never remember her name – wasn't there. Maybe she'd gone to lunch, but if so, someone should've been covering for her until she got back. At the very least, she could've left a note that said when she'd return. But there was nothing. The woman's absence irritated her. She'd hoped to ask her if anyone had found her reading glasses and turned them in. She had no intention of taking a seat in the waiting area and flipping through old magazines with wrinkled covers and torn pages until the woman returned. Debra had things to *do*. She had a *life*.

Fuck it.

She walked around the semicircular counter, intending to look for her glasses herself, go through every drawer if she had to. But when she got to the other side, she saw that the space wasn't empty. The office chair was pushed up to the desk, and the woman – Katherine? Kathy? – was crouched on the floor, hunched over something. Her head was pointed away from Debra, so she couldn't see what the woman had, but she was making wet chewing noises. Debra's subconscious sent up another warning, this one louder than the last.

Get the fuck out!

Debra heard this warning, but she hesitated. No more than a second, two tops. But it was enough for – Kate? – to realize she was there. The woman sat up on her knees and turned to look at Debra. Her nose, mouth, and chin were slick with blood, as were her hands. She held a bloody thing that was mostly a skeleton with a few scraps of fur and flesh clinging to it. The woman – Katie! Her name was Katie! – drew the mutilated remains to her chest and glared at Debra with wide, wild eyes.

"You can't have any, bitch. It's all mine!"

Her voice was a high-pitched shriek and bloody spittle flew from her lips as she yelled. There were bloodstains and tufts of skin and fur on the carpet in front of the woman, and Debra knew she'd been working on the animal – a cat? – for a while.

Debra no longer gave a shit about her glasses.

She held her hands palm out in a warding gesture, and she began to back up slowly. She wanted to turn and run, but she knew better than to take her eyes off Katie, and she also knew that if she started running, she might trigger a predatory response in the woman, prompting her to attack. No, she *had* to go slow, regardless of how fast her heart was beating (very) or how much adrenaline was coursing through her veins (a lot).

The woman continued glaring at her, but she made no move to rise to her feet. A soft sound was coming from her throat, and while Debra wasn't certain, she thought the woman was actually growling at her.

She'd taken three steps backward when she bumped into something. An involuntary squeal of fright escaped her lips, and she whirled around to see the clinic's director standing there. She couldn't remember this woman's name, but she recognized her. She was always here, and today she'd observed Debra's entire session with Lori for some reason. Probably some kind of performance review thing, she'd decided. Lori wasn't bad, but she could use some improvement, that was for sure.

Debra's first response was to enlist the director's aid, and she hooked a thumb over her shoulder in Katie's direction.

"Do you see what she—"

She broke off when the details of the director's appearance registered on her awareness. The woman was covered in blood from head to toe. She looked like she'd been bathing in the stuff, swimming in a goddamned pool of it. Not a lake, an *ocean*....

The director smiled and held up a pair of glasses, lenses speckled with blood.

"Are these yours?" she said.

The woman's long braid swayed behind her under its own power, as if she had a large gray snake growing out of the back of her head. The sight of the thing moving independently made Debra feel queasy. It was unnatural. *Wrong*. It couldn't be and yet it was, and that idea – that something that should be impossible might be real – was more terrifying than these two women combined.

The braid whipped out from behind Melinda's back and lashed Debra across the face. The impact stung like hell, and she stepped back, shaken. She brought her hand to her cheek as if by touching it she could somehow lessen the pain.

Katie's growling became a snarl then, and Debra felt the woman slam into her from behind. Her shoulder screamed in agony, and a burst of white light filled her vision as Katie's weight bore her to the floor. She hit hard, and she felt something snap in her chest. A rib? She couldn't catch her breath, and her mouth gaped open and closed like a fish on land as she tried to draw in air. She thrashed back and forth in an attempt to dislodge Katie, but the woman grasped her shoulders tight and held on.

The director knelt in front of her face and smiled, lips sliding away from blood-slick teeth.

"I imagine your shoulder must be hurting a great deal right now. Don't worry. We can fix it. There might be a little discomfort at first, but it'll be over in a few minutes. You'll feel much better afterward." Her smile widened. "In fact, you won't feel anything at all."

The director dropped Debra's glasses to the carpet and then both she and Katie went to work. As it turned out, the director had lied to Debra. She felt more than a little discomfort, quite a fucking lot, in fact.

★   ★   ★

Melinda did her best to wipe her hands clean on the carpet before she stood, but there was only so much she could do to get the blood off — there was so *much* of it. And really, why bother? She was covered in it, her clothes dark, sodden, and heavy. Besides, she rather liked the feeling of blood on her skin, and while she hadn't had a chance to view herself in a mirror yet, she suspected 'blood-drenched maniac' was a good look for her.

When she was on her feet, she regarded Debra's corpse. Working together, she and Katie had torn off Debra's left arm and cast it aside. It now lay several feet from the body, fingers half curled, thumb slightly extended, almost as if Debra was signaling approval of their work from the great beyond. They'd removed most of the muscle in her left shoulder and had discarded it, too. Katie had taken a couple bites of it, but she found the meat too tough and chewy, and she was now hunkered over Debra's remains, gnawing on a length of intestine. While this admittedly drastic therapy was quite messy, Melinda thought it fast and effective. Debra's shoulder pain had been thoroughly and completely resolved.

As she stood watching Katie work on her grisly meal – it *was* lunchtime, after all – she pondered what to do next. She'd killed Dennis – torn the business manager's throat out with her teeth – before coming out to the reception area to help Katie deal with Debra, and there was no one else currently in the clinic. The other PTs were at lunch, and no clients had been scheduled for this time. People would soon be coming, though. Her employees would return from lunch, and the afternoon clients would begin to arrive. She supposed she and Katie could attack them as they entered, and while that would be fun, she couldn't escape a nagging feeling that there was something else she should do. Something important.

It had been a strange day so far. She and Katie were always the first to arrive, and while Melinda usually beat her to the office, today had been one of those rare occasions when Katie got there before her. She had been seated at the reception counter when Melinda entered the clinic. Melinda wasn't much for empty pleasantries at the best of times, and today she especially wasn't interested in chatting with Katie. She and Carlo had had a fight last night, a real knock-down-drag-out that had come close to ending their relationship. Things had been better between them this morning, if still strained, and while she was hopeful they would return to normal soon, she was worried the fight had been a symptom of deeper relationship issues that needed to be addressed.

The fight had started because Carlo had said he was too tired when she'd wanted to make love last night. He'd been putting her off sexually for a while now, but when she'd confronted him about it, he'd said she was making something out of nothing. He still loved her, still wanted her. He was simply tired. He ran his own construction company, and he put in long hours, often doing physically demanding work alongside his employees. Of course he'd be too tired for sex sometimes. Melinda knew that. But *every* time she wanted to fuck? She was starting to worry that he was having an affair.

So when Katie greeted her as she entered the clinic, she hadn't bothered smiling, only nodded and hoped Katie would get the message and leave her alone. But Katie hadn't taken the hint.

"I've got something cool to show you," she'd said. "*Really* cool."

Melinda had intended to ignore Katie and keep on walking until she reached her office, which was located across the hall from Dennis's. She'd enter, close the door behind her, and try to get it together before her first client of the day arrived. But she didn't do that. Instead, she walked over to the reception counter to see what Katie wanted to show her. *Why* she'd done this, she wasn't certain. Maybe, despite her determination not to interact with anyone this morning, she needed some positive human contact. Or maybe she'd decided that just because she felt shitty was no reason to treat Katie poorly. Whatever the reason, she was at the counter, and she waited for Katie to reveal whatever it was she wanted to show her. *It damn well better be cool,* she'd thought.

Katie had something inside a plastic shopping bag sitting on her desk area behind the counter. She stuck her right hand inside the bag, but instead of pulling out whatever object it contained, she quickly withdrew her hand, reached out, and rubbed her fingers rapidly back and forth over Melinda's lips.

"What the *fuck*?" She stepped back in alarm, raised a hand to her lips, touched them, looked at her fingers, saw they were smeared with thick, sticky red.

"It's cat blood," Katie said. "Awesome, right?"

Melinda was beyond horrified. She had two cats herself – Puddin' and Lightfoot – and the idea that Katie would smear ketchup on her and claim it was cat blood for some sick fucking joke was....

She heard the plastic bag rustle, then watched as Katie lifted a dead cat – *half* a dead cat – up for her to see.

It's out of the bag, Melinda had thought. *The cat. Is out. Of the bag.*

The blood (definitely *not* ketchup) felt warm and tingly on her lips, and she had the sensation that her skin was absorbing it somehow, pulling it into her. Or maybe the blood was forcing its way in, invading her. Either way, it didn't matter. What mattered was that it felt good. Felt fucking *great*, in fact.

She'd started laughing then, and Katie joined in. They both looked at the cat's head – open staring eyes, small blood-flecked tongue sticking out of its mouth – as if they expected it to say something. It remained silent, of course, but the look on its dead face was so ridiculous that the women's laughter intensified, becoming shrieks of hilarity.

That had been hours ago, and while Melinda still felt fantastic, as if she was flying high on the greatest drug ever created, she felt unsettled as well. Restless. There was something she needed to do, she and Katie both, but she couldn't—

And then the dark infection that had entered her body via tainted cat blood began whispering to her. She listened intently for several seconds, and when the voice fell silent, she smiled. She knew what they had to do.

"Lunch is over, Katie. Time for you and I to get back to work."

Katie spat out the length of intestine she'd been chewing on and stood, giving Debra's ravaged body a last regretful look, as if she felt guilty about wasting so much food. Then she turned to face Melinda, her stomach bloated, full to bursting with cat and human meat. Melinda noticed the woman's face had changed. Her eyes were now amber and larger than before, and tufts of downy hair covered her cheeks. No, not hair. *Fur.*

They say you are what you eat, Melinda thought. In Katie's case, it seemed to be *you become what you eat.*

"You want me to take the rest of her out back to the dumpster?" Katie asked. There was a soft, fluttering hum to her voice, almost a purr.

"I don't think so. Her corpse livens up the place – so to speak. No, you and I are going to take a little trip to pick up a new friend."

She felt her braid quiver against her back. It was excited, ready and raring to go. She reached around to the back of her head and stroked the base of the braid.

In a moment, she thought. *Be patient.*

"Okay," Katie said. "But can we maybe stop and get some snacks along the way? I'm starving."

Melinda smiled. "I think that can be arranged."

★   ★   ★

It was beginning to rain by the time Lori pulled into Woodlawn Cemetery. The rain wasn't heavy, but it was steady, and Lori activated her windshield wipers. *What a cliché,* she thought. *Rain in a cemetery.* She might've thought the Cabal had arranged the rain in order to provide a suitably gloomy atmosphere for her, but from what she'd experienced so far, the Cabal wasn't this unoriginal.

If I have to be stalked and harassed by fiendish otherworldly mystics, at least they're creative ones, she thought.

She hadn't been here in almost fifteen years, but she remembered the way so well, she thought she could drive it with her eyes closed.

Woodlawn was one of only a handful of cemeteries in town, and it was smaller than the others. It was enclosed by orange brick walls all the way around, and its only entry and exit point was through a pair of black wrought-iron gates, which were left unlocked and open every day from nine a.m. to nine p.m. The ground here rose and fell in modest hills and dips, and there were few trees. Those that were present were young, with thin trunks and even thinner branches, leaves still mostly green, but some edging toward fall colors. She remembered more trees, much older and larger than these, and she wondered if they'd been cut down and replaced by younger ones since the last time she'd been here. Probably. Cemeteries were depressing enough as it was. Who wanted to be greeted by a bunch of dead and dying trees?

A narrow access road wound through the cemetery grounds, the asphalt old and cracked. They'd replaced the trees but couldn't be bothered to repair the road? Cheap-ass bastards. The road was only wide enough for one car to drive on, but there was no one else in the cemetery – at least, she couldn't see any other vehicles – so she didn't have to worry about having to pull off to the side so another car could pass. More importantly, she wouldn't have to worry about anyone seeing her here. No one would know who she was or why she'd come, but she still didn't want any eyes on her. This was going to be hard enough as it was. She didn't need a goddamned audience.

The headstones were of different sizes and fashioned from different colors of stone. Most were in the typical rectangular shape, but some were shaped like larger obelisks or spires, and others were more stylized in design, carved to resemble a heart or – in one extremely depressing case – a cradle. The headstone she was looking for was a modest one. No pictures of angels carved onto its face, no sentiments like *Always in our hearts* or *Gone to be with the Lord*. Just gray rock with simple letters and numbers etched in its surface.

And there it was.

Up to this point, Lori hadn't felt much of anything. She'd been numb, operating on autopilot, desperately trying not to think about Katie holding the mutilated body of the dead cat out to her.

Want some?

But now that the grave – Aashrita's grave – was in sight, she felt a lance of pain behind her right eye. The first sign of a stress-induced migraine, she thought. The rain wasn't helping either. It always played hell with her sinuses.

She parked her car and got out, leaving her purse on the passenger seat. She had a small umbrella in the glove box, but she left it where it was. The rain wasn't coming down that hard, and it was cool but not cold out. She had a red windbreaker in the back seat, but she didn't want to have anything to do with that color right now, so she left it, too. As rain hit her — especially her uncovered head and bare arms — she hoped the sensation would provide a kind of buffer that would insulate her from her emotions. So many awful things had happened to her since Goat-Eyes had first approached her in the grocery store, but none of them was worse than this was going to be.

She stepped onto the grass, careful to avoid walking across people's graves as she made her way to Aashrita's headstone. She did this out of a quasi-superstitious politeness more than from any actual belief she would be disrespecting the spirits of the dead by tramping on their graves. But given everything she'd experienced since last night, she figured better safe than sorry.

Her bad knee always ached when it rained, and it throbbed now, buckling a little with every step. She was grateful for this pain, too. It was an old friend, and as such was — in a weird way — a comfort to her now. The pain wouldn't serve as a distraction from her thoughts about Aashrita, though. How could it, considering Aashrita had been there when she'd sustained the injury responsible for that pain?

She was surprised to see one of the new, skinny trees had been planted close to Aashrita's grave. Too close, she thought. The base of the trunk was less than a yard from the headstone. As the tree grew, would its roots grow around Aashrita's burial vault, or would they worm their way through tiny cracks in the concrete, widening them until they'd breached the vault and could slither toward the casket — and its occupant? When Lori reached Aashrita's grave, she stepped off to the side to avoid standing on her friend's resting place, body angled so she could face the headstone. Fifteen years of exposure to the elements had worn the edges of the letters and numbers somewhat, but they were still easily legible. AASHRITA DHAWAN. That was all, aside from her birth and death dates. There was no sign anyone had visited the grave recently. There were no flowers, and the grass could use some trimming. Lori wondered if the sound of a lawnmower would disturb the dead's sleep, or if they would welcome sounds of life, however impersonal those sounds might be. She felt an urge then to say hello to Aashrita, but she couldn't bring herself to do so.

She felt memories pushing at the threshold of her consciousness, demanding that she pay attention to them. But she'd spent so many years suppressing them – sometimes so successfully that she forgot Aashrita had ever existed – that she was afraid to let them in. She feared they'd overwhelm her, inundate her, *drown* her....

She experienced a powerful urge to run back to her car, get in, drive away, and never look back. But she forced herself to remain where she was, forced herself not to look away from Aashrita's headstone.

Start with one memory, she told herself. *Just one.*

She closed her eyes and waited for a single memory to emerge from the roiling maelstrom in her mind.

★　　★　　★

She opened her eyes and gazed upon the face of a man without any eyes of his own.

"Have you figured it out yet?" the Driver asked.

In the light cast by the mass of firebabies slowly swirling above her, she saw the Driver held a knife large enough to be a machete, the blade slick with blood. *Her* blood, judging by the fiery lines of pain that crisscrossed her naked body.

There was no way he could see her take in the knife, but he said, "I didn't have time to clean it off after cutting that cat in two before using it on you. Sorry. You might want to put some antibiotic ointment on those cuts later."

"If you don't die from blood loss first," Goat-Eyes put in.

"Excellent point," the Driver conceded.

The woman stood on the Driver's right. She wore a metal gauntlet on her left hand, needle-like spines covering the fingers. The spines, like the Driver's blade, dripped with blood. Rauch stood on the Driver's left, his neck gills opening and closing so fast they buzzed like a hummingbird's wings. He held a flail that looked as if it had been made from the craggy gray skin of some reptilian creature. It too was streaked with blood.

She looked past her three tormentors and saw the crimson-robed figures of the Cabal standing shoulder to shoulder on the tower's upward-curving spiral, observing her with silent intensity. She tried to move her arms and legs, felt the shackles' restraint, heard the chains rattle.

"I was in the cemetery," she said, her voice a soft dry rasp.

The Driver smiled.

"There's nowhere you can go that we can't find you."

"Not even death would permit you to escape us," Goat-Eyes added.

"You're ours until we release you," Rauch said.

"And we won't do that until the Intercessor is satisfied," the Driver finished.

He turned to face the assembled Cabal, raised his hands high above his head, and shouted, "Everyone?"

Hundreds of the red-robed mystics spoke through the firebabies in a single thunderous voice, their words so loud Lori felt the X-cross vibrate against her body.

"Confess and atone — or suffer."

Lori spoke again, her voice louder and clearer this time. Her words still came out as barely more than a whisper, but she had no doubt the entire Cabal could hear her.

"Tell me what I did and I'll fix it…if I can."

The Cabal was silent for several long moments, and then the chamber was filled with the roar of riotous laughter.

The Driver, Goat-Eyes, and Rauch were laughing too as they raised their implements of torture and stepped toward her. Seconds later, her screams joined the thundering cacophony of sound within the Vermilion Tower.

★   ★   ★

She woke to wet and cold. Aashrita's headstone lay in front of her, but something was wrong with it. It lay sideways, as if someone had knocked it over. Had she done that? She didn't remember going close enough to the headstone to touch it, let alone shove it onto its side. And even if for some bizarre reason she'd wanted to knock it over, the thing was made of solid stone. No way was she strong enough to….

That's when she realized she was lying on the ground. The headstone wasn't sideways. *She* was. She remembered being in the Vermilion Tower again, and for an instant she felt the pain of the wounds that had been inflicted on her there. She was about to scream, but the pain receded so swiftly that within an instant it was as if she'd never experienced it at all. She pushed herself into a sitting position with trembling arms and attempted to wipe water from her eyes and face, but the rain was still coming down and her actions accomplished nothing.

She had been dragged back to the tower in the middle of the day without having to fall asleep first. If the Cabal could pull her there whenever they wanted, what would happen if they did so while she was driving? It wasn't as if she'd had any warning. One moment she was conscious, the next she was manacled to that goddamned X-cross again. If she passed out while behind the wheel, she'd wreck, injuring herself and possibly others. That was a really nasty new wrinkle to this game.

And that's what it was beginning to feel like to her – a game. A sick one with life-or-death consequences, but a game nevertheless. One that she was being forced to play without knowing the rules. She thought of how the Cabal had laughed when she'd asked them to just tell her what they wanted her to do. Maybe, she thought, her not knowing the rules was part of the game, too. If so, it was an even shittier game than she'd thought.

She stood, legs weak, but they supported her. She'd been out in the rain long enough that she was soaked from head to toe, and she wondered how long she'd been unconscious, how much time had passed in the real world compared to within the Vermilion Tower. She supposed the details didn't matter much, but then again, maybe the details were all that mattered in this game. How could she know? She was grateful she hadn't passed out during her conversation with Reeny. Her sister would've been on the phone to nine-one-one within seconds, and Lori would likely have woken up in a hospital.

She looked at Aashrita's headstone once more, focused on the letters that comprised her name. She needed to remember everything about Aashrita, not just that day at soccer practice when she'd been the goalie and Lori had fucked up her knee, destroying any chance at a college soccer career. She recalled the details of that day without difficulty. It was what had happened in the days and weeks afterward that mattered, she was sure of it. If only she could fucking *remember*.

She lowered her gaze to read the information beneath Aashrita's name. Birth date, death date. Aashrita had died when she was seventeen. They'd been the same age – their birthdays were only six weeks apart – so that meant Aashrita had died during their senior year of high school. That sounded familiar, more like the memory of a memory than the thing itself, though. What had the cause been? Accident? Illness? Suicide?

Migraine pain erupted in her head, so intense and crippling that she fell to her knees once more. She clapped her hands to her head and squeezed, as if trying to keep the contents of her brain from exploding outward. Through the agony, she thought, *Guess suicide it is.*

She hoped this realization would be the key to unlock the rest of her memories about Aashrita's death, but she experienced no sudden influx of images and emotions, no tidal wave of data crashing into her with psyche-obliterating force. There was nothing.

I'm sorry, Aashrita. She meant this to be an apology for forgetting how her friend had died, but she sensed there was more to it than that. Much more. Before she could explore this feeling further, though, she caught a flash of black out of the corner of her eye.

Oh no.

She didn't want to look, but she knew she had to. She directed her gaze at the slender tree next to Aashrita's headstone, saw a shadow creature clinging to the thin limbs like an ebon spider, looking at her with its featureless dark face. Another flash of black, and she turned to see a second shadow creature half-crouched behind a neighboring headstone, long multijointed fingers folded over the top of the stone, sharp black nails clicking against it in eager anticipation. Within moments, a dozen more of the things were visible, most partly hiding among old headstones and young trees, but some standing out in the open, clawed hands at their sides, held slightly away from their bodies like Wild West gunslingers ready to draw on a foe.

Lori got to her feet, turned, and ran toward her Civic. Her shoes slipped on the wet grass, but she managed to keep from falling. She'd left the car unlocked, and when she ran around to the driver's side, she opened it, threw herself inside, pulled it shut, and locked it behind her. She hadn't looked back to see if the shadow things had pursued her, but of course they had. They closed in on her car from all sides and slammed into it en masse. The vehicle rocked back and forth, and she screamed. The sound of her terror seemed to energize the shadow things further, whipping them into a frenzy. They began slapping, punching, clawing at her windows, doing so with motions so rapid it sounded as if her car were being bombarded with baseball-sized hailstones. Up close, in the gray light of the overcast rainy day, the shadow things appeared even more awful than they had in her apartment last night. They'd seemed dreamlike then, things that existed half in nightmare, half in the real world. But now they fully inhabited the waking world, the contours of their forms clear, their dark substance possessing depth and a certain fluid solidity, as if they were formed from living, animated oil. Horrible black faces smooth, without even the suggestion of eyes, noses, or mouths, hatred radiating off them like heat from a blazing inferno. Their voices – sound issuing from nonexistent mouths – were like the violent crashing of waves against an arctic shore, the howling shriek of gale-force winds tearing across a midnight desert, the deep rumbling crack of stone being rent asunder by vast seismic forces.... If these voices spoke words, she couldn't discern them, heard only raw, malignant rage, the entirety of it directed at her. And just as last night, she began to feel strength flowing out of her, and she realized with horror that the shadow things were somehow feeding on her, siphoning away her life bit by bit.

She had to do something; she knew that if she remained here much longer, the shadow creatures would shatter the Civic's windows, rush into the car like a flood of darkness, and finish her off. She had no way to fight them, though. She didn't know whether physical weapons like knives or guns would have any effect on them, but since she had neither, it scarcely mattered. She didn't have any tools in her car that could be used as weapons, either. No crowbar, not even a goddamned hammer or screwdriver. And she certainly wasn't capable of fighting them hand to hand. She was fit, but she had no combat training of any kind, and even if she had, there were simply too many of the damn things for one person to deal with, no matter how skilled at fighting he or she was. She couldn't defend herself, and in only a matter of moments....

She realized then that she'd been wrong. She *did* possess one weapon, and if she wanted to survive this attack, she needed to use it – *now*.

She put her foot on the brake and stabbed her finger toward the ignition switch. The Civic's engine turned over, and she put the car in drive. She removed her foot from the brake, put it down on the accelerator, and the vehicle leaped forward. She couldn't see the access road clearly because of the shadow creatures crouched on her hood and roof, their clawed hands pounding on the windshield. She gripped the steering wheel tightly and did her best to maneuver through the cemetery without hitting any headstones or trees. Her path was erratic and weaving, and she couldn't go fast enough to dislodge the shadow creatures that clung to her car. She'd left the others behind, but a quick glance at the rearview showed they were running after her, and as slow as she was moving, she knew they'd catch up to her soon. Some escape this was turning out to be.

Fuck it.

She angled her Civic off the path and pointed it toward the brick wall that enclosed the cemetery. She had a relatively unobstructed route to the wall, and she jammed the accelerator to the floor. The car began to gain speed as it moved forward, and she yanked the steering wheel to the right and left as she went, doing her best to avoid the few headstones in her way. She clipped one with the edge of her front bumper, but the impact wasn't enough to slow her down significantly. She mentally apologized to whoever lay buried beneath the headstone she'd damaged, and then forgot about it as she continued to accelerate toward the wall.

The shadow things hanging on to her car showed no indication that they were alarmed by what she was doing, and they continued pounding at the Civic's windshield and side windows. Cracks were beginning to appear in the glass, and Lori knew she had only seconds left before the creatures broke through.

The pale orange-brick face of the wall grew larger in her vision, seeming to almost shimmer, as if she was viewing it through tears. She realized then what a ridiculous plan this was, if it could even be called a plan. She'd started driving toward the wall out of instinct, hoping to scare off the shadow creatures, or if they wouldn't scare, to injure them when the car crashed into the wall. But either the things weren't intelligent enough to know what she was doing, or they didn't care. Maybe the impact wouldn't harm them, or maybe they didn't fear injury. Maybe they possessed no drive for self-preservation, only a need to attack and kill. Even if the shadow creatures were as vulnerable as humans – which she doubted – she couldn't possibly build up enough speed to do them any real harm when she crashed. The most likely outcome of her grand attempt to flee was that she'd hit the wall, the vehicle's airbags would go off, and she'd be momentarily stunned, giving the shadow creatures the few last moments they would need to smash through the car windows and get their clawed hands on her.

But her sense of self-preservation was highly developed, and as the wall loomed close, she was unable to stop herself from stomping on the brake. She gripped the steering wheel even tighter, closed her eyes, and waited for the collision to happen.

CHAPTER SEVEN

And waited.

And waited.

The Civic came to a stop, but it felt as if the car had continued moving longer than should've been possible given her proximity to the wall. Keeping her foot on the brake, she opened her eyes. She registered darkness first, and she felt a rush of panic, believing that so many of the shadow creatures now clung to her car that they completely covered the windows. But then the Civic's automatic headlights came on and they cut through the darkness, illuminating a glossy-smooth length of road. She saw no other light outside – no streetlights, no building lights, not even any stars.

She had a sudden sick feeling she knew where she was.

Pain hit her then, fiery lines of agony that covered her flesh, which made her skin *burn*. She glanced down at herself, and by the dashboard lights she saw she was naked, her body covered with cuts, welts, and bruises – just as she'd been the last time she was here. Blood flowed freely from the worst of the wounds, but none of them appeared life threatening, and she decided to ignore them for the time being. Her wrists and ankles hurt, and the skin was red and swollen. *From the manacles,* she thought.

Somehow, she had found her own entry to the Nightway, and this time she'd brought her car with her. However, it appeared none of the shadow creatures had managed to accompany her. None were visible in the headlight beams, and none clung to the car, pounding their clawed hands on the windows. The silence was as eerie as it was welcome, though. All she could hear now was the sound of the Civic's idling engine combined with the frantic beating of her heart and the rapid in-out, in-out of her breathing. Then again, maybe the shadow things *had* transitioned to this starless void with her, only they'd moved away from the car, taking refuge in the dark where they would be perfectly camouflaged, shadows lost in shadow. Maybe they were even now watching her from their concealment, waiting for her to be foolish enough to think herself safe. They'd wait for her to open her door and get out of the car. Maybe she'd do so to check the damage that the Civic had sustained during her improvised escape. Or maybe she'd step out of the car to assure herself that this place was real, that she wasn't merely imagining it. Whatever the reason, once she opened the door, they would attack, finally getting their opportunity to sink their claws into her flesh and tear her to pieces. But it didn't feel like they were out there. It felt as if she were entirely alone in this desolate darkness.

Only one way to find out.

She lowered the driver's-side window the merest crack. Cold air filtered into the car, along with a strange odor, almost metallic, like the smell of ozone that lingers after a lightning strike. No shadow creatures rushed toward her car, no curving ebon claws slid through the opening between the upper frame of the door and the slightly lowered window. Encouraged, she lowered the window down to the halfway point, and just as before, no attack came. It looked like she *had* left the creatures in the real world, and she wondered what had happened to them when the Civic had vanished. Had momentum carried them forward into the wall? She hoped so, and when they hit, she hoped it had hurt like hell.

She began to shiver in the cold air filtering into the Civic's interior, so she raised the window all the way up and turned on the heater. The car's engine had been running long enough to produce warm air immediately, but the change in temperature provided only partial comfort. Her wounds still throbbed, and she was getting blood all over the seat. She obviously possessed the same body as she had the other times she'd been in this reality, and she wondered what had happened in the Vermilion Tower when she'd appeared on the Nightway in her car. Had this version of her disappeared from the tower, leaving the Cabal to stare at an empty X-cross and wonder what had just happened? Or had the two versions of her merged? Whichever the case, she liked the idea of those red-robed fuckers standing around and scratching their asses as they tried to understand how she'd Houdini-ed herself away from them.

She didn't know what to do now. Could she return home by closing her eyes once more and willing herself there? If she did, would she and her Civic appear in the same place relative to where they'd been when they'd left? Probably outside the cemetery wall, and likely in the street. If so, the shadow things would still be close by, and she had no doubt they'd scent her somehow and come after her again. They might even be able to find their own entrance to the Nightway and continue their pursuit of her. There was no way to know what the goddamned things were capable of.

Speaking of pursuit, would the Driver get in his big black car and start racing up and down the Nightway in search of her? Possibly. Probably.

Certainly.

Regardless of whether the shadow creatures, the Driver, or both came after her, it wouldn't be wise to stay here. Best to get moving, even if she didn't have a destination in mind. After she'd gone several miles, she could try to transition back to the real world again. With luck, she'd reappear far enough from the cemetery to throw off the shadow creatures, at least for a while. She took her bare foot off the brake and pressed it to the accelerator. She started slow at first. There were no painted lines to mark the road's edges, and it was difficult to tell where the Nightway ended and whatever lay beyond it – obsidian-colored soil or pitch-black rock – began. As she drove, she wondered if she'd slipped all the way into full-blown madness, and if so, she wondered if she cared.

Humming to herself and not thinking about Aashrita, why she'd visited her friend's grave, or what she'd hoped to accomplish there, she pushed the accelerator down farther and the Civic began to pick up speed.

★ ★ ★

The Shadowkin mill about the cemetery, searching for Lori, sniffing for her trail like dogs that have lost the scent of their prey. They do not possess the capacity for rational thought, not in the way humans understand it, and are thus incapable of reasoning out where Lori has gone. All they know is that she was here and they almost had her, and now she is not here.

Each time the Shadowkin are near Lori, they feed on her energy, growing stronger, more *real*. But even with their increased abilities, they cannot now sense her presence. Without her, they have no focus, no purpose. They are lost, and this frightens and angers them. Without Lori to hold them together, the Shadowkin begin to drift apart, leaving the cemetery one by one, moving out into the town in search of other food, and just as importantly, something to vent their anger upon.

Something to *hurt*.
Something to *kill*.

★ ★ ★

It was an old joke that mail carriers get invited into the residences of horny customers on their routes to deliver quite a bit more than bills and sales flyers. Wife doesn't answer her phone when you call during your lunch hour? Your baby doesn't look like you? Blame the mailman.

Norman Palmer was well aware of this cliché when he took a job with the postal service as a carrier, and other, more seasoned employees teased him about all the ass he'd get on the job. Not just the male carriers. The women joked about it, too. Norman had figured they were all just razzing the new guy, and he didn't expect more out of his job than doing a lot of walking while his mind wandered. Norman dreamed of being a professional cartoonist, and he figured he could work on ideas for cartoons in his head while he walked, and then draw them later. A steady paycheck, regular exercise, *and* time to think about cartoons seemed more than enough to expect from his job.

But it turned out that the stories were true. He *did* get a lot of ass.

Not every day, but a couple times a week, sometimes more. Bored housewives whose husbands were at work and whose kids were at school would open the door when he stepped onto their porch to put their mail into the box. Sometimes they'd be dressed in tight T-shirts and shorts or maybe low-cut tops that displayed their cleavage. Maybe they'd be wearing a T-shirt and panties or sexy lingerie or nothing at all. They would ask him how he was doing, how his day was going, invite him in for a cool drink when the weather was warm, a hot drink when it was cold. And when he accepted their offer and went inside, they gave him a hell of a lot more than liquid refreshment.

He was young – only twenty-five – tall and broad-shouldered. He had a man's body and a boy's face, and a lot of women found the combination irresistible. It didn't hurt that he had a larger than average cock, either. He didn't know for sure, but he suspected the women on his route told their friends – their best friends, the ones they could trust – about what he had to offer. Word of mouth is the best kind of advertising.

As far as Norman was concerned, he was living his absolutely best life. He didn't know how long it would last, though. Husbands might become suspicious and the women would decide not to put their marriages at risk anymore. And one day he wouldn't look so boyish, and then he might not receive as many invitations to come inside – might not receive any. But until then, he was going to enjoy every minute he spent with other men's wives. When he'd turned fifteen, his dad had given him some advice. *Fuck as many women as you can as often as you can. Because once you get married, you'll be lucky to get laid once a month, if that.* Norman had taken his father's advice to heart, and he intended to have as much sex as he could while he could.

This rainy afternoon he was in bed with Camille Barnes. She was almost twice his age and carried a few extra pounds, but she had large breasts and she fucked like a teenager. She was one of those older women who tried to appear younger by dyeing their hair in colors favored by millennials – in Camille's case, a bright blue – and getting tattoos and piercings. Camille wore a nose stud, and she had an elaborate tattoo of a phoenix on her back, red flames trailing from its wings, eyes blazing with inner fire. Whenever he fucked her from behind, as he was doing now, he couldn't escape the feeling that the phoenix was glaring at him, demanding he plow the bird's mistress harder, faster, deeper. For this reason, he often kept his eyes shut while screwing Camille in this position, or sometimes he'd let his gaze wander around the room – anything so long as he didn't have to look at that damn bird.

Camille was on her hands and knees, pushing herself back against him as he thrust himself into her, her large breasts making slapping sounds against her chest as they flopped back and forth. She had her head down as if she was concentrating, and she kept up a running monologue while they fucked.

"Yeah, that's right, that's good, keep it up, keep going, don't stop, get in there, fill me up, fuck me harder, that's good, right there…."

He supposed a lot of guys might be turned on listening to a woman responding like this while they were screwing, but he found it kind of distracting, to be honest. It was like she was trying too hard to have a good time instead of just having it. But each to their own, right?

The first time a woman brought him into her marital bed, he thought he'd feel self-conscious at best and like an absolute piece of shit at worst.

But it turned out he hadn't felt much of anything. In fact, the idea that he was fucking another man's woman on the same bed that the two of them had sex on was kind of kinky. Besides, most of the bedrooms he was invited into had been decorated by the women, so they felt more like the wives' spaces than the husbands'. Camille's bedroom was done in variations of blue. Everything – the walls, the curtains, the carpet, the bedclothes – was different shades of blue. The air *smelled* blue too, like she was using some kind of air freshener or something. The décor was a little much for him, but he wasn't here to admire Camille's aesthetic taste. He was here to fuck this woman until she screamed.

Camille had opened the bedroom window several inches, high enough so they could hear the rain – she *loved* the sound of falling rain – but not so far that water got inside. It wasn't raining so hard that the sound would mask Camille's X-rated monologue and her cries and shouts as she approached orgasm. But if she didn't care if her neighbors heard them fucking, why should he?

His postal uniform – along with his underwear and socks – lay on the floor where Camille had dropped them after undressing him. She'd met him at the door wearing only a skimpy black bra and panties, and they lay next to his uniform. Camille had removed them seconds after she'd gotten him naked. His carrier bag stuffed with mail sat propped up against the wall near the clothes. Whenever he was invited into a woman's bedroom, he always brought his bag and put it where he could keep an eye on it. He was a professional, after all.

Camille wanted to switch positions, and a moment later, she lay on her back, legs up in the air and spread wide, mashing her left breast with one hand and furiously working her clit with the other while he continued drilling her. Both of them were slick with sweat, and Norman was wondering if she would squirt when she came today. Sometimes she did, sometimes she didn't.

He was so absorbed in his work that he didn't notice a tendril of darkness slide through the tiny spaces in one of the window screens, pushing its way silently between the curtains, and begin slithering into the room. The Shadowkin arced downward toward the floor, moved across the carpet, then stretched upward along the side of the bed. The tip of its tendril reached to the top of the bed near Camille's left shoulder, and then, swift as a striking cobra, it lunged toward her mouth. She'd been in the process of her sexual monologue – words coming faster, voice pitched higher, breathing more rapid as she got closer to climax – so her mouth was open when the Shadowkin's tendril came at her, and it jammed itself past her teeth, over her tongue, and down her throat. Her eyes went wide with surprise, and she tried to scream, but the Shadowkin's thick, dark substance filled her throat, preventing her from making any sound or, for that matter, taking in air. The Shadowkin continued flowing into her, doing so rapidly, and by the time Norman was aware there was some kind of weird-looking snake-like thing crawling down Camille's throat, the last of the Shadowkin's substance had come through the window screen, shot toward Camille, and vanished into her.

Her eyes rolled back in her head and she removed her hands from her breast and clitoris and grabbed Norman's wrists. His hands were palm down on the mattress, supporting him while he'd been fucking Camille, only now he wanted nothing more than to pull out of her and throw himself backward off the bed in order to get away from her and the thing inside her. But her hands tightened around his in twin death grips, and he couldn't free himself. The woman might've been twice his age, but damn, she was strong!

He watched in horror as bulges appeared on her upper and lower abdomen, and he realized the black stuff – whatever the hell it was – was racing through her, down her alimentary canal, into her stomach, then her intestines, and from there—

Her body arched against him, her muscles tightened, and she threw her head back. The tail end of the Shadowkin had penetrated deeply enough inside her that she was able to breathe again, and she used that breath to scream. It struck Norman that she was caught in the throes of pain so intense that it seemed like a grotesque parody of an orgasm. Something was happening inside her – something *bad*. He still couldn't pull free from her grip, felt her fingernails cutting into the flesh of his wrists, but his cock – still inside her – began to deflate. Then he felt something tickle the opening of his penis, almost as if a finger was poking him from inside her.

Good Christ. The tentacle-thing had burst through her intestines, into her uterus, and had slid down her vaginal canal, where it was now fondling him.

"No!" he shouted. "No, no, no!"

He gritted his teeth, put everything he had into yanking his arms free of Camille's hands, but she continued holding him fast, her grip like iron.

And then the Shadowkin entered him.

Norman had never been catheterized before, but it had always seemed to him like one of the most painful things a person – especially a man – could endure. But this was worse than anything he could've imagined. It was like molten fire had been injected into his penis, and he screamed without being aware that he did. He redoubled his efforts to pull free from Camille's grip, but she continued holding on to him tight, so tight he felt the bones in his wrists grind together. If this continued, they might well break, but he didn't care about that. He had worse things to worry about.

Her body began spasming more violently, as if she were caught in a massive seizure. Then her head snapped forward, and her eyes focused on him. For an instant, he saw awareness in them, along with absolute terror. And then her mouth opened wide and she vomited a torrent of dark blood onto him. It splashed onto his chest, so hot it almost burned, and then her eyes rolled white once again, her head fell back on the pillow, and her body – breasts and belly also splattered with blood now – fell still. Her grip loosened and he was finally able to pull away from her. He yanked his arms free so hard that he fell backward, slid off the foot of the bed, and hit the floor. He didn't feel the impact, though. The agonizing fire in his penis – which had now spread to his lower abdomen – overwhelmed all other sensation. He saw the black stuff, looking like a thick ebon snake, protruding from the end of his cock and stretching up onto the bed where it was still in the process of exiting Camille's dead body. He instinctively grabbed hold of the thing, intending to pull it out of him, but its surface was slick with Camille's blood, and it slid through his hands with ease. The pain intensified as the dark tentacle pushed its way further into his body, and he no longer possessed the ability to think or act. His hands fell away from the tentacle's blood-slick surface, and he lay back against the carpet and screamed. He saw the tail end of the tentacle wiggle into him, and once it was inside, his dick went fully limp, like a balloon that's had all the air let out of it. He continued screaming, unaware that blood now bubbled up from deep inside him and ran down his chin and the sides of his face. He felt a sharp piercing pain just below his sternum, followed by an awful pushing and tearing sensation. A small fissure opened in his skin, followed by a trickle of blood. And then a clawed black hand burst upward in a spray of blood.

As Norman died, he saw the Shadowkin pull itself free from his body, and as the great dark rushed in to claim him, he had time for a final thought.

Should've worn a condom.

And then he was gone.

*   *   *

Blanche Tucker was eighty-three years old, and she could still get around on her own – more or less. She lived in a retirement community, Sunrise Hills, a stupidly bland name, but the place was a hell of a lot better than a full-fledged nursing home. She didn't drive anymore, so she relied on Uber and Lyft to get from point A to point B. Her vision was okay, and while she wouldn't be running any marathons in the future, she could walk just fine. Her mind wasn't as nimble as it once was. Her thoughts came more slowly these days, and she couldn't always remember things right away, but she showed no signs of dementia, thank the lord. Overall, her health was good. At least, as good as it could be given her age. She took a handful of pills in the morning and another handful at night, which was a pain in the ass, but they kept her functioning, so she put up with them.

People marveled at how active and mentally alert she was at her age. *You should thank the lord for your good health,* one of the other residents at Sunrise Hills had once told her. She'd received similar expressions of wonder combined with envy from other people. But although she *was* grateful for her health, she lived in a constant state of dread. For the thing about getting older was that each day brought her another day closer to death. This was true for everything that lived, of course, but only human beings were aware of it, and most could ignore this cold reality and get on with the business of living. But when you reached a certain age – which Blanche had done a while ago – you knew that there were fewer days ahead than behind. Each tick of the clock brought you closer to death, and while you didn't know when the big event would occur – unless you took your own life, of course – you knew it would be sooner rather than later. It didn't help that you got to watch so many friends and family members go before you did. Her husband (heart attack at sixty-nine), their only child (heroin overdose in her thirties), her sister (massive stroke in her mid-seventies), her best friend (breast cancer in her fifties). The parade of death kept marching on, and one day you'd have no choice but to join it.

So Blanche was paranoid about her health, always alert for any sign there was something wrong with her – *seriously* wrong. She washed her hands obsessively, used hand sanitizer when she couldn't wash. She checked her pulse multiple times a day, monitored her bowel movements, never forgot to take her pills, and exercised to the degree of which her old body was capable. She ate right, avoided fat and sugar, stayed away from caffeine, and visited her doctor regularly. Too regularly. Whenever she had the least little concern about her health – a pain in her stomach, a stubborn cough that held on too long – she went to her doctor's office. She went so often that during her last visit, the doctor had suggested that she make a regular appointment to come in once a month to be checked out, but otherwise she wouldn't come in unless she was running a high fever or was in excruciating pain. And the doctor had emphasized *excruciating*. She'd reluctantly agreed, although she doubted she'd be able to stick to the plan. As soon as her throat got too dry or her hands began to ache – as soon as *anything* happened – she'd be back in. She couldn't help herself. The doctor had never used the word *hypochondria*, but she knew that's what the woman was thinking. The doctor was half Blanche's age. *Wait'll you hit your eighties,* she thought. *Your definition of hypochondria will change then.*

She'd decided to do some early Christmas shopping for her great-grandnieces and nephews, and she'd gone out even though it was raining. A lot of the residents at Sunrise Hills wouldn't set foot outside if the weather wasn't absolutely perfect. Not Blanche. She'd put on her coat, grabbed her umbrella, called an Uber, and had the driver drop her off at a small shopping plaza not far from downtown. There was a store there called Blue Elephant Toys that specialized in items you couldn't find in big box stores, funky educational toys, as well as playthings designed to exercise children's imaginations. No Barbies or Pokemon here. She'd spoken with the owner the last time she'd stopped in, and the woman had told her the store carried a curated selection of toys. Blanche liked that word. *Curated*, like in a museum.

She stood outside the store now, the building's overhanging roof protecting her from the rain, so she didn't need to use her umbrella. The Uber driver had dropped her off here, but after paying and getting out of the car, she hadn't gone inside the store. The instant she stepped out of the car, she started having trouble catching her breath. She told herself that nothing bad was happening. She got winded sometimes, especially if she pushed herself too hard, and she'd spent the morning cleaning her apartment and doing laundry. *Did too much, that's all.* She only needed to stand here a few moments and give her lungs a chance to relax. She'd be fine then, and she could go into the toy store and find something that, hopefully, would delight the children on Christmas morning. But as she stood on the sidewalk in front of the Blue Elephant, rain pattering on the overhang above her, making a rushing-hiss sound as it came down on the parking lot, she still couldn't catch her breath. In fact, it was becoming more difficult for her to draw in air at all. Her pulse raced. She could feel it fluttering at the base of her throat, pounding in her temples.

You're having a panic attack. You've worked yourself up to the point where you're afraid you can't breathe, and now that's what's happening. A self-fulfilled prophecy.

If she could relax, calm herself, her breathing should return to normal and she'd be okay.

She was well aware of the weight of her purse hanging from her shoulder, of the phone she kept inside. She could pull it out, call nine-one-one, wait for paramedics to arrive and tend to her, take her to the hospital if necessary. If she waited too long to call, if she was stubborn and denied the possibility that she was experiencing a medical crisis, she might die right here, now, in front of a store that sold playthings for children. Wouldn't that be a lovely surprise for the next child whose mother brought him or her to the store? *Mommy, why is that old lady lying on the sidewalk? Is she asleep?*

She didn't want to be weak, didn't want to give in to her fear. But she didn't want to die, either. She reached into her purse and grabbed her phone. But before she could remove it, she saw them. They came running across the parking lot, lean, long-limbed creatures formed of featureless darkness. A half dozen, maybe more. They wove between parked vehicles, slashing out at them with clawed hands, digging gouges in the metal, shattering window glass. But the damage didn't end there.

As the creatures moved on, the vehicles began to lose their shapes, melt and liquefy, the falling rain hastening this process until they lost structural integrity entirely, sagged, and collapsed into piles of thick, metallic-colored goo. Within seconds, the shadow things destroyed a dozen cars in this fashion, and they continued destroying more as they headed in Blanche's direction. She understood instantly what she was witnessing. These were creatures of death, and they were coming for her at last. She didn't intend to stand there and wait for them, though. She'd spent eighty years and change avoiding them, and she didn't plan on giving in to them now. She turned and rushed inside the Blue Elephant, concerns about her breathing and heart rate forgotten. She had more immediate threats to contend with.

The toy store wasn't crowded. It was a small shop and it was early afternoon on a weekday. There was a woman in her twenties or thirties – it was hard for Blanche to judge people's ages if they were significantly younger than her – at the register, and a man she guessed was in his sixties looking at a display of build-it-yourself robots. The lighting was bright inside the Blue Elephant, to make the wares seem more appealing she guessed, and there were shelves containing realistic-looking stuffed animals, challenging puzzles of both the 2-D and 3-D variety, toys and games designed to inspire and sharpen a child's imagination and creativity, and best of all, not a mindless fashion doll or violent video game anywhere.

Blanche realized she must've made more noise than she'd thought when entering, for both the girl at the register and the middle-aged man turned to look at her. They both seemed concerned, and she figured she must look like a crazy woman to them – face pale, expression alarmed, gasping for breath and trembling with terror. She opened her mouth, intending to tell them what was coming, to exhort them to hide, but nothing came out. Part of this was due to her trouble catching her breath, but she also had no idea what words to say. How could she describe what she'd seen, what was coming for them, for *her*? She didn't have to, though, for an instant later the glass door shattered and death's dark emissaries flooded into the store. She tried to run, but the best she could manage was an unsteady, teetering walk. She heard the sounds of displays and shelves being knocked over, heard thick *plaps* as items liquefied and dropped to the floor. The girl at the register screamed, and the man in front of the robotics toys gaped in stunned disbelief.

Blanche turned down the first aisle she came to, this one containing shelves of toys based on a historical theme, dolls, games, and activities focused on different time periods from Ancient Egypt all the way to the American Revolution and beyond. The shadow things spread throughout the store, but none of them followed her. She'd gotten lucky, for the moment at least, but she doubted her luck would hold out long. Still, she didn't intend to give up. She hadn't lived as long as she had to surrender to death without a fight, even if she couldn't put up much of one at her age.

The monsters destroyed toys and the shelves upon which they were displayed, both melting as she'd seen the vehicles in the parking lot do. One of the things slashed the middle-aged man on the arm, and he cried out in pain and clapped a hand to the wound. His voice began to drop in tone, and Blanche watched as his face began to soften and sag. He looked at her, eyes stretching downward as his features melted, lips surrounding the long oval of his mouth twitching as if he wanted to say something, perhaps beg for her help, and then he collapsed like a broken water balloon, clothes and all. Reduced to a spreading puddle of organic and inorganic material.

The same thing happened to the girl behind the register, only she'd attempted to run toward the back of the store, where presumably a rear exit was located. One of the creatures clipped the back of her head with its claws, the impact sending her sprawling forward. She burst apart into splatters of glop when she hit the floor.

Blanche had reached the far end of the historical toy aisle when one of the creatures came running after her. She knew it was going to get her, knew she would die in the same horrible manner as the man and the girl. But still she kept moving, kept fighting, trying to eke out a few more seconds of life before she fell into eternal night. One good thing about becoming a human version of a rapidly melting ice cream cone – at least her death would be over swiftly.

She felt claws rake her back, slice through her coat and top, cut deep lines in her skin. The pain was excruciating, and she thought of how her doctor had used that very word and she almost laughed. The sensation of dissolution itself was curiously painless, and as her body liquefied, she waited for her consciousness to fade, like someone slowly turning off a light set to a dimmer switch. She struck the ground, broke apart into fragments that quickly began to lose what little solidity they had left. But even in this state, her consciousness continued on, and after several moments it showed no sign of dissipating. She realized with a horror deeper than anything she'd ever felt before that there were some things worse than death. Much, much worse.

She lay there, an unmoving sentient puddle, as the Shadowkin continued destroying the Blue Elephant.

★   ★   ★

Sharilyn Boland glanced at the digital clock on the dashboard of her Corolla. Three-oh-one. She was officially late for her shift at Go Mart. *FML*, she thought.

It had been raining for the last several hours, and it showed no sign of letting up. Her car was ancient, and the windshield wiper blades were long past the point of needing to be replaced. The one on the driver's side was the worst. The wiper's rubber strip had torn halfway off, and it flopped around on the glass, doing little to clear away the rainwater. Because of this, Sharilyn was driving five miles under the speed limit, earning her angry looks from drivers stuck behind her. To make things worse, her gas tank was dangerously low. She thought she had enough fuel to make it to Go Mart, but she didn't know if she'd have enough to get home. And although Go Mart was a convenience store with gas pumps out front, she didn't have enough money to buy fuel. She'd just have to hope the gods of transportation would look kindly upon her later.

Sharilyn was twenty-one and lived with her grandmother. Her parents had split up when she was in middle school, and she had no idea where her dad was these days. The last time she'd heard from him, he'd been living in Arizona, but that was several years ago. Her mom was bipolar and a barely functioning alcoholic, and it was all she could do to take care of herself. So Sharilyn had gone to live with Grandma. She loved her grandmother, but she was desperate to get her own place. She was taking business classes at the community college in Waldron – when she could afford them – and working two jobs, and she still didn't have enough money to get her own place, even if she had a roommate to share expenses.

She'd started her morning at five a.m., when she'd gotten up, showered, ate a cold Pop-Tart, and headed off for her morning shift as a server at Rise-N-Shine, a restaurant that specialized in serving breakfast food all day. Mornings were Rise-N-Shine's busiest time, and when her shift ended, she was exhausted. She had to keep hustling, though, and she'd changed out of her Rise-N-Shine uniform shirt and into her Go Mart one in Rise-N-Shine's restroom before leaving. She wished she had time to run home and shower. She smelled like bacon grease and stale coffee, but there was nothing she could do about it. She'd just have to hope the customers at Go Mart wouldn't notice.

And to top it all off, she was congested and feared she was catching a cold. With her, colds often turned into sinus infections, and she definitely did *not* need one of those right now. She couldn't afford to miss work. For that matter, she couldn't afford an antibiotic, either.

By the time she reached Go Mart, she was already stressed. When she saw Darlene's Prius parked in front of the store, she groaned. She was tempted to drive on past Go Mart and call in sick – which technically wouldn't be a lie as she *was* sick of dealing with Darlene's bullshit. But she thought there was a good chance she'd get fired for calling in sick at the last minute, and she needed the money, so she reluctantly pulled into Go Mart's parking lot and drove around the side of the building where employees were supposed to park. After she turned off the engine, she sat there for a moment, listening to the rain hitting the roof of her car. Maybe it wasn't Darlene's Prius after all. Hers was hardly the only one in town, right?

There was a pounding on her car window then, and she jumped, startled. She turned to see Darlene leaning forward, her face close to the window. She didn't have an umbrella and her long black hair hung down the sides of her face in wet strands. She made a half circle gesture, and Sharilyn knew Darlene was asking if she could go around to the passenger side and get in. Sharilyn didn't want to let her, but Darlene was drenched, and she looked cold, too. Reluctantly she nodded and pressed the control on the arm of the door to disengage the car locks. Darlene gave her a grateful smile, then she hurried around the back of the car. When she reached the door, she opened it, slid into the seat, and closed the door behind her.

"God, I'm so *wet*."

Darlene wasn't the type to make double entendres, but Sharilyn couldn't help wondering if that was how she'd meant the comment. They hadn't been together sexually for over a month now.

"I can't talk," Sharilyn said. "I'm late for work."

She didn't like how icy her tone was, but she couldn't help it. The last thing she wanted to do right now was deal with her crazy ex.

Darlene ignored her statement. No surprise there.

"It's *so* good to see you, Shar."

Her voice was soft and Marilyn Monroe-breathy, almost a little girl's voice, which clashed with her sharp features and startlingly green eyes. This contrast had been one of the things that had initially attracted Sharilyn to Darlene. Now she found it repulsive.

"You need to stop doing this shit," Sharilyn said. She glanced briefly sideways at Darlene, but she didn't want to meet those green eyes, didn't want to give her the slightest sign of encouragement.

Then why the hell did you let her into your car? she thought.

She told herself to shut the fuck up.

"I miss you," Darlene said. There was sadness in her voice, along with an edge of petulance, like a child frustrated she couldn't have what she wanted *right now*.

Sharilyn had actually met Darlene here at Go Mart. Darlene had filled up the tank of her Prius, and afterward she'd come inside to buy a diet soda and a bag of peach rings – gummy candies that Sharilyn couldn't stand. Darlene was eight years older than Sharilyn, and she carried herself with an easy confidence that Sharilyn envied. Darlene smiled as she placed her items on the counter for Sharilyn to ring up, and she looked directly into her eyes and held her gaze without looking away. Sharilyn had taken that as an invitation.

"Do you really like those things?" Sharilyn held up the bag of peach rings. "They're way too sweet for me."

"I love them," Darlene said, still holding her gaze. "They're great after sex."

The comment had caught Sharilyn off guard, and she lost her grip on the bag of candy. It hit the counter, and both women looked at it for a moment, then looked back at each other. An instant later they started laughing.

They'd dated for nine months after that. Darlene had begun suggesting she move in with her after the first week they'd been together. In retrospect, Sharilyn knew she should've seen this as a red flag. Suggesting soon became urging which then became a combination of pleading and nagging. Darlene was an elementary school art teacher, and whenever she wasn't working, she wanted to spend time with Sharilyn. She resented Sharilyn working, resented her spending time with friends or with her grandmother. Darlene wanted her to quit her two jobs.

I may not make a ton of money, but I make enough to support the two of us. If you didn't have to work, you could spend more time on school. You could take out loans to pay for classes, and I can help you out financially too. The more time you study, the higher your grade point average will be when you graduate, and then you'll have a better chance of getting into a really good law school.

Sharilyn's ultimate career goal was to become a lawyer, and Darlene's argument was tempting. But Sharilyn knew that Darlene's primary motivation for making it was to free up more of her time so she could spend it with her. It wasn't that Darlene didn't care about Sharilyn's education, but it was definitely a secondary consideration for her. Sharilyn had almost given in. Even if Darlene claimed a lot of her time, she figured she'd still end up with more hours to study than she had right now. Grandma knew she was a lesbian and was completely cool with it, although she wasn't completely sold on Darlene as a partner for Sharilyn. And Grandma was still old-fashioned enough to believe two people should take the time to thoroughly get to know one another before taking such a big step as cohabiting.

On the other hand, maybe Darlene's neediness wouldn't be so bad if they were together more often throughout the week. Then again, maybe it would remain the same or perhaps even get worse. She realized then that she'd begun to think of Darlene as an emotional black hole, an endless void that could never be filled, no matter how much time and attention a lover gave her. The following day after having this realization, Sharilyn broke up with her.

Darlene, surprisingly, had seemed to take it well. She didn't argue, cry, yell, promise that she'd change, or tell Sharilyn that she'd regret this decision for the rest of her life. She'd asked Sharilyn if she was sure this was what she wanted, and when Sharilyn said it was, she'd said okay.

To say Darlene's reaction was anticlimactic was an understatement, but Sharilyn had been so relieved that she hadn't questioned it. But of course it wasn't over between them – not by a long shot.

Darlene began sending texts, leaving voicemails, having presents delivered to her grandmother's house – flowers, jewelry, cute stuffed animals, gourmet chocolates.... She'd park her Prius across the street at night and watch the house, hoping to catch a glimpse of Sharilyn, who'd peek through her bedroom curtains periodically throughout sleepless nights to see if she was still out there. Darlene began following her after that, driving two or three cars behind Sharilyn, trying not to look too obvious and failing. Darlene had never stalked her at work before, though, and she'd never tried to make actual contact – until today.

"You need to move on," Sharilyn said. "For both our sakes."

"I love you."

Sharilyn said nothing. What was the point? Darlene refused to hear anything she didn't want to hear. "I have to go."

Sharilyn opened the driver's-side door and stepped out into the rain. She planned to go inside, start working, and hope Darlene got the message and left. She didn't know what else to do.

She ran around the side of the building – as much to get away from Darlene as to get inside where it was dry – but when she was only a few feet from the entrance, she stopped. There were people running across the parking lot toward the building. No, not people. Shadows shaped like people. Their movements were too fluid to be human, and their arms and legs seemed to stretch and contract as they moved, as if they were made of rubber. The sight of them sent a wave of revulsion through her. These things were a violation of everything she believed to be real. They should not, could not exist. In short, they were *wrong*.

It was hard to gauge their exact number. They moved fast and they didn't run in straight lines, crisscrossed in front of one another as they came, making it difficult to count them. There were perhaps a dozen of them, maybe more. A man – ball-capped, bearded, and beer-bellied – had parked his pickup in front of one of the pumps and was busy fueling his vehicle when the shadow things reached him. He hadn't seen their approach, but some instinct warned him at the last instant, and he turned just as the first raised a clawed hand to strike.

He didn't have time to scream.

Sharilyn thought the creature would slash the man with its claws, but instead its substance stretched, lost definition, become amorphous, and flowed over him like a wave of darkness. And when it rolled past, the man was gone. Destroyed or absorbed, Sharilyn didn't know, and really, what did the particulars matter? Gone was gone.

With each death they caused, each bit of destruction they wreaked, the creatures grew stronger, as did their ability to interact with and affect reality. The others also lost their forms, and they all flowed together, merging into a single large mass of black. They washed over the gone-man's pickup, and it too disappeared. The edge of the dark wave caught part of the gas pump, and half of it vanished. The residue of gas in the partially disintegrated hose splashed onto the ground as the black wave rolled on toward the building.

"What the *fuck* is that?"

Darlene was standing at Sharilyn's side. Her attention had been so focused on the shadow things that she'd been unaware of the other woman's approach. Darlene's voice jolted her out of her paralysis, and she grabbed the woman's hand and dragged her inside the store. The man at the register – a skinny guy with curly red hair named Ray – looked over at them as they entered.

"Where the hell have you been, Sharilyn? My shift ended fifteen minutes ago!"

Sharilyn didn't acknowledge his words, didn't even look at him. The wave was coming, and she and Darlene had to get as far away from it as they could.

There were only a few customers inside the store – a heavily tattooed man perusing the snack cakes, a woman around Darlene's age getting a bottled water from one of the coolers at the back, and an old dude with a thick white beard thumbing through an issue of *Guns & Ammo* in front of the magazine display. The three of them looked over when Ray shouted and when they did, they saw what was rushing toward Go Mart's entrance. The tattooed man gaped, the woman screamed, the old guy shouted, "Fuck me!" and Ray said, "Jesus Christ!"

There was no sound of breaking glass or display shelves being overturned. The dark wave had absorbed the gone-man and his truck in absolute silence, and Sharilyn knew the same thing was happening now. She pictured the shadow wave flooding into the store, sucking in everything it touched with eerie silence, including Ray and the others.

Sharilyn was heading toward the rear of the store, hoping to reach the stockroom where there was an exit she and Darlene could escape through. Part of her realized that she could move faster if she wasn't pulling Darlene along behind her, but she didn't consider letting go of her hand.

I guess I still love her after all, she thought.

They had almost reached the door in the back, the one with the sign that said *Employees Only,* when Darlene screamed. Sharilyn knew she shouldn't turn and look, but she couldn't stop herself. She saw a wall of blackness rushing toward them, and she had just enough time to tighten her grip on Darlene's hand before it engulfed them.

★   ★   ★

The Shadowkin continue spreading throughout Oakmont, causing havoc in different ways depending on the situation. Their choices aren't conscious ones, but rather reactions to stimuli in the environment around them. Sometimes they cause damage solely with their claws, tearing chunks out of physical objects or inflicting terrible wounds on their victims. Other times, they loosen molecular bonds, attack on a mental or spiritual level, or dissolve pieces of reality itself. The Shadowkin have a single function – to break everything down, and that's exactly what they do, in one fashion or another.

Oakmont and its residents die haphazardly, incrementally, and there is nothing anyone can do to stop it. Anyone currently in our reality, that is.

CHAPTER EIGHT

Justin Nguyen sat at a table in front of a window, watching the rain come down as he sipped his second double scotch. It was lunchtime, but he hadn't eaten anything. When he'd first gotten to the bar, he'd intended to order food – something greasy, carby, and artery-clogging. What did eating healthy matter now? Besides, he could use some comfort food. But when a server came over to take his order, he realized something. By eating, he was providing nourishment for his body. *All* of it, his tumors included. He lost his appetite after this realization, and all he ordered was a double scotch. He'd meant it to be the only drink he had, but it had gone down fast and easy, and it felt so good, he'd ordered another. Why not? He needed to live it up while he could, right?

He let out a bitter bark of a laugh, then took another sip of his drink.

One nice thing about being diagnosed with cancer – it made his relationship problems seem like not so big a deal. For weeks, he'd been frustrated by Lori's inability to commit fully to their relationship, as well as her blindness when it came to the issue of Larry. He'd tried to explain to her that keeping her ex-boyfriend as a roommate was just a way for her to maintain a buffer between them. He felt she was keeping Larry in her life on purpose, as an excuse for not completely committing to him. To *them*.

He'd almost decided not to call her today and tell her about his diagnosis out of spite over last night's disastrous phone conversation. But he was scared – fucking *terrified* – and he'd needed to talk to someone. And did part of him hope that his diagnosis would make Lori feel sorry for him, prompt her to direct more of her emotional energy toward him? Probably. He supposed even cancer had a silver lining, tarnished and thin though it might be. The truth was, he was still in shock after receiving the news that his own body was in the process of trying to kill him. He kept finding himself breathing shallowly, as if he was afraid that taking full breaths would agitate the cancer cells that had invaded his lungs, causing them to reproduce even faster.

He wore a white button-up shirt with the sleeves rolled up, navy-blue slacks, and black shoes. Normally he wore a tie to work, but today's tie was lying on the passenger seat of his silver Corolla. He hadn't bothered to put it on before his doctor's appointment, and he hadn't felt like doing it afterward. He might just let the fucking thing sit in his car all day. He hadn't decided yet.

His doctor had done his best to reassure him, to tell him not to give up hope. He would be referred to an oncologist, of course, and the doctor spoke of treatment options such as chemotherapy, immunotherapy, radiation therapy, pulmonary lobectomy, pneumonectomy.... All of it sounded horrible to Justin, and after a bit he'd stopped listening.

He'd never been to the Curious Keg before. The bar was located halfway between his doctor's office and BioChem Diagnostics. He'd taken a half-day off for his doctor's appointment, and he was trying to decide if he should call off for the rest of the day or if he should go in and hope work kept his mind off his cancer. They both seemed like shitty choices to him right now. Maybe more scotch would clarify matters. He drained the rest of his drink and held up the empty glass to signal his server. When she came over, he said, "One more of the same, please."

She looked doubtful, like maybe she thought he'd had enough for now. He was ready to argue with her, but she smiled, nodded once, took his empty glass and headed for the bar. Justin wondered if she'd seen something in his expression that had told her to keep her damn mouth shut and go get his drink. If so, good. Cancer Man didn't need any lip from the waitstaff.

The Curious Keg was only a step or two above a dive bar, the kind of place with grimy windows, sticky floors, graffiti carved into tabletops, and an omnipresent odor of cleaning chemicals that didn't quite mask the faint smell of urine. He imagined his lungs were like this. Not a complete wreck yet, but well on their way. The place was only half full, and Justin didn't know if that was due to it being too early for a full crowd, or if the place was always like this. Most of the customers looked like blue-collar workers drinking their lunch the same as he was, while some looked as if they might be unemployed or homeless. Shabby clothes, unkempt appearances. He knew he was stereotyping, but he didn't care. As an Asian man, he'd been stereotyped plenty in his life. People who thought English was his second language even though he'd been born and raised in the

United States, people who thought he possessed a genius-level intellect simply because of his race, women who expected him to be emotionally reserved and have a small penis. After a lifetime of that shit, he figured he'd earned the right to stereotype others a little.

The server brought his third drink, and he thanked her without taking his gaze from the window. The rain was coming down heavier now, and he could hear the sound of it striking the pavement outside, a muted *ssssssshhhhhhh*. Cars drove by on the street outside, and Justin wondered how many of their occupants were dealing with their own small tragedies today. Maybe all of them, he thought.

He sometimes wondered why he kept trying with Lori. She was smart and extremely empathetic – which made her perfect for her career – but she lacked a capacity for introspection. She remained focused on the present while still looking toward the future, but when it came to examining the past, forget it. It was like she had some kind of mental block, almost as if the past didn't exist for her. If he hadn't gotten his CT scan results back today, if he'd called her solely to discuss last night's conversation, she would've acted like it was no big deal, almost as if it had never happened at all. It was one of the qualities about her that he found most inexplicable – and maddening. He was a big believer in looking back at one's past, to try to learn from one's mistakes in order to become a better person. Without introspection, people continued to follow the same destructive patterns of behavior they always fell into. How was that any way to live a life?

He'd contemplated breaking up with Lori from time to time. Logically, she wasn't a good match for him and vice versa, but despite this – or maybe in a weird way because of it – he felt a powerful draw to her that he couldn't explain or deny. He supposed logic didn't mean dick when it came to matters of the heart. A cliché, maybe, but that didn't make it any less true.

He wished Lori were here with him now. Even if they only sat quietly and watched the rain fall, her presence would be a great comfort to him.

He found it ironic that at work he'd run hundreds of medical tests for physicians. Nothing on the level of CT scans, of course. Just basic blood panels mostly. He wondered how many people had gotten bad news from their doctors because of test results he'd sent over. Had some of those results basically been a death sentence? He didn't know, but he thought it likely.

Still gazing out of the window, he watched a white Jeep Cherokee SUV enter the parking lot and pull into an empty space next to his vehicle. A pair of women got out, the driver swinging her door open so violently that it smacked hard into the Corolla's passenger-side door.

"Goddamnit!"

Justin jumped up from his seat and rushed toward the door. His server called out to him – *Probably thinks I'm trying to skip out on the check,* he thought – but he ignored her. He was in the grip of a white-hot rage that had come upon him suddenly and without warning. Some of it was due to the amount of alcohol he'd had on an empty stomach, but much of it was a reaction to the news he'd received from his doctor. He'd lost control of his body, control of his *life*. He was not going to sit by and watch some careless stranger put a dent in his goddamned car and not do something about it. He had to prove there were still some things in this world that he could stand up to, that he didn't have to roll over and accept like a whipped dog.

He was already shouting when he plunged out into the rain.

"What the fuck do you think you're doing? You can't just—"

His words died in his throat and he stopped and stared at the two women. He hadn't fully registered their appearances when they'd first gotten out of the SUV, but now he did, and he had no idea what to make of them. Both women had been dry when they'd gotten out of their vehicle, but neither carried an umbrella, and they were quickly getting soaked. But that wasn't what he found so strange about them. Their clothes were covered with dark reddish-brown stains that looked like blood – a lot of it. They looked like they'd gotten caught in a slaughterhouse explosion. The rain, heavy as it was, wasn't doing much to wash the stains from their clothes. The older woman wore her long gray hair in a braid, which hung down her back. The braid swayed back and forth idly, and it made Justin think of the way a horse's tail swishes lazily as it fends off flies. The younger woman had tufts of fur growing in scattered patches on her skin, her eyes were amber and shaped like a cat's, and when she opened her mouth, she revealed upper and lower incisors, the teeth long and sharp.

"Meow," she said, then grinned.

Justin forgot about the dent in his car door. All he wanted was to go back into the bar, find a table where he couldn't see the window, and hope these two women wouldn't follow him inside. He started to back away from them, but before he could get very far, the younger woman rushed toward him and grabbed hold of his left arm. He felt claws extend from her fingers and sink into his flesh. Not deep, but far enough to hurt. He reflexively tried to pull away, and she pressed the claws in deeper. He cried out in pain, and he looked at his arm, saw blood welling from the points where her claws were embedded in him, the rain washing it away even as it left his body.

The woman gave him a lazy, contented smile and made a fluttering thrum in her throat. Was she *purring*?

The older woman stepped closer to him. He saw no sign of sanity in her eyes, only glittering madness. That complete lack of rationality was more terrifying to him than the younger woman's catlike features. Even though his arm would become little more than shredded meat if he yanked it free from the younger woman's cat claws, he almost did it, so afraid was he of the insanity that peered at him through the older woman's eyes.

"It's nice to meet you."

The older woman's voice held no indication of insanity, though. It was calm, almost soothing. "I'm Melinda, and my friend with the extremely sharp claws is Katie. We've been sent to collect you."

Justin had no idea what the hell she was talking about.

"Sent by who?"

Melinda frowned as if the question had caught her off guard.

"I'm…not sure," she admitted. Her smile faltered for a moment, but returned full force. "I just know we were supposed to come here and fetch you."

"I don't want to go with you." He'd meant this to come out as a strong statement of defiance, but instead it came out as a frightened, pleading whine.

"She's not talking to you," Katie said.

Katie, he thought. *Katie-Cat. Here, Katie-Katie-Katie!*

With her free hand, Katie tapped a clawed index finger to his chest. "She's talking to *them*."

He didn't know what she meant at first, but then it came to him. She was referring to his cancerous cells.

Melinda leaned her head close to his chest. Rainwater streamed down her face, and she blinked periodically to clear it from her eyes.

"Hello in there, little friends." She spoke in a raised voice, as if she wanted to make sure the cancer heard her. "Ready to come out and play?"

He looked down at his chest, almost as if he expected the malignant cells to answer, their tiny voices speaking in unison from inside his lungs. He heard nothing, of course, but that didn't mean there was no reaction to Melinda's question. Fire erupted in his chest, and he gasped and doubled over. He tried to breathe, but he couldn't draw in any air. It was as if his lungs had ceased working.

I'm going to die, he thought frantically. *I'm going to suffocate right here because my goddamned lungs have betrayed me.*

The pain intensified. Now it felt as if dozens of worms were trying to chew their way out of him, burrowing through muscle and skin. So great was his agony that he would've screamed and screamed.... Screamed until his vocal cords tore apart and blood bubbled past his lips. But his lungs still refused to take in air, and the only screaming he could do was in his mind.

When the pain reached its zenith, he expected his chest to explode outward in a spray of splintered bone, shredded lung tissue, and bright red blood. Sparkles danced in his vision, and his ears were filled with a roaring sound. He swayed on his feet, dizzy, and he knew he was close to passing out. But the pain stopped then, and his lungs began working once more. He drew in a deep, gasping breath. His vision cleared and his dizziness began to recede. He took several more breaths, and when he felt strong enough, he intended to pull away from Katie – to hell with the damage he'd do to his arm by yanking it free of her claws – and run back into the bar for help. But when he tried, his body refused to obey him. His chest felt strange, the skin thick and tight. Even before Melinda's braid whipped around and lashed open the front of his shirt, he knew what he would see. His chest was covered by a mass of swollen dark-red tumors. His cancer had come out to play.

Words came out of his mouth then, but they weren't his.

"Rain feels good. Cool. Wet. We like."

Katie retracted her claws and removed her hand from his arm. The wounds she'd created hurt like hell, the pain made worse by the rain striking them, but these injuries were of no concern to him now.

Melinda spoke, but not to him. Her gaze was fixed on the swollen crop of tumors spread across his chest. "Would you like to go for a ride with us?" she asked.

"We're going to see Lori," Katie said, baring her sharp feline teeth.

"We like much," the tumors said with his voice. *"Much-much."*

"Then let's go."

Melinda turned and walked back to the SUV, her braid wagging like a happy puppy dog's tail. Katie headed for the vehicle's passenger door, and Justin's body began following her, limbs moving stiffly, the tumors unaccustomed to operating him yet. He tried to exert control, force his body to stop moving. But when he tried, his lungs seized up and he was once more unable to draw in air. The message was clear. He did as the tumors wanted, or they would cut off his breath. And if they cut it off long enough, he would die. He stopped resisting, his lungs relaxed, and he was able to breathe normally again. His consciousness was now merely a passenger in his body, an ineffectual observer, and he was surprised by how little this alarmed him. In many ways, it wasn't all that different from how he'd walked through the world all his life.

Once the two women were in the vehicle, Justin – or rather his body – climbed into the back seat. The tumors didn't put a seat belt on. Perhaps they didn't want to feel restricted by it, or maybe they didn't know what it was. An image passed through Justin's mind, the SUV colliding with something – another vehicle, a tree, a light pole – the force of the impact slamming him into the back of the seat in front of him.

His body reached for the seat belt, pulled it across his chest, and clicked it into place.

Maybe he and the tumors didn't have to be enemies after all. Maybe they could work together. After all, they *were* part of him – and he part of them. Instead of adversaries, they could be a team.

He heard many voices in his mind then, speaking as one.

Team. Yes.

Justin smiled and settled in for the ride.

★　　★　　★

How are you doing? Let me know soon as you can.

Larry sent the text, and although he knew Lori was likely too busy with a client to text him back right away, he held his phone for several moments, hoping a message from her would appear. It didn't, and he put the phone down on the table.

After his interpreting gig had finished, he'd decided to stop in at a funky little coffee shop called Grinders. It was too late for lunch and too early for dinner, so he just got a large latte and a blueberry muffin. Back when they'd been dating, Lori used to get after him about his irregular eating habits. He didn't keep to a regular meal schedule. He ate whenever he was hungry, and he ate whatever he felt like at the time. He listened to what his body told him, and today it had told him blueberry muffin. It had been a long time since he'd visited a doctor, but he felt healthy and he kept his weight down, so he figured he was doing something right.

Grinders was a small place located in a strip mall only a couple miles from the clinic where Lori worked. There were six tables, each large enough to accommodate four customers, and an old couch with red velour upholstery was positioned near the front window. Only half of the seats were filled. A couple of people wore suits and worked on laptops, while the remaining customers were dressed more casually. They also had laptops, along with open textbooks and notebooks. College students, Larry guessed. He looked like one of the business types in his gray suit, wine-colored shirt, and gray-and-red-striped tie, but he felt he had more in common with the college kids. He was in his thirties, though, and he doubted the students saw any difference between him and the other 'older' customers. The thought depressed him.

He took a bite of his muffin – it was a little dry but it tasted all right – and as he chewed, he thought about the interpreting job he'd just completed. He'd been so concerned about Lori that he hadn't been able to focus on his work, and he'd made mistakes that he hadn't since his first signing class in college. He'd felt like a fucking idiot, and his embarrassment and frustration had only caused him to screw up even more. He'd managed to muddle through, but he wouldn't have been surprised if the event organizers had decided not to pay him. As it was, he was half-seriously contemplating not cashing the check they'd given him.

Only two baristas were on duty at the moment, a man and woman the same age as the students. They were probably students themselves, he thought, working to help pay for college. He'd worked as a waiter during his own college years, and he knew what it was like to have to serve irritating, rude customers with a smile and a pleasant tone, and he appreciated anyone in a service position that was able to remain positive during an interaction with a customer, whether that came to them naturally or they had to fake it.

The young man who'd taken his order was a hair under six feet, with light reddish hair cut close to his scalp and a well-trimmed mustache and goatee. A lot of men that age affected a scruffy lumberjack look, but Larry wasn't a fan. It was hard to kiss a man when you had to battle your way past facial hair so thick that you needed a machete to cut a path to the lips. The barista wore black-framed glasses that made him look intelligent, and he wore a black T-shirt beneath a green apron with the Grinders logo on it. He'd seemed genuinely friendly when taking Larry's order, and Larry had enjoyed talking to him. Sometimes Larry could get a vibe when a man or woman was interested in him, but he'd picked up nothing like that from the barista. It was a shame. He was really cute. Then again, he was probably ten years younger than Larry, maybe more. Not an insurmountable age difference by any means, but he knew if he attempted to chat up the boy, he'd only fuck it up, worried as he was about Lori.

No cock for me tonight, he thought.

He didn't feel especially bad about this. He fucked the same way he ate – whenever his body told him to. And he had others things besides sex on his mind right now.

When he'd woken this morning, he'd almost called and cancelled his gig. He didn't feel comfortable leaving Lori alone after last night. But he was also afraid that if he stayed home to be with her, he'd be feeding into her…what? Delusion? Fantasy? He wasn't sure what to call it. Despite what the police and the crime tech had said, he wasn't certain that someone had broken into the apartment last night. Why would someone go to the trouble of forcing open the patio door and entering the apartment, only not to take anything? And if whoever it was had really wanted to get to Lori, it wasn't as if the door to the master bathroom was made of thick, solid oak. It was a cheap, flimsy thing, easy enough to break open if you put your back into it. And why had this theoretical invader departed before he'd gotten home? If he, she, or they had been pounding on the bathroom door the way Lori had described, they wouldn't have heard him coming up the stairs and opening the door. But he sure as hell would've heard them. But he'd heard nothing at all. If Lori's car hadn't been in the parking lot, he might've thought she hadn't gotten home yet, it was so quiet.

Even if someone *had* sneaked into the apartment last night, no way did he believe it was a group of fucking shadow monsters. And he didn't think the weird dream she'd had of a tower filled with otherworldly beings held any special significance. As for the goat-eyed woman Lori had encountered at FoodSaver, she'd probably been suffering from some sort of mental illness, maybe a physical deformity too, which accounted for the weird shape of her pupils. Then again, it was possible Lori had hallucinated that encounter as well. He knew she had some memory problems, at least when it came to the subject of Aashrita Dhawan and the girl's death. She'd told him of the incident on several occasions, only to completely forget she'd spoken to him about it. Hell, it seemed like she sometimes forgot about Aashrita altogether. The first time this happened, he'd tried to repeat what she'd said to him, but she quickly became drowsy and fell asleep. She hadn't quite passed out, but it had been close to that. Afterward, he'd decided not to push her on the matter. Maybe one day she'd come to terms with her guilt and be able to remember permanently. Maybe she wouldn't. Everyone dealt with trauma in their own way.

But because he had experienced her remembering about Aashrita only to almost instantly forget again, it wasn't a big leap to imagine that she might have other psychological issues – like believing she was being persecuted by some bizarre group of mystics that called themselves the Cabal. He'd listened to and supported her last night without judgment because she'd been so freaked out. But if he kept up the pretense of believing her story, he feared he'd only strengthen her delusion, which in turn would only make it harder for her to break free from. So he hadn't woken her this morning, had left a note for her in the kitchen. Now he was beginning to wonder if he'd done that more for his own sake than hers. Maybe he hadn't wanted to deal with an ex-girlfriend who was beginning to go crazy. They might not be lovers anymore, but they were friends. He shouldn't have abandoned her like that. Who knew where she might be right now or what state she might be in?

He picked up his phone and tried to call her, but he only got her voicemail.

"It's me. I'm just calling to see how you're doing. I'm worried about you. Please call me as soon as you get this."

After he disconnected, he checked his texts and saw she hadn't replied to the message he'd sent. He then slipped the phone into his pants pocket.

He was beginning to have a bad feeling now, and yeah, maybe he was overreacting, but he didn't care. He needed to see Lori, to speak to her, to reassure himself that she was okay.

He'd only eaten a couple of bites of his muffin and had a few sips of his latte, but he was too anxious to want more of either. He reached for them, intending to throw them both away as he left the shop. But before he could take hold of either, someone walked over to his table, pulled out the chair opposite his, and sat down. It was a woman. And she had eyes like a goat's.

Larry had read about people whose mouths fell open in surprise. He'd never experienced this reaction before, nor had he ever witnessed anyone else having it happen, so he'd always figured it was bullshit. But his mouth fell open now and he thought, *I'll be damned. It really does happen.*

He couldn't believe how much her eyes resembled those of a goat. No, not *resembled*. They *were* goat's eyes, large and watery, and they examined him with a detached, cold, and altogether alien intelligence. *Like the woman Lori saw in the grocery store,* he thought. *No, not like. The same woman.* He was getting over his initial shock at seeing the woman, and he now noticed that the skin around her weird eyes was soft and doughy. She exuded a strong body odor too, the stink so intense that it made him gag, and for a moment he thought he was going to spew latte and bits of chewed-up muffin onto the table. The blue sweatshirt she wore was almost disappointingly bland. A...*being* like this should be garbed in clothes that presented a sense of dark glamour – a black leather bustier with a high-collared cape, maybe.

"I'm disappointed in you, Larry." Her voice sounded normal, conversational even, as if they were two friends having an intimate personal conversation. "I thought you were Lori's friend. Her *best* friend. Best friends believe each other, support each other. They listen. That's your problem. You don't truly *listen*."

He was only partially aware of what she was saying. He was too mesmerized by her eyes to fully concentrate on her voice. It wasn't just the weird rectangular shape of her pupils, although that was some of it. But what had captured his attention was how black those pupils were, a black so dark, so deep, that it seemed to go on and on forever. Those eyes held endless voids within them, and he felt the darkness calling to him, threatening to draw in his awareness, his mind, his very self, and swallow it whole.

"You fascinate me," Goat-Eyes said. "You have two professions, one based in sound, the other in silence. Do you love both, or are you merely reluctant to commit fully to one or the other?"

These last words snapped him back to himself. As a bisexual person, he often got the *Why don't you pick a side?* question from both straight and gay people. He'd given up trying to explain that it wasn't about sides, wasn't about choices. No one ever understood, not really, except other bisexual people – and Lori. She'd accepted who he was without question, and that was one more thing he loved dearly about her. So when Goat-Eyes said he was unable to commit to sound or silence, it had struck a very raw nerve in him.

He found his voice for the first time since she'd sat down.

"They're different aspects of the same thing," he said.

"Are they now?" Her mouth stretched into a slow smile. "Let's find out, shall we?"

She reached toward her face, touched the doughy flesh around her eyes, and with thumbs and forefingers peeled off a pair of dime-sized pieces of thin, whitish skin. She held them out, as if for him to examine, then she flicked her hands forward and released the scales. They flew toward him like tiny shuriken, and he thought they were going to strike his eyes. But they veered off at the last second, and curved toward the sides of his head. An instant later he felt sharp pain in his ears, as if someone had inserted long needles into his aural canals. It hurt like a bitch, and he cried out in pain. He felt a wiggling-squirming sensation, and he had the impression that something inside him was being rearranged by the flecks of Goat-Eyes' skin. Then, as suddenly as it had come, the pain stopped.

Goat-Eyes smiled. "Now you can hear everything…and nothing."

At first he had no idea what she was talking about, but then the sounds within the coffee house began to grow louder. The cute barista was taking the order of a young woman wearing a short-sleeved top that displayed her colorfully tattooed arms.

"THAT'LL BE THREE DOLLARS AND NINETY-EIGHT CENTS," the barista said.

Each syllable was like a cannon blast, a thundercrack, and he winced, gritting his teeth against the pain caused by the barrage of sound. The woman opened her wallet, removed a debit card, and inserted it into the reader on the counter. Each of these motions produced deafening sounds, and when the card reader began beeping, the noise loud as a fire engine's siren, Larry moaned. He pressed his hands to his ears, pressed them *hard*, but this did nothing to shut out the noises assaulting him.

The conversation of the two people at the table next to his, talking about how their respective supervisors were assholes. The hiss of the espresso machine behind the counter, the whirring of a coffee grinder. People sipping their drinks, chewing pastries or cookies. The gurgling in their stomachs as acid churned. Air rushing through their nostrils, down into their lungs, then back up to be exhaled. The thudding of their hearts, the whooshing of blood flowing through their veins, the combined sounds of hundreds of bodily processes at work. He could even hear the crackle of electricity shooting between neurons in their brains, the soft moist tearing sound of cells dividing, the even softer sound of old cells dying.... All of it rushing in on him like a tsunami, invading him, overwhelming him, drowning him....

He let out an anguished cry – the sound of his own voice so loud he thought his brain might liquefy in his skull. He jumped up from the table, only partially aware of everyone else in the café – including the cute barista – looking at him with a mixture of puzzlement and alarm. He ran toward the door, bumping into tables on the way, knocking over people's drinks, causing them to spill, customers yelling and cursing as he hurried past. He kept his hands to his ears, for all the good it did, and opened the door by slamming into it with his shoulder. He plunged out into the street—

—and was hit by ten times the amount of sound that he'd experienced inside the coffee shop, a hundred times, a *thousand*. Cars and trucks passing by on the street, engines roaring, brakes squealing, horns honking. Pedestrians' shoes click-clacking on the pavement. A rumble of an airplane flying somewhere off in the distance. He heard disembodied voices and jumbled musical notes, and he realized he was hearing cell phone conversations and radio broadcasts, picking up the signals as if he were some kind of receiver. It was too much, too much. He couldn't remember his name, who he was, possessed only the vaguest sense that he existed at all. Everything was sound and sound was pain and that pain had become his entire world, the center of his existence. *He* was pain, and pain was *him*.

He thought he was screaming, but he couldn't hear his own voice over the sounds of the citizens of Oakmont going about their day. Some pedestrians glanced at him with pity, some with alarm, but all avoided him. Hands still clasped to his head, he fell to his knees, wailing, tears streaming from his face. He wanted to lean over and pound his head against the sidewalk until he was dead, anything to escape the mad cacophony buffeting him. He almost did it, too, was on the verge, when the sound suddenly ceased.

The relief was so immediate, so profound, that he gasped and nearly collapsed. Tentatively, he took his hands from his ears, waiting for the pain to return, but it didn't. He looked at his palms, expected to see them covered with blood, as if something deep in his brain had ruptured. But his hands were clean. He rose to his feet, legs shaky, head swimming with vertigo.

It's over, he thought. *Thank Christ, it's—*

But it wasn't.

All the sounds that had overwhelmed him simply didn't return to their normal volume. They continued to diminish, growing softer, less distinct, until finally they cut out altogether. The world around him continued to move – people passed him on the sidewalk, vehicles drove on the street – but it did so in utter silence.

Just as he'd feared, the unimaginable din of the heightened sounds that had plagued him until a moment ago had damaged something inside him – his hearing. He was now as deaf as the people he interpreted for. He'd long thought that if he ever lost his hearing, he'd be able to deal with it, no problem. He already knew how to sign, and he was an okay-if-not-great lip reader. And he was around deaf people all the time. They and their culture weren't alien to him. He figured he'd be able to adjust to being deaf fairly well, certainly much better than the average person. But the silence terrified him. He felt as if a large part of who he was had just died. How could he play music if he couldn't fucking hear? And he couldn't interpret anymore if he couldn't hear people speak the words he needed to relay through sign language. Not only had he lost one of his primary senses – one he relied on more than the others combined – he'd lost the ability to do his job or pursue his artistic passion. He'd lost the things that made him who he was.

But then he began to become aware of something within the silence. Not sound, of course, but something like it. It reminded him of being aware of a signal that's just out of the range of human hearing. You could *feel* it. It might make the hair on the back of your neck stand up, might make you wince and grit your teeth, make you look around to see if you could pinpoint the origin of the non-sound. But of course you never could. This non-sound was like that, and it quickly grew stronger, more intense. Shivers began to run up and down his spine, and a cold fluttering took up residence in his gut. He felt a headache building rapidly, and he thought of Lori's migraines, hoped his headache didn't grow into one of those monsters. But *damn* did it hurt. Another wave of vertigo came over him, different than the last. He felt imbalanced in every part of his body, as if his very atoms were quivering so violently the binding forces between them might break and he'd fall apart into nothing.

He became aware of a deeper non-sound then, one so vast it seemed to permeate all creation. It was the silent scream of the universe dying, a scream that had started less than a nanosecond after the Prime Event and which had continued ceaselessly for trillions of years. The universe was born to die, and it had been doing this since the beginning of time and would continue to do so after time itself had become a meaningless, forgotten concept. Hearing the deathscream of all existence was far more agonizing than the heightened sounds of before had been, for this non-sound affected him on a mental and spiritual level rather than merely a physical one.

He remembered what Goat-Eyes had said.

Now you can hear everything…and nothing.

She hadn't spoken metaphorically. He *had* been able to hear everything before, and now he could hear Nothing with a capital *N*. He was hearing the unvoice of Nonexistence, of Nullity, of the Void, of Oblivion…and it wasn't simply killing him – although it was doing that as well – it was *obliterating* him, reducing him to nothing piece by piece, bit by bit, and he knew that soon there wouldn't be anything left of him. The consciousness that thought of itself as Larry Ramirez would be gone, and capital N Nothing would take its place.

Wild, unreasoning, animal terror gripped him. Although the thinking part of his mind knew he couldn't escape the unsound, the instinctive part, the part that, when confronted with danger, reacted first and saved thinking for later, shrieked at him to flee, and that's what he did. He ran into the street, mouth wide open as if he was screaming at the top of his lungs, but he could not hear his own voice, had no idea if he was producing any sound at all. Cars swerved to avoid him, the drivers behind their windshields looking shocked, confused, angry. When he reached the middle of the street, the rational part of his mind started functioning again, and it informed him that he had done something extremely foolish. Vehicles continued streaming toward him, and he knew he was in serious danger of being struck by one.

The deathscream of All receded in his consciousness as survival instinct kicked in, but he was still aware of it in the back of his mind, and he knew he always would be. He needed to get the hell out of the street before—

A big black car of indeterminate make came racing toward him. He caught a glimpse of the driver, a man wearing sunglasses even though it wasn't particularly sunny this afternoon. He thought then of what Lori had told him of her dreams – no, her *nightmares* – of riding along the Nightway in a black car driven by a man who had no eyes. He didn't question that this was the same man driving the same car. He could sense it, and even if he hadn't been able to do so, the bastard's cruel grin would've told him the man had come to kill him.

The black car came at him *fast*, so fast that he wasn't sure he'd be able to avoid it. He was tempted to stand there and let the vehicle run him down. Now that he'd heard the deathscream of the universe, he understood in the deepest level of his being that death was the ultimate end product of life. There was no point in continuing, of delaying the inevitable. The only reason he didn't let the car hit him was because he feared the universe's deathscream would follow him down into nonexistence and he'd never be free of it.

The black car was mere inches from hitting him when he threw himself to the right. At first he thought that despite his expectations he was going to make it, but then the edge of the vehicle's front bumper struck his left foot. The impact spun him around, flipped him over, and he hit the asphalt on his back. Pain shot through his body like lightning, and this time when he cried out, he was able to hear his own voice. His cry was a needle that punctured the bubble of silence, and the sounds of the world rushed in upon him once more. He heard the screeching of tires as drivers fought to avoid hitting him, and he heard people on the sidewalks shouting, although he couldn't make out what they were saying. He still heard the non-sound of the universal deathscream, though, and he knew he always would. It was part of him now.

He hurt all over, but he pushed himself up on all fours anyway, ignoring the fiery pain in his left leg and his back's shrieking protests. He faced the direction the black car had gone, but he saw no sign of it. He turned his head toward Grinders, and among the crowd that had gathered on the sidewalk, he saw the goat-eyed woman. She smiled at him as her hands began moving.

Next time, she signed.

Then she turned and began walking away. Larry tried to follow her with his eyes, but a wave of weakness came over him and his arms could no longer support him. He fell to the ground, and the impact – while mild – sent fresh pain shooting through his injured body. He heard people running toward him now, heard someone shout, "Call nine-one-one!" and then he felt himself slipping away into darkness. He didn't know if he was dying or merely losing consciousness, and right then he didn't care. But whatever was happening to him, wherever his spirit might end up, he knew the universal deathscream would be there to keep him company.

And then darkness rushed in and he knew no more.

CHAPTER NINE

"Tell me again why we have to go to the mall?"

Maureen McGuire sat behind the wheel of the police cruiser. It was raining, not *too* heavily, and the windshield wipers were doing a good job of keeping the glass clear. It was overcast, almost dark enough to be twilight, and she had the headlights on. The lights might not be absolutely necessary – it wasn't *that* dark – but Maureen believed in being proactive when it came to safety. When you were a cop, especially if you'd been on the job as long as she had, it was too easy to become lazy, to start cutting corners, to think that just because you're a cop, nothing bad can happen to you. Like doctors who don't believe they'll ever get sick or judges who think they'll never be found guilty of a crime. That was why she always followed the rules. She drove to the speed limit – unless it was an emergency – and she always used her turn signal, always came to a full and complete stop at intersections. So if it was even close to dark enough to turn on the headlights, that's what she did.

Next to her, her partner said, "Because we have work to do there."

Rauch didn't look at Maureen as he answered, and his tone was relaxed, almost amused, as if he were enjoying some joke that she wasn't aware of. Maureen didn't turn to look at him, though. She always kept her eyes on the road when driving. She wanted to ask, *What kind of work?* but she didn't. If Rauch wasn't in the mood to go into detail about something, no amount of coaxing could get it out of him. Rauch liked to play things close to the vest, and while this frustrated Maureen, she'd learned to live with it during their time working together.

She frowned. Just how long *had* they been partners? She couldn't remember. Not all that long, she supposed. At least, that's what it felt like. She honestly had no idea, which was weird. Weirder still, for most of her career she'd driven a cruiser solo. Oakmont wasn't a big city, and there wasn't enough money in the budget to hire so many officers that they rode two to a cruiser. Maureen hadn't ridden with another cop since she'd been a green-as-they-come rookie. So why was she now partnered with Rauch? And hadn't they been working the night shift yesterday? Yeah, they had. So what were they doing working this afternoon, too? She'd never been assigned a day shift immediately following a night one before.

Her frown deepened as she realized she couldn't remember going home last night. She remembered responding to a break-in call at that woman's apartment. Her name escaped Maureen now, but she remembered what she looked like well enough, and also the layout of her place. But as to what she and Rauch had done after leaving the woman's apartment.... She didn't have a clue. Had she and Rauch been driving around ever since then? Again, she didn't know, but she had a feeling that Rauch hadn't been with her the entire time. Sometimes he was there and sometimes he wasn't. Where he went or what he did while he was gone was yet one more thing Maureen didn't know.

Maureen was divorced, and the two children she'd had with her ex were grown and long on their own. She'd never remarried, so if she had been out all night, there was no one in her life to notice. The thought depressed her.

They were less than a mile from the mall when they hit a red light. Maureen braked to a stop and turned to look at Rauch, intending to ask him to explain what the hell was going on, because *something* sure as shit was. Rauch continued looking straight ahead, but before Maureen could speak, three slits opened in Rauch's neck. They spread wide, revealing red flesh inside, and they remained like that for a moment before closing. Maureen was revolted by Rauch's— What were they? Gills? But she wasn't alarmed by them. She had the feeling that she'd seen this happen before, had seen it a lot of times. She couldn't remember when, precisely – big surprise – but she felt certain she'd witnessed the slits opening and closing before, sometimes faster, sometimes slower. And while she didn't know for sure, couldn't with her terrible memory, she thought she'd never asked Rauch about them, that it had never even occurred to her until now that she should ask, that something wasn't right – was in fact terribly *wrong* – about her 'partner'. But she still didn't find the words or the will to speak. It was as if some kind of force was keeping her from thinking or talking about certain things, subjects that Rauch might not wish to address.

Rauch's neck gills opened and closed twice more before the light turned green and Maureen remembered to remove her foot from the brake and put it down on the gas pedal. The cruiser pulled into the intersection and neither Rauch nor Maureen spoke for the next few minutes. When they drew near one of the mall's entrances, Maureen slowed, hit the cruiser's right turn signal, and turned into the lot. The mall's official name was the extraordinarily pretentious Horizon's Edge, but no one seemed to remember why it had been chosen. Almost everyone in town simply referred to it as *The Mall*. Whoever had designed the parking lot had been overly optimistic. Maureen had never seen all the spaces filled. Even at Christmas, only a third to a half of the spaces were ever used by customers. Today was no exception. There were only a handful of cars in the lot, and almost all of them were parked close to the main entrance. The building was two stories high, long, and made of dull whitish-gray brick, which made it look more like a prison than a shopping center.

"Pull up to the entrance," Rauch said. "Use one of the handicapped spaces."

It was illegal for them to park there, and while Maureen would usually never do such a thing on her own, she did so now at Rauch's command. She didn't know why she felt compelled to follow the man's orders, but she was and she did. Once they parked, Maureen left the engine running, headlights and wipers on.

"Now what?" she asked.

Rauch turned to her, and she saw that not only was the man smiling, he was holding a phone up, the screen facing Maureen. On the phone was a photo of a woman Maureen didn't recognize – a petite blonde dressed in a gray blazer and looking every inch the professional working woman – her arm draped around the shoulder of a young brown-haired boy.

"Who are they?"

Rauch's smile widened, and his neck gills began opening and closing rapidly, making wet flapping sounds, like the noises a fish might make flopping around on the bottom of an angler's boat.

"They're who we've come here to see. Well, who *you've* come to see. You've got a message to deliver to them – a very *special* one."

Then he laughed, and after a moment, Maureen – although she didn't know why – began laughing too.

★   ★   ★

Maureen walked through the mall, scanning her surroundings as she went. Situational awareness was important when you were a cop, and it had long become second nature to her. She took in the people – mostly old folks and mothers with young children at this time of day – walking past her, heading in the opposite direction. She glanced into the shops as she walked by, her gaze zeroing in on the registers to make sure no one was being robbed. People avoided meeting her eyes, and those who did looked at her quickly and then looked away. People treated cops like predators whose attention they didn't want to attract, and while this response was one of the things she liked least about her job – after all, she'd sworn to serve and protect these people, not frighten them – their reluctance to focus their attention on her was useful now. No one questioned the presence of a cop in public. An *armed* cop. They just wanted to go about their business without said cop hassling them. This meant no one would think to stop her before she reached the play area, before she could complete the task she'd come here to do. She was a little fuzzy on *why* she had to do it, though. Rauch had explained it to her in the car, and it had seemed to make perfect sense at the time. But now that she was inside the mall, alone, she was no longer so certain of her mission. Maybe she should go back to the cruiser and talk with Rauch some more, make sure she fully understood what she was supposed to do, and why it was so important. Rauch had stressed that it was absolutely vital that she complete the task she'd been sent to do, that the Balance depended on it. Maureen didn't know exactly what the Balance was or why it was so important, but Rauch had made a big deal of it, and Maureen saw no reason why the man would lie. She trusted her partner, even if she couldn't remember when they'd become partners. Still, she didn't feel right about the job she'd come here to do, felt unsettled, doubtful. Good cops knew when to rely on their gut, and hers was telling her she needed to rethink the situation, get a better handle on it, get some *clarification*. Because once she got to work, she would be fully committed, no take-backs.

She stopped walking, was about to turn around, when a recent memory flashed in her mind. She saw Rauch sitting in the front passenger seat of the cruiser, the upper half of his body turned so that he could face Maureen.

Do you understand what I've told you?

Yes, Maureen had answered.

Good. And just to make sure you don't have second thoughts....

Rauch's neck gills had widened. He'd closed his mouth, tightened the muscles in his neck, and a chuffing sound had filled the cruiser as jets of black gas shot forth from the slits. A black cloud enveloped Maureen's head, cutting off her vision. The gas smelled sour and rank, like spoiled milk and rotten meat. She'd been caught off guard, and she inhaled the noxious stuff before she could stop herself. As bad as the shit stank, she hadn't coughed, and the cloud quickly dissipated. She'd felt calm then, relaxed, compliant, happy – even eager – to do whatever Rauch asked of her.

The memory of that awful stench wiped away her doubts as effectively as if she'd gotten a fresh dose of the gas. She'd come here to do a job – an important one – and she intended to see it through. She unsnapped the safety strap on her side holster, put her hand on the butt of her Glock, and continued on toward the play area.

★　★　★

"Look at me, Mommy!"

Brian climbed on top of the bulbous yolk of a gigantic over-easy egg and jumped. Reeny watched as he landed on a section of egg white. The plastic was slick, and his feet slid out from under him and he went down on his butt. She rose from the bench where she'd been sitting, intending to go to him and see if he was hurt. But he got up laughing, stepped off the egg, and started running toward an equally gigantic waffle covered with plastic syrup and a plastic pat of melting butter. Her assistance not required, Reeny sat back down and marveled at how resilient children could be. Why couldn't people keep that quality and take it with them into adulthood? It would make getting through life a hell of a lot easier.

She'd intended to take Brian to the park after picking him up from preschool, but the rain had necessitated a change of plan. Instead, she'd brought him to Horizon's Edge. A silly name for a cheap, tacky place that always smelled like greasy fried food, popcorn, soda, and cotton candy. Unlike some kids, Brian wasn't tired after school. He was always revved up, so Reeny took him to the park to burn off some of that energy before she took him home. If she didn't, he'd run around like a little lunatic and drive her crazy while she tried to make dinner. But the weather being what it was, she'd brought Brian to the mall today. More especially, to the play area, not far from the food court. And maybe its proximity to food was why it had been designed in such an unusual way. Instead of standard play equipment to climb on, jump on, or slide down, the area contained giant plastic sculptures of breakfast food: eggs, pancakes, waffles, sausage links, muffins, tall glasses of milk and orange juice, and even a mug of coffee. The drink sculptures were too large for children to climb, so they mostly ignored these, although occasionally some kids would chase each other around them. Running, climbing, and jumping were the primary activities children could engage in here, and while school-age children would tire of the breakfast sculptures quickly, toddlers and preschoolers didn't need much in the way of outward stimulation in order to make their fun – thank god.

There were maybe a dozen kids playing, a roughly even mix of boys and girls, running around, laughing, and yelling while their tired parents sat on benches positioned around the play area. Some, like her, were watching their children have fun, while most gazed down at their phones. She watched Brian fall into a game of tag with several other children, smiling at the easy way they played together. If only adults could make friends so easily. Brian looked like his father – lean, narrow-faced, thick brown hair – but he didn't have his father's athletic grace, not yet anyway. Charles owned and operated a cleaning company called We Got It Maid. But he'd been on both the football and basketball teams in high school, and now he ran several miles each morning and played doubles tennis with her at the weekends. She hoped Brian would inherit his father's physical abilities. She'd been awkward and clumsy growing up, and she hoped her son could avoid having to deal with other kids teasing him because he wasn't good at sports. Neither she nor Charles were shallow people, at least she hoped they weren't. They didn't judge others by their physical gifts. What was inside a person's mind and heart was infinitely more important than whether they could do a layup or hit a fastball. But the reality was that the fast, the strong, and the agile had an easier time of it in this world – certainly when they were young – and as a mother, she wanted her child to have the best life he could.

Her thoughts drifted toward Lori then. Her sister had been on her mind ever since their lunch earlier, and she hadn't been able to concentrate on anything else. She was worried about Lori – deeply worried – and she wondered if she'd made a mistake by not staying with her after their talk at A Taste of Thai. Maybe she should've canceled the afternoon's showings and invited Lori over to her house where they could've continued talking. Maybe she should've tried to convince Lori to check herself into a hospital for a psychiatric evaluation. Lori's mental health had been good for the last…had it really been seventeen years? But Aashrita's death during their senior year in high school had hit her hard, and it had taken her some time to recover. Sometimes Reeny thought Lori had only partially recovered. By unspoken agreement, they didn't talk about Aashrita, but every once in a while one of their parents would bring up the subject, and when that happened, Lori became distant, distracted, almost as if she went into a kind of trance. Reeny didn't need to be a psychologist to know her sister had unresolved issues regarding Aashrita's death. She'd tried talking to Lori about it a couple times over the years, but she'd gotten nowhere, had only elicited blank looks and silence, so she'd given up. Now she wished she hadn't. Maybe if she'd been more persistent, had been able to convince Lori to get help, she wouldn't be having delusions about being persecuted by some otherworldly secret society.

She'd texted Lori a couple times to see how she was doing, but she'd gotten no response. She'd called and left voicemails too, with the same result. She'd tried calling Get Moving! in case Lori's phone was dead, but no one answered. She told herself that Lori was there, just so busy helping clients that she hadn't had time to get back to her. She'd call or text when she got a chance. These thoughts, however, failed to reassure Reeny.

Maybe she should collect Brian and drive over to Get Moving! and see for herself how Lori was doing. If nothing else, it would make her feel better. She started to stand—

—and that's when she heard the first shot.

Reeny's head snapped toward the direction of the sound and her eyes searched frantically for its source. Someone screamed – she didn't see who – and another shot split the air. More screams, and still she couldn't see the cause for these cries of fear and shock. She thought she might be in shock herself, sitting frozen on her bench, gaze darting this way and that as she tried to determine the location of the threat. Her eyes fell upon a small body lying on top of the large plastic waffle. The girl lay face down, the back of her light blue T-shirt dark and wet with blood. Not far from the girl, she saw a little boy lying on the floor, arms splayed outward, the red ruin that had once been his face pointed toward the ceiling. Someone was shooting, she realized. At kids. Someone was *killing* kids.

She didn't yell, didn't scream. Instead she jumped to her feet and began running toward the last place she'd seen Brian playing tag with the other children – over by the giant mug of coffee. Hysteria bubbled beneath the surface of her consciousness, and she fought to keep it at bay. She couldn't help her son if she surrendered to the terror blazing like a wildfire within her.

It's happening, she thought. *Right here, right now.*

These days, everyone in America lived with the possibility that they and their loved ones might get caught up in the wave of gun violence that had swept through the country over the last several years. Now it had finally come to Oakmont.

She didn't see Brian as she ran toward the mug. She was aware of other people as only blurs or smudges, ill-defined objects that took up space but which couldn't be identified or named. Some of these objects moved, some remained motionless. Some were quiet, and some made sounds as equally indistinct to her as their forms. And then just like that, everything snapped into place, and she saw children, saw mothers – and even a few fathers – running, some toward each other, some away, fleeing without intention or direction as they tried to escape death.

Another gunshot, and this time when she looked in the direction of the sound, she saw a middle-aged police officer standing in a shooting stance, gun gripped in both of her hands, just like cops did in the movies and on TV. Was she trying to stop the shooter? She saw the body of a young mother lying on the edge of the egg sculpture, her blood splattered on the white plastic, a squalling infant lying on the floor near where it had fallen. Reeny experienced a momentary impulse to run toward the baby, pick it up, and carry it to safety, but she shoved the feeling aside. As cold and cruel as it was, Brian was *her* child, and he was her first responsibility. She shut out the baby's cries and kept moving.

She called Brian's name, shouted it as loud as she could. She could barely hear her own voice over the tumult all around her, and she doubted Brian could hear her. She'd just have to keep looking.

Another shot.

She winced, expecting to feel a bullet slam into her back, but nothing happened. Had someone else gone down, injured or dead? Another child or parent? She prayed the shooter had missed this time, but from what she'd seen of his work so far – weren't these killers always men? – he hit whatever he aimed at. Maybe that last shot had come from the cop's gun, though. Maybe she'd managed to take out the shooter. Reeny was tempted to turn and look, eager to get visual confirmation that this nightmare was over, that they were safe. All who hadn't taken a bullet yet, that is. But she forced herself to keep moving forward. She couldn't afford to take a chance that the shooter had been stopped. She had to find Brian, had to protect him, make sure he was safe.

She shouted his name again, loud as she could this time, and she almost burst into tears when she heard him cry out, "Mommy!"

He'd been hiding behind the giant sausage link. Now he came running around it toward her, tears streaming from his eyes. He held out his arms to her, wanting her to scoop him up and carry him away from this awful place, and that's exactly what she intended to do.

Another gunshot.

Brian's head jerked as a bullet struck the side of his neck. Blood sprayed the air, his body went limp, and he started to collapse. As he went down, time seemed to slow to a crawl, and Reeny got a good close look at her dead son's face. His eyes were wide in what appeared to be almost comical surprise, and his lips had contracted into a small *O*, creating an overall grotesque cartoonish expression. *This is death*, she thought. Sudden and stupid, without even a shred of dignity. A split second ago this had been her son, Brian, a boy who loved to eat Cheerios only when they'd floated in milk long enough to get soggy, who loved TV shows with happy talking animals whose adventures were simple and not too scary, who begged her to read the same book to him every night – a collection of silly poems about food – and who slept on his stomach, head to the side, knees drawn up, butt in the air. A boy who laughed too loud and ran in the house no matter how many times she reminded him to walk. But he wasn't Brian anymore. Now he was only meat.

Time returned to normal speed then and Brian hit the floor and slid several inches before coming to a stop, leaving a smear of blood to mark his path. She staggered toward him, her vision narrowing until it seemed she was looking at him from the far end of a very long, very dark tunnel. Her vision went black for a moment, and when it was restored, she was on her knees next to him, holding his hand, gripping it tight without any memory of how she'd gotten there. She examined Brian's wound with numb, almost clinical detachment. The bullet had torn a chunk of meat from his neck, severing an artery in the process. Blood flowed from the wound, so much of it. The heart stopped pumping when you died, so the blood flow should stop soon, too, right? She wondered how long it would take. A minute or two? Longer?

She felt something warm flowing down her face. At first she thought some of Brian's blood had hit her, but when she reached up to touch her face with her free hand, her fingers came away wet but not red.

You're crying, she thought.

People were still screaming and shouting, running away from the ridiculous play area in all directions. She heard footsteps approaching her, the stride slow and deliberate. She looked up and saw the cop walking toward her. The woman held her gun in her right hand, down at her side, and the expression on her face was one of puzzlement and, perhaps, some small portion of regret.

As soon as Reeny saw the woman, she knew she was the shooter. There never had been anyone else. She'd killed her son and now she was going to kill her. Good. The horrible reality of Brian's death hadn't fully hit her yet, but it would, and soon. She didn't think she could survive that kind of pain, and she wanted to die before she could experience it.

The cop stopped when she reached Reeny. She looked at her, then at Brian, then back to her.

"I have a message for you," she said. "Actually, it's for your sister." She paused and frowned, as if trying to recall the words, wanting to get them just right.

"Confess and atone."

She raised her gun, but instead of pointing it at Reeny, as she hoped, the cop placed the muzzle against the underside of her jaw and pulled the trigger. There was blood of course, and this time a fair amount splattered onto Reeny, much of it on her face where it mingled with her tears. The cop went down and hit the floor with a dull thud. She too was only meat now.

The bitch had cheated Reeny out of her own death, *and* she'd escaped without ever having to face justice for what she'd done, killing not only Brian but the others that she'd shot before him. Reeny wanted to scream at the staggering unfairness of it all, was on the verge of doing so, when she felt Brian's small hand grip hers. Startled, she looked down and saw that his eyes once more gleamed with life and awareness, and his mouth stretched into a wide grin, displaying flecks of blood on his teeth.

"Or suffer," he said.

It took her a second to realize he was finishing the cop's message.

He sat up. Blood ran down the side of his face, on to his neck, soaked into the collar of his shirt. He continued holding onto Reeny's hand, his grip tightening to the point of being painful.

"Let's go see Aunt Lorlee," Brian said. "We need to give her the message."

"Yes," Reeny said thoughtfully. Then stronger, anger in her voice. "*Yes.*"

★　　★　　★

Driving on the Nightway was beyond surreal. There was the monotony of moving through a world of unvarying blackness, a realm where the only things that were real were what the headlights of your vehicle touched, as if the light solidified the darkness, forced it to coalesce so that you'd have something to drive *on*. She wondered what would happen if she turned off her headlights. Would the surface of the road suddenly become insubstantial, would her car plummet downward through an endless void, tumbling end over end forever? It was not a theory she wanted to test.

Without markings to delineate the sides of the Nightway, Lori had to drive more slowly than she'd have preferred – thirty-five, forty miles an hour – to ensure she didn't veer off the road into whatever lay beyond. She had the heater blowing full blast, but the air that emerged from the vents was barely warm, as if the Nightway refused to let those who traveled it get too comfortable. The blanket she had wrapped around her body helped somewhat, but she still shivered from time to time. Why she couldn't have entered this world wearing her clothes, she didn't know. Then again, considering they'd been soaked from her standing outside in the rain at the cemetery, maybe it was a good thing her clothes hadn't come through with her. She'd be freezing if she'd had to wear those wet things. She supposed that was one thing to be grateful for – along with escaping the shadow creatures, of course. She hurt, too. The wounds she'd suffered at the hands of the Cabal, wounds which hadn't followed her into the real world, had returned to her body the instant she appeared on the Nightway. None of them were life threatening – she hoped – but the pain was distracting.

She wished she'd gassed up her car recently. She had only a quarter of a tank, and while she was in no danger of running out of gas any time soon, the fuel wouldn't last forever. She didn't relish the idea of being stranded on the Nightway, gas tank bone dry, sitting behind the wheel, and wondering what the hell to do next. Her best defense in this place was to keep moving, and when she could no longer do that, who knew what would find her – and what it would do to her when it did.

The landscape around her wasn't completely featureless, and she wasn't entirely alone on the Nightway. She'd see shapes on either side of the road sometimes, things that looked as if they might be natural features – hills, perhaps, maybe trees too, although it was difficult to tell for certain. Occasionally she'd pass an artificial structure like the Vermilion Tower, something that had been created by the hands of whatever beings dwelled in this place. Sometimes these structures would be entirely dark, and she'd only get a basic impression of their forms as she drove by. Other times, they'd be lit somehow, giving her a clear look at them. At one point, she passed what looked like a gas station cast in the glow of fluorescent lights, except instead of fuel pumps, strange insectile creatures were bound to metal poles by strips of leather, rubber hoses protruding from their mouths. Another time she passed something that resembled a greenhouse – all glass and bright light. It was huge, nearly a mile long, and the plants inside, large-leafed things with thick stalks covered with long black thorns, swayed slowly as if in time to music she couldn't hear.

She passed other vehicles as well. Not many, but enough to let her know that she wasn't alone out here. She couldn't decide if that knowledge was comforting or terrifying. Maybe a little of both. One of the vehicles – if that's what it was – was a silver sphere about twice the size of her car. It was comprised of segmented plates, and it made her think of the way an armadillo rolled itself up into a ball when threatened. There was no obvious way for an operator to see out – no windows of any kind – but the sphere maintained a steady course as it rolled along, so its driver had to have some kind of method for navigating. Another vehicle she passed was of more familiar design, but no less alien for that. It was a covered wagon, like something out of the Old West, drawn by a team of four horses. But the wagon was constructed entirely from bone, its covering stitched-together patches of dried skin, and the horses – large, thick-bodied things – were wreathed in orange flame. There was no sign of a driver, and she wondered what sort of passengers rode within the wagon. She was glad the occupants weren't visible to her, though. She had a strong suspicion that if she could see them, she'd wished she hadn't.

Each time a vehicle passed her, she held her breath, fearing that it might be driven by one of the Cabal, out searching for her. She didn't relax until the vehicle was in her rearview and dwindling fast.

She wondered where the air in this world came from. She had no trouble breathing, although the air felt flat and stale. But this place didn't appear to have anything close to a natural ecosystem, so how was there oxygen? Wherever it came from, she was glad for it. It wasn't like her car was an airtight spaceship with its own air supply.

She'd started driving because she hadn't known what else to do, and while she didn't know how long she'd been on the road – her car's digital clock kept flashing 00:00, as if time had no meaning here – it seemed as if she'd been driving for a while. Was she getting anywhere? Was there any*where* to get to? She'd hoped that after some time, she'd snap back to the real world, as she'd done before, but it hadn't happened yet, and she was beginning to fear that it might not. She could end up stuck here, a permanent resident of this awful non-place. She wondered what Reeny would think about her disappearance, what their parents, Larry, and Justin would think. She realized she'd thought of Justin last, as if he was an afterthought, and wasn't that a sad commentary on their relationship?

She tried turning on the radio, but all that came out was a chorus of half-audible voices chanting words in a language she didn't recognize – the same as what she'd heard on the Driver's radio when she first appeared on the Nightway – and she turned it off.

She kept feeling something scratching at the back of her mind, something trying to get her attention. She suspected it had to do with her visit to Aashrita's grave, or more precisely, why Aashrita had died so young. But thinking about Aashrita made her head hurt, so she turned her thoughts away from the subject whenever her mind began drifting toward it. There would be time for her to remember later, after she found a way to return home. She knew she was lying to herself, that deep down she didn't want to remember, was scared to fucking death of what would happen if she allowed herself to remember. But she didn't care. She'd lie to herself a thousand times over if it would protect her from the pain the memory of Aashrita's death would surely bring.

It was during one of these moments, when she was purposely turning her mind away from thoughts of her dead friend, that something dashed out into the road in front of her. She had an impression of a multi-limbed thing that was formed of pale white flesh, but before she could make out any further details, she slammed into the creature head on. She heard the dull thud of the impact, and she was thrown forward the same instant the airbag deployed. She felt the bag envelop her as the car spun and skidded, tires making almost no sound as she slid across the Nightway's slick surface. She had no time to think, no time to react, could only let the car's momentum do with her what it would.

CHAPTER TEN

The motion stopped, and she sat there as the airbag began deflating. When it pulled away from her face, she drew in a gasping breath. Her nerves jangled with adrenaline, and she felt her pulse pounding throughout her entire body.

I hit something, she thought. *Oh my god, I hit something.*

Her car had come to a stop with its front end pointing almost ninety degrees away from the thing she'd struck, so she could see it. The car's engine had died, one of the headlights was out, and the other seemed dimmer than it had only a few seconds ago. The Civic's front end was dented inward, and the hood had buckled, although it hadn't broken free from its latch and flown upward during the crash. She sat there several moments, stunned, trying to gather her thoughts. Her chest and wrists hurt from smacking into the airbag, but considering what might've happened to her if she hadn't had airbags, she figured the pain was a small enough price to pay for her continued existence. She started shaking, and she knew her tremors had nothing to do with the vehicle's internal temperature.

She thumbed the seat belt release. It didn't do anything at first, and she thought it was broken, but she tried it again, and this time it worked. Not thinking clearly, operating on automatic, she opened the driver's-side door, and – grabbing hold of the blanket – got out of the car. A sharp pain shot through her right knee as she put weight on it, her old soccer injury making itself known. She thought of Aashrita again, but the instant she did, the thought drifted away, and it was like she'd never had it at all. The air held a bone-chilling dampness, and she wrapped the blanket about her naked body, not that it did much to keep out the cold. The smooth surface of the Nightway felt strange beneath her bare feet, like ice but not as slippery, and there was a constant low-level vibration, almost a hum, as if some kind of energy flowed through the road's glossy ebon surface. She walked around to the front of the car to see what she'd hit, limping because of her bad knee, and immediately regretted doing so.

The remaining headlight of her Civic wasn't pointed directly at the thing, but the light from the beam still illuminated the creature's form, if only dimly. It was ten feet long and roughly shaped like a scorpion. But instead of being covered in a chitinous exoskeleton, it had pale, almost bone-white skin. The first half of its body was humanoid, the head hairless, eyes receded into hollow sockets, jutting cheekbones, lips pulled away from sharp white teeth. Instead of pinchers, it had a pair of long lean arms that ended in large clawed hands. Smaller limbs protruded from the creature's midsection, six of them, only these were bent at odd angles, giving them a more insectile appearance. The upward curving tail was a head and torso that looked exactly like the front of the thing – as if the creature was a pair of conjoined twins – except the torso had no arms and the head hung upside down. The thing was injured, the arms on its left side broken, and blood dribbled from the mouth of the tail-head. Half of the front head's face was crushed, and blood ran freely from one of the eye sockets.

Lori found the thing revolting on a primal level, and she instinctively took several steps back to move closer to the driver's-side door, but her attention was transfixed by the alien abomination, and she made no move to get back inside the car. Aside from a slight spasmodic twitching in the tail, the creature was motionless. Had the impact killed it? She hoped so.

She didn't know whether the thing had been traveling on the Nightway under its own power or if it had come from the dark land beyond the road, and she really didn't care. All that mattered was that it posed no threat to her. She had a thought then. What if there were more of these creatures out there in the darkness, watching her at this very moment, trying to determine whether she was dangerous, if it was safe to attack and take revenge for their dead companion?

She didn't know if the Civic was still operable, but she couldn't stay out here, exposed and unarmed. There might not be any more scorpion things out there, but there could well be other predators about, and she'd rather not meet them if she didn't have to. She turned to reach for the car door, but in doing so she twisted the upper half of her body, changing the distribution of her weight on her legs, and her soccer injury screamed in protest. The pain made her gasp, and her leg gave out from under her. The blanket slipped off her shoulders as she started to go down, and she flung herself against the Civic, hoping to grab hold of the roof and steady herself. But her hands found no purchase on the smooth metal and she fell. She landed on her knees – hard – and she felt something crunch inside her injured knee. This time the pain was so intense that she cried out in a near-scream, and tears filled her eyes. She flopped over onto her side to take the pressure off her knee, and while this lessened the pain somewhat, the relief was minor. Her knee was on fire from the inside, and she whimpered like a child.

She became aware of two things in that moment. One was a pair of headlights off in the distance, some sort of vehicle heading toward her. The other was the sound of a large form pulling itself across the Nightway's slick surface, a heavy, ominous sliding that could only mean one thing. Not only was the scorpion creature not dead, it could still move – and it was coming for her.

The creature made a high-pitched sound as it came, a powerful keening like it was in great pain. She hadn't purposely harmed the thing, but she nevertheless felt a pang of guilt, as if its condition was entirely her fault.

Jesus, here she was, naked, alone, bruised and cut, being stalked by some monster on a highway in an alien dimension, and she was feeling sorry for it. *Better toughen up, bitch, if you want to continue breathing.*

She carefully sat up, and using the side of the car to brace herself – doing her best to keep weight off her bad knee – she pulled herself up into a standing position. She saw one of the creature's clawed hands come into view around the front of the car, and she began hopping toward the rear of the vehicle, keeping her hands on the Civic's roof to support herself. She reached the rear quarter panel when the creature's front head became visible. It fixed its one good eye on her, and its keening died away, replaced by an angry hiss. Now that the thing was closer, she could smell it, and she nearly vomited. She was already nauseated as a result of the crash, and the beast's stink was like a pile of used tampons that had been baking for hours beneath a blazing sun. It was overpowering, so much so that for a moment she was overwhelmed with revulsion and unable to move.

Light washed over her, and she heard the sound of an approaching car engine. One of the Cabal coming for her, maybe the Driver himself? At this point, she'd almost welcome it if it was.

Headlight beams played over the scorpion thing, and as if realizing it might have competition for its prey, its hiss became a shriek of fury, and its hands slapped the road as it began pulling itself toward her with increased speed, its wounded limbs seemingly little impediment to forward motion. That got Lori moving again. If she could've run, she would have, but with her injured knee, the best she could do was hop around to the rear of her car, hands on the trunk, and continue on to the other side of the vehicle. The scorpion thing continued its angry shrieking, accompanied by the *slap-slap-slap* of its palms on the ground, and the heavy sound of its body being pulled along behind.

She glanced back at the approaching vehicle. The headlights loomed larger now, and their illumination dazzled her eyes. The vehicle itself was a dim shape behind those lights, their glare making it impossible to discern any details about it. She wondered if the driver would pass on by, sparing only a curious look for the naked woman fighting to survive an attack by some monstrous thing. For all she knew, on the Nightway a sight like this might be perfectly normal, of no more than fleeting interest to one of its travelers. Or maybe whoever – or whatever – was behind the wheel would turn out to be a worse threat to her than the scorpion thing. Maybe it would be best if the vehicle *did* continue on past her. It didn't, though. It was close enough now that she could see it was a van, but she could make out no other details, not with its headlights shining in her eyes. The van slowed to a stop a few yards from her, and the driver got out.

He was a black man in his late thirties, of medium height, stocky, short hair, and a neatly trimmed mustache and goatee. He wore a black T-shirt that said PEST DEFENSE in white capital letters, along with a pair of black satin shorts. Sticking out from the shorts were a pair of prosthetic legs that looked like jointed metal rods and which terminated in plastic feet inserted into a pair of red sneakers. The man started toward her with a rolling gait, swaying side to side as he moved forward. She was uncomfortably aware of her nakedness, but there wasn't anything she could do about it now. Besides, what did personal modesty matter when a malformed human scorpion was trying to kill her?

The Civic rocked then, and Lori looked toward the scorpion thing and saw the monster pulling itself on top of the roof. Instead of following her around the rear of the car, the fucking thing had decided to take a shortcut. Once on top of the car it hissed at her again, and its muscles tensed as it prepared to launch itself at her.

The man – who up to this point had barely glanced at her, who'd kept his gaze focused on the scorpion thing – made no move toward the creature. He stopped walking when he was within a few feet of the car, opened his mouth wide and coughed forth a dark cloud. At first Lori thought he'd expelled some kind of gas, but then she heard the buzzing and saw the cloud was comprised of hundreds of small black beetles, all of which flew straight toward the scorpion thing. The insects engulfed the creature before it could attack Lori, and it began shrieking as beetles gathered on its pale flesh and started eating. It thrashed and swatted at the insects, and its tail stabbed downward, the head at the end of it attempting to tear masses of beetles away from its shared body. But the secondary head only succeeded in providing the beetles with easy passage down its throat and into its interior. The creature shrieked from two mouths now, and its exertions became so violent that it rolled off the Civic and fell to the glossy surface of the Nightway. It rolled violently back and forth in a desperate attempt to free itself from the beetles, but there were simply too many of them. Within seconds, they completely covered the creature, which no longer screamed from either mouth, as both were filled with ravening insects.

It was over quickly after that.

The scorpion thing's exertions lessened before ceasing altogether. The creature lay motionless on the road while the beetles continued their work. Before long, the insects began to take flight once more, only a few at first, but more joined them until the insects' departure became a mass exodus. The insects flew back toward their host, who once again opened his mouth wide to allow their return. Lori watched in revulsion as the beetles disappeared down the man's throat without any seeming discomfort on his part. She turned to look at the scorpion thing and saw it had been reduced to a scattered pile of bones, the muscle and sinew that had held them together gone, and she closed her eyes and concentrated on keeping her stomach contents where they were.

She heard the man walk with his lurching gait, and a moment later she jumped, startled, as she felt her blanket being draped around her shoulders. She opened her eyes and saw the man smiling at her. Grateful, she drew the blanket tight around her body and put the majority of her weight on her uninjured leg. Her bad knee still hurt like hell, but at least she managed to remain standing.

"Let me guess," the man said, voice low and sonorous. "The fucking Cabal, right?"

Surprised, Lori nodded.

The man shook his head.

"I *hate* those assholes."

★   ★   ★

"Want me to turn up the heater some more?"

"No, thank you. I'm fine."

Lori sat in the van's passenger seat, blanket wrapped around her, seat belt buckled. The dashboard vents blew a steady stream of warm air, but it couldn't touch the core of cold at the center of her being. She wondered if she'd ever truly feel warm again.

She glanced over at her benefactor. He'd introduced himself as Edgar Mullins, and as the business name on his T-shirt – PEST DEFENSE – suggested, he was an exterminator. Or at least he had been, back in the real world. Although the longer she spent on the Nightway, the more it was beginning to seem real and the more Earth began to seem like a dream. If she stayed here long enough, would she forget about Earth entirely and come to think of the Nightway as the only reality that mattered, maybe even the only one that existed?

The van was Edgar's work vehicle, white, with PEST DEFENSE painted on the sides, below that a cartoon image of a black man in coveralls thrusting a sword into the midsection of an equally cartoonish human-sized cockroach. The vehicle's interior smelled of harsh chemicals, and metal canisters in the back rattled and clanged against each other as Edgar drove. Lori wondered just how toxic the air she breathed was, but she didn't really care. Being stranded without a working car on the Nightway was far more dangerous than huffing pesticide fumes.

Edgar could get around fine on his prosthetic legs but he needed help to drive. He had a handle to the left of the steering wheel that allowed him to control acceleration and braking, and a knob on the steering wheel, which made it possible for him to operate it with his right hand while the left was busy with the handle controls. Edgar drove with an easy confidence, and she guessed he'd been using the equipment for some time.

He had the van's radio on, the volume turned low, but Lori could still hear the eerie, indecipherable chanting coming from the van's speakers.

"How can you stand to listen to that?" she asked. "The sound makes my skin crawl."

Edgar answered without taking his eyes off the road. "You get used to it. And sometimes, I think I can almost make out what they're saying, you know?"

Lori didn't know, but she didn't want to discuss the Nightway's sole radio program any further.

The collision with the scorpion thing had wrecked her Civic. She'd tried starting the engine, but she couldn't get it to turn over. And even if it had started, one of the front quarter panels had been smashed against a tire, making it impossible to steer. So when Edgar had offered to give her a ride she'd accepted, although not without hesitation. He seemed ordinary enough, but she knew he was hosting hundreds, maybe thousands of carnivorous beetles inside his body, so many that they couldn't possibly all fit inside him, and yet somehow they did. The insects had made quick work of the scorpion thing, and they'd be able to devour her even faster if they wished. Sitting next to Edgar was like sitting next to a ticking time bomb. If he wanted her dead, all he'd have to do was open his mouth and let his beetles out to do their thing.

If he wanted you dead, he'd have killed you already, she thought. Then again, maybe his beetles' tiny bellies were so full after killing the scorpion creature that the insects wouldn't be hungry again for some time. Maybe Edgar wanted to keep her in reserve until his friends' appetites returned. It was a risk she felt she had to take, though. If the beetles did decide to eat her, at least her death would be brief, if agonizing.

"Thanks for coming to my rescue," she said.

"No problem. I couldn't just let the damn thing kill you. I hate void crawlers. Fucking things are worse than a million roaches. And did you get a whiff of it?"

"Yeah. I don't know if I'll ever get the smell out of my nasal passages."

"Right? And given what I used to do for a living, I was exposed to all kinds of horrible smells. But void crawler stink is the absolute *worst.*"

Luckily, she hadn't been injured seriously when her Civic hit the scorpion thing...the void crawler. Her knee throbbed, but now that she was sitting, it felt a little better. She had a couple of other aches and pains, but they were minor for the most part. She was surprised she didn't have a killer of a headache, but so far, so good.

"So what brings you to the Nightway?" Edgar asked. "I assume you're new here or you'd have known to watch out for void crawlers. No offense."

"None taken. I *am* new to the Nightway. If you hadn't stopped to help me, I'd be dead."

She told him her story then, glossing over some of the details but making sure to hit the high points.

When she finished, he said, "Sounds like you've been through a lot. I hate to tell you this, but you probably have more to go through yet, and it's going to get worse. Maybe a *lot* worse."

His words didn't exactly cheer her up.

"How about you?" she asked. "Have you been here long?"

"Yeah. I don't know exactly how long, though. Time doesn't operate the same way here as it does back home."

"What is this place?" she asked. "Do the laws of physics even work here?"

"When they're in the mood. The Nightway is like a path between worlds, one that circles the outermost edge of the Gyre. Because of that, reality here is…situational."

Lori didn't understand, but she didn't ask for further explanation. There was only one thing that really mattered to her right now. "How do we get back to our world?"

"The Nightway has on and off ramps, just like a regular highway. The trick is finding them."

"I didn't have any trouble getting back before."

"That's because the Cabal brought you here. At first, they can only hold a person in this dimension for so long. But the more you come to the Nightway, the more you adjust to it and the longer you stay. If you get home and stay home, you'll be okay. But if you enter of your own free will – like you did this last time – you're stuck here. Unless you can find an exit."

"You said you hate the Cabal. Have you dealt with them too?"

"Sure have. Fuckers."

Edgar drove in silence for a time, and Lori waited for him to say more.

It took a while – so long she thought he would say no more on the subject – but then he finally started speaking.

"My story's pretty much the same as yours. I didn't see any Shadowkin, though. I had encounters with weird people, some of the same ones you've met, some different. They all had something wrong with them – one eye way bigger than the other, extra fingers on each hand, a forked tongue like a snake's – and they had red pinky nails, too."

Lori had checked Edgar's left pinky before getting into his van, and she'd been relieved to see it wasn't painted. Then again, she supposed that didn't necessarily mean anything. All a member of the Cabal had to do to go incognito was remove the polish from their finger. The thought wasn't a comforting one.

Edgar continued. "They all gave me the same message yours gave you: *Confess and atone – or suffer.* But the bastards wouldn't tell me what I'd done or how I could fix it. One of them said it wouldn't be a true confession if I had to be told what to say, and if the confession wasn't true, atonement wasn't possible. Whatever the fuck that means. I'd find myself in the Vermilion Tower on and off, and several members of the Cabal would torture me while the rest looked on. Things started happening in the real world, too. Bad things."

She didn't like the sound of that, not at all.

"The Cabal did something to my friends and family. They started to change, become crazy...*evil*. They began hurting people. Killing them. All to get to me and give me that goddamn message again. My wife, my two kids, my brother, my mom, my best friend...."

The man's voice had grown thick and Lori thought he might start crying. But all that came out was a lone tear, and he wiped it away before it could get halfway down his face.

"I tried, but I couldn't figure out what I'd done. Or at least, what the Cabal *thought* I'd done. The next time I found myself in the Vermilion Tower, they locked me up in a small chamber. I wasn't alone, though. They gave me some new friends. Hundreds of them, as a matter of fact."

"The beetles," Lori said.

Edgar nodded.

"This'll probably sound stupid since I'm an exterminator, but I've always hated insects. Damn things creep me out big time. Maybe that's why I chose to make a living killing them, I suppose. The beetles – big black ones like none I'd ever seen before – crawled all over me, taking little bites out of my flesh. Not enough to kill me, but it hurt like a motherfucker."

In the dim glow of the dashboard lights, she could see small scars and pockmarks on his face, neck, arms, and hands. She tried to imagine the pain he must've experienced, and she was glad she couldn't.

"I tried to knock them off me, tried to crush them with my hands, stomp on them, but there were so many. Too many to kill them all. I bled from dozens of wounds, dozens *upon* dozens, and of course the beetles triggered my phobia, and I was terrified as well as in pain. I screamed myself hoarse, and I kept screaming after that, except it came out as a sort of whispery rasp. I started talking to the beetles then. Guess I'd kind of lost my mind a little. I begged them to stop hurting me, told them they could have anything they wanted if they just left me alone – or better yet, helped me escape the tower. They told me they would. For a price."

She felt a cold heavy weight settle in her stomach.

"Oh god."

He nodded. "They didn't take my legs right away. First they entered me and rearranged some things inside so they could remain there without killing me. It hurt so bad, I wished they *would've* killed me. When it was over, I lay on the cell floor, barely conscious. When one of the Cabal came to check on me, the beetles flooded out of my mouth and attacked her. I don't know what sort of powers the Cabal possess, but evidently immunity to flesh-eating beetles isn't one of them. Once she'd been reduced to a skeleton, the beetles went back inside me, and I hauled ass out of there. The beetles had to kill a couple more Cabal members on the way out, but I made it. There were vehicles in the courtyard. Only a couple looked like regular cars, though. I stole one of them and raced off down the Nightway, pedal to the fucking metal. Eventually, I got lucky and found an exit. I made it back home, and the instant I did, the beetles came out to take what I owed them. They didn't wait for me to park – goddamn impatient things – and I lost control of the vehicle. I guess I hit a telephone pole. I don't know. I'd lost consciousness by then. Cops found me, called for an ambulance, and after the docs amputated what was left of my legs – which wasn't much – I spent a few weeks in the hospital, after which I left with these."

He reached down and tapped his right prosthesis. "All in all, it was the best deal I ever made."

Lori wondered if she could ever become so desperate that she'd be willing to make such a sacrifice. Based on what the Cabal had done to her so far, she thought she might.

One thing about Edgar's story was encouraging, though. It was good to know members of the Cabal – whatever they were – weren't all-powerful. They could die just like anyone else.

"How did you end up back here?" she asked. "Did the Cabal bring you back?"

"Nope. Once you learn to navigate the Nightway on your own, it's harder for the Cabal to pull you into it themselves. They can, however, keep harassing you in the real world, which is what happened to me. They continued changing people I knew and sending them after me. Finally, I couldn't stand others getting hurt because of me, and I hopped in my van and started searching for an entrance to the Nightway. It took a while, but eventually I found one. I've been driving this road ever since."

"Can't the Cabal find you easier here? After all, this is where they live. You'd think it would be where they're most powerful."

"They're still after me, all right, but they seem to have a harder time finding me on the Nightway. Don't know why. Maybe something about the Nightway itself interferes with their senses? Whatever the reason, I'm just grateful for it. Gives me some breathing room, you know?"

Lori thought of the vibrations she'd felt beneath her bare feet when she'd stood on the Nightway's surface. If Edgar was right, she'd be safe from the Cabal as long as she kept moving. She doubted things would prove to be that simple in the end, but for now she'd enjoy remaining hidden from the Cabal for however long it lasted.

"Are you still trying to figure out what you need to confess?" she asked.

"I've mostly given up at this point," he admitted. "If I run across a new potential avenue of information, I check it out. Otherwise...." He let his voice trail off.

On one level, it was a comfort to meet someone who'd also had run-ins with the Cabal. But hearing that Edgar had never been able to discover what the Cabal wanted from him made her despair of ever being able to learn what they wanted from her. Would she end up like Edgar, wandering the Nightway for the rest of her life, trying to keep the Cabal from finding her? And what about what he'd said, about how the Cabal had transformed people he knew and set them against him? Had that happened to the people she knew and loved back home? Larry, Justin, Reeny.... The thought made her sick. She had to learn what transgression she'd committed that the Cabal wanted her to confess, then discover what she needed to do to make everything right again – if that was even possible at this point.

"It may take me a while, but I should be able to find an exit for you," Edgar said. "It'll let you out at the same place you left. It's how they work." He paused, then added, "Most of the time."

They drove on in silence for a time after that, both lost in their own thoughts. Eventually, Lori spoke again. "I hope you don't take this the wrong way, but why are you helping me? You could be putting yourself in danger by doing so – assuming the Cabal are looking for me."

"They are, no doubt about that. And there are other reasons you might be dangerous to me. You could be one of them in disguise or something else pretending to be someone you're not. Transformation and deception are a way of life on the Nightway. Way of death, too."

"So why *are* you helping me?"

"I got friends."

He opened his mouth and stuck out his tongue, displaying a cluster of beetles clinging to it. He closed his mouth, and when he spoke again, he did so normally. Lori had no idea how he could do so with those insects on his tongue. The thought made her shiver with disgust.

"After they took their payment from me, they decided to stick around. Don't know why. Maybe I make a good home for them. Whatever the reason, they're happy to help me out – especially if there's a meal in it for them. So I got more protection than most folks who travel this road. I can afford to take a chance on you. Besides, if helping you means I get to fuck over the Cabal, so much the better. I'll do anything to hurt those bastards."

"Anything?"

He turned to look at her and gave her a frown. "Do you have something in mind?" He sounded half suspicious, half intrigued.

"You said you searched the Nightway for answers to what the Cabal thinks you did, but so far you haven't had any luck."

"That's right."

"Any place you *haven't* tried yet?"

Edgar didn't answer right way. He gripped the steering wheel tighter, and she could see conflicting emotions warring on his face.

"Just one," he said. "I've never been there, but I've heard about it from people like us, stranded on the Nightway, running, searching...." He took a deep breath, then said, "They call it the Garden of Anguish."

"Sounds like fun," Lori said. She meant this sarcastically, but Edgar responded as if she was serious.

"You wouldn't think so if you went there. There's no place worse on the Nightway. None."

Considering what she'd experienced on the Nightway so far, she thought that was saying something.

"But it's a place where I could get the answers I need?"

"Yes. But there's a good chance you wouldn't survive the asking."

"Which is why you never went there?"

"No. I've never gone there because I'm afraid I *would* survive."

Lori didn't know what to make of his response. But she knew one thing: if her friends and family were in danger from the Cabal, she had to do whatever was necessary to save them.

"Take me there."

He gave her a sideways glance. "You did hear the name, right? The Garden of *Anguish*?"

"I did. I still want to go there."

He considered for a time, tapping his fingers on the steering wheel nervously and chewing his lower lip. Finally, he said, "Okay. But I'm just going to drop you off. I won't step into the Garden with you."

"Could you wait for me and give me a lift to an exit when I'm finished?"

"What the hell do you think I am? A goddamn cab driver?" He sighed. "Fine. I'll wait. And if you survive with enough of your mind intact, I'll take you to an exit. If you don't—"

He broke off, cocked his head as if listening to something only he could hear. A moment later, he turned toward her. "My friends say they'll be happy to devour you if you live but your mind's destroyed. They promise to make your end as quick and painless as possible."

She felt a cold twist in her gut.

"Tell them thanks, but I'll need to think about it."

Edgar nodded. A faraway look came into his eyes then, and she thought he was likely delivering her message to his 'friends'.

They continued on toward the Garden of Anguish. Lori hoped they'd get there before she could change her mind.

★   ★   ★

Edgar was right about time passing differently on the Nightway. They could have traveled for days or merely hours. There was no way to tell. She couldn't check the time on her phone. She'd retrieved it, along with her purse, from her wrecked Civic, but the device wouldn't work on the Nightway. And since the sky was nothing but unbroken blackness, it seemed like they traveled in an eternal now, where time was frozen and forward movement only an illusion. Time still existed for her body, though, and she became hungry and thirsty. Edgar had some energy bars and bottled water in the back of his van – he said he made supply runs to Earth from time to time – and he offered her some. Later, when she had to pee, he pulled over to the side of the road. He told her not to go very far from the van, and he stood outside with his back to her to keep watch. He didn't have a gun or anything, but with his friends inside him, he didn't need any other weapons. The ground felt like hard black sand beneath her feet, and she had to squat to do her business. She was only halfway through when she heard something big and heavy let out a chuffing breath not far from her. Her urine stream cut off instantly, and her head whipped in the direction of the sound. Before she could react further, Edgar opened his mouth and his beetles flew forth. They streaked past Lori toward whatever had made the noise. She couldn't see it, but she heard it shriek as the beetles fell upon it. There was a loud thud as it hit the ground and began thrashing, trying to dislodge the insects, no doubt, but its actions did no good. Seconds later it fell still, and a couple moments after that, she heard the beetles as they buzzed lazily back toward their host. Whatever that thing out there had been, it was nothing but bones now. She thought she was too shook up to finish peeing, but she did. When she was done, she stood and hurried back to the van.

"What the fuck was that?" she asked Edgar.

He cocked his head in the way he did when listening to his friends. He smiled. "They say it was delicious."

★   ★   ★

They passed several vehicles as well as a couple structures – one that resembled an upside-down pyramid, another that looked like an arrangement of gigantic crystalline shards floating in the air. She didn't ask Edgar what these structures were, and he didn't volunteer the information.

After a time, Lori said, "What *is* the Cabal? What do they want from us?"

"I don't know for sure," Edgar said. "I've asked around the Nightway, and I get different answers from different people. Some say the Cabal delight in tormenting people, that they feed on our suffering, and that the whole 'confess and atone' bit doesn't mean anything. It's just a lie to cover their true intentions."

"Do you believe that?"

He shrugged. "Some days I do. Others I don't. Who the hell can know for sure?"

The idea that the Cabal tortured their victims solely for the pleasure of it didn't feel like the right explanation to Lori. Or at least, it wasn't the complete explanation. The Cabal might enjoy the pain they caused, but during her encounters with them, she'd sensed a driving purpose behind their words and actions. More than that – an urgency – as if there was a vital importance to what they were doing, even if she couldn't understand it.

"What else have you heard?"

"That they're not real. They're demons created by the minds of disturbed individuals racked by guilt and shame over something awful that they've done."

Lori pondered this for a moment. It was an idea that was equally comforting and disturbing. Comforting in the sense that if the Cabal was a projection of her own subconscious, then that meant it could be possible for her to exert control over them somehow. But it also meant that she was, on some level at least, insane. Still, this explanation didn't make sense to her. Her mind wasn't more powerful than any other person's. She was smart, but she was no genius, and it wasn't like she had psychic powers or anything. How could she create actual living beings? No, more likely the Cabal and the Shadowkin were realistic illusions. And if so, did that mean the Nightway was an illusion, too? That Edgar was? Was she in reality lying in a bed in some mental hospital imagining all this? The last scenario seemed the most realistic of those she'd considered so far, but it still didn't feel right. Or maybe she simply didn't want to believe it. Who would?

"There's one other explanation I've heard," Edgar said. "It's kind of out there, though."

Lori laughed. "Like the others are more believable?"

He gave her a sideways glance, smiled. "True. Well, some say the Cabal's purpose is to maintain the Balance."

She frowned. "The balance between what?"

"Between what we think of as the real world and what's called Shadow."

"Like in *Shadow*kin?" she asked.

He nodded. "Each moment of time is like an entire separate universe. As one moment gives way to a new one, the old moment begins to die. The dark energy produced by these deaths creates a realm all its own. It's like...." He paused, considering. "Like part of a shoreline being eroded and falling into the ocean. Except in this case, it's the falling that *creates* the ocean. Does that make sense?"

"Not really," she admitted. "But go on."

"Some creatures thrive in Shadow, whether they're things born there or people who can sense it and move back and forth between it and the real world. The creatures native to Shadow feed on the death of all those moments in time that create their world. They break it down, and process it so it can then go on to feed the Gyre. They kind of pre-digest its food for it. The Shadowkin are such creatures. They're ravenous, mindless things." He tapped his chest. "Not all that different from insects in a lot of ways."

Lori wanted to ask him what the Gyre was, but she didn't want to stray too far from what she really needed to know. "So why do the Shadowkin seem so drawn to me?"

He shrugged. "That I don't know."

"Okay, then can you tell me how the Cabal figures into all of this?"

"The creatures natural to Shadow can be greedy. Their hunger is never sated, and they try to find their way into the real world to feed on it. Destroying it, breaking it down. The Cabal exists to make sure that doesn't happen. They work to keep Shadow and the real world separate as much as possible, although even with all their efforts, there are still some places where the worlds intersect."

"What about the Nightway?"

"It's connected to both Shadow and the real world. And to neither. Basically, it's its own thing."

That didn't make any sense to her, but she decided to let it go. "So what you're saying is that, according to this explanation, the Cabal are really the good guys?" She couldn't keep the disbelief out of her voice.

"I wouldn't go that far. I don't think they give much of a damn for either world or the beings that inhabit them. All they care about is the Balance, and they'll do whatever is necessary to maintain it, without any concern for who they might hurt in the process. They're like sociopathic doctors who don't give a shit about their patients, only about solving medical problems."

"So if this explanation is true, that means the Cabal thinks we've both done something to upset the Balance between Shadow and the real world?

"Or at least threaten it," Edgar said.

She mulled this over for a time. If the Cabal were like doctors, it would make sense why they were so enigmatic in how they went about their work. They'd be like surgeons, operating very carefully, in limited, controlled ways, so they could fix a problem without causing additional damage. It was a concept she was well familiar with as a physical therapist. Therapy needed to be specifically targeted to a client's needs, without making their condition worse or causing any new problems.

So the Cabal are basically the PTs of the universe, she thought, and despite the situation, the notion made her smile. "So if we can figure out what we did to screw up the Balance...." she began.

"We can confess and, more importantly, atone," Edgar said. "Easier said than done, though. I've been trying to figure out what the hell I did for years, and so far, I haven't had much luck."

The thought that she might end up like Edgar, as a sort of Flying Dutchman of the Nightway, endlessly on the run from the Cabal while trying to figure out what they wanted her to do, sounded like a kind of Purgatory to her, if not actual damnation. She'd prefer to avoid that fate if she could.

"We're here," Edgar said.

CHAPTER ELEVEN

Lori peered through the windshield. At first she saw only a glow of blue-white light spread against the darkness, but then she began to make out shapes – lots of them. She thought they might be trees, but they were too uniform in size to be organic. As the van drew closer, she saw what she was looking at were wooden poles about eight feet in height, with a crosspiece on top to form a large letter T, topped with a fluorescent light. There were dozens of poles, spread out alongside the road and continuing back into the darkness, making it impossible to guess how many there might be. There were objects on the Ts, and these objects had heads, arms, and legs. She realized then that she wasn't looking at Ts – she was looking at *crosses*, all of which had people affixed to them.

"Fuck me," she said softly.

Edgar said nothing. He pulled the van to the side of the road and turned off the engine and the headlights. Everything went dark for a moment, but then individual fluorescent lights came on above the crosses, bulbs attached to lengths of metal that rose from behind the wooden structures and curved downward to hang above them, illuminating the people on the crosses in pools of blue white. The people were naked and represented a mix of ages, races, and body types. Men and women were equally present. The people were bound to the crosses by tight coils of barbed wire around their wrists and ankles, but as painful as that looked, it was nothing compared to the other condition they all shared. Their abdomens had been slit open from sternum to crotch, and their internal organs were now external ones. Viscera spilled forth from body cavities and hung down past the victims' feet, entrails making soft, glistening piles on the ground beneath them. The lower halves of their bodies were streaked with blood, and the ground around the base of the crosses was soaked with the red stuff. But as horrifying a sight as the mass crucifixion was, far worse was the fact that each one of these men, women, and children were still alive. Pain-filled eyes blinked as tears flowed freely, mouths opened and closed silently as if their owners were trying to speak but could not. Bodies writhed in agony, some of their exertions so violent it was clear they were trying to shake themselves free. But all they did was cause the barbed wire to dig deeper into their flesh, fresh blood flowing from those new wounds. Lori didn't understand how anyone could survive like this for any length of time. They should all be dead. But they weren't, and she supposed she shouldn't have been surprised. This was the Nightway, after all.

She experienced an urge to tell Edgar to start the van, pull back onto the road, and drive away from this awful place as fast as he could. She almost did it, too. But she thought of her family and friends, of what the Cabal might be doing to them at this very moment, and she said nothing. They both sat there for a moment, gazing at the nightmarish tableau. Then Edgar got out of the van, and a couple seconds later, Lori did the same, keeping the blanket wrapped around her more for the security of it than any sense of modesty. Self-consciousness about her own nakedness seemed almost obscene among so many unclothed and violated bodies.

Edgar came around to the passenger side of the van, opened the door, and leaned inside. He opened the glove box, retrieved an object, then stepped back and closed the door. Lori saw that he held what looked like a gun in his right hand. At least it was shaped like a gun, but it was white and made of a number of smaller pieces that had been put together.

Those are bones, she thought. *Small ones, like you'd find in a foot or hand.*

"What's that?" she asked.

"That's just in case," Edgar said.

"Good idea."

The two of them walked around to the other side of the van and surveyed the scene before them.

"God*damn,*" he said. "And I thought void crawlers stank."

Lori was too busy gagging to respond. The air was filled with the coppery tang of blood, so strong she could taste it. When she'd been a child, she'd bit the tip of her tongue while talking to a friend in her parents' kitchen. She tried to recall which friend it had been. *Aashrita?* Maybe. It hadn't hurt all that much, but it bled like mad, and her mouth quickly filled with blood. Terrified, she'd tried to cry out for help, but all she succeeded in doing was spraying blood all over (Aashrita) her friend, who immediately started screaming.

The smell here was bad, but equally horrifying to Lori was the low buzzing thrum that hung heavy in the air. Flies covered the victims' exposed organs, crawling across them, traveling back and forth between the crosses, searching for just the right place to lay their eggs. She glanced at Edgar. He gazed upon the bodies nearest the edge of the road, swaying slightly, as if in time to music only he could hear. The man had said he hated bugs, but that was before he became a host to a legion of them. Perhaps because of his little hard-shelled friends, the flies' droning sounded quite different to him than it did to her.

She caught movement out of the corner of her eyes, and her first thought was a cloud of flies had abandoned one of the corpses and was coming toward them. She raised her hands, intending to fend off the insects, but when she turned in that direction, she saw no mass of flies streaking toward them. Instead, she saw a figure – a person, or something shaped very much like a person – walking with sandaled feet across the blood-soaked ground. There was something about the way the figure moved, a subtle grace that Lori thought of as feminine, although it was difficult to gauge gender given the way he or she was dressed – a loose-fitting brown robe cinched at the right shoulder like a toga, leaving the left arm free, and beneath this a plain white shirt with long wide-cuffed sleeves. The figure wore a head covering that looked something like an unadorned bishop's miter, made of simple white cloth, with thin strips hanging down on either side. The outfit looked like something that might've been worn around the time of the Roman Empire, but the cloth looked relatively new, and it was clean. Not a spot of blood on it. The person's face was covered by a white cloth mask, which had no openings for eyes, nose, or mouth. Lori found the effect eerie, especially once she noticed the figure's hands were covered by white gloves, its feet by white socks. What if there was no person beneath the cloth? What if there was simply nothing?

The figure stopped when it was within five feet of them. It had kept its arm at its sides the whole way, and it made no move to raise them now.

"Welcome. I am the Haruspex, and this—" the figure gestured toward the crosses and the people bound to them, "—is the Garden of Anguish. Have you come seeking knowledge?"

Edgar said nothing. He'd warned Lori that he was going to drop her off and leave, and yet here he was, standing next to her. It was clear, however, that he didn't intend to take the lead in dealing with the Haruspex.

"Yes," Lori answered, throat so dry she could barely get the word out.

"This is good. If you had stopped for any other reason, I would have been forced to kill you both and use you as fertilizer for my crop. Rules, you know."

The Haruspex's voice was calm, soothing, genderless, and devoid of all emotion save for a mild pleasantness. Lori watched the area of the mask over where the Haruspex's mouth should be, but she saw no sign of lips moving.

"What's a Haruspex?" Lori asked. "I'm not familiar with the term."

The cloth-faced creature regarded her for a moment with whatever senses it possessed.

"It's a Roman word. A Haruspex was a priest who divined knowledge by examining the entrails of sacrificed animals. Although in my case, I don't do the interpreting. That you do yourself. My Garden is like a buffet in that sense. I supply the meat – you serve yourself."

A breathy *sss-sss-sss* came from the Haruspex, and it took Lori a moment to realize the creature was laughing, or at least doing its version of it.

"Exactly how does this work?" Lori asked.

"The process is simple," the Haruspex said. "Just start walking among the crosses until one of the bodies speaks to you, both literally and figuratively. Everyone has someone waiting for them in the Garden. Someone *special*."

Edgar winced at this, and she understood why he didn't want to accompany her into the Garden. He feared confronting whoever was waiting for him within. She felt the same, but if she was to have any hope of finding some way to restore her life to normal, she had no choice but to enter the Garden and face whatever she found there.

"What do I do after I go in?" she asked.

"It all depends on which of my beautiful flowers stops you," the Haruspex said. "Since the earliest days of your species, if one wished to gain insight into that which was hidden, one needed to peer inside the greatest mystery of all – a living body. What makes its heart beat, its lungs breathe, its blood flow…. What makes it love, makes it hate, makes it afraid? Where is the soul, and once it is located, what secrets might it share with us? Can it tell us what is happening now, far away from our sight? Can it show us that which is to come, and how to ensure those events come to pass – or how to prevent them from occurring? Can it show us the past, shadows of memory we can barely recall, nightmares we lived but fear to revisit?"

These last words hit Lori like a hammer blow. She wanted to remember what had happened to Aashrita and why, but she was also deeply terrified of discovering the truth.

"All of these things can be learned in my Garden. All you have to do is be brave – or foolish – enough to enter."

The Haruspex had no visible mouth, but Lori heard the smile in its voice as it spoke this final sentence.

So far, Edgar had listened without saying anything, but now he asked, "And what is the price for this knowledge?"

"Price?" the Haruspex said. Lori heard the smile in its voice again. "What makes you think there's a price?"

"Because there's *always* one on the Nightway," Edgar said.

Lori looked at the man's prosthetic legs and thought of the price he'd had to pay for the beetles' help in escaping the Vermilion Tower.

"Of course, you are correct," the Haruspex admitted. "The price for knowledge gained here is a simple one. You must help me tend to the Garden."

"What sort of 'help' would I have to do?" Lori asked.

"That will be revealed when all your questions have been answered," the Haruspex said.

"That's bullshit," Edgar said. He turned to Lori. "You know that, right?"

"Maybe," she said. "But what choice do I have? I need to *know*."

"No, you don't. You can come with me. You can run."

It was a tempting offer. She had no way of knowing what would happen to her inside the Garden, or even if she'd survive the ordeal. And she had no idea what sort of price she'd have to pay for the knowledge she sought. Knowledge that she needed, even if she didn't want it.

She thought of Aashrita's headstone, rain running down its face, over her name and her birth and death dates.

"I have to," she said.

Edgar looked at her for a long moment before nodding.

"Then it is settled," the Haruspex said. "I have already prepared the auguries for you. All part of the service."

Lori had thought both of the Haruspex's hands had been empty, but now she saw the being clutched a long, wicked-looking knife in its right hand, the blade covered with old, dried blood, as if it had never been cleaned. Had the blade been there before? Had it just appeared? Really, what did it matter? It was there now.

She held the blanket tight around her as she began walking between the rows of crosses. The cloth did little to keep her warm, but she didn't know if that was due to the temperature here or if it was caused by her fear. Either way, she wished she had a sweater. A warm jacket would be nice, too. Most of all, she wished she had some fucking shoes. The ground here was gritty and sandy, as she'd experienced elsewhere in this realm, and it hurt to walk on with bare feet. But that wasn't the main reason she wanted shoes. It was so the flesh of her feet wouldn't come into contact with any of the blood that had been spilled here, of which there was a copious amount. It made the sand clump together in a manner that reminded Lori of what litter did when cats peed in their box. The thought was so ridiculous she almost laughed, but she stopped herself. She feared if she started laughing now, she would never be able to quit.

The blood-stink was worse this close to the bodies. No, not bodies. *People.* They weren't dead yet, although they probably wished they were. She knew she would if she were in their place. There were other odors here, too. A smell like raw chicken, which she assumed came from the victims' exposed organs. The musky scent of shit and the ammonia smell of piss, both the result of crucified bodies expelling whatever waste remained within them. Another reason to wish she had shoes. The Garden wasn't silent. People moaned and whispered, drew in slow, painful breaths, mumbled prayers to whatever gods might exist to put them out of their misery. But if there were any such gods, it seemed they weren't listening.

The crosses were arranged in neat rows regularly spaced from one another. It felt like she was walking through some nightmarish version of a cornfield, except the stalks held more than just ears – they had entire bodies on them. She felt laughter threatening again, and this time she bit her lip hard, hoping the pain would help her hold it back. She tasted blood, and she thought once more about that time she was a child and had bit her tongue.

"That was really gross."

The voice was so soft, Lori almost didn't hear it. She stopped and turned in the direction she thought the voice had originated from. *A girl's voice,* she thought.

There, two crosses to her right, hung a brown-skinned girl, nine, maybe ten years old. Like all the others in the Garden, she was bound to her cross with barbed wire, and her flat tummy had been sliced open, her innards splayed onto the ground at her feet. Flies crawled over her organs, infested her open body cavity, buzzed around her head, landed on her face, scuttled across the soft flesh there.... Despite her condition, the girl's eyes were wide open and alert, and she watched Lori with intense interest.

Lori experienced no shock of recognition upon seeing the girl, but she did feel a sort of tickle at the back of her mind, along with a tightening in her gut.

You don't want to do this, she thought. It was true. She didn't. But she walked over to the girl and stood before her anyway.

"Do you know me?" she asked.

"Oh yes," the girl said. Her voice was weak, but this close Lori could hear her well enough. The girl leaned her head to the right, then the left. Lori had the sense she was trying to draw her attention to something, but she didn't—

Her gaze focused on the girl's inner forearms, first right, then left. They were sliced open from wrist to elbow, the cuts deep. Unlike her abdominal wound, which bled freely, the blood around these cuts was old and crusted.

Lori's head swam and her vision blurred. She took several steps back from the girl, her movements awkward, clumsy. She felt numb, disconnected from her body, and she thought she was going to faint. She fought to hold on to consciousness, and while for several seconds the outcome was in doubt, she managed to remain aware and on her feet. When her vision cleared, she saw the girl was now a young woman, probably in her late teens. Lori recognized this version of her, just as she'd recognized the previous one, but this time she was able to give her a name.

"Aashrita," she said.

The young woman gave her a weak smile. "Yes," she breathed.

Was this the real Aashrita, somehow brought back from the dead, or was it something that only looked like her? Lori hoped the latter but feared the former was the truth. She felt memories beginning to crowd at the threshold of her mind, screaming to be allowed in. This was why she had come here, why she'd gone to Aashrita's grave in the first place – to get answers. All she had to do was allow the memories to come. But she couldn't. It wasn't a matter of choice, a mere exercise of willpower. She simply could not allow the memories in, knew if she did, they would destroy her. The mental struggle was too much, and pain erupted in her skull as a migraine flared to sudden life. It hurt so much that tears streamed from her eyes, and her vision narrowed to pinpoints. She had to get out of here – now.

She turned to flee, the blanket falling away from her naked body as she did. But she only managed a few hobbling steps on her bad knee before something flew over her head, came down around her bare waist, and started pulling her backward. She fought it, gritted her teeth, put all of her strength into moving forward. She reached down to take hold of whatever it was that had wrapped around her and felt something soft, spongy, and wet. She looked down in revulsion and saw that her hands were slick with blood. A cord of some kind pressed tight against her flesh, bumpy and pinkish-pale. It was a length of intestine, she realized. Aashrita's.

Lori continued to move forward. Another loop of intestine wrapped around her left wrist, and yet another encircled her right. Still she fought, although her movements were almost completely restricted now. The intestines were slick, though, so if she could manage to wriggle free….

A last loop came down over her head and pulled tight around her throat, immediately cutting off her air. She tried to reach for the portion of intestine choking her, hoping to loosen it so she could draw in a breath. But her arms were held away from her body, and regardless of how hard she struggled, she couldn't budge them. She was restrained in four places now – waist, wrists, and neck – and the intestine, flexing like a giant constrictor, lifted her off her feet.

When she'd been a kid, she'd read somewhere that together the human large and small intestines measured around twenty-five feet. That had sounded so long, and she'd found it hard to believe that all of it could fit inside a person. She had no trouble believing it now, though.

Aashrita's intestines raised her several feet higher, turned her around to face the young woman and brought her closer until their noses practically touched. Flies now buzzed around both their heads.

Aashrita's eyes bored into hers, shining with eager anticipation. "I'd like to say I don't want to do this to you." Aashrita's weak voice was stronger now. "But that would be a lie."

The coil of intestine wrapped around Lori's neck began to squeeze tighter. Her lungs blazed with fire and her head pounded so violently she thought it was going to explode. Darkness crept into her vision, and she realized she was going to die – strangled by the internal organ of a girl she'd worked so hard and so long to forget. She was surprised by how little this distressed her.

I deserve it, she thought.

She fell into blackness, and there, in the great nothing, her memories broke free at last.

★   ★   ★

Lori sat on her parents' front porch, right leg resting on a pillow her mother had brought out and put on a stool for her. A pair of metal crutches lay on the porch next to the chair. It was late afternoon in September, but the day was summer-warm, and she wore a T-shirt and shorts. No shoes. Despite the temperature, she had a fuzzy blanket draped across her legs. She didn't want to look at the angry red incision on her knee, didn't want to gaze upon the swollen, puffy flesh there. The knee throbbed with pain, but she'd discovered it was worse – or at least felt worse – when she could see the incision site, so she kept it covered whenever she could. It helped. Her pain meds helped more, and while she would've loved to take some now, her next dose wasn't due for two more hours. She'd just have to tough it out until then.

Even though her meds had nearly worn off, she still felt spacy, and she sat looking out at the street, headphones in, listening to an Alicia Keys song on her MP3 player, and not thinking about much of anything.

After the accident during soccer practice, she'd needed to have a knee replacement, and now she had to wear a CPM – Continuous Passive Motion – machine to slowly move and strengthen her leg several hours a day, as well as doing physical therapy. At first, both had hurt like hell, even with pain meds, but the pain had continued to decrease as the days went by. At this point in her recovery, she didn't use the CPM much, and she could get around without her crutches, unless she was tired or her knee started hurting too bad. She'd originally come outside so she could walk up and down the street and exercise her knee, as her physical therapist had told her to do. But once she'd gotten outside and felt the warm air, she'd said to hell with it and sat down on the porch and put her leg up. She was finding it increasingly difficult to stay motivated when it came to her rehab. Sure, she wanted to get back to the point where she could get around normally all on her own. But no matter how hard she worked, she wouldn't be able to play soccer again, so really, what good were the painful exercises her PT wanted her to do? No matter how religiously she did them, she'd never be able to get back her full strength and speed. And if she tried to play, she'd risk screwing up her knee replacement, and she did *not* want to go through another operation and long recovery period.

So basically, her life sucked.

She'd sit out here for a half hour or so, and then go back inside. With any luck, her mother wouldn't realize she hadn't actually gone anywhere. Lori promised herself she'd go walking tomorrow, but she knew she didn't mean it.

So she was in a dark frame of mind when she saw Aashrita coming down the sidewalk. Aashrita lived a couple blocks from Lori's house, and while Lori only had one sibling – Reeny – Aashrita had four brothers and sisters, two of each, all older than her. She needed to escape the chaos in her house on a regular basis, and when she did, she'd walk over to Lori's place and the two of them would hang out. It had been that way for the better part of a decade now, but Lori hadn't seen Aashrita since the accident during soccer practice. Aashrita hadn't visited her in the hospital, nor had she been over to the house since then. She had sent a get-well card, however, a small one that had come in a blue envelope. When Lori had opened it, it had begun playing music – soft and slow – in electronic tones, and it had contained a single printed word: *Sorry*, below which Aashrita had signed her name. Lori hadn't replied. No calls, no texts, no emails. She'd been so damn angry at Aashrita that she hadn't wanted to talk to her, see her, or even think about her.

So Lori was not pleased when Aashrita reached her parents' front walkway, turned, and started walking toward the porch. Toward *her*.

If she'd had full mobility back, she would've gotten up from the chair, quickly gone inside, and shut the door before Aashrita could reach the porch. But she didn't want Aashrita to see her awkward movements as she reached for the crutches and tried to get to her feet, so she remained seated.

Lori tried to read Aashrita's face as she approached. She saw several different emotions there – fear, hope, anticipation, guilt, shame, defensiveness – all swirling together in an uneasy mix. Like Lori, Aashrita was also dressed in T-shirt and shorts, only her shirt was the one given out by the Oakmont Recreational Soccer League. Had she worn the fucking shirt on purpose, intending to mock her, or had she simply been unaware of the ramifications of wearing it to visit the girl whose knee she'd fucked up so badly it'd had to be replaced? Either way, it was a pretty shitty thing to do.

Aashrita came halfway up the porch steps and stopped, as if reluctant to come any closer. Maybe she felt she needed permission to step all the way onto the porch. Maybe she wanted to keep her distance to avoid getting an up-close look at the damage she'd caused to Lori's body.

"Hey." Aashrita's voice was tentative, the word almost a question. *Are you willing to talk to me?*

Lori did *not* want to talk to her, wanted to tell her to turn around and get the hell out of there. But she found herself saying hey back, her tone neutral, noncommittal.

"How are you, uh, doing?" Aashrita asked.

Lori felt grim satisfaction upon seeing how uncomfortable she was. Bitch *should* be uncomfortable.

"I'm all right. Getting better every day." She spoke these words with a cold edge that she didn't bother trying to hide.

"Good. Glad to hear it."

Lori didn't respond to this. She just looked at Aashrita, watched her grow ever more uneasy as the silence stretched between them. She liked seeing Aashrita this way, liked seeing her *hurt*. If only a little.

"I'm sorry I didn't come over sooner. I...was afraid you wouldn't want to see me. You know, because of the accident."

Was it an accident? Lori thought. *Or were you tired of not being the best on the team, so you decided to take out the competition?*

Lori knew this wasn't fair of her. Aashrita had never shown any sign of being jealous of her before, and honestly, had Lori *really* been the best player on the team? She'd been good, one of the best, but *the* best? That was debatable. This was a reasonable way to look at the situation, an *adult* way. But she didn't want to be reasonable. She was angry, and she wanted to lash out at the girl who had robbed her of her future.

With a magician's flourish, she pulled the blanket off her legs and tossed it aside.

"So what do you think? Pleased with your handiwork?"

Aashrita flinched as if Lori had slapped her.

Lori continued speaking, her voice becoming louder and angrier as she went on.

"I'm never going to be able to play sports again – not unless I want to risk fucking up my new knee. Hell, right now it's all I can do to walk up and down the street a couple times. It still hurts like a bitch, too – especially if I use it too much. My physical therapist says it won't hurt forever, but I think he's full of shit. I think it's *always* going to hurt. Maybe not as much as now, but I think the pain is never going to not be there. I'll have it – and the scar – to remind me of you for the rest of my life. Better than signing my senior yearbook, right?"

Lori knew she was being cruel, but she couldn't stop herself. And part of her didn't want to stop, wanted to keep on hurting Aashrita.

"Don't know what I'm going to do about college now that a soccer scholarship is out of the question. Maybe I'll get a job at a fast-food place after graduation instead. 'Would you like fries with that?' How'd I do? Think I got what it takes?"

She thought Aashrita might get angry and lash out at her. Lori wanted her to, wanted to get into a shouting match with her, wanted to yell and scream and cuss her out. But Aashrita said nothing. Her eyes shimmered with tears, but they did not fall, not yet.

"I'm sorry, Lori. It was an accident. I didn't mean it. I'd do anything to take it back."

"Well…. There is one way you could make it up to me."

Aashrita wiped the nascent tears from her eyes and gave Lori an uncertain half-smile.

"What is it?"

Lori's words came out of her mouth like daggers of ice. "Go kill yourself, you brown bitch."

She shocked herself, perhaps more for the racist barb she'd hurled than for telling Aashrita to commit suicide. She was deeply ashamed, but at the same time she felt dark satisfaction at knowing how much her words had hurt her friend. Her *former* friend.

Aashrita's eyes went wide and the tears came now, flowing fast and free. She looked at Lori for several seconds, mouth open as if she might say something. But then she whirled around and ran down the walkway. She kept running when she reached the sidewalk and didn't look back.

Lori almost called out for her to stop, almost shouted that she was sorry, that she hadn't meant it. But she remained silent and watched Aashrita go, not knowing it was the last time she'd see her friend alive.

* * *

Lori fell out of the memory and found herself looking into Aashrita's face – the version of the woman whose exposed intestines had a life of their own. They were still almost nose to nose, and the loops of organ still wrapped tight around Lori and held her above the ground. The loop coiled around her throat had loosened a little, just enough so she could breathe, but only shallowly. A cloud of flies still buzzed around them.

"You didn't know depression ran in my family, did you?" Aashrita said. Her voice started out weak but grew stronger and more forceful as she went on. "My family was in denial of it. They self-medicated – Dad with booze, Mom with drugs. My brothers and sisters used both in various amounts and combinations. And when my parents saw I was quiet, moody, and withdrawn, they assumed it was nothing but normal teenage angst. Nothing to be concerned about." She released a bitter laugh. "No therapy or antidepressants necessary. 'She'll grow out of it,' they told each other. 'It's just a phase.' They knew better when they found me in the bathtub later that night. The water was long cold by the time they entered the bathroom, but it was still red. I'd used a pair of garment scissors to slice deep vertical gashes in my forearms, just like I'd read on the Internet you were supposed to if you wanted to do it right. The scissors lay on the bathmat, blood on them still wet.

"You know what the funny thing is? The racism didn't bother me all that much. You kind of get used to it after a while. It hurt because it came from *you*. You called me a brown bitch not because you were racist, but because you knew how much it would hurt me to hear those words come out of your mouth."

"I didn't mean to hurt you," Lori said. "No, that's a lie. I *did* want to hurt you. I blamed you for my knee getting fucked up, and I wanted to get back at you in some small way. I was a stupid, self-absorbed teenager wallowing in pointless anger."

While she would've hopefully found her way out of that emotional state on her own eventually, Aashrita's death – and the guilt and shame she felt over the way she'd treated her friend the afternoon before she killed herself – had shocked her out of it. She'd stopped focusing on herself after that, dedicated herself to helping others. As a PT student in college and as a professional working at Get Moving!, she'd come to have a much better understanding of how people could react emotionally to receiving a chronic injury. Her own experience with such feelings gave her far more empathy for her clients than a lot of other PTs had. But while her guilt had motivated her to make positive changes in her life, it had also caused her to bury the memory of Aashrita's suicide, and sometimes she didn't remember Aashrita at all. She remembered now, though, and she wouldn't allow herself to forget again.

"You say you wanted to get back at me in a small way?" Aashrita's voice burned with barely restrained anger now. "Well, small actions can have pretty goddamn big consequences!"

Lori said nothing for a moment. She looked into Aashrita's eyes as the woman's words sank in.

"You're what I need to confess to and atone for," she said. "I mean, what I did to you. You were teetering on the edge, and I thoughtlessly pushed you over. I'm so, so sorry."

"You can't confess to me. I already know what you did. But congratulations on your little epiphany anyway. There's more you need to know, though. A lot more. Think you're ready?"

Lori answered truthfully. "I'm not sure."

Aashrita's smile was cold. "Too bad. You don't have a choice."

Aashrita's brow furrowed in concentration, and her facial muscles tensed. Lori heard a wet tearing sound, and Aashrita let out a cry of pain. The lower end of her intestine came slithering out from her body cavity, disturbing the flies gathered there. The intestine swayed like a viperous snake, and Lori realized she was looking at Aashrita's colon. She'd caused it to tear free from her anus, and now it was rising further upward, snaking between their two bodies.

"We've covered the past," Aashrita said. "Now I need to show you the present and the future. I wouldn't be much use as an augur if I confined myself solely to what was, would I?"

Lori tried to protest, but the colon shot toward her mouth, slid past her teeth, and wiggled its way down her throat. And then it began pumping something thick and sludgy into her. She tried to scream, but all that came out was a muffled moan.

Images began to flash across her consciousness. She saw Shadowkin moving through the streets of Oakmont, destroying anything in their path, including people. There were so many, far more than had broken into her apartment last night, and more than she'd seen at the cemetery. Three times that number, maybe more. They moved so swiftly, killed so many.... They were far stronger now than they'd been when they'd broken into her apartment. They'd fed on her then, taken some of her strength. And had they retreated afterward so that they could digest what they'd taken? She thought so.

The images changed then, and she saw Melinda, Katie, and Justin riding together in Melinda's white SUV. Melinda drove, her gray braid swishing back and forth behind her head while Katie – who now had tufts of fur on her face, along with cat teeth and cat eyes – scanned the sidewalk for something. Or some*one*. Justin sat in the back, face expressionless, his shirt open to reveal a chest covered with a mass of misshapen, discolored growths. What the hell had happened to them, and how had they ended up together? But she knew the answer to that, didn't she?

The Cabal.

The images in her mind changed yet again, and now she saw the inside of Horizon's Edge Mall, saw people running, mothers with children mostly, saw bodies and blood.... Reeny was on her knees, tears streaming from her eyes, mouth open in a silent scream as she cradled the limp body of Brian. Lori's nephew had blood on him, a lot of it. Near Reeny and Brian lay the body of a uniformed police officer, gun in hand, the top of her head blown off. There was lots of blood on her, too, but her features were clear enough, and Lori saw she was one of the two officers that had come to her apartment last night to investigate the Shadowkin's break-in. Officer...McGuire. She'd never learned the woman's first name, but that didn't matter. All that mattered was poor Brian and her devastated sister. Lori focused on them, tried to reach out mentally to Reeny, to let her know she was not alone in her grief.

Then Brian opened his eyes.

Lori felt almost giddy with relief. He wasn't dead! He was only wounded, and despite all the blood, evidently not too seriously, for he sat up easily, displaying no sign of distress. He started speaking, and although these visions came with no sound, she could tell by the increasingly angry expression on Reeny's face that whatever her son was saying, it was making her furious. What the hell—

The vision faded, was replaced by yet another.

This time she saw a scene of Oakmont viewed from above, as if she were flying over the town. There wasn't much left, just some scattered buildings here and there. Most of the structures had been destroyed, reduced to broken brick and concrete, splintered lengths of wood, shards of shattered glass, bent and twisted metal. The ground was torn up too, as if dozens of tanks had rolled through, treads churning the soil. It looked as if a mass of tornadoes had swept through Oakmont, their merciless winds pulverizing everything in their path. There were bodies, too, so many of them, some more or less intact, some only partials, others smears of bloody meat and crushed bone. There were no signs of life, not even animals – no dogs or cats, no birds.

She tried to scream, needed to release the horror she felt, but the sludge from Aashrita's colon was still being extruded into her, and it clogged her throat, and she could make no sound. And then the coils of intestine grew slack and she slipped through them. As she fell to the ground, the end that had been forced into her mouth came free, and she was able to breathe again. She pushed herself onto her hands and knees, her body shaking so violently that it was all she could do to keep from collapsing back onto the ground. She opened her mouth to scream at last, but instead a torrent of thick black liquid shot forth. The muck that came out of her smelled foul – and tasted worse – and the sensation caused her to vomit even harder. She continued vomiting, abdominal muscles contracting painfully, spine arched and rigid, for what seemed like hours. But eventually the flood of sludge became a trickle, and then she was dry heaving. She felt the blanket being draped over her body, and she might've flinched at the unexpected contact if she hadn't been so physically spent.

"You okay?" Edgar said. "Sorry – stupid question. Of course you aren't. Want to try and stand?"

She realized her migraine was gone, not a trace of it remaining. That at least was something. She nodded weakly, and Edgar gently helped her to her feet. Her legs were wobbly, and Edgar kept hold of her left arm to steady her. She saw he'd tucked his strange weapon into the waistband of his pants to leave his hands free. *Is that a gun in your pants or are you just glad to see me?* she thought, and almost laughed, but she was too weak. She didn't want to look at Aashrita, partly out of shame for what she'd done to the girl, but also because of what this version of Aashrita – whether it was truly her or some kind of monstrous duplicate – had done to her. She'd helped her remember, had showed her visions that she didn't understand, but which she knew were important. But she had violated her in the process in an unspeakably horrible manner. She looked, though. She felt she owed her that much.

Aashrita was still bound to the T-cross, but her flesh now sagged on her frame, flowed slowly downward like melting wax. Her features were distorted, almost unrecognizable, but her eyes remained unaffected and they fixed on Lori. The anger that had blazed within them a moment ago was gone. Lori saw sadness in them now, along with love and…was that forgiveness? Lori didn't know for certain, but she desperately hoped so. Then the eyes liquefied, just as the rest of Aashrita's body was doing. In a sudden rush, the meat slid off her skeleton all at once. The bones quickly followed suit, and the mass puddled at the base of the cross, where it slowly began to be absorbed into the gritty black soil. Lori saw that the sludge she'd vomited was doing the same thing, disappearing into the ground. When both the vomit and Aashrita's remains were gone, the fluorescent light attached to her cross flickered and died. The flies that had been clustered on Aashrita's body had taken to the air when she began to melt, and now they flew off in search of new hosts for their eggs.

Lori realized then that she hadn't seen Larry in any of the visions that Aashrita had shown her. Did that mean he was okay, that the Cabal hadn't done anything to him? At least, hadn't done anything to him *yet*? She hoped so. If even one of her family and friends was safe, it would be something she could hold onto, one small glint of hope in what was otherwise becoming an increasingly dark picture.

"Have you gotten what you came for?"

Lori turned, startled. She hadn't heard the Haruspex approach. As she looked upon the being's featureless cloth face, it struck her that this creature was perfect for tending the Garden of Anguish as it was kind of a scarecrow, albeit one garbed in more sophisticated-looking clothing than most.

"Yes," she said.

The Haruspex inclined its head in a nod. She saw that it still held the wicked-looking knife in its right hand down at its side, almost as if trying to conceal it, or at least not draw attention to it.

Edgar drew his bone gun and held it down at his own side, ready to use it if necessary.

"I am gratified." The creature pointed to Aashrita's cross with its free hand. "Look."

Both Lori and Edgar turned toward the empty T-cross and saw a thin tendril emerging from the soil at the base of the structure. At first Lori thought it was a plant of some kind, but then she realized that the tendril wasn't made of vegetable matter. It was made of meat. She watched as it slowly snaked up the cross, thickening and broadening as it went.

"It shall take some time," Haruspex said. "But eventually this cross will have a new occupant. I'll be interested to see who it is. It's always a surprise, but I like that. It keeps my job interesting."

"Is it…going to grow another Aashrita?" Lori asked.

Lori found the thought appalling, but in a strange way comforting as well. If Aashrita could be regrown, it meant she wasn't really dead, didn't it?

"No," the Haruspex said. "Each of my lovely flowers is unique. Once gone, they can never return. Only a new bloom can take their place."

Lori found the Haruspex's flower analogy to be exceptionally creepy, given that its 'garden' consisted of disemboweled naked people lashed to crosses by coils of barbed wire.

"Thank you for your help," she said. "But I think it's time for us to go now."

She looked to Edgar for confirmation, and he nodded.

The Haruspex stepped closer to them.

"Before you depart, we need to discuss the matter of your fee."

The Haruspex had said that in return for the knowledge she would gain, she must help out in the Garden. At the time, it hadn't seemed like too steep a price, but now….

"My Garden is thirsty," the Haruspex said. "It needs to drink in order to remain strong and healthy, for new life to grow."

The Haruspex raised its knife.

"The Garden thanks you for your contribution."

In a flash of insight, Lori understood that the Haruspex intended to water his Garden with her blood. Edgar's too, most likely. She didn't react – didn't scream, didn't try to run. She was too stunned by the visions Aashrita had shown her to think straight. She'd pushed her best friend to commit suicide, and she felt having her throat cut and bleeding to death was only fair.

The Haruspex stepped toward her, but before the creature could strike, Edgar shoved Lori aside, putting himself between her and it. He opened his mouth wide and black beetles poured forth to engulf the Haruspex. The creature staggered backward, arms flailing. Lori waited to hear the

Haruspex's shrieks as the beetles began devouring it, but the creature gave no scream, made no sound whatsoever. The insects tore at the fabric that comprised its body with their mandibles, tearing threads apart, but as swiftly as the damage was done, the Haruspex's body repaired itself, the threads rejoining and pulling tight once more. Eventually the insects gave up and began detaching themselves from the Haruspex and flying back to their host, entering his mouth once more and disappearing to wherever it was inside his body that they dwelled. The Haruspex had no mouth to smile with, but Lori heard deep satisfaction in its voice when it spoke.

"Your pets can do nothing to me. I am not made of flesh and bone."

The Haruspex raised its knife and stepped toward Lori once more. This time, Edgar raised the bone gun, aimed at the Haruspex's cloth face, and fired. As close as Lori was to the man, the sound was deafening, and she flinched.

The bullet struck the Haruspex at the point between where its eyes would've been if it had possessed facial features. The round penetrated all the way through the Haruspex's head, exiting the back in a spray of old dried leaves and feathers. The creature didn't react right away, and Lori feared the damage it had sustained would not in any way slow the thing down. But the Haruspex's grip on the knife slackened, and the blade fell to the ground. An instant later, the Haruspex joined it there, collapsing into a boneless, unmoving pile of cloth and stuffing.

A wail went up from the cross-bound – hundreds, maybe thousands of disemboweled men, women, and children – voices joining in a chorus of sorrow, as if they were in mourning for their lost master, and why not? What's a garden without a gardener? The sound was deafening, and the power of the cross-bound's unified grief was overwhelming. Lori wasn't sorry that the Haruspex was dead, but she found herself crying anyway in response to the ocean of sadness that surged around them.

Edgar kept his weapon trained on the Haruspex and they waited to see if this injury would repair itself, like those the beetles had inflicted upon the creature. But it seemed that the Haruspex was not immune to the bone gun's special ammunition. It looked like the creature was, if not exactly dead, then no longer functional, and they started for Edgar's van.

"Goddamn Nightway," Edgar said.

Lori silently agreed.

CHAPTER TWELVE

Once they were back on the road, Lori said, "That gun you used. Is it really made of bone?"

"Yep. It's called a Gravedigger Special. Picked it up during my travels when I was searching for a weapon to use against the Cabal. It fires the teeth of people who've died horrible, agonizing deaths. Their suffering is distilled into the teeth, and it's released when they hit their target. Few things can withstand a concentrated dose of another being's pain."

"Why didn't you use the gun on the Haruspex right away? Why sic your bugs on him first?"

"I only have so much ammo, and it's not easy to come by. You have to extract the teeth yourself – *as* the person is dying. I had eight rounds when we got to the Garden. Now I have seven."

Lori glanced at the glove box where the Gravedigger Special was once more stored. She wondered what it would be like to touch one of the bullets. Would you be able to feel the suffering contained within? Would the tooth burn your fingers or would it be cold as Antarctic ice? Whichever was the case, she didn't intend to find out.

She sat back in the seat and gazed out of the windshield as she thought about what she'd learned in the Garden. She didn't understand how Aashrita's death – and her role in it – had disrupted the Balance between Shadow and the real world, but the specific details didn't matter, she supposed. What mattered was that she should do what the Cabal had continually urged her to – confess and atone. But confess to *who*, atone *how*? Aashrita was dead. Twice dead if that version of her in the Garden really had been her. There was no way Lori could make any kind of amends to her. Her parents then. As far as she knew, they were both still alive and still lived in Oakmont. If she went to them, told them about her last conversation with Aashrita and asked for their forgiveness, she was confident it would count as confessing. As for atoning…. That she wasn't so sure about. But that was okay. The most important thing was that she go to Aashrita's parents and confess. The rest would fall into place afterward. She hoped. And she hoped that if she found a way to atone, the transformations the Cabal had thrust upon Justin, Melinda, and Katie would be undone. And as for Brian...maybe he would return to being a normal, *living* boy. She had to believe there was a chance of saving her family and friends, otherwise, how could she continue on?

Now that she'd decided on her next move, she needed to find a way back to the real world, and more specifically to Oakmont. She needed an exit.

When she told this to Edgar, he said, "I've been looking for one since we left the Garden. What did you think I was doing? Psychically jacking off?"

"Is that really a thing?" she asked, intrigued.

Edgar sighed.

"You can help. Keep your eyes peeled for any place that looks like heat distortion. You know, the way the air seems to ripple above a road when it's really hot out? That's a sure sign of an exit. Or an entrance. You'll get a tingly feeling on the back of your neck, too."

Lori tried to concentrate on looking for an exit, but she couldn't stop thinking about what she'd learned in the Garden. In one way, it was a relief to have her memory of that day on the porch with Aashrita back. She felt as if a piece of herself had been missing for years without her realizing it, and now she felt whole. She hardly felt good about it, though. The denial she'd engaged in for so long had caused her to become a person who went through life unaffected by the events that occurred around her, by the people she interacted with, because what did the present matter when it would soon be the past? She thought of Edgar's explanation for Shadow, how it was a realm where time went to die, a place where each tick of the clock passed through before being ultimately swallowed by entropy. She was like that too in her own way. Not only did she not try to hold on to the present, she actively consigned each moment to the past as swiftly as she could, and did her best never to think about it again. She'd always considered her forward-looking approach to life to be one of her strengths. But now she saw that it was the reason why her life was, if not exactly a mess, then stagnant. She'd let go of her romantic relationship with Larry without any great difficulty, and she'd fallen into their currently ill-defined friendship just as easily. She'd started dating Justin, but she wasn't really committed to that relationship, even to the point where the revelation of his cancer hadn't affected her all that much. She loved Reeny, but she didn't spend much time with her or her husband, Charles. And while she liked being an aunt, she didn't spend a lot of time with Brian, either. As for her parents, even though she lived in the same town as them, she hardly ever saw them. Not because there was bad blood between them, but because she rarely thought about them. It was almost like they'd ceased to exist the day she'd left home for college.

Everything that had happened since Goat-Eyes had confronted her in FoodSaver had been a nightmare, but one thing her experiences with the Cabal had done for her – they'd kept her grounded in the here and now, prevented her from dismissing and forgetting them as she'd done to so many events in her life. She knew it was possible to become too focused on the past, though. If someone wasn't careful, they could become obsessed with it, could end up drowning in guilt and remorse. But if a person ignored the past entirely, they never learned from their mistakes, left behind wreckage as they plowed through life at full speed. Forgot friends. Forgot the hurt they'd caused them, the insults, slights, disappointments, and betrayals. The deep, deep wounds, which were sometimes fatal.

Like with Aashrita.

She would find a way to atone for what she'd done. Not for herself, and not for the fucking Cabal, but for the girl who had once been her very best friend in the world.

"Shit," Edgar muttered.

Lori looked at him.

"What?"

"Don't you hear that?"

At first she had no idea what he was talking about, but then she realized the wordless voices on the radio, which she'd gotten so used to that she didn't pay attention to them anymore, sounded different. They were louder, faster, higher pitched. They sounded distressed, alarmed.

"What does it mean?" she asked.

"That someone's coming – for us."

An instant later, light shone in the rearview mirror. She turned around to look out of the back window and saw a pair of headlights off in the distance.

"And there they are," Edgar said.

"It could just be someone else traveling the Nightway," Lori said.

"Could be," Edgar said. "But it isn't. Forget about them and keep looking for an exit. We're going to need one sooner rather than later, I think."

A lone beetle emerged from the corner of his mouth, as if it was concerned about what was happening and had decided to emerge and check on the situation on behalf of the others. Edgar swept it up with his tongue, brought it back into his mouth, and sealed his lips tight to keep the little bastard where it belonged. The sight nauseated Lori, and she started to thrust it from her mind, but then she stopped. She didn't want to forget things anymore, wanted to deal with them head-on, no matter how unpleasant they might be. She owed it to Aashrita.

She did her best to focus her attention on the road ahead of them and keep watch for the rippling in the air that Edgar had said marked an exit. She couldn't help taking a look backward now and then, and each time she did, she saw the headlights of the vehicle behind them were closer.

"Can you go any faster?" she asked Edgar, worried. "Like, even a little?"

The van's engine was already rumbling loudly, and the vehicle shook and bounced as it flew down the Nightway.

"This is all she's got. It's an extermination van, not a goddamn race car!"

Edgar held the steering wheel tight, and despite his earlier advice for Lori to keep looking for an exit, his gaze kept flicking toward the rearview mirror to check how close the vehicle pursuing them had come. And it *was* pursuing them, she believed that now. The radio voices were practically screaming with urgency.

She turned around to look through the rear window once more. It was hard to judge distances on the Nightway, given the darkness and lack of visible landmarks. The vehicle was close, though. A couple of hundred feet, maybe closer. She couldn't make out the shape of the vehicle yet, but the headlights were set low and far apart. *A car,* she thought. *A big one.* And who did she know traveled the Nightway in a large vehicle, one resembling a midnight-black Cadillac? It had to be the Driver. How had the eyeless fucker found them? Edgar had said the Cabal had a more difficult time locating people on the Nightway than they did in the real world. Maybe the Driver had gotten lucky, or maybe they'd stayed at the Garden of Anguish long enough for the Cabal to get a fix on them. Or maybe the Cabal had guessed where she'd go in search of the answers she needed, and the Driver hadn't managed to reach the Garden before they departed. It didn't matter how the Driver had found them, though. It only mattered that he had.

"There!" Edgar shouted.

Lori whipped around to face the front, expecting to see another pair of headlights barreling toward them. Instead she saw a shimmering curtain of distortion ahead, on the left side of the road. They'd found an exit. Edgar yanked the steering wheel hard to the left, and the van's tires squealed. Lori could feel the van tilt to the right, and for an instant she thought Edgar had turned too sharply and the vehicle would tip over.

And that's exactly what it did.

The passenger-side window's glass shattered as the van hit the ground. The side of Lori's head smacked the remains of the window, and she felt sharp pain from the impact, as well as from glass cutting her skin. Canisters of pesticide clanged as they bounced around in the back, striking one another. What would happen if the chemicals were released? Would she and Edgar be poisoned? Could they die?

The van slid along the slick surface of the Nightway for a dozen feet before coming to a stop. The engine died, and the voices on the radio – which were shrieking now – cut off. Lori and Edgar were both belted into their seats, a fact for which Lori was grateful; otherwise Edgar would've landed on her. Edgar tried his seat belt release and found it jammed.

"Get us out of here!" he said.

Lori thought he was speaking to her, but then his beetles surged forth from his mouth. Half of them scuttled onto his seat belt and began furiously chewing at the tough fabric. The other half crawled down toward her and began working on her belt. She hadn't tried her release yet, but as fast as the beetles worked, she knew she'd be free within seconds. While the beetles chewed, Edgar tried to open the driver's-side door, but he couldn't get any leverage and was unsuccessful. He hit the window control, and luckily, it still worked. The window went down, and he grabbed hold of the doorframe just as the beetles finished chewing through his seat belt. He dropped some, but his grip held. Grunting with effort, he maneuvered his body around until he was able to pull himself through the open window and out onto the side of the van, which, Lori supposed, now counted as the vehicle's roof.

The beetles working on her seat belt finished, and then they all took to the air, flying up and out of the open window, presumably to join their master. A second later, Edgar reached down for her.

"Take my hand!"

As Lori contorted herself into a position where she could do as Edgar wanted, light flooded the van's interior. The Driver had arrived.

Lori popped open the glove box and grabbed hold of the Gravedigger Special. Then she took Edgar's hand, and the man pulled her up. She used her feet to help propel herself upward, and a few seconds later she was outside, crouching on top of the van next to Edgar, gun held tight. She hadn't been able to grab hold of the blanket as she exited the vehicle, and she was naked and cold. She hadn't grabbed her purse either, which meant it – and her phone – were still somewhere in the van. She didn't remember seeing her purse as she climbed out, and even if she had, retrieving it hadn't been her first priority. Getting the fuck out of the van had.

The beetles hadn't re-entered Edgar's body. Instead they buzzed angrily around his head, as if ready for battle. Lori thought that if she survived this, she might actually grow to like the carnivorous little fuckers.

She saw the car that had pulled up close to them was indeed the Driver's vehicle. He got out, leaving his engine running and the headlights on, and he walked toward them. He wore his crimson robe – *Must be a pain in the ass to drive in,* Lori thought – with the hood back. He had on a pair of sunglasses, but he removed them and tucked them into a pocket, revealing the smooth, pulsating patches of flesh that covered his eye sockets.

"Thanks for making it easy for me to catch up," the Driver said, smiling. He looked at Edgar and his smile widened. "Hello, old friend. I'm surprised to find you in Ms. Palumbo's company. Helping her was a mistake, you know. You might have thought you've been evading us all these years, but we've always known where you were. We could've reclaimed you whenever we wished. We hoped that giving you a long leash might help you discover what you did to upset the Balance and how to correct it. It appears that hope was in vain, though. Pity."

Edgar pointed at the Driver and shouted, "Eat him down to the fucking bone!"

The beetles surged toward the Driver in a large black cloud.

The Driver's smile didn't falter as the beetles came at him. He then did something Lori hadn't thought possible – he opened his eyes. The patches of skin stretched tight and split apart, blood running down his cheeks like red tears. The Driver had no eyeballs in his sockets, only twin pools of darkness. The ebon substance blasted forth from the Driver's head to engulf the beetles, and they disappeared inside it, the buzzing of their wings suddenly muffled, as if the insects still flew, only now they were very far away. The darkness rushed back inside the Driver's head, curling into his sockets like sentient smoke. When it was back where it belonged, the skin patches resealed, became smooth and unbroken, but the blood that had fallen onto his cheeks remained there.

The beetles were gone.

Edgar stared at the Driver in shocked disbelief.

"You motherfucker!" he shouted.

Before he could react any further, another pair of headlights appeared in the distance. This vehicle, however, had flashing red-and-blue lights on top.

Rauch, Lori thought.

She heard the rumble of a motorcycle engine then, and she turned to look in the other direction and saw a single headlight approaching. *Goat-Eyes,* she guessed. Who else would it be?

Did the Cabal have a way to contact each other, some kind of telepathy or simply a Nightway version of cell phones? Whichever the case, she felt certain the Driver had informed his fellow mystics of their location, and they were hauling ass here as fast as they could. How many had been traveling the Nightway in search of them? Just these three? More? Would the entire fucking Cabal converge on them in the next few minutes?

Lori thrust the Gravedigger Special toward Edgar, but he didn't take it, didn't even seem to notice she was offering it to him. He jumped off the van, clearly intending to confront the Driver, but when he hit the ground, he cried out in pain and his right prosthesis snapped. Lori didn't know if it broke or became unattached, but either way, Edgar fell onto his side with an *oompf.*

"Graceful," the Driver said, amused.

Anger flared bright in Lori, and she raised the Gravedigger Special, pointed it at the Driver, and fired. The weapon roared and bucked in her hand, and she thought for sure that the round had gone wild. But the tooth-bullet struck the Driver on the left shoulder. He staggered backward, letting out a cry of pain that Lori found deeply satisfying.

"Son of a bitch, that *hurts!*"

A dark stain appeared on the shoulder of the Driver's robe, and Lori wanted to cheer. Whatever kind of being the Driver was, he bled just like anything else when he was hurt.

She was going to take another shot – hopefully this time she'd get the bastard in the heart – but before she could squeeze the trigger, Rauch came racing toward her in his police cruiser, lights flashing and siren blaring. She realized he intended to hit the van, and she had no choice but to jump. She threw herself into the air and was on the way down when the cruiser slammed into Edgar's van, sending both vehicles spinning.

She landed on her feet, her bad knee screaming in agony, and then she hit the ground and rolled. She came to a stop lying on her side, her hands empty. She'd lost her grip on the Gravedigger Special when she landed, and she didn't see the weapon in her immediate vicinity. It was then that she remembered Edgar. He'd been lying on the ground too, in front of the van, when Rauch—

She pushed herself up into a sitting position, ignored the pain blazing in her knee, and frantically searched for Edgar. She feared she'd see his broken body lying near the two wrecked vehicles, but he was on his feet and very much alive. Well, on his *foot*. His damaged prosthesis hung from his knee at an odd angle, forcing him to hop on his other one.

He was heading for the Driver. The mystic had pressed his left hand to his shoulder wound in an attempt to slow the bleeding, but the dark stain was still spreading. His teeth were gritted, features contorted in pain, and she remembered what Edgar had told her about the Gravedigger Special's ammunition.

It fires the teeth of people who've died horrible, agonizing deaths. Their suffering is distilled into the teeth, and it's released when they hit their target. Few things can withstand a concentrated dose of another being's pain.

She was glad the fucker was hurting. She'd make him – and the rest of the goddamned Cabal – experience all the pain in the universe if she could.

Rauch, wearing his police uniform, exited the cruiser, seemingly unhurt after ramming his vehicle into the Pest Defense van. *Too bad,* Lori thought.

The rumble of the motorcycle engine grew louder, and an instant later, Goat-Eyes joined the rest of them. Like the Driver, she wore her Cabal robe, and Lori wondered how she was able to drive her bike without getting the hem's fabric caught in the back wheel. It seemed to Lori that it would take as much supernatural power as anything else the Cabal did.

Goat-Eyes pulled her motorcycle up to the Driver's car, parked, and dismounted.

The gang's all here, Lori thought.

Ignoring the protestations of her knee, she rose to her feet. Whatever was going to happen next, she'd be damned if she'd face it lying down.

She looked around once more for the Gravedigger Special and this time she saw it, gleaming white against the Nightway's glossy ebon surface, ten feet to her left.

Goat-Eyes had a cord of braided leather wrapped several times around her waist. A handle protruded from the coils, and Goat-Eyes took hold of it and yanked. The cord slipped loose, and when Goat-Eyes flicked her wrist, Lori realized she was holding a whip. It cracked loudly and flames burst to life along its length. Lori had to admit the effect was impressive. Goat-Eyes kept cracking the whip as she approached, and every time she did, the flames burned higher and hotter.

Smiling in triumph, the three Cabal members closed in on Lori and Edgar. Only the Driver was unarmed, but considering what his non-eyes could do, Lori knew he didn't need any other weapon.

"Come with us willingly, Lori," the Driver said, hand pressed to his shoulder wound, voice tight as he fought against the agonizing pain caused by the tooth-bullet. "If you do, I promise no harm will come to Edgar. We'll leave him here without so much as mussing a hair on his head."

"Of course, there's no guarantee a predator won't get him after we depart," Goat-Eyes said.

"But that's not our problem," Rauch said. "Besides, he's a wily veteran of the Nightway. If anyone can survive its dangers on foot – literally one foot – it's him."

"Don't do it," Edgar said, wobbling as he continued to try to maintain his balance. "You can't trust them. They'll probably kill me as soon as they get you out of here."

"We wouldn't do that," Goat-Eyes protested. "We still have need of you."

"By *need*, you mean you want to take him back to the tower and torture him," Lori said.

Goat-Eyes shrugged. "One person's torture is another's bliss. We do what we must to maintain the Balance."

The trio had continued moving as they spoke, and now they were less than fifteen feet from Lori and Edgar. Lori glanced at the Gravedigger Special again, tried to calculate the odds of her being able to get hold of the gun before the Cabal members could attack. She was no great mathematician, but she figured her chances were piss-poor.

Edgar extended his hands in a warning gesture.

"Stay back! Not all of my bugs are dead. They've multiplied since I escaped you, and I still got a fuck-ton inside me. If you so much as take another step closer, I'll—"

Rauch raised his gun and fired.

Edgar's head jerked as a bullet pierced his skull and entered his brain. The impact knocked him off balance and he fell to the ground, blood jetting from his wound. He turned to look at Lori one last time, but his eyes were already starting to glaze over, and she didn't know if he actually saw her. Then he slumped over and fell still, mouth open, no beetles emerging from it.

"You idiot!" the Driver shouted. "He was bluffing – he didn't have any more beetles inside him!"

"How was I supposed to know?" Rauch said. "He sounded very convincing."

Goat-Eyes stared at Edgar's body. The whip fell from her hand, and when it hit the ground, its flames extinguished.

"Do you have any idea what you've done?" she said, nearly screaming the words.

Edgar's sudden death shocked Lori to her core. She hadn't known the man long or well, but he'd been a friend to her, helping her when she'd most needed it, and without any concern for his own safety. Fury at the Cabal – especially Rauch – overwhelmed her, and while the three mystics argued, she started toward the Gravedigger Special. She tried to run, but her fucking knee wouldn't allow her to do more than a sort of shuffling hobble. She expected to hear Rauch fire his gun once more, expected to feel a bullet slam into her, but he didn't. As if from a distance, she heard him arguing with his two companions, and she prayed the three would remain distracted just a few moments more.

Her knee gave out on her before she reached the gun, but as she fell, she stretched out her right arm as far as she could. As she smacked down onto the Nightway's cold, smooth surface, her hand came down on the Gravedigger Special. She grabbed it, rolled onto her side, aimed at Rauch, and fired.

The tooth-bullet struck Rauch in the throat, and his head jerked backward. Blood jetted from his neck slits, and when the agony contained within the tooth was released into his system, he screamed. More blood gushed from his mouth, and for an instant he looked like some kind of grisly fountain. Then his body went limp and he fell to the ground.

"Fuck you!" Lori shouted in triumph.

The Driver and Goat-Eyes gaped at their companion's corpse, and Lori wondered if they'd ever seen one of their own die before – or if they'd even believed any of them *could* die until this very moment.

By her count, the Gravedigger Special had five rounds left, and she intended to use them all. She aimed at the Driver, but before she could pull the trigger, she felt a tremor shudder through the ground beneath her, far stronger than the mild vibration that constantly hummed in the Nightway's surface. She'd lived in Ohio all her life and had never experienced an earthquake, but she knew that was exactly what was happening now.

The four vehicles – the overturned van, the Driver's car, Rauch's cruiser, and Goat-Eyes' motorcycle – shook and bounced. The motorcycle fell over with a crash, and both Goat-Eyes and the Driver fell too, unable to maintain their balance.

The tremors intensified, and Lori felt the ground actually ripple beneath her, as if the Nightway momentarily became water. She heard cracking sounds like breaking ice, and she watched as fissures – some small, some large – opened in the road's obsidian surface. She couldn't stand, couldn't move. All she could do was hold tight to the Gravedigger Special so she wouldn't lose it again and let the tremors do with her what they would. She had no idea how long the quake lasted, but eventually the tremors lessened before finally ceasing altogether.

She lay still for several moments, heart pounding, body bruised and aching. Her knee still hurt like hell, but she had more important things to concern her right now. She pushed herself into a sitting position and saw that the tremors had bounced and rolled Edgar's body, and now he lay face down, arms splayed at awkward angles. His damaged prosthesis had broken entirely off and lay some distance away, while the other was now bent at a forty-five-degree angle. As she gazed upon her friend's corpse, she became aware of a tickling sensation on the back of her left hand. She looked down and saw a black beetle – one of Edgar's, she presumed – crawling on her skin. Ordinarily, the sight of such an insect on her body might've freaked her out, but she was emotionally numb after everything that had happened in the last several minutes. So instead of shaking her hand to dislodge the beetle, she raised it to her head and tilted it to encourage the insect to crawl off. She felt it scuttle onto her head, where it nestled into her hair and fell still. Maybe one of Edgar's friends had escaped being swallowed by the darkness inside the Driver's head. Or maybe Edgar had had one last beetle inside him after all, and the earthquake had shaken it loose. Either way, a piece of him had survived, and she didn't intend to leave it behind.

She looked up then, startled to see the Driver standing over her. He still had one hand pressed to his shoulder wound, but he held out his other hand, and without pausing to consider whether it was a good idea, she took it and let him help her to her feet. He winced in pain from the effort but did not cry out. Goat-Eyes walked over to join them. Her face was ashen, as if she was terrified, and the Driver didn't look much better.

"What the hell was that?" Lori asked.

The Driver spoke first. "Edgar died before he could discover how he upset the Balance and take action to correct his mistake. And now that the Imbalance cannot be rectified by any other means—"

"The Intercessor has decided to step in," Goat-Eyes finished. Her voice was respectful, almost worshipful, but also suffused with fear.

Lori remembered hearing that word – *Intercessor* – in the Vermilion Tower.

"Isn't that your people's god or something?" she asked.

"The Intercessor is much more than a mere god," the Driver said. "It is the ultimate keeper of the Balance between worlds. The members of the Cabal act as its agents, but when we are unable to correct an Imbalance ourselves, the Intercessor rouses from its slumber to tend to the task itself."

"It hasn't woken for millennia," Goat-Eyes said. "In all that time, we haven't failed to fulfill our duties."

"Until now," Lori said.

"Yes," the Driver said.

Lori remembered seeing the Vermilion Tower for the first time, when the Driver had brought her to it. She had been struck by the structure's spiral, almost organic-looking, shape, and she'd imagined it as the horn of a gigantic beast whose body was almost entirely hidden beneath the ground. She realized then that her imagining had been right. The Vermilion Tower *was* part of the Intercessor, and the creature was now awake.

"The earthquake...."

"Was the result of the Intercessor pulling itself out of the ground," Goat-Eyes said.

Lori thought of the Cabal members she'd seen within the tower, hundreds of them. Had any of them managed to escape before the Intercessor had begun to wake? What of those that had been caught inside? Had they been tossed around like pieces of straw in a hurricane as their god began to move? If so, how many of them had survived? Not that she gave a damn what happened to them, considering the way they treated the people they abducted.

"Why would you let it come to this?" Lori asked. "If you just handled Imbalances yourselves instead of goading us into trying to figure everything out, something like this would never happen, and the Intercessor could go on sleeping forever."

"We are unable to directly address an Imbalance," Goat-Eyes said.

"Why the fuck not?" Lori demanded.

"Because we don't know what causes them!" the Driver shouted.

Lori stared at him, shocked.

He went on, speaking normally once more, although she sensed this restraint took an effort. "The Intercessor communicates with us psychically, in jumbled images that aren't always easy to interpret. We can usually determine who has created an Imbalance, where on Earth they live, and how to find them. But we do not know what they have done specifically to upset the Balance. We only know that they have, and that only they can repair the damage that they've caused."

"It is said that long ago, the Intercessor told us everything," Goat-Eyes said. "But by knowing too much, we risked interfering too directly, which we sometimes did, making an Imbalance worse than it was originally."

"Sounds like a fucked-up system to me," Lori said.

"Perhaps," the Driver admitted. "But it has served us well enough for several thousand years."

"Until today," Lori said.

"Yes," the Driver agreed. "Until today."

"So what happens now?" she asked.

"The Intercessor will travel the Nightway until it finds an exit," Goat-Eyes said. "It will use its power to widen the gateway until it is large enough to pass through. It will then go to your world – to Oakmont, specifically.

There, it will rectify the Imbalance."

"You said the Intercessor was awakened by Edgar's death," Lori said. "Why would it go to Oakmont instead of his hometown?"

"Because Edgar would not have died if *you* hadn't come to the Nightway on your own," the Driver said. "That was something we did not anticipate. Since you caused his death, however indirectly, his Imbalance has been added to yours. This now makes Oakmont the focal point of *both* your transgressions."

"What will the Intercessor do?" Lori asked, but before either Goat-Eyes or the Driver could answer, she remembered the final vision Aashrita had revealed to her in the Garden of Anguish – an aerial view of Oakmont, flattened as if by a series of massive tornadoes.

"Oh god," she whispered.

"The destruction of your town will be total," the Driver said. "But if the Imbalance isn't corrected, the Shadowkin will overrun your entire world, devouring everything until nothing remains. Oakmont is a small price to pay for saving your planet."

It didn't seem that small to Lori. Thousands of people lived in Oakmont, and if what Goat-Eyes and the Driver were telling her was true, they were all marked for death.

"There are two Imbalances in your town," the Driver said. "And now Edgar's can never be fixed. The Intercessor can tolerate a single Imbalance in one location. It's like a wound that will never heal but which will not, itself, prove fatal. But the Intercessor cannot abide two Imbalances, especially when one is as serious as what you caused."

"We know the Shadowkin are involved somehow," Goat-Eyes said. "They're drawn to you because you've become the living embodiment of Imbalance. The negative energy you emit is like food and drink to them. It's made them grow stronger, given them the power to affect matter in your world."

"So you know whatever I did is serious, but you don't know what it is," Lori said.

"Precisely," Goat-Eyes said.

"Then what fucking use are you?" Lori sighed. "If I go back to my world and fix the Imbalance I created...."

"The Intercessor may return to its slumber," the Driver said.

"*May?*"

The Driver exchanged a glance with Goat-Eyes before turning back to Lori. "It's our best guess at this point."

Lori was about to tell the Driver where he and Goat-Eyes could shove their best guess when a new tremor hit. This was different than the others, a single solid *thoom*.

The Driver and Goat-Eyes – both of whom had always seemed in total control – now looked scared shitless.

Thoom.

Lori saw a crimson glow off in the distance, and for a moment she thought the sun was rising. Except there was no sun in this place.

Thoom.

The crimson glow swayed from side to side, and Lori understood that she was seeing the tower – the Intercessor's horn – lit up. The behemoth was using it to light its way, like a fish that lived in the darkest depths of the ocean used bioluminescence to help locate its prey.

Thoom.

Both Goat-Eyes and the Driver had been looking toward the crimson light, but now the Driver turned toward her.

"Go! We'll do what we can to slow down the Intercessor!"

Thoom.

Lori turned toward the shimmering curtain that marked the exit and ran, pain in her knee be damned.

CHAPTER THIRTEEN

She'd forgotten it had been raining back home, but she remembered the instant she reemerged into her world and cold water pelted her naked body, the raindrops' impact making her cuts and bruises sting. The sky was dark, but not nearly so much as on the Nightway, and she saw buildings flanking her on the right and left, saw cars moving past her, coming toward her.

The exit had let her out in the middle of a street.

Drivers honked their horns, some in warning, some in irritation, some in approval of seeing a naked woman in their midst. Lori still gripped the Gravedigger Special – which now held only five rounds – and out of reflex she pointed it at a car coming toward her. It was a black Kia Soul, just like the kind Larry drove. The vehicle stopped and the driver put on the hazard lights, while the drivers behind laid on their horns, angry at having to deal with the sudden obstacle. The driver lowered his window and stuck his head out.

"Why the hell are you naked?" Larry asked.

Grinning in relief, Lori lowered the gun and ran toward Larry's car, bare feet slapping wet pavement. Once she was inside, Larry took off his leather jacket and handed it to her. She draped it over herself like a blanket and shivered as Larry turned on the heater and cranked it to full blast. Warm air gusted from the vents, and Lori closed her eyes and sighed. It was the first real warmth she'd felt since finding herself on the Nightway again, and it was like heaven.

Drivers continued to honk, and Larry turned off the Kia's hazards and began moving forward again. Lori opened her eyes and looked at him.

"Thanks for picking me up," she said. "But how the hell did you know where to find me?"

"This."

Larry's phone rested in the cupholder. He picked it up, swiped his thumb across the screen to unlock it, and then handed it to Lori. She took the phone and saw a text message displayed.

Lori. Franklin Street where it intersects Hawthorne. 4:37 p.m.

She saw the sender's name: *Aashrita*.

"Isn't that the name of the friend of yours who...." Larry began.

"Yes."

Lori felt no pressure to dismiss the memory of her friend – and she felt no migraine threatening – and this was such a relief that she almost cried. It seemed Aashrita might've forgiven her after all and was looking out for her from the other side. She texted back *Thanks* and received an immediate reply.

What are friends for?

Smiling, Lori put the phone back in the cupholder.

"So...you're getting texts from dead people now," Larry said.

"Guess so."

"And you're appearing out of thin air without any clothes on."

"Yep."

"Sounds like you've had an interesting day so far."

"You could say that."

"My day was eventful, too."

"You go first," Lori said.

She listened as Larry told her about his encounter with Goat-Eyes and almost getting run down by the Driver, how he'd slipped into unconsciousness afterward. He woke up just as the paramedics arrived. They examined his leg, pronounced it badly bruised but not broken, and suggested he see a doctor for a more thorough diagnosis. He said he would, and when the paramedics determined he was otherwise uninjured, they departed. His leg hurt, but he could get around on it okay. He'd holed up in a library after that, a place where he could be around people and feel safe, or at least safer. He figured the Cabal would leave him alone if others were close by. It was a stupid assumption, and she wanted to berate him for putting those people in danger. Better he had gone somewhere where he'd be alone, in case Goat-Eyes, the Driver, or another of the Cabal approached him again. She said nothing, though, and when he finished talking, she understood why he hadn't appeared in the visions Aashrita had shown her. Unlike Melinda, Katie, Justin, Reeny, and Brian, he'd managed to resist the Cabal's influence.

"So how about you?" Larry asked.

She quickly filled him in.

"So there's some kind of Godzilla-sized monster heading for town? That's...fucked up."

"Sure is."

"How long before this thing – the Intercessor – gets here?"

"I don't know. I don't think it moves very fast, and the Driver said once it reaches an exit, it'll have to make it big enough for itself to go through. I have no idea how long that'll take."

"So we have some time, but not a lot," Larry said.

Larry had continued driving while they spoke, not heading toward any place in particular. As they traveled, Lori saw dark shapes slinking through alleys, peering over the edges of rooftops, crouching behind parked cars.

Shadowkin. So many of them.

Some were bolder than their brethren, running down sidewalks, darting down streets. One dashed in front of Larry's car, pausing for an instant to turn and look in their direction, featureless black face regarding them – regarding *her*. Goat-Eyes had said the creatures fed on the energy she emitted because she embodied the Imbalance, and it seemed like this creature recognized her. She thought it would veer toward them and attack – leap onto the hood, smash through the windshield with its clawed hands, grab her by the throat and drain the life out of her. But the Shadowkin turned away and continued across the street. It ran inside a secondhand clothing store, and Larry kept driving. She turned around in her seat as they passed the store, hoping to see what the Shadowkin was doing inside, but they were moving too fast, and she couldn't make out any details through the store's window. A second later, several people ran out of the building, shouting and screaming. One woman trailed behind the others, left arm streaked with blood. She only managed to make it a few steps outside before clawed hands thrust through the doorway, sank their talons into her shoulders, and yanked her back inside.

Shaken, Lori turned back to Larry.

"Jesus," she said.

"Yeah. And it seems like their numbers keep increasing. It reminds me of that old Mickey Mouse cartoon, the one where he's a sorcerer's apprentice and he brings a broom to life to do his chores for him. The broom won't quit working, so he uses an ax to chop it to pieces. But all the pieces become new brooms and they…." He broke off. "Sorry. I'm rambling, aren't I? I'm just—"

"Terrified," Lori said.

"Out of my fucking mind."

Periodically, they saw police cruisers and paramedic vehicles racing through the streets, lights and sirens going. They saw a couple officers in a parking lot surrounded by Shadowkin. The officers had their guns drawn and were firing at the creatures without effect. Larry turned a corner before Lori could see how the situation played out, and she was grateful. She had a pretty good idea how that little drama was going to end.

"You all right?" Larry asked.

"Not in the slightest. If the Cabal is right, I somehow caused all this to happen."

How many people had died at the hands of the Shadowkin since she'd been traveling the Nightway? Dozens? Hundreds?

"It's not like you let the Shadowkin into our world on purpose. Whatever happened, it was an accident. You can't blame yourself."

Intellectually, she knew Larry was right. Emotionally, however, she felt totally responsible for the carnage that had come to Oakmont. She told herself that – in this case, at least – her predilection for ignoring the past could be useful. She should do her best to focus on what was ahead of her so she could do what needed to be done to fix things before the Intercessor arrived. It was like she told her clients. *It doesn't matter what caused your injury. It only matters what you do to recover from it.*

She looked through the windshield at the rain hitting the glass, at the road beyond, and tried not to see the living shadows hunting prey on the streets of her town.

Oakmont was light years away from being a big city, and the people who lived there weren't used to this level of violence. She thought of the final vision Aashrita had shown her, Oakmont lying in ruins, everyone dead. If the town's residents thought the Shadowkin were bad, they would be in for one hell of a surprise when the Intercessor arrived – unless she could find a way to stop that from happening.

The Driver and Goat-Eyes had claimed the Cabal had no choice but to operate the way they did. Maybe that was true, but she didn't care. Not only had they fucked with her, they'd assaulted her friends and family, transformed them in monstrous ways, all in an attempt to force her to realize what she'd done to upset the Balance and what she needed to do to fix it. Edgar had tried to help her, and he'd lost his life doing so.

She reached up to touch her head, felt the hard bump of the beetle nestled in her hair. At least something of Edgar remained, however small.

"You said you felt you'd made peace with Aashrita in the Garden," Larry said.

"Yes. I hope so, anyway."

"But that didn't prevent the Intercessor from waking up and hitting the road."

"Which is why I think reconciling with her wasn't enough. It might've been an important part of the puzzle, but there's still a piece missing. I think I need to tell her parents what I did, let them know how ashamed and guilt-ridden I was – and still am – for what I said to her that day on the porch."

"So if you confess to them, does that count as atonement?"

"I don't know. Maybe? I can't think of anything else to do."

"All right, let's go home so you can grab some clothes and—"

"There's no time for that. We need to see Aashrita's parents as soon as possible."

She didn't know how long they had before the Intercessor managed to break through into their world, but whatever time they had, she knew they couldn't afford to waste it.

"Okay. Tell me where to go."

Lori did, and Larry executed a U-turn in the middle of the street – almost hitting a delivery truck – and pushed the Kia's gas pedal to the floor, roaring back in the direction they'd come from. Lori hoped they weren't already too late.

★   ★   ★

"You sure this is where you want to stop?"

It was after five p.m., and Reeny had parked her Altima in the lot of a small shopping center, near an ice cream shop called Sprinkles. The wipers moved back and forth in a steady rhythm, keeping the windshield clear enough to give her a good view of the place. The lights were on inside, and three people sat at a small round table – two women, one man. Since the spots directly in front of the shop had been taken, she'd had to park a couple of rows back, and she couldn't make out any specific details about the trio. She'd never been to Sprinkles before. Brian's favorite ice cream place was the Cold Stone near where they lived. She hadn't even known there was an ice cream shop here until Brian had told her to pull into the lot.

"This is the right place," Brian said. "They're inside. I can feel them."

She didn't know who *they* were, and she really didn't care. She was becoming increasingly concerned for her son. His voice had a strange, flat quality to it, and his manner seemed older than his years. Quite a bit older. Then again, she supposed being resurrected was bound to mature a person.

Without saying another word, Brian unfastened his seat belt, opened the door, and got out of the car. He shut the door behind him and started walking toward Sprinkles, oblivious to the rain. Reeny had an umbrella in the car, and she wished he'd waited for her to grab it, but then again, the rain would hopefully wash away the worst of the blood from his neck wound, so that was good. She decided to forgo the umbrella as well, for the same reason. She got out, shut the door, and started running after Brian. Even if she'd carried the umbrella, she still would've run. She always did, and her husband Charles never failed to tease her about it.

Are you afraid you're going to melt? You might get a little cranky sometimes, but you're hardly the Wicked Witch of the West.

After the...*incident* at the mall, she and Brian had gone looking for Lori. But they hadn't been able to find her. Reeny tried calling her, but she didn't answer. They drove to Get Moving! and found the place swarming with police and reporters. Then they tried Lori's apartment, but when they knocked, no one answered the door.

As they drove away from the apartment complex, Brian said, "I don't understand. I should be able to sense her. It's why I'm here. But I can't."

She hadn't been sure what he was talking about, but it didn't matter. All she cared about was that she had her son back, and together they would punish Lori for her role in causing his temporary she didn't want to think the word *death*, didn't want to engage with the awful reality of it, so she let her thought drift away. She wasn't certain exactly what Lori had done to contribute to Brian's...current condition. But Brian insisted his aunt had done *something*, and as much as Reeny loved her sister, she believed her son. She had to. She was his mother, after all.

But after failing to find so much as a trace of Lori, Brian said that they needed help. She could tell by the irritation in his voice that this was galling to him. She didn't like it either, would've preferred to continue searching with Brian, just the two of them. Keep it in the family, you know? But Reeny didn't object. If Brian wanted something, it was her job as his mother to make sure he got it, whatever it was. Hence, their stopping at Sprinkles. She wondered if Brian simply wanted to take a break from their search, maybe discuss a new strategy with her over ice cream. Could he still eat? She wasn't clear on how this whole coming back from the dead thing worked.

Brian reached Sprinkles' door and pushed it open. An old-fashioned jingling of bells announced their presence, but there was something off about the sound, and Reeny realized it was some kind of recording. She found this sad. Was Brian only a recording too, a facsimile, an imitation of the boy he'd been? She didn't want to examine this thought too closely, so she put it aside and followed her son into the shop.

The first thing she noticed was the blood. It was *everywhere*. On the floor, the walls, the ceiling.... A half-dozen bodies in various states of mutilation lay on the floor, where they hadn't been visible to her from the car – four adults and two children. There was blood on the front counter and on the large menu hanging on the wall behind it.

Three living customers sat at a table, each holding ice cream cones. Reeny couldn't tell what flavors they had, but their ice cream was dotted with blood. Sprinkles, indeed.

One of the women had a long gray braid that undulated in the air like a serpent. The other had clawed hands, sharp teeth, and uneven tufts of fur covering her skin. The man looked as if he suffered from some kind of hideous skin disease. His shirt was open, exposing a lumpy mass of discolored growths on his chest. There were smaller ones on his neck, face, and hands, as if whatever was wrong with him was spreading outward from his chest to infect the rest of his body. Their clothes were soaked with blood, and if Reeny had had any doubt who was responsible for the dead bodies scattered on the floor, she no longer did.

The three looked at Reeny and Brian as they entered, and the cat woman hissed. The one with a braid put a hand on the woman's shoulder.

"It's all right, Katie." She smiled. "They're our kind of people."

Reeny hadn't recognized Justin at first. Part of that was due to the obscene growths covering his flesh, but a bigger part was that he was so out of place in this nightmarish scene – the blood, the bodies.... She didn't know Justin well. Lori hadn't been seeing him all that long, and while Reeny had invited them over for dinner once, Justin hadn't talked much about himself. He'd talked about his job as a lab tech, when he talked at all. Justin had struck Reeny as a nice enough guy, not particularly complicated – which was a point in his favor after Larry, who was *all* complication – but he'd also come across as anxious, almost neurotic, and she didn't think he and Lori were going to work out as a couple. This was fine with her, as she thought her Sissy could do a lot better.

"Hello, Justin," she said.

He started to speak but was overcome by a sudden burst of violent coughing. Small black chunks were expelled from his mouth to land on the table, as well as on the ice cream cones of his companions. Neither of the women seemed bothered by this, and the cat woman even licked one of the gobbets from her cone and purred as she chewed it. Reeny had heard the expression *coughing up a lung* before, but this was the first time she'd actually seen it happen. Brian seemed delighted by the man's discomfort. He clapped his hands and laughed as the man struggled to get control of himself.

"Sorry," Justin gasped when his coughing fit subsided. "We're still having some trouble adjusting to each other." His voice changed then, sounded like a chorus of voices speaking in unison. "*Trouble, yes.*"

We're? Reeny thought.

"You two know each other?" the woman with the braid asked.

"Yeah," Justin said. "She's Lori's sister. The boy's Lori's nephew, Brian." His voice changed again. "*Lori bitch. We no like.*"

The woman with the braid smiled, displaying her teeth. "Well isn't that just *wonderful*," she said. "Won't you join us? Justin, would you please pull up a table for our new friends?"

Justin rose, shuffled over to the nearest table – the surface of which was speckled with blood – and dragged it over next to the trio's. The table's metal legs slid through blood on the floor and made streaks on the tile. He then brought over a couple chairs and set them down. There was blood on them too, and he tried to wipe it off with his hand but only managed to smear it around. He gestured for Reeny and Brian to sit.

Brian did so without hesitation.

"Would you like some ice cream, sweetie?" Reeny asked him.

"Yes," he said.

Brian might not be able to digest ice cream, she thought, or even taste it, but maybe he'd enjoy the texture. She walked over to the counter, stepping carefully around both blood and corpses. When she was behind the counter, she saw a seventh body, that of a young woman wearing a blue apron with the Sprinkles logo on the front. There were copious amounts of blood on the floor, but no sign of the girl's head. She wondered where it was.

She made Brian a cone with a double scoop of butter pecan – his favorite – and took it over to the table. She didn't get any ice cream for herself. She didn't need the calories. And she didn't have much of an appetite at the moment.

When she handed Brian the cone, he looked at it for a moment, then he looked at her. It took her a second to get the message, but when she did, she bent over, ran her fingers through a pool of blood on the floor, straightened, then held her hand over Brian's ice cream. Blood dribbled onto the butter pecan like strawberry syrup, and when the ice cream was completely covered in crimson, Brian said, "Thank you."

Reeny smiled, nodded, then lowered her hand. She wanted to go back to the counter and get a fistful of napkins to clean off the blood, but she didn't. Instead, she let her hand hang down to her side so she wouldn't get the remaining blood on her clothes.

Brian lifted his treat to his mouth, extended his tongue – which had become a mottled gray – and began licking. Reeny sat down, and the cat woman, Katie, looked at the woman with the braid.

"So these two are after Lori, just like we are?" Her voice was a feline purr, and Reeny found it soothing in its way.

"Yes," the Braid-Woman said. She turned to Reeny. "I'm Melinda, and this is Katie. You already know Justin."

"I'm Irene, and this is my son Brian." She glanced at Brian, saw his mouth was smeared with blood and ice cream. "People call me Reeny. It's a nickname from when I was a kid."

"What did Lori do to you?" Melinda asked. "I assume she did *something* or you wouldn't be here."

"She.... There was a shooting at the mall. Brian.... Lori caused it. I don't know how, exactly, but she was responsible."

"We're going to make her pay," Brian said happily.

A part of Reeny that was still fully herself – a part buried deep down in her psyche – protested that Brian would never talk about his Aunt Lorlee like this. Not only was it out of character, it was creepily adult. This part also told her that sitting in an ice cream shop with corpses strewn about the place was not, in any sense of the word, normal. Something had happened to Brian, had happened to her. Something *bad*. They weren't themselves anymore; they were…what? She didn't know. She only knew they weren't right, and that they should get up and leave this place immediately, before things became even worse than they already were.

But then she remembered what it had felt like to hold her dead son in her arms, and cold anger swept through her, wiping away her doubts and fears.

She smiled at her son. "Yes, we will."

"So you've heard the same call we have," Melinda said.

"Not that we've been able to do much about it," Katie said. "We've looked all over this goddamn town for your sister, but we haven't been able to track her down. That's why we came in here – to take a break and try to figure out where she might be. Do you know where she is?"

"No," Reeny said. "I've tried calling her, but it always goes to voicemail."

"Same," Melinda said.

"It's like she vanished off the face of the fucking Earth," Justin said. "*Gone-gone.*"

"It's extremely frustrating," Melinda said. "We were created – or maybe I should say *re*-created – to go after your sister and convince her to…." She frowned, as if trying to remember. "To do something, but we can't find her."

Brian had continued working on his disgusting ice cream while the adults spoke, but now said, "I know where she's at."

They all turned to look at him.

"Go on, sweetie," Reeny urged.

"She's back in this world again. She just got a text message from a friend. A *dead* friend. I'm sensitive to that kind of thing since I'm dead too."

Melinda, Katie, and Justin all leaned forward, eager to hear what Brian had to say.

"Tell us more," Reeny said. "Do you know exactly where she's at right now?"

"Better," Brian said, grinning. "I know where she's *going*."

★   ★   ★

Lori and Larry passed her parents' house on the way to Aashrita's.
Everything looked normal from the outside, but that didn't necessarily
mean her mom and dad were safe. She pictured Shadowkin swarming
through the house, claws sinking into her parents' flesh, tearing them apart
as if they were tissue paper.

"Do you want to stop?" Larry asked. "Just for a minute, to make sure
they're okay?"

She was tempted. She knew Larry cared about her parents too. His
mother had died when he was a teenager, and his father hadn't really
spoken to him after he came out as bisexual. Lori's parents adored Larry
and had become like a second mom and dad to him. Sometimes Lori
thought they were more upset that she and Larry had broken up than
she was.

"I'll just call them. Can I borrow your phone?"

Larry nodded, and she took his phone from the cupholder and called
her mom. She picked up on the second ring.

"Hey, Mom."

"Lorelai! Thank god! I've been trying to call you all afternoon."

"Sorry, I lost my phone. I'm using Larry's. How are you and
Dad doing?"

"We've been frantic! After what happened at the clinic, we thought...
well, we thought the worst."

Lori frowned. "What do you mean?"

Her mom told her about the murders at Get Moving!

"The police have no idea what went on there. And that's not all. Have
you been watching the news? The whole town's going crazy! There was a
shooting at the mall, and some kind of terrorists are running around killing
people. Where are you? Come over here so we know you're safe. Bring
Larry, too."

She wasn't surprised that her mom didn't say anything about Justin.
Her mom and dad felt lukewarm toward him at best.

"I've got something to do first, Mom. But I'll be there as soon as I
can, okay?"

"Have you heard from your sister? I've been trying to call her, too, but
she hasn't answered."

Lori thought of the visions Aashrita had shown her, saw Reeny sobbing as she held Brian's dead body.

"I haven't," she said truthfully. "I'll let you know if I do. Try not to worry about her. She's probably fine." She hated lying to her mother like this, but she could hardly tell her the truth.

She once more promised that she and Larry would be over soon, and then ended the call. She would've loved to go to her folks' house and hole up there until this all blew over. But she knew if she didn't find a way to reset the Balance between Shadow and the real world, no one in Oakmont – maybe in the whole damn world – would be safe.

Lori's parents weren't rich, but they lived in one of the more upscale sections of town, the kind of place where larger, two-story houses sat too close to one another, and there were no streetlights because residents thought they were too garish. The Dhawans lived a couple of streets away from the Palumbos, and their house was even larger and nicer. At least, it *had* been the Dhawans' house back when she was a senior in high school. But after Aashrita's death, she hadn't seen or spoken with her parents, not once. Not even at Aashrita's funeral, which she'd barely been able to make herself attend. For all she knew, they'd decided to move sometime in the last fifteen years. She imagined herself and Larry knocking on what she believed was the Dhawans' front door, only for their knock to be answered by a man or woman she didn't recognize.

The previous occupants moved out years ago. No, I don't have their new address. Sorry.

Then there would be nothing she could do to stop the Intercessor, and all of Oakmont would be well and truly fucked.

She thought she might have trouble recognizing the Dhawans' house after all these years, but she knew it the instant she saw it. She felt a wave of sadness move through her. She and Aashrita had spent most of their time together at Lori's house, but that didn't mean she hadn't gone to the Dhawans' before, and she found herself feeling a strange emotion, homesickness for someone else's home.

She pointed to a white two-story with black shutters.

"This is it," she said.

Larry pulled into the house's upward-sloping driveway, parked, got out, and walked around to the passenger side of the car to open the door for Lori.

"All ashore who's going ashore," he said.

It was still raining. His hair was plastered to his head and water droplets clung to his beard.

Lori tucked the Gravedigger Special into the inner pocket of Larry's leather jacket, and got out. The rain felt cold on her head, face, hands, and legs, but she barely registered the sensation. Her mind was laser-focused on what she'd come here to do.

She hurried to the front door, Larry following close on her heels. She hadn't asked him to accompany her, but she was grateful for his presence. When they reached the porch, Larry stood a couple steps back to give her room. She faced the door – a big white thing that looked as if it had been freshly painted recently – raised her hand, and knocked. She felt the beetle in her hair shift positions, and she wondered if it had done so to get more comfortable or to get a better view of the events about to transpire.

No one answered right away, so she knocked again, a bit louder, more forceful.

"Maybe we should break a window," Larry said. "I could climb inside and unlock the door in case something has, you know, happened to them. With all the Shadowkin running around…."

Lori was seriously considering it when the door finally opened, and she saw Aashrita's mother for the first time in seventeen years.

Rajini Dhawan was a handsome East Indian woman in her sixties, with gray hair she wore pulled back in a bun. The hair startled Lori. She remembered Rajini with long, beautiful black hair. She was short, only an inch or two over five feet, and she was heavier than Lori remembered. She wasn't obese by any means, but her face was rounder, her body plumper. She wore a long-sleeved black pullover sweater, navy-blue slacks, and a pair of black flats. She had on earrings and several thin bracelets, but on her fingers only a wedding band. Rajini was an anesthesiologist, and Lori remembered Aashrita once telling her that her mom didn't wear any other rings because of how often she had to wash her hands at work.

"Hi, Dr. Dhawan," Lori said. "You probably don't remember me, but—"

"Of *course* I remember you, Lori. It's good to see you, but I must ask: are you wearing anything under that jacket, because it doesn't look like you are."

Lori almost laughed in relief. She hadn't known if Aashrita had told her parents about the awful things she'd said on the day before she ended her life, but she'd always feared she had. It was why she hadn't spoken to Aashrita's parents at the funeral, and why she'd avoided Aashrita's siblings as well. She hadn't been able to bear the thought of their looking her in the eyes and thinking, *This is the girl who caused Aashrita to kill herself.* She'd been afraid that Rajini would look at her that way now, but the woman hadn't, and she began to hope that maybe Aashrita hadn't said anything to her family about her cruel words. That, or if Rajini knew, she'd long ago decided to forgive her.

"It's a long story, Dr. Dhawan." She remembered Larry was standing behind her, and she half turned toward him to acknowledge his presence. "This is my friend, Larry Ramirez."

"Nice to meet you," Larry said. He grimaced then, perhaps aware of how ridiculous social niceties were in this situation.

Rajini favored him with a smile before facing Lori once more. "Why don't you come in and get dry? Are you in trouble? Do you need help?"

"Actually," Lori said, "we are and we do."

Before she could say anything more, a pair of vehicles came speeding down the street toward the Dhawans' house – a white Jeep Cherokee and a red Nissan Altima.

"Shit," Lori said.

She watched as the vehicles drew closer, neither slowing. Reeny was in the lead, and when she reached the Dhawans' yard, she went over the curb and onto the grass. Melinda followed close behind. Lori thought they were going to keep coming and ram into the porch in an attempt to hurt them, but at the last instant, Reeny veered off and hit the brakes. The Altima slid on the wet grass, tires churning the ground to mud. Melinda braked abruptly too, but she managed to maintain better control of her vehicle, and it didn't slide nearly so badly.

"What in the *hell*?" Rajini said.

Lori wanted to tell her to run inside and call nine-one-one, but she doubted anyone would come to their aid. Oakmont's police force was doubtlessly overwhelmed dealing with the Shadowkin attacks throughout town.

The passenger-side door of Reeny's car opened, and Brian stepped out. Lori already knew what to expect since Aashrita had shown her visions of the transformations her nephew, her sister, and the others had gone through. Larry did too, in general, since she'd told him about the visions. But knowing what to expect and experiencing it were far from the same thing.

Brian's clothes were covered with dark stains that Lori knew were blood – some of it his, some of it not. His skin was a pale grayish white, and he moved with awkward, stiff motions, as if he was having trouble remembering how to operate his body. But worst of all was the expression on his face. His mouth was twisted into a cold, mirthless smile, and his eyes were flat and unfeeling like a doll's.

"Hi, Aunt Lorlee!"

His voice was awful too, a hollow echo that sounded as if it came from very far away.

Reeny got out of the car next, but other than being soaking wet, she appeared normal. For an instant, Lori hoped that Reeny had escaped being changed by the Cabal, but then she saw the raw hatred contorting her sister's features, the sheer loathing that burned in her eyes, and Lori knew that while Reeny looked unchanged on the outside, she had been transformed within. Reeny walked over to stand next to her son, put a hand on his shoulder, and together they stared at Lori.

Melinda, Katie, and Justin got out of the Cherokee and joined Reeny and Brian. They too fixed their gazes on Lori, but their faces displayed different emotions – amusement from Melinda, hungry excitement from Katie, and jealous resentment from Justin. All three of them were covered with blood, and their bodies had been transformed in different ways. One thing about the Cabal: you couldn't fault their creativity. Melinda's braid had been animated with a life of its own, and it whipped the air behind her like the tail of a restless animal. Katie *was* an animal, or at least she possessed aspects of one – a cat, Lori judged. It made sense. Her personality had already been like a feline's in many ways. And Justin.... Jesus Fucking Christ, poor Justin! If she hadn't already known it was him, she never would've recognized him. His body was completely covered by tumors, so many that his nose was no longer visible, and his mouth was a thin, barely perceptible line. His eyes remained unobstructed, though, and somehow that was the worst of all. She saw no love for her within them, only blazing anger that was growing hotter by the moment. His breathing was rough and labored, and when he coughed, it sounded as if his lungs were filled with wet gravel.

"Oh god," Rajini said, and then she slammed the door shut and locked it, leaving Lori and Larry to face the others on their own.

Smart woman, Lori thought.

Larry didn't take his gaze off the five nightmares confronting them as he spoke in a hushed voice. "What do we do now?"

Lori didn't answer him. Instead she addressed the others.

"You've come to deliver a message to me," she said. "I already know what it is. I damn well ought to by now. I've heard it enough. But you might as well get it out of your systems. So get on with it."

The five spoke in unison, as if they'd rehearsed. "Confess and atone – or suffer."

Lori clapped.

"Bravo. Message received loud and clear. That's why I've come here to the Dhawans' – to fix the Imbalance I created. That means there's nothing left for you to do. You've played your parts and played them well. Now go away and let me play mine."

Melinda smiled. "We don't care what we were *supposed* to do, and we don't give a *fuck* about the Imbalance. We're writing our own script from now on, and in this next scene...we're going to kill you."

"And worse," Katie said, rough cat tongue licking an elongated incisor.

"I'm going to eat your heart," Brian said. "I bet it'll taste like candy."

"And you'll eat every bite of it," Reeny said to her son, "just like the good boy you are."

Hearing her sister speak like that hurt Lori more than all the tortures the Cabal had put her through combined. This was Reeny, not just her sister but her very best friend.

Not anymore, she thought.

Justin spoke next, pausing every few words to catch his breath.

"You know what...the best thing about...cancer is? It *spreads*. That makes it...the gift that keeps on giving. I'm going...to pass it along to you." His gaze flicked to Larry, and his tumor-covered brow furrowed. "And to *him* – your emotional crutch...of an ex-boyfriend." His voice changed then, became a chorus. "*We join with you. Much-much happy.*"

The Cabal had turned Justin and the others into monsters in order to goad her into discovering the nature of the Imbalance she'd created and then fixing it. But the Cabal had done their job too well. Reeny, Brian, Justin, Melinda, and Katie were like machines that had been created to perform a specific task, and they intended to keep performing it, even if it was no longer necessary. They wouldn't stop until she was dead – and if she died, so did everyone in Oakmont.

Lori drew in a deep breath, released it.

"Let's get started then. I'm on the clock."

She drew the Gravedigger Special from the leather jacket's inner pocket and stepped off the porch and into the rain.

CHAPTER FOURTEEN

The Gravedigger Special had five rounds left. Five people, if you could still call them that, stood in the Dhawans' yard, ready to attack her. She wondered if this was somehow linked to the concept of Balance – five enemies, five bullets – or if it was only a coincidence. Either way, she couldn't afford to waste any ammo. She needed to make every shot count.

She blinked to keep the rainwater out of her eyes. The water was cold against her skin, but she barely noticed. From the porch, Larry said, "Uh, I'm not sure this is a good idea, Lori."

"It's a terrible idea," she said without looking at him. "But it's the only one I've got."

The woman she'd been less than twenty-four hours ago would've waited for one of the five to attack her, and when that happened, she might not have been able to bring herself to fire the gun. Now she raised the Gravedigger Special, aimed it at Katie – who she judged to be the most immediate threat – and pulled the trigger. But as she lifted the gun, Melinda gave her head a quick shake and her braid snapped forward. It shot toward Lori, lengthening as it came, and it wrapped around the wrist of the hand holding the weapon. The braid yanked at the same instant Lori squeezed the trigger. The gun bucked in her hand as it went off, and she thought for certain that the shot would go wild. Instead, it struck Katie in the left eye.

Thanks, Melinda, she thought.

Katie yowled as blood gushed from her wound. Her head jerked back, she staggered a couple of steps, and then went down. She lay on the wet grass, rain pelting her still form. Everyone looked at Katie's body, and Lori waited to see if the woman would change back to herself in death, but evidently that was something which only happened in movies because she remained half-cat.

Lori thought of the Katie she knew, the woman she worked with, the one who was full of life and laughter, who liked to gossip and tell dirty jokes. She supposed that woman had died the moment the Cabal had gotten to her, but that didn't make Lori feel any better about what she'd done.

Melinda, Reeny, Brian, and Justin stared at Katie's corpse as if they couldn't quite believe what they were seeing. They'd been transformed, were strong and filled with hate. How could one of them have been brought down so easily?

Melinda turned toward Lori then, features twisted by fury. "You *bitch!*"

She pulled her head back and her braid began to retract, pulling Lori with it. She stumbled forward, almost went down, but she managed to stay on her feet. The braid squeezed tighter around her wrist as it pulled her toward Melinda, and she knew the woman was trying to force her to drop the Gravedigger Special. Lori hadn't taken her finger off the trigger, and the gun discharged. She didn't get lucky this time, and the bullet struck no one. She now had three rounds left.

Out of the corner of her eye, she saw movement across the street. She turned her head and saw dark forms crouching on the roof of the house opposite the Dhawans'. Three, no, four of them. The Shadowkin had reached this neighborhood, and it looked like some of them had taken a ringside seat to the latest episode of *Lori Fights to Save the World*.

She saw another flash of movement then, this one to her right. At first she thought it was another Shadowkin, attacking her from behind. But it was Larry. He stepped in front of her, grabbed hold of Melinda's braid with both hands, and pulled. In that moment she loved the dumb sonofabitch more than ever.

She also took hold of the braid with her free hand and added her strength to Larry's. Maybe if the grass had been dry, they would've been able to slow or even stop Lori's progression toward Melinda. But it wasn't, and neither she nor Larry could get any traction. They slid forward as Melinda pulled, almost as if they were slow-motion water skiing. Then Melinda tossed her head back, giving her braid a fierce yank. Lori and Larry lost their footing and fell forward. She and Larry continued sliding toward Melinda, who was grinning in triumph. Larry tried to hold on, but the rain had made Melinda's hair slick and he lost his grip. He rolled to the side as Lori shot past him, and when she reached Melinda, the braid raised her up into the air until her bare feet dangled several inches above the ground. Melinda held Lori by the right wrist, just below the hand that held the Gravedigger Special, and she couldn't aim her gun at the woman. The weapon was useless.

Melinda had to raise her head to look Lori in the face. Lori gazed into her eyes, searching for any sign of the person she'd once been. Their relationship had been prickly at times, but Lori had respected her as a boss and colleague. She was tough on both her clients and staff, but she'd built a strong practice that had helped a lot of people. Lori couldn't reconcile that woman with the one grinning at her now. This Melinda wasn't a person so much as a force of nature, no different than the rain falling on them. She was hatred, aggression, and cruelty personified. She was, in short, evil.

"I'm not surprised you were able to take Katie out so easily," Melinda said. "She always was more sizzle than steak. But I'm far stronger than her." Her grin widened. "Meaner, too. So if you think—"

While Melinda talked, Lori felt feather-light movement in her hair. It crept down the back of her neck, onto her shoulder, then up the arm that Melinda was holding her by. She watched as the last of Edgar's friends made its way onto Melinda's braid and began scuttling along it, picking up speed as it went. The beetle disappeared from sight as it followed the braid down to where it was attached to Melinda's head. It reappeared on top of her head, ran over her forehead, onto her nose, and before the woman was even aware it was happening, the beetle crawled into her right nostril and vanished up her nose.

Melinda's braid flailed about wildly as her shriek grew into a scream. Blood gushed from both nostrils, and she brought her hands to her face and pressed them against her nose in a vain attempt to stop the flow. Lori leaned back against the ground, took a two-handed grip on the Gravedigger Special, and aimed it squarely at Melinda's chest. But before she could fire, Melinda's screaming became a high-pitched ululation, and her body began spasming. Fresh gouts of blood jetted from her nose, her eyes rolled white, and she collapsed to the ground. Her braid continued moving for a moment, then it too fell still. An instant later, the beetle emerged from Melinda's left ear. It was coated with thick blood, but the rain washed the gore off the insect. The beetle took to the air, flew toward Lori, landed on her head and once more nestled in her hair. She thought she knew what the insect had done. It had entered through Melinda's nostril, burrowed its way up into her brain, and started eating as fast as it could. A nasty way to go, but at least it had been fast and she hadn't wasted another tooth-bullet. She still had three.

She looked at the house across the street and saw more Shadowkin had climbed onto the roof to watch the action. There were ten now, maybe a dozen. And there were Shadowkin on some of the other roofs too.

She'd been so focused on Melinda that she'd lost track of the others. She looked around and saw Reeny and Brian standing off to the side, watching and waiting. She saw Justin and Larry grappling with each other. Justin gripped Larry's shoulders and Larry had his hands around the other man's throat. Justin's neck was so swollen with tumors that Larry's fingers had sunk so far into the spongy discolored flesh that they weren't visible. Larry's features were scrunched up with effort and his arms were shaking. He was putting everything he had into strangling Justin. For his part, Justin kept his hands on Larry's shoulders, gripping them tight, yes, but not in a way that would cause any damage. Why wasn't he fighting back? An instant later Lori understood why.

Justin let out a violent cough and a spray of black particles hit Larry's face. Larry drew in a reflexive breath, and then he began coughing too.

"Fuck," Lori said softly.

Larry let go of Justin's throat and stepped back. He kept coughing, so violently now that his entire body shuddered.

Lori didn't think. She raised the Gravedigger Special and fired. A tooth discharged from the gun's barrel, streaked across the yard, and buried itself between Justin's shoulder blades. She expected him to cry out in agony as the pain stored in the tooth was released into his system. But he didn't. Instead, he simply fell apart. He collapsed into a pile of tumors – no blood, no bones, just a mound of obscene growths of varying sizes that lay on the grass, getting struck by rain that could never cleanse or purify them.

Lori was horrified by the way Justin died, but she was more concerned for Larry. He was coughing so hard that she feared he couldn't breathe. She ran to him, forgetting for the moment about Reeny and Brian. When she reached Larry, she put her free hand on his back, as if that would do any good at this point. She looked down at the ground and saw dark blood on the grass, dissipating in the rain. More joined it as Larry coughed, splatters thick as mucus, and that's when she knew it was too late for him.

His coughing subsided somewhat and he managed to look at her. His mouth was smeared with red, and his eyes were bloodshot, the capillaries broken from the violent exertions of his coughing. He smiled weakly. "I just…wanted to help."

He coughed one last time, blood spraying the leather jacket of his that Lori wore, and then he collapsed into the grass, bloodshot eyes unblinking as rainwater pelted them.

Lori felt as if she'd been kicked in the stomach. For a moment, she couldn't breathe, and then she drew in a shuddering gasp of air and released it in a loud sob. She fell on her knees next to Larry, folded her body over his, wrapped her arms around him. His death was her fault, just as Edgar's was. She hadn't hurt Larry intentionally, of course, but that distinction meant dick right now. He was dead, and she was to blame.

"You look really sad."

She glanced up and saw Brian standing close by, smiling at her. Reeny stood next to him, her expression unreadable. Brian's smile widened.

"I like it," he said. "It's funny."

The Gravedigger Special – which Lori still held – had two rounds left. One for Brian and one for Reeny. Lori's grief over Larry's death flared into anger, at herself, the Cabal, this whole damn fucked-up situation, and she saw Brian and Reeny as symbolizing everything that had turned to shit in her life.

The Shadowkin crouched on the rooftops across the street leaned forward, as if eager to see what would happen next.

Lori intended to fire the bone gun two last times, but before she could squeeze the trigger, headlight beams illuminated the three of them. They all turned to look as a BMW pulled into the Dhawans' driveway. The driver parked, and when he got out of the car and stepped into the rain, Lori saw that it was Aashrita's father. Saakar Dhawan was a gastroenterologist in his early sixties, a tall man with a goatee that was still primarily black. He wore a gray suit and tie, and Lori assumed he had come home after a long day of seeing patients or performing colonoscopies. He gazed at the carnage spread across his lawn and then looked at Lori, Reeny, and Brian.

"What the hell is going on here?" Dr. Dhawan demanded. "Who are you people?"

"I like you," Brian said. "You make me laugh."

The boy fell onto all fours then and began running across the lawn like an animal toward Saakar. The man stood motionless and gaped in disbelief.

"No!" Lori shouted. She started to go after him, but Reeny slammed into her from behind, knocking her to the ground. As she hit, her right knee gave its familiar scream of protest. Reeny then straddled her back, put her hands on her shoulders and pushed down to prevent Lori from rising.

"Dr. Dhawan!" Lori shouted. "Run!"

The man didn't move, just kept staring at Brian, and when the boy reached him, Brian launched himself into the air, grabbed hold of Saakar and buried his teeth in the man's throat. Saakar struggled, tried to grab hold of Brian and shove him away, but whatever Brian was now, he wasn't human, and he was far too strong for Saakar to fend off.

"Get off me!" Lori shouted to Reeny. "I have to help him!"

But even as she spoke these words, she knew it was too late.

Saakar fell to the ground, and Brian kept tearing at the man's throat in bestial fury, blood jetting from torn arteries. As Saakar bled out, his exertions began to lessen, and he fell still. Brian didn't stop, though, kept biting and gnawing at the ragged ruin that had been the man's throat. Lori's stomach gave a sickening lurch when she realized her nephew was ripping chunks of meat from Saakar's body and swallowing them.

"He gets so hungry after school," Reeny said, her voice distant, dreamy. "We didn't have time to go home, so he didn't get a snack. We stopped and had ice cream with our new friends, but that was just sugar and empty calories. A growing boy like Brian needs something more substantial in his belly."

Hearing her sister talk like this filled Lori with a profound sense of loss. The Reeny she knew and loved was gone, destroyed by the power of the Cabal and replaced with this lunatic who didn't care that her undead son was a flesh-eating monster.

Lori still held the Gravedigger Special, and now she shifted hard beneath Reeny to free her gun hand. She raised the weapon and pointed it backward at Reeny. She didn't squeeze the trigger right away, though, didn't know if she could do it. Sure, she and Reeny squabbled sometimes, like all siblings do, but they'd been there for each other all their lives, offering love and unfailing support. Even if Reeny's mind had been warped by the Cabal, she was *Reeny*, wasn't she? Her real self was still in there somewhere – it had to be. It might still be possible to heal her mind and bring her back to herself. But that wouldn't happen if Lori killed her – especially if she couldn't bring herself to pull the goddamn trigger in the first place.

But lives other than Reeny's were at stake. Everyone in Oakmont, maybe the entire world, was in danger as long as the Imbalance between Shadow and the real world existed. She had to confess her sin – it was the only way to fix the problem – and now that Saakar was dead, there was only one person left who she could confess to: Rajini. And she had to do it fast before the Intercessor arrived. Because once it did, she feared nothing she could do – nothing anyone could do – would be able to stop it.

I'm sorry, Sis.

Before Lori could fire, the Shadowkin across the street starting leaping off the roofs, landing on yards, running toward the Dhawans' yard. Lori didn't know why they'd waited this long to act. Maybe the scent of Saakar's blood was driving them, or maybe they'd enjoyed watching the humans fight for a time, but now they were bored and intended to get in on the action themselves.

As the Shadowkin dashed into the street, Lori shouted, "They're coming!"

Reeny looked at the rapidly approaching Shadowkin, but she didn't react.

"Brian's in danger, Reeny. If those creatures get hold of him, they'll tear him apart!"

That got Reeny moving. She reached out, yanked the Gravedigger Special from Lori's grasp, and sprung to her feet. She started running across the lawn toward Brian, who still had his face buried in Saakar's neck. "We have to go, sweetie," she called. "Now!"

The boy was so occupied with his grisly feast that he paid no attention to his mother.

Lori got to her feet and watched as the Shadowkin, perhaps attracted by Reeny's sudden movement, veered toward her. As swiftly as the creatures moved, Lori was certain they'd catch Reeny before she could reach Brian. And while Reeny had the Gravedigger Special, the weapon only had two rounds left. Even if she successfully struck two of the Shadowkin with the remaining tooth-bullets, there were at least a dozen more she'd have to contend with.

She was as good as dead.

"Lori!"

Lori turned to see Rajini standing in the open doorway of her house. "Hurry – inside!"

Lori didn't need to be invited twice.

Moving as fast as she could with her injured knee and ignoring its protests of pain, she headed toward the house. She heard Reeny fire the gun's last two rounds, but she knew it wouldn't do her any good, not against so many Shadowkin. Once Lori was inside the house, Rajini slammed the door shut and locked it. Lori ran into the living room to look out of the picture window, Rajini joined her, and they watched as the Shadowkin flooded over first Reeny and then Brian. Reeny disappeared beneath their claws, but Lori heard her scream. Thankfully, it didn't last long. Brian never stopped feeding on Saakar, even when the Shadowkin's claws began tearing into him. He made no sound as the monsters killed him, maybe because he'd already died once that day, and doing it a second time meant little to him.

Lori turned away from the window to face Rajini. She felt tears threatening, but she couldn't let them come, not yet. She still had work to do. She reached out and took Rajini's hands.

"I'm so sorry about your husband. But I've got something very important to tell you. Something I should've told you a long—"

Lori's words were cut off as the picture window exploded. A lone Shadowkin leaped into the living room, slammed into Rajini, and knocked her to the floor. Her hands were yanked out of Lori's, and before Lori could do anything, the Shadowkin went to work on Rajini with its black, clawed hands. Unlike Brian, Rajini screamed when the Shadowkin tore into her. Blood sprayed the air as the Shadowkin savaged Rajini's body, the blood faded in midair, and Rajini began to vanish as well, almost as if the Shadowkin wasn't killing her so much as *unmaking* her. When the Shadowkin finished its awful work, nothing of Rajini remained. No clothes, no gobbets of meat, no splintered bone, not even a patch of wet blood soaking into the carpet. It was like she'd never existed at all.

The Shadowkin rose to its feet then and turned to regard Lori.

It's all over, she thought. There was no one left for her to confess to. She couldn't fix the Imbalance, and the Intercessor would soon come and destroy everything. She didn't want to be here when that happened, so she walked toward the Shadowkin, arms spread. "I'm all yours," she said.

The Shadowkin made no move toward her. It looked at her for a moment, then turned and leaped back through the broken window.

Lori stood there, waiting to see if another Shadowkin would jump inside and finish her off. When none did, she stepped up to the broken window and looked outside. The Shadowkin in the yard were dispersing, moving off in different directions to search for other things to destroy.

"What about me?" Lori shouted. "What's *wrong* with me?"

But she knew what was wrong. The Shadowkin had grown so strong that they didn't need her anymore.

The departing Shadowkin didn't react to her words, just kept going, and soon the yard and street were empty of them.

Lori looked out at the falling rain. There were no bodies on the lawn now. The Shadowkin had cleared them away, reducing them to nothingness, as had happened to Rajini. She wished she could join them in oblivion.

*　　*　　*

Lori, still clad only in Larry's jacket, stood before Aashrita's headstone once more. A metallic blue Lexus was parked nearby. It was Rajini's car. Lori had found the key in the Dhawans' kitchen. She didn't think Rajini would mind that she'd borrowed it. The woman certainly had no use for it anymore.

The goddamned rain was finally starting to let up, had become a light sprinkle. She was still wet and cold, though, and she couldn't stop shivering. That was okay. She deserved to feel uncomfortable. That's why, in a weird way, she was grateful for her bum knee. It throbbed like hell and she could barely put any weight on it. She didn't have any pain medicine – that was in her purse on the Nightway, along with her phone – but even if she'd had pills, she wouldn't have taken them. She wanted to feel the pain. Needed to.

"I'm sorry," she said, eyes focused on Aashrita's name carved into the stone. "I didn't mean to get your parents killed. I didn't mean to get anyone killed. And I'm sorry I never got to confess what I did to you. I'm sorry because I wanted to stop the insanity that's been happening, but I also wanted to take responsibility for what I did, to stop hiding from it. Hiding from *you* – or at least the memory of you. But I failed, and I'm so, so sorry."

She waited, half expecting to hear Aashrita's voice, especially after interacting with her – or a version of her – in the Garden of Anguish. But the only sound came from the falling rain.

Given everything that had happened, she would've expected to have a killer migraine right now, but her head felt fine. She would've welcomed the pain, though, felt it was the least she deserved. "We never get what we want in this life, do we?" she said.

Aashrita, of course, didn't respond.

"One thing I don't understand about all this." Lori paused, then gave a bitter laugh. "Okay, one of the *many* things I don't understand, is why if my urging you to kill yourself created an Imbalance between Shadow and the real world, the Cabal waited so damn long to do anything about it. If it was such a big deal, if it was going to cause so many problems – maybe even threaten the world – why not try to fix it right away? And why did it take the Shadowkin so long to show up? Seventeen years seems like a hell of a long time. I suppose the Imbalance might've taken a while to build up to critical mass. Maybe the Cabal didn't detect it until recently because of that. But – and I don't want you to take this the wrong way – how could what I did to you upset the Balance? You and I, we're just two people. How could anything we do or anything that happens to us have any real impact on anything?"

She heard Aashrita's voice then, maybe for real, or maybe it was only a memory. Either way, the voice repeated the words that Aashrita had said to her in the Garden.

You say you wanted to get back at me in a small way? Well, small actions can have pretty goddamn big consequences!

"What I did had serious consequences, that's for damn sure, but it wasn't small. Not to you, and not to me."

She heard Aashrita's voice again; this time she was sure it wasn't a memory.

Then maybe it was something else you did. Something more recent, perhaps.

The idea stunned Lori. She'd assumed the action she had to confess and atone for had to have been the worst thing she'd ever done. But what if that wasn't the case? What if what she'd done to Aashrita had nothing whatsoever to do with the Imbalance? Something small…. Like if you were walking on a mountain trail and accidentally kicked a stone that went over a cliff and started an avalanche. So what small thing had she done recently that could've caused the current situation?

In her mind, she saw a pair of eyes. Sad, haunted eyes, with threads of darkness that passed through the whites like storm clouds moving across a morning sky.

Can I ask you a question?

No, not like storm clouds. Like *shadows*.

Like Shadow*kin*.

She'd been suffering from a migraine at the time, had barely been able to think. The man's question hadn't fully registered on her consciousness, and she'd said no automatically and continued on to the pharmacy and the relief that awaited her within. If the man had approached her another day, she would've stopped, listened to what he had to say, and if she could, she would've helped him.

But would she have? Would she *really*?

Probably not.

The answer shamed her, but it was the truth. She'd do exactly what she'd done: written the man off as a beggar or someone who, if not completely crazy, was not right in the head and wanted to talk to her about whatever nonsense was rattling around in his skull. She'd ignore him and keep on keeping on. And just as she'd done, she'd forget all about him because he was in the past, and Lori Palumbo liked the past to stay where it was – dead and buried, where it could do no one, especially her, any harm.

So by not listening to the man's question and answering it if she could, she'd kicked a stone over a cliff edge, and now, a week later, Oakmont was in danger of being crushed by a damn big avalanche – maybe the biggest that there'd ever been. But how could she make things right, and was it already too late? The Shadowkin were rampaging through the town, and the Intercessor was on its way. How could she hope to find the man – the Questioner – in time to stop what was happening? Hell, he could've been killed or unmade by the Shadowkin already, and if so, there was no way she could confess to him, let alone atone.

She wrapped her arms around herself in a futile attempt to generate some warmth, and once again focused her attention on Aashrita's headstone.

"Looks like that last vision you showed me is going to come true after all. I wonder how long it takes to destroy an entire town. I suppose it all depends on just how big and powerful the Intercessor is."

"It's *very* big and *very* powerful."

She turned to see the Driver coming toward her. His red robe had been torn to shreds, and it was something of a miracle that the scraps of cloth still managed to cling to his body. His flesh was cut, bruised, even burned in some places, and his left arm hung limply at his side, as if broken. One of the skin patches that covered his eyes had been torn, and a dark smoke-like substance curled forth and rose into the air. Even seeing him hurt like this, her first reflex was to reach into the jacket for the Gravedigger Special – a more than appropriate weapon to be used in a cemetery – but she found the inner pocket empty. Then she remembered: Reeny had taken the gun at the Dhawans' and fired the last two rounds. Even if Lori still had the Gravedigger Special, it wouldn't matter. What good was a magic gun without any bullets?

"Where's Goat-Eyes?" she asked.

The Driver looked at her for an instant, as if he was unsure who she was referring to. But then he understood. "She's still on the other side of the entrance to the Nightway, doing her best to hold off the Intercessor."

Entrance? Right, the one near the cemetery wall that she'd used to escape the Shadowkin during her first visit to Aashrita's grave. She assumed that was how the Driver had gotten here.

"I didn't know you guys were that powerful," she said.

The air was cut by a scream and then an object came hurtling toward them. It struck Aashrita's headstone so hard that the impact broke the marker in two. The object bounced off, hit the trunk of a nearby tree, ricocheted, hit the ground, and rolled for a half dozen feet before finally coming to a rest less than three yards from where Lori stood. Steam rose from the object as if it had been exposed to superheated air. It was a head. More precisely, Goat-Eyes'. Roughly half of the head was a gleaming white skull, but the other half was more or less intact. The woman's remaining goat eye was wide open, and for some strange reason it looked less disturbing in death than it had in life.

"We're not," the Driver said, his voice tired, defeated.

Another sound echoed through the cemetery then, unlike anything Lori had ever heard before. It was like the high-pitched whine of a jet engine crossed with the racheting-pounding of the world's largest jackhammer. Lori clapped her hands to her ears to muffle the sound, but it didn't help. The sound seemed to be coming from inside her head as much as outside. The noise even bothered the Driver. He gritted his teeth in pain and pointed to the far side of the cemetery, where the entrance to the Nightway was located. She didn't see anything right away, but then she became aware of a crimson glow. The light grew larger, brighter, and she saw the air shimmer all around it. There was a shape within the red light, sharp and pointed. It hung high in midair, a hundred feet, maybe two hundred. It was difficult to estimate. After the experiences she'd been through in the last day, she thought she understood what it meant to feel terror, but now – looking at the tip of the Intercessor's horn as it worked to make the entrance large enough for its titanic body to pass through – she understood she'd known jack shit about terror.

That noise.... Was it the sound of the entrance being forced open wider, or was it the voice of the Intercessor, bellowing to the world that it was coming? Maybe the sounds were one and the same, she thought.

The Driver's lips moved, but Lori couldn't hear him. She stepped close, lowered her head to his, and turned her right ear to his mouth.

"It's over," he said. He shouted these words, and she could still barely hear them. "Nothing can stop the Intercessor now."

"I think I know what I did," she yelled back. "It happened a week ago, but I don't know how to fix it."

More of the Intercessor's horn protruded into the real world. She tried to estimate just how much. Ten feet? Twenty? Would the Intercessor have to continue slowly widening the entrance, or would there come a point where the strain would be too much and the entrance would suddenly open the rest of the way, like the lid of a jar that was stuck? You strain to open it, giving it all you have, and just when you think the goddamned thing is never going to loosen, it suddenly moves, and after that it comes off easily. She supposed she'd find out soon enough.

"Do you remember the exact time and place?" the Driver shouted.

"Yes, but like I said, it was—"

The Driver pressed the flat of his palm against her chest and shoved – hard. Lori stumbled backward, her bad knee gave out on her, and she fell....

CHAPTER FIFTEEN

And fell....

And fell....

It felt as if she dropped for hours, the world around her a hazy-gray nothing, the entire universe one vast cloud bank.

Finally, after what seemed like forever, her bare ass hit something solid. Pain jolted through her tailbone and up along her spine, and she let out a loud, "Fuck!"

A woman holding hands with a toddler boy shot her a dirty look. Lori realized her face was more or less level with the child's, and the mother seemed to hover over them both like a giant.

"Watch your language!" The woman's upper lip curled in distaste. "And put some clothes on, for godsakes. And why are you all wet? Never mind. I don't want to know."

She turned away and continued on, dragging the boy with her. He looked back at Lori, eyes wide. He mouthed a word that she thought was *fuck*, but he said it so softly, she wasn't sure.

She put her hands down, felt the cold hardness of concrete. *I'm sitting bare-assed on a sidewalk,* she thought. Cars passed by, going in both directions. *Dry* cars. It wasn't raining. It looked like it hadn't rained in some time.

She rose to her feet. Her injured knee still hurt like a motherfucker, and now her tailbone felt as if she might've broken it. When she was up, she checked the leather jacket to make sure it was zipped all the way, then she tugged it down to make sure it covered as much of her nether regions as it could. That accomplished, she tried to get her bearings.

She was downtown, on the same street where she worked. Everything seemed normal. Not only wasn't it raining, there were no Shadowkin causing havoc everywhere. If she were to go to Woodlawn Cemetery right now, would she hear that terrible sound, see the awful sight of the Intercessor's horn forcing its way into this reality? Or would the cemetery by calm, peaceful like here?

Now that she wasn't in immediate danger, the full impact of what had happened hit her. They were all dead – Aashrita's parents, Melinda, Katie, Justin, Larry, Reeny, and Brian…. Grief overwhelmed her, and she felt dizzy, light-headed. She moved toward the building closest to her, one that housed a store called Fresh Air Vape. She leaned back against the wall next to the store's entrance, fighting tears. She knew that if she allowed herself to start crying, she wouldn't be able to stop. She'd fall to the sidewalk, put her hands to her face, and sob uncontrollably. She couldn't afford to surrender to her grief, not yet. The Driver had sent her here for a reason, and she had to keep herself together until she—

A woman came walking down the sidewalk toward her – a woman wearing a blue smock. Her face was pale, eyes squinted almost closed to shut out the worst of the light. She swayed a bit as she walked, as if she was having difficulty with her balance. Lori recognized the woman, of course. It was her. And she knew what was wrong with her other self. She was suffering from a migraine, a bad one, and she was out of her medicine and heading to the pharmacy, desperate to get a refill on her prescription.

Somehow, the Driver had sent her back in time to last week. She'd known the members of the Cabal were powerful, and supposed if they could pull her across dimensions, they could send her back in time a week. Still, the realization of what the Driver had done was staggering, and she found herself unable to do more than stare as her other self walked past. The Lori-That-Was didn't look in her direction, showed no sign of noticing her. No surprise, given how much pain she was in.

She watched herself go, then saw an older man step out of an alley and into the other Lori's path. White hair, mustache, brown suit, fedora, ugly yellow tie…. She recognized him, of course – the man with the shadows in his eyes – and she knew at once that he was the reason the Driver had sent her here.

"Can I ask you a question?" the man said to her other self. When she didn't answer, the man stepped directly in front of her and repeated his question.

"No," Past-Lori said and continued on her way.

The man watched Lori's other self go, his shoulders slumped in disappointment, or perhaps defeat. Other-Lori glanced back at him once, but she faced forward once more and kept walking.

Lori stepped away from the wall and hurried toward the man.

"You can ask me," she said.

The man turned toward her, and when he saw her face, he frowned in confusion. She thought he might say something – *Aren't you the woman that just ignored me?* But he didn't. She looked into his eyes and saw darkness swimming there. An instant later, Shadowkin emerged from his body – heads, hands, moving in and out of him rapidly, as if they were trapped within him and trying desperately to free themselves. Then as quickly as it happened, it was over. The Shadowkin submerged back into the man, although she still saw the shadowy threads moving across his eyes.

The man pressed a hand to his chest.

"Do you know what I'm supposed to do with these things?" he asked.

Lori could only look at him, completely at a loss for words.

He sighed. "I didn't think so. Thanks anyway."

He turned away and re-entered the alley from which he'd emerged.

This was it. The moment she'd upset the Balance, the one she had to confess and atone for. And she'd just fucked it up.

She hurried into the alley after the man, gritting her teeth against the pain in her injured knee. The alley was clean for the most part, so she didn't have to worry about cutting her bare feet, but even if the alley had been strewn with broken glass, rusty nails, and used hypodermics, she wouldn't have hesitated to enter it.

The man was already halfway down the alley by the time she caught up to him.

"Wait!"

She reached for his shoulder, intending to take hold of it and stop him. But a shadowy clawed hand emerged from his back and took a swipe at her. In her mind, she heard an inhuman voice shout, *Ours!* She jumped back, but not in time to avoid being struck. The Shadowkin's claws struck her right shoulder, slicing through the leather of Larry's jacket and into the skin beneath. The impact of the blow knocked her hard against the alley wall. She hit, bounced off, lost her balance, and fell. Fresh pain flared in her knee, but it was nothing compared to the fiery agony that now burned in her shoulder. She sat up and looked at her injury, saw torn flesh through the ragged opening of the jacket's shoulder, saw blood – lots of it.

She looked for the man, but didn't see him. He'd reached the alley's other end, walked out, turned right or left, then continued down the sidewalk. She needed to get up and get moving if she didn't want to lose him for good. She tried to rise, but her bad knee refused to support her weight, and she slumped back down. She took a deep breath and tried again. This time she concentrated on the faces of those who had died. Except they weren't dead in this time, were they? And if she could change what happened, prevent the Shadowkin from wreaking havoc in the real world, the Cabal would never intervene, and Larry, Reeny, and all the others would live. It was this thought that gave her the strength to get on her feet and stay there. She pressed her left hand to her shoulder wound to slow the blood loss as best she could, and then began hobbling down the alley.

She could move, but not very fast, and she almost lost sight of the man several times. The pain in her shoulder and knee merged into a single throbbing sensation of agony that suffused her entire body. It only made sense. She'd failed to confess and atone, and now she was suffering. The thought initially made her laugh, but this sent off a fresh wave of pain, and she instantly regretted it.

This slow-speed chase continued for several blocks until they reached the worst section of the Cannery District. Here, the buildings were run-down, many of them unoccupied, windows broken or boarded up. Most of Oakmont's residents stayed away from this part of town, and only the homeless or drug users looking for a secluded place to feed their addictions came here. Before Goat-Eyes had approached her in FoodSaver, she would've been nervous about coming here. Now, after everything she'd seen and done in the last day, this place seemed about as dangerous as a child's playroom.

The man never looked back once the entire time Lori followed him. She called out to him several times, but he never responded. Maybe he was hard of hearing, or maybe he didn't want to have anything to do with her after her past self had blown him off like that. But she thought he didn't respond because he was filled with Shadowkin and all he could hear were their voices whispering in his mind.

Eventually he stopped in front of a building with a faded sign over the entrance that said this was *The Respite*, below it the tagline *Living Redefined*. Like so many of the buildings in this neighborhood, The Respite had long been abandoned, and she wondered if the man was homeless, if this was the place where he sought shelter when the weather got bad. He walked up the concrete steps, opened the door – which creaked and sagged on its hinges – and went inside.

There was no traffic in this neighborhood, and Lori limped across the empty street, hand still pressed to her shoulder wound. She didn't know how much blood she'd lost, but she felt weary, and she was having trouble keeping her eyes open. She'd been through a lot in the last twenty-four hours, and her mind and body were exhausted. That, combined with her blood loss, made her want to go find an alley of her own, lie down, close her eyes, and rest. Whether she slept, passed out, or died didn't matter to her at this point. She was just so fucking tired.

She forced herself to keep going, though, and when she reached The Respite's front steps, she walked up them, each step taking a major effort. When she got to the door, she took hold of the handle and tried to open it, but it wouldn't budge. She wasn't just tired. She was weak, too. She tried again, gripping the handle with both hands now. The blood coating her left hand made her grip slippery, but she pulled harder this time, and the door came open with a loud creaking sound.

She entered.

She stepped into a dark hallway, the only illumination the faint dingy light filtering through the small dirty window set into the door. The paint on the walls was flaking off, the plaster beneath cracked and crumbling, and the carpet under her feet was moldy and threadbare. There were numbers on the doors she passed, metal ones nailed to wooden surfaces. They'd lost whatever luster they once possessed years ago, and now looked as if they'd been burned into the doors. She could make out a few numbers, guess at others. 1-A, 1-B, 1-C, and so on. The air was stale, flat, dead, and she breathed through her nose, hoping to filter out any nasty particles that might be floating around her. She knew it wouldn't work, though, that the best she could hope for was to minimize her exposure to whatever was in the air by breathing slow and shallow. The precaution made her feel a little safer, and even if it was an illusion, she'd take it, and gladly.

There was a smell in the air, one that underlay the mingled scent of mold and rotting wood. It was so different from anything she'd smelled before that her mind could find no comparison for it. The closest she could come up with was a crude approximation. It smelled *black*, and while she'd never experienced synesthesia before, she thought that, or something very like it, was what was happening to her. How else could a color have a smell?

This was the last point where she could turn back, her one and only opportunity to turn around, hobble down the hallway, push open the entrance door, and return to the street. Once outside, she could keep walking and never look back. She almost did it, and to hell with the consequences. Instead, she continued forward.

Halfway down the hallway, one of the unit doors was open. She pressed her left hand to her shoulder wound once more and walked toward the apartment. When she reached it, she stopped at the doorway and peered inside. The room was empty of furniture, but trash littered the floor. Empty beer cans and liquor bottles, crumpled fast food wrappers, syringes, and in one corner a dead rat. Chunks of plaster were missing from the walls, and graffiti covered the area that remained intact. Huge stylized letters formed words Lori couldn't decipher, along with crude images of erect penises, swastikas, and anarchy symbols. The wall on the far side of the room had a large jagged crack in it that ran from floor to ceiling. It was two inches wide, three in some places, and it was pitch dark inside. Looking at it, Lori a felt a profound sense of wrongness, as if she was seeing something that should not exist. She thought of what Goat-Eyes had told her on the Nightway.

There are locations on your planet where the barrier between it and Shadow are more permeable than others. Oakmont is one such place.

A Thin Place, Goat-Eyes had called it. Lori was looking at proof of this right now – a crack in reality, one that opened into Shadow.

The man stood in front of the crack, regarding it.

"I come here sometimes," he said. "Into this building. When it's too cold out or when it's raining too hard. Sometimes there are other people in the building. If it's too crowded, I move on, look for someplace else. A couple of days ago, we had a real bad storm, remember? Rain, wind, lightning, the whole show. I hauled ass over here, and when I got inside, I was surprised to find no one else was here. I thought for sure others would come looking to stay warm and dry. I figured the storm must've come on too sudden for anyone else to get here, and I decided it was my lucky day, and I was going to have the whole place to myself. I picked a room at random – this one – went inside. And I found this." He nodded toward the shadow-filled crack on the wall. "I'd never seen anything like it. It seemed kind of real and unreal at the same time, you know? I got closer so I could get a better look." He laughed, shook his head. "Dumbest goddamn thing I ever did. See, there was something alive inside the crack. Something that wanted out. But they couldn't do it on their own. They needed a kind of…anchor to take hold of, something they could use to pull themselves into our world. They used me as that anchor. They all rushed into me at once, maybe a dozen in all, and once they were inside, they made themselves at home. Coming into our world took a lot out of them, and they needed a place to hole up for a while and rebuild their strength. I've been walking around town the last couple days, trying to figure out what to do about these damn things. They're *wrong*, you know? They shouldn't be loose in our world. They don't belong here. I wanted to find some way to get them out of me and send them back to where they came from. But I had no idea how to do it. So I started asking people if they knew what I could do. I asked everybody I met, but either they didn't have any answers for me, or they ignored me."

He glanced over his shoulder at her.

"Like you did."

How did he know that this version of her was the same woman he'd just met on the street? Some instinct or insight granted to him by the Shadowkin dwelling inside him? Probably.

He turned back to the wall.

"You were the last straw. After you wouldn't talk to me, I decided there was nothing I could do about the shadow things, so I came back here. See, they're strong enough to come out now. They're hungry for our world, and if I can't send them back, I have to let them out. There's nothing else I can do. I'm like an egg, and it's time for them—" He broke off, doubled over, grimaced in pain. "—to *hatch*."

He straightened, threw his arms wide, and screamed. Dark clawed hands emerged from his body, followed by heads, shoulders, torsos…. As the Shadowkin tore themselves free from the man's body – a man whose name Lori had never learned, she realized – he faded a bit more, as if the Shadowkin were leeching away his life, his very existence, as they departed their temporary host.

Unable to do anything to help the poor man, Lori turned and left, moving as fast as her injuries permitted. She was frightened by the prospect of what the Shadowkin would do to her once they had fully emerged, but she was also filled with despair. She knew now what she'd done to upset the Balance, but she also knew that if she'd originally stopped and listened to the man's question, it would've made no difference. Either way, he'd returned here, to the place where the Shadowkin had entered him, to release them. The creatures had clawed their way out of him – just as they were doing now – and began roaming around town, feeding, growing in strength over the course of a week until they were strong enough to start causing some real damage. And there was nothing she could've done to stop it. For all their efforts at manipulating her, for all the lives it had cost, the Cabal had failed – and so had she. Everything would happen the same way it had before, and in the end the Intercessor would appear and destroy Oakmont before the Balance between Shadow and the real world could be disrupted any further. And if the entire planet had to be destroyed to maintain that Balance, so be it.

The Shadowkin flooded into the hall, moving as a single dark mass as they came after her. She would be their second meal in this new world of theirs – after the man – and they intended to enjoy her to the fullest. There was no way she could outrun them on her best day, let alone when she had a fucked-up knee and was low on blood. She was within arm's reach of the entrance when they fell upon her. They swarmed around her, encircling her with absolute darkness. She could do nothing now but wait to die.

But in the darkness, she heard a voice. It was Aashrita.

You're stronger than he was, and you know more about the ways of Shadow. There's still one thing you can do – if you hurry.

What did Aashrita mean? What could Lori do to stop the Shadowkin now? How—

Then it came to her, and in the darkness, she confessed.

"I ignored the man when I should've listened. I did not help him then, and I could not help him now. But there is one thing I can do." She steadied herself for what was about to happen. "I can become your prison."

She opened herself to the Shadowkin, drew them inside her, heard their angry howls of protest, and she smiled.

CHAPTER SIXTEEN

When the darkness cleared, Lori found herself standing in Woodlawn Cemetery once more, the Driver at her side, the glowing horn of the Intercessor in the sky above them. The terrible sound of reality being torn asunder had stopped, and as she watched, the Intercessor's horn began to slowly withdraw. After several moments, it was gone.

The rain still fell, but it was only misting now. Soon, she knew, it would end, and the storm – both literally and figuratively – would've passed.

The Driver turned toward her and gave her a weak smile.

"I take it you were successful."

"In a way," she said.

Her knee still hurt and her shoulder throbbed like hell, but otherwise she felt surprisingly good.

"Did I fix it?" she asked. "All of it?"

The Driver's smile faded.

"I'm afraid it doesn't work that way. You've restored the Balance between Shadow and your world, but your actions have otherwise not changed the past. The destruction the Shadowkin wrought – the people who died – all of it still occurred."

For an instant, Lori had allowed herself to hope that her friends and family – along with all the people killed by the Shadowkin – would be returned to life. But now that hope was crushed.

"Why the hell did I do it then? What was the point?"

"The Intercessor left," the Driver said. "That was the point."

She wanted to yell some more, to take out her anger at the unfairness of it all on the Driver, but she didn't. He was right. So many more would've died if the Intercessor had come all the way into her world. She reminded herself of something she sometimes told her PT clients. *Focus on what you do have, not on what you don't have.* Cold comfort, maybe, but it was all the comfort she was going to get.

She sighed.

"Now what happens?"

The Driver shrugged.

"That's up to you. For the rest of your life, you'll have to fight the Shadowkin inside you. And eventually you'll need to find a way to safely dispose of them before you die. Otherwise, they'll be released and start killing all over again."

That, she decided, would be a problem for another day. She wondered if her eyes had threads of darkness running through them now. She supposed they probably did.

"You could always join us," the Driver said. "All of us in the Cabal were once as you. We all did something to upset the Balance, and we all had to confess and atone. And we all paid a heavy price to do so."

"No thanks," she said. "I couldn't do your job. I don't think I have it in me to be that cruel."

This time the Driver smiled in dark amusement.

"You might surprise yourself."

Only scraps of his robe remained, but he still had a pocket left. He reached into it now, withdrew a phone, and handed it to Lori.

"I retrieved it from Edgar's van before I entered the cemetery. You can call a cab to pick you up." He examined her critically for a moment. "On second thought, maybe you should call an ambulance."

She felt a tickling sensation on her scalp then, and she remembered the beetle hiding in her hair.

"You said Edgar never fixed the Imbalance he created, and since I caused his death, his Imbalance was added to mine, like I'd inherited it or something. Did I fix his Imbalance too?"

"No, but your actions have helped you shed his Imbalance, so it's no longer your responsibility."

"Maybe not," she said. "But unless it's fixed, it could go bad, like mine did, right? Maybe bad enough to rouse the Intercessor again."

"It *is* a possibility," the Driver admitted.

"Then I think I'll see what I can do to find out what Edgar did and try to fix it. He was a big help to me on the Nightway, and I'd like to return the favor if I could."

"The Cabal can assist you…" the Driver began.

"Uh-uh. Your 'help' cost the lives of too many good people. If I'm going to do this, I'll do it on my own. I've got more resources to draw on now."

"Then this is farewell," the Driver said.

Lori gave him a nod, and the man walked away, heading back toward the entrance to the Nightway. When he was gone, Lori called nine-one-one and told the dispatcher where she was – *Yes, the cemetery*, she repeated – then she sat down next to Aashrita's broken headstone.

She felt the Shadowkin inside her. They raged in fury at being imprisoned, clawed at the cage within her mind that locked them away.

Hush, she thought, and after a moment, they settled down and grew quiet.

She smiled, closed her eyes, and waited for whatever would come next.